SMALL TOWN WITH A BIG CITY DISEASE

SMALL TOWN WITH A BIG CITY DISEASE

By

Mike Rogers

Self-Published with help from

Midnight Express Books

SMALL TOWN WITH A BIG CITY DISEASE

ISBN-13: 978-0692532157 (Midnight Express Books)
ISBN-10: 0692532153

Disclaimer: This is a work of fiction. All characters are totally from the imagination of the author and depict no persons, living or dead; any similarity is totally coincidental.

Published by
MIDNIGHT EXPRESS BOOKS
POBox 69
Berryville AR 72616
(870) 210-3772
MEBooks1@yahoo.com

Book cover design: Q. Wilson
Email: inmarkdesign@gmail.com

Cover model: Anthony Rogers   (501) 231-8056

SMALL TOWN WITH A BIG CITY DISEASE

By

Mike Rogers

Acknowledgements

I would like to first and foremost give thanks to the God of our beginning.

As black people, I feel we spend too much time in debate as to who God is, and not enough time in actions, giving thanks and praise in our works of faith, to the God we say we love. Secondly, I would like to give thanks to all the brothers of FCI Memphis who I've spoken to over the last fourteen years (1994-2008) of my life as an inmate coordinator of the many cultural events, roundtable discussions, African American History Classes, Great Book Courses, and other social gatherings that we managed to maintain as a vanguard of dedicated individuals at FCI Memphis. I cannot even begin to count the number of brothers who have played super important roles in my development as a man of better understanding. I only hope that I gave as well as I have received. Bro. Yah Yah, Bro. Che, Mr. Risher, Bro. Blakney, Bro. Tony Muhammad and all the brothers of the Nation of Islam, past and present, all the El's and Bey's of the Moorish Science Temple, past and present and to those more progressive brothers of the Christian and Sunni Communities who would at times break ranks and come fellowship with me, I thank you as well. I give special thanks to all the young brothers who I took a special interest in mentoring, who have listened to my countless hours of trying to teach you things, that at times, it may have seemed, I didn't fully understand myself. In always trying to have something new and more compelling to tell you, I had to constantly upgrade my own knowledge and I thank you for making me learn. There's too many of you jokers to even attempt to try and name, and I would feel remiss, if I left one of you out, so, I give thanks to all my young warrior brothers who have participated in the various programs, be it Kwanzaa, Juneteenth, Dr. King, Malcolm X, Marcus Garvey, Haile Selassie and all the other celebrations of culture or other achievements of black people we observed. To my family, I give thanks and ask that you learn to love yourself as you have loved me over the years. I know that if you loved yourself as much as you have loved me, I could then rest peacefully, because I know you're going to be all right. To the CO's of FCI Memphis who have always shown me respect to a considerable degree, I thank you as well. I understand that your job dictates some of your actions, and for those of you who did not allow your job to dictate all of your actions, I thank you for keeping it always professional. Lastly, to the brothers that critique Small Town With A Big City Disease during our Great Book 2 Class, I owe you very special thanks. You were my first review board and though we were not always in agreement, you all loved the book. Through your encouragement and inspiration, I was able to write Part 2 to this ongoing saga. I thank you brothers, Antwan Ruff, Carey Blakney, Marcus Walker, Patrick Kimble, Walton Foster, Aveyon Watkins, Keith Parker, Kenneth Latham, Shannon Lee, Erick Lacy, Mervin Anderson, Perry Honorable, and I'm sure I missed someone. If so, brother, please forgive me. Also, thanks to all the brothers who read the book as friends of those in the class and told me you loved it as well. Can you imagine brothers, if a guy like Michael Rogers could make it to what some people refer to as the top of this literary world? You know we would need a larger stage, for surely, I would never leave you behind. Mom, Dad, I love you. I never fail because of you, but thanks to you, I've always been able to rise when I've failed because of me. I thank God for you and the love and care you've always shown me. Because of the memory loss illness and death, we may be apart. Still, in the spirit of the love you gave me, we'll be together forever. Thanks for the love. If I missed anyone, please forgive me and do write and tell me so I'll remember next time. Oh yea, Michael Rogers Jr., Gamba Hondo, I love you son. I'm still trying to make you proud.

About The Characters of This Book

As a quiet, and shy, middle sibling of six brothers and a sister, I grew up in Pine Bluff, Arkansas, as a product of the seventies. With five older siblings, an active father, and loving Christian mother, our family home was always filled to capacity with the many character traits of family friends who came to visit for a moment and oftentimes ended up staying for weeks at a time. As an avid reader and thinker, I saw and recorded many events that I overheard in conversations between my older sibling and their friends during visits or those things that occurred around me and within me during the early seventies and eighties. I grew up in an era when the neighborhood legends were guys named Michael Burks, Grizzle Hound, Big Earl, Scacehead, Dirty Red, Lock, B.C., Bobby Jet, Piss Mo, Shag, Saint, Too Tough Bob, Blue Boy, L.D, Bobby Joe, and an assorted list of other toughs and wanted to be toughs. I remember afro wearing men and women of black social clubs who were really Eastside and Westside cliques of young militants that rode together. The women of this era were just as bold, with even sharper tongues and quicker wits and razors than the men. Based on the many characters of my youth, I've comprised the characters of this book in memory of their spirits. It was my desire to draw from these spirits in hopes to tell this story and to keep their names alive. Each character in this book is comprised of many characters from my youth and some of the things I've heard them say or do. Though this is a work of fiction, my characters are based on real people who I love and admire as the legends of my youth and upbringing. In trying to tell this fictional story, I have called on some of these old and newer street names of Pine Bluff legends to help me. In calling on these names, I've tried to inject some of the many character traits of these old and newer legends into the story I've told. If it seems that I may have belittled or said something derogatory about certain characters, I only want the reader to remember, that this is a work of fiction, and that my characters are not any one person but rather a compilation of many people into one. In trying to tell this story it has not been my intent to belittle anyone but rather, to pay homage to some of the brothers and sisters who I remember of my youth by mentioning their names in a book that they helped to inspire. Again, I caution the reader to remember, that this is a work of fiction, and I'm simply saying hello to old friends.

FOREWARD

Small Town with a big city disease is not your typical urban novel. Written by Mike Rogers a native Arkansan, the author has created a new genre of literature. The novel begins with the betrayal of a young and naive black boy from rural Arkansas. Trained and ready after he leaves prison, this young man along with his comrades takes on all the vices plaguing the black community. From skinheads, drug dealers, crooked cops and politicians, there's no backing down for the men of Pine Bluff as they take to the streets in this gritty, and well written, believable drama. With names and characters from the actual streets of Pine Bluff, Arkansas this work of fiction, by the first time author, is so believable that some may think it's true. The reader will fall in love with the characters of Broke, Cream, Brick, Lil' Shelia, Sherry, Borilla, Louis X, Clean, Doretha, Lil' Brick, Angie, Eddie Jr., Lee Lee, Roundhead, Michelle and others. These will become their heroes as the reader cheer and cry for them as they overcome the odds against such foes as Fast Money, Piss Mo, Grizzle Hound, Cass an Asian drug dealer and his crime partners Samson & DeLil'ah, Skinheads who fight to run blacks out of the rural town where it all begins, and crooked cops who protects Fast Money. With short exciting action filled chapters, Small Town With A Big City Disease is a must read for all readers and especially the urban reader who loves a good story. Michael Rogers has no peers when it comes to telling the kind of triumphant and believable story that inspires the black man and woman to stand up for themselves against all odds. With vast knowledge and understanding of the social ills facing the black community, Mike Rogers tackles these issues in ways that are compelling and provocative. He leaves the reader with a sense of pride, in not only his/her race but within themselves, as those who are ultimately responsible, for changing not only their own conditions, but in doing so, are ultimately responsible for changing America and the world as a whole.

BROKE

Chapter 1

Michelle sat nervously at the detective's desk. She stared around the room as if afraid that unseen eyes were watching her. Detective Jones watched her as he cradled the receiver of the phone to his ear after receiving a call. A fat balding sexagenarian, detective Jones cast an approving eye at the sexy redbone sitting across from him. She was a friend of a friend who had come to give a statement. According to the friend, Michelle was a crack addict or crack-head as the friend had referred to her. Judging from her appearances, Detective Jones found it hard to believe. Still, he had seen many beautiful women go from sugar to shit after becoming addicted to crack cocaine. As sweet as this one looked, Detective Jones figured she was still in her sugary stage. Detective Jones cleared his throat as he hung up the phone.

"So you say you're involved with a drug dealer."

"Uh huh"

"And his name is Broke"

"Uh huh"

"And you want to make a statement against him"

"Uh huh"

Michelle answered each question with her eyes glued to some imaginary spot on the floor between her legs. Her legs were slightly parted as she leaned forward with her arms resting on her knees. This caused her fat butt to spread in an arched position as if she was about to lift up off the chair. Detective Jones couldn't help the erection he got from staring at the sexy woman. He was like a lion in the jungle when it came to vulnerable women. Even though he preferred them much younger than Michelle, he couldn't help fantasize about abusing her in ways that she could never imagine. Detective Jones fidgeted with some papers on his desk before reaching in the desk drawer and removing a tape recorder that he placed on top of the desk.

"Okay Michelle, now I'm going to need more than just Uh huh when I turn on this recorder. You understand?"

"Uh huh"

Detective Jones sighed as he hit the switch on the tape recorder. He recorded Michelle's statement with more passion in how she constantly licked her lips while speaking then he had for the words that she spoke.

Michelle finished her statement and sat staring around the room to keep from staring into the lustful eyes of the detective. Detective Jones suddenly cleared his throat after realizing that he was staring and that Michelle was no longer speaking.

"Thank you Michelle," detective Jones cleared his throat before speaking and placing the tape recorder back into the desk drawer. "This should be enough for a warrant," he said. "If your story checks out, you won't have to worry about Broke hitting you again for a long time."

"Thank you," Michelle said shyly as she stood to leave. "Can I go now?"

"Yes you can leave"

Detective Jones couldn't help the moan that escaped his lips as he watched Michelle stand with the dress riding up her thighs, until he could see the red bikini panties that she wore. Her thick yellow thighs were oiled and shiny causing him to momentarily lose his composure.

Michelle smiled shyly at him, as she pulled at the hem of her dress, tugging it down and patting it straight.

Michael Rogers

Chapter 2

Pine Bluff was a small town with a big city disease. It was constantly ranked at the top of the nation for its number of murders per population size. It was presently ranked number eleven in the nation as one of the most violent poverty-stricken cities in which to live. Pine Bluff was like one big violent neighborhood or project in the big cities. That's why Broke was thankful that he had a girl like Michelle. Not only was she beautiful, Michelle was also smart. If not for her, he would have a tough time adjusting from the quiet comforts of Altheimer to the turbulent and harsh conditions of the Pine Bluff lifestyle.

Broke first met Michelle in an Altheimer nightclub called the Jig Joint. The Jig Joint was a popular one room club that catered to the more adventurous partygoers. It was packed on weekends with those that came to party from Altheimer, Pine Bluff and the smaller towns surrounding Altheimer. The partygoers came to the club for many reasons. Partygoers came in search of country girls, country drug money or just plain ol' country fun. The night Broke had met Michelle, Michelle had come to the club with a friend. She later told Broke that the friend was her cousin. Broke still couldn't believe the sexy redbone woman had chosen him over all the slick money making hustlers in the club. He never asked her, but Michelle answered his concerns one day, when she told him that she was a simple girl from Des Moines, Iowa, that loved her some country bumpkins as she called Broke.

Broke stared around cautiously for lurking State Troopers as he pulled a blunt from his shirt pocket. He fired up the blunt and inhaled deeply after putting the short body 98 Seville he was driving on cruise control. He set the cruise control for sixty-five miles per hour. He took the car off cruise control ten minutes later and adjusted his speed to fifty-five miles per hour as he approached the Arkansas Bridge. Broke turned the music down as he crossed the old bridge that would take him across the Arkansas River from Altheimer to Pine Bluff. He liked to ride in silence when crossing the bridge. The sounds of the tires rolling across the bridge and the whistling sound that came from the bridge structure as the car passed across it was like music to his ears. In his eighteen years of existence, Broke had crossed the bridge many times. Growing up in Altheimer, a small town of less than a thousand people, Broke still got a sense of excitement whenever he crossed the bridge that was just beyond the halfway point between Altheimer and Pine Bluff, Arkansas. His hometown of Altheimer was fifteen miles outside of Pine Bluff. Altheimer was farm country. Pine Bluff, with its' population of over fifty thousand people was considered the city by those who traveled there from the many small towns that surrounded it from all sides. The same sense of excitement and adventurous spirit that Broke once got when traveling to Pine Bluff with his parents as a child, he now got in the form of adrenalin rush as a young man making the trip on his own. Broke finished off the forty ounce bottle of beer he was drinking. He rolled down the window in preparation to toss the empty bottle.

The trip from Altheimer to Pine Bluff seemed much shorter now that Broke was older. As a child staring out at the open fields of cotton and soybean from the back window of his father's car, the fifteen-mile trip seemed much longer. The trip was now a one blunt, one forty ounce and six rap songs ride. Broke tossed the empty forty-ounce bottle into one of the many open fields that ran the length of the trip. He retrieved the half of blunt he had stubbed out in the ashtray and lit it up. He was still five miles outside of Pine Bluff when he finished the blunt and tossed the end portion called the roach out the window. The smell of summer filled the car through the driver window that Broke left open to clear the marijuana smoke and smell out the car.

The summer breeze across open fields brought back fond memories to Broke. He was still a farm boy at heart. Even though he had moved to Pine Bluff to live with his girlfriend, Broke still loved the country. If not for the insisting of his girlfriend, Broke never would have left Altheimer. He missed the smell of his mother's country breakfast while sitting on the porch in the morning with his father before going fishing, hunting, or off to work in the fields. The work had been hard but it had made a man out of Broke. At eighteen years of age, he now had a physique that men of any age would be proud to own. Broke stood over six feet tall with a chiseled frame of muscle and brawn. He was a physical specimen that put one in mind of a Zulu warrior. His strong African features made some people think he was from Africa. With his wide nose and sable dark skin, Broke was not your average black man or boy. That's why his uncle Ray had named him Broke. He said Broke had broken his way out of his tightwad daddy's balls, and that he had broken the mold of men when he was born.

Even though Broke was very much a man in the physical sense, he was still naive when it came to the world outside of the Altheimer farm community. Though he could easily navigate his way around as a hunter in the woods of Altheimer, he was more like the prey in the jungle he now called home. He was still learning by trial and error but what he didn't understand was that in the city of Pine Bluff, your errors is most often what led to your trials, and sometimes these trials could cause you your life.

Michael Rogers

Chapter 3

Broke entered Pine Bluff with his ailing father on his mind. It was for this reason that he had driven back to his parent's house earlier in the day. He had planned to spend the night at home with his parents. That was before he had received a call from Michelle and she had asked him to do a favor for her and her cousin.

Broke was passing the University of Arkansas at Pine Bluff (UAPB) when his cell phone vibrated in his pocket. He answered the phone with a smile.

"Yo, Broke, what's up."

"Hey, what's up, Fast Money," Broke spoke excitedly into the receiver with the smile on his face. He felt important because he could do something for Fast Money. He had no idea of the treachery that lurked within the heart of the man to whom he was speaking.

Fast Money was with Michelle the night Broke first met her in the Jig Joint. As a naive country boy, Broke was impressed by Fast Money's city slick ways. He would smile like a chess-cat whenever Fast Money would stop by Michelle's apartment.

Broke never questioned why Fast Money had a key to Michelle's apartment. Neither did he question why Michelle would always take the phone into the other room whenever Fast Money would call. He never questioned anything that Michelle done.

"Yo, you got that package," Fast Money asked Broke?

"Yea, I got it," Broke said. "I'm on my way."

"All right B, I'll wait for you, I'm with Michelle now."

"All right Money, I'll be there in a minute."

Broke hung up the receiver to the phone with the smile still on his face. His chest was swelled with pride. He was happy because Fast Money needed him. He was proud of the fact that he could do Fast Money a favor.

Broke didn't see anything wrong with bringing Fast Money the ounce of marijuana that Michelle had asked him to bring. Michelle knew about Broke's white friend Billy who supplied him with drugs. He figured she must have told Fast Money. Everyone down south knew that the white boys had the best weed. Everyone just didn't have the white connection that Broke had with his friend Billy. Michelle had told Broke that she would be at Fast Money's house. Broke knew where Fast Money lived. He had been there with Michelle when she was waiting to have the utilities connected.

Broke pulled into the yard of the half-brick home ten minutes after hanging up the phone with Fast Money. Fast Money's car was in the driveway but there was no sign of Michelle's car. Fast Money was waiting in the open doorway for Broke as he parked his car in the driveway and got out.

"What's up my nigga?" Fast money had a smile on his face as he extended his hand to Broke.

"What's up Fast Money" Broke shook Fast Money's hand as he stepped into the house with a wide grin on his face like he was shaking hands with the president.

"Same old shit', Fast Money said.

"Where's Michelle at?" Broke asked the question as he stared around the room after Fast Money had shut the door.

"Shell had to make a run to the store" Fast Money said before asking Broke to let him see the shit. "I hope it's that real," Fast Money said as Broke begin to fumble around in his pants in search of the package he had hidden beneath his balls.

"I got that white boy shit," Broke said trying to sound hip. "You know how I get down. If it ain't good I don't fuck with it." Broke pulled the bag of weed out his trousers and handed it to Fast Money.

Fast Money opened the bag of dope and stuck his head into the bag sniffing the contents like a dope dog. "Man, this that shit!" he said excitedly.

Broke stood proudly before Fast Money. He was smiling like a kid that had just given his parents a report card filled with A's. He was still smiling when he took a seat on the love seat across from Fast Money.

"Man, you the truth!" Fast Money said as he fingered the dope in the bag before placing the dope sack on the table in front of Broke. "I'll be right back," Fast Money said. "I got to go and get the money out the car. I must've left it over the visor."

Fast Money walked quickly towards the door before Broke could say anything in response. Broke stared around the house while waiting for Fast Money to return. To him the house seemed void of personality as if no one lived there. It didn't seem to have that lived in feeling that Broke got from his parent's home. Maybe it's just me Broke was thinking as he stood. The forty ounces of beer he had drunk on the drive to town were beginning to take effect; Broke emptied his bladder in the bathroom down the hall. He was rubbing his hands dry after washing as he walked back into the living room. Where the hell is Fast Money he was thinking.

Boom! Get down! Get down! Get down!

"What the fuck," Broke muttered. The door blew open. He stared dumbfounded as the room filled with menacing looking cops dressed in black suits with guns drawn and pointed at him. Ten or more of them rushed into the room. The frighten Broke stood frozen with his hands in the air as the cops screamed at him to lie face down on the floor which he did with the help of a fat black cop who slammed him down. Broke was quickly handcuffed and left lying on the floor on his stomach. The cops ransacked the house after finding the ounce of marijuana on the coffee table.

"Bingo! We got something" The fat black cop that had slammed Broke onto the floor emerged from the bedroom holding a bag of white rock like substance. The cop walked over to Broke and kneeled down beside him on the floor. "Mr. Hudson, you have the right to remain silent."

"That ain't my shit!" Broke screamed.

"You have the right to speak with an attorney."

"That ain't my shit!

"This ain't my house! I didn't do nothing!"

Broke was screaming at the top of his voice as he strained to turn and look up at the cop. The fat cop stood suddenly and walked over to a desk across the room. He fumbled around in the desk drawer and retrieved some papers. He walked back over to Broke holding the papers in his hand.

"Are you Lonnie Hudson," the cop asked?"

"Yes sir," Broke said, hoping the cop had found something to exonerate him.

The cop tossed the papers on the floor beside Broke and again began to read him his rights.

"If you can't afford an attorney one will be appointed to you free of charge."

Broke listened to the cop in a dazed and confused state of mind; he couldn't take his eyes off the utility bills and rent receipts addressed to the house in his name.

Chapter 4

Broke was arrested and taken downtown where he was booked into the city jail. He was charged with marijuana possession and possession with intent to deliver cocaine. Broke tried calling his mother and then Michelle when he was allowed to use the phone. He tried calling both numbers all weekend but never got an answer. By Sunday, he was a total wreck. Broke was more concerned about his mother not answering her phone then he was with Michelle. His mother was always home. It was not like her not to answer her phone. Broke wondered if his ailing father had made a turn for the worse.

Broke sat back on his bunk after eating Sunday's lunch. He was listening to the jailhouse sounds of inmate singing and storytelling. The only time the place was quiet was during feeding time. Every time a new arrival came onto the cellblock, the place would liven up as the inmates that had been there for over a week begin to pump the new arrival for the latest news from the streets. If the prisoners weren't catching up on street news, they were either singing old R&B classics or jailhouse preaching about the white man and his wicked ways.

Broke listened in silent agony, as he lay on his back in the hard bunk while staring up at the ceiling. His cellmate who was an older man had tried on several occasions to break Broke's silence. After two days of the silent treatment, the older gentleman had finally grown tired of Broke sulking in his own misery. He was not deterred by the hard look Broke was giving him as he begin to speak in a concerned voice to Broke as if he was talking to his own son. "Listen son" the man said. "I don't know why you're here but I can see you're taking it hard, so I imagine this is your first time in jail."

Broke was about to tell the man to fuck off as he gave him an even harder stare from his top bunk position. He softened his stare as he looked into the caring eyes of the older gentleman who reminded him a lot of his father. The man was soft spoken with a professional mannerism that made Broke wonder why the man was in jail.

"I've been around a lot longer than you son, so there may be some things I know that you don't know. I may have some answers to the problems you're facing or about to face. You don't seem like these other boys I've seen come through here. Is this your first time in jail?"

Broke nodded yes.

"I figured that," the man said. So tell me son, what great crime have you committed against humanity that brought you to jail." The man asked the question jokingly with a smile.

Broke started at the beginning and told the man everything that had happen to him the day of his arrest.

"Son, what I'm about to tell you may not be what you want to hear." The man took a seat on the commode after covering it with some newspaper. "First off, you were set up to be a fall guy from the very beginning of your relationship with the girl you mentioned." This guy you know as Fast Money, I know him as Leon James. Leon is a shyster, wannabe pimp, drug dealer, gambler and all around bad guy. He's originally from Nashville, TN. He moves around a lot but has made Pine Bluff his base of operation. Men like Leon have no honor or merits. They have no respect for the game they play or any respect for themselves in how they play the game. Whereas some players will pay a retainer fee up front to a lawyer in case of trouble, guys like Leon will set them up a fall guy to give to the police as a trade for a drop charge or time reduction if they get arrested and charged with a crime. While you were enjoying the pleasure of one of his girls, she was also setting you up by using your social security number amongst other information that she got out your wallet, probably while you were sleeping, to set up the house in your name in which you were busted."

Broke couldn't believe what he was hearing. Him and Michelle had made passionate love every night. She told him that she loved him. There must be some mistake, Broke was thinking. Broke was finally able to find his voice and interrupted the man.

"I never signed for no utilities at that house, but everything was in my name. How could they do that without my signature?" Broke asked the question as he sat up in bed.

"Son, the utility companies don't care who they give accounts too. All they want is an address and deposit with proper identification from someone that lives in the house. I'm sure that Fast Money probably have someone at the utility company and the owner of the house is probably some fictitious owner that he uses as a front for a house he bought in their name for such purposes as to rent out to unsuspecting fellows like yourself. It's not as hard as you think."

"Won't they have to prove in court that I lived at the house? Broke asked.

"If you decide to take the matter to court you may expose Fast Money and the girl but you won't be able to get off from under the charge. You see son, Fast Money, also have cops on his payroll. Probably the one that found the crack cocaine and read you your rights. Right now you're in trouble, but if you decide to fight the charges, you'll only be in deeper trouble. Fast Money and the girl will come to court against you. Make no mistake about it. Now you can say you never signed anything, but believe you me, the girl will say you told her to sign for you."

Broke listened intensely to the man as he debated on what he should do. There was no way he could do years in prison for something he didn't do. He wished he could speak with his father. Broke knew that his father would know what to do.

"Man this stuff crazy," Broke said. "Ain't no way they can charge me with that dope they found. My finger prints not on the bag. How they gone charge me with some stuff that I never even seen. This shit crazy," Broke said again.

"My advice to you young man is to take a plea. Try and make the best deal possible with the prosecutor."

Broke stared at the man as if he was crazy. "Cop a plea for what?" Broke asked. "Shit, I didn't do nothing. Why should I cop a plea for something I didn't do."

"You got to weigh your options son. You're young and it's your first time being in trouble. I'm only telling you to cop a plea because if you decide to fight your case in court, it might be turned over to the Federal Government. Believe me, you don't won't to go Fed. If you do go Feds, the Feds will bring witnesses from every jail in a fifty-mile radius to lie in testimony against you. The Feds don't even attempt to play fair. You can easily go from being charged as a small time dealer as you are right now by the state, to being prosecuted as a kingpin in the Feds."

Broke shook his head as he thought about what the man was saying. He couldn't believe that this was happening to him. At any moment, he hoped to wake up from what had to be a nightmare dream.

"I have a Fed case myself son. That's why I'm trying to talk to you. The Feds are looking for cases like yours. Simple, open and shut cases that some overzealous prosecutor can use to pad his resume. I'm waiting for the Feds to pick me up on Monday. My case began as a simple firearm possession charge that was thrown out of the state court last week for lack of evidence. The Feds picked the gun charge up after the state dropped it for lack of evidence the gun was mine. Because I have a felony record, the Fed's are charging me with constructive possession of a firearm that was found under the passenger seat of my son's car. Mind you son that my record is twenty years old. Here I am, sixty-five years old and haven't been in trouble in twenty years and these fools trying to give me fifteen years for a gun I had no idea was in my son's car. My son has even shown papers for the gun and tried to claim ownership, but the Feds still want to prosecute. That's how the Fed's work, they don't care about the truth. Some overzealous federal prosecutor with greater aspirations like most federal prosecutors to be a federal judge, probably see my case as an easy win that he can pad his credential with. Forget about my innocence or the twenty-five thousand dollars I've spent in lawyer fees to fight the trumped up charges. It's all a scam son. The lawyers, prosecutors and judges are all in cahoots together. You can fight them and you may win, but if you lose, it could cost you your life. As a first time offender, I know a few years in the state pen may seem like a lifetime, but trust me, it's a lot shorter than doing ten years in the Feds. You're still young, you can learn from this experience, life is filled with challenges. This is your first lesson and first challenge. Learn from the lesson and meet the challenge."

Broke gave a long sigh and laid back in his bunk with his hands behind his head after the man had finished speaking. He thought about what the man had said for most of the night and most of the day on Monday. His mind was made up on Monday when he was finally able to reach his mother by phone. Broke's mother told him that she believed in him and knew that somebody was lying on him. She also told him that she had been at the hospital all weekend with his dying father. She told Broke that the doctors had given his father less than a week to live. Broke was devastated by the news. He couldn't stop the tears that started to fall as he held the phone to his ear while sobbing loudly. Broke cried off and on all day and on into the night.

Broke was appointed a lawyer the next morning. His bail was set at fifty thousand dollars. Broke knew his parents had the money. But there was no way he would ask his mother to leave his father's side for even a moment to raise the bail. He knew that at any moment his father would die. Broke's father meant the world to him. He wanted his mother to be there by his father's side. If only he had not left his parent's house to go and be with Michelle on the night he was arrested. None of this would be happening and he would be there with his mother at his father's side. It was the guilt of leaving his father and the desire to be by his side on his deathbed that helped Broke to make his decision to cop a plea.

Broke told his lawyer to make him a deal with the prosecutor that would allow him to visit his dying father in the hospital as part of the plea. The lawyer was all but too happy to make the deal. Broke had always heard that justice was swift. He just didn't know how swift. In just six days time, he had went from being a free man in love, to a man now about to sign a plea deal for four years in state prison for an ounce of crack cocaine that he had never seen. Life's a bitch and then you die. Broke shook his head as he signed the papers his lawyer placed before him.

***

Broke stood at his father's side later that night. He had tears in his eyes as he held his father's hand. Broke was at least grateful to the cops for allowing him to take off the handcuffs. He didn't want his father to go to his grave with the last image of his son being that of him in handcuffs. His father managed a weak smile as if assuring Broke that he would be all right and for him not to worry. His mother sat to the opposite side of the bed with her hand on his father's arm. She watched through teary eyes as the only man she ever loved took his last breath as he looked into her eyes for the final time. Broke was broken by his mother's wail which caused his knees to buckle. Tears flooded from his eyes like rain. Broke would do anything to correct this scene. The sight of his mother crying over his dead father's body destroyed something in Broke. That was the night he lost his innocence and became a man. He was ready to face his trials and tribulations. On that night he swore he would never be the victim again. Broke said goodbye to his mother for the last time at his father's funeral. The cops signaled for him after he hugged her and promised her that he would be all right and not to worry.

Chapter 5

The next time Broke would visit his father would be at his father's gravesite three years later when he got out of prison. The graves of his mother and father were side to side. Broke's mother couldn't live without her true love. The pain of losing both her husband and son had weighed too heavy on her fragile heart. Broke's mother died six months into his incarceration.

Broke was sitting on the front porch of his parent's home smoking a blunt as he contemplated his future. He had been home for a week and had spent this time fishing, camping and getting the house in shape. His body was rock hard from prison weights and his mind was as equally impressive. Broke had spent his time wisely in prison. He could have been home much earlier but had decided after his mother's death to flatten his sentence. He didn't want to be on paper where he would have to report to some parole officer every month with the possibility of going back to prison if he violated the conditions of his parole. He had seen enough of that while in prison. It seemed every week someone was returning to prison after violating the terms of their parole.

Broke was no longer the naive country boy he was of three years ago. He was now twenty-one years of age with the insight of an old man. Broke had been mentored well by the old heads who had looked out for him while he was in prison. He had also learned the art of boxing from his uncle Brick. By the time Broke had left prison he was the best boxer in the Arkansas prison system. Couple that with what he had learned from his father as a boy and Broke was a lethal weapon of mass muscles and brain.

Brick who was doing a life bid for murder had taught Broke how to box as a form of discipline and a way for him to channel his pent up anger and frustration. Broke's first few months in prison were spent in and out the hole for violent outbursts against both guards and inmates who mistook his youthful age and quiet demeanor as signs of weakness. Brick, who was like the prison revolutionary George Jackson, had taken Broke under his wings and placed him in the cell with him. Brick taught Broke about black history at night and showed him how to box while in the gym during the day. Broke showed Brick how to use a knife. It was one of the many things his father had taught him during the many hours they had spent together in the woods.

Broke done his three years at Cummins prison. Cummins was one of the worst prisons in Arkansas and the United States as a whole. The inmates were responsible for growing their own food and had to tend the fields each day. Some men dreaded the work. Broke loved to be in the open fields chopping or pulling up weeds. Being in the fields brought back memories of his early childhood when he and his father would work the fields together.

Broke was finishing up the blunt he was smoking when he noticed a cloud of dust behind a car speeding fast down the turn row that led up to his house. He recognized the car as belonging to his cousin Borilla.

Borilla was a big, black and naturally strong, eighteen year old country boy who worshipped the ground Broke walked on. The two of them had worked-out everyday together on the free weights Broke had removed from the shed and placed underneath the shade tree since coming home. Borilla reminded Broke a lot of himself three years ago. He was naturally built but since he had been working out with Broke on the free weights he had become even more sculptured.

"What up cuz," Borilla was smiling broadly. He leaned out the car as he sped up in front of the house. Broke waited until the dust had settled before walking out to the car.

"What up boy!" Broke said smiling.

Borilla had two girls with him. "Who dat," Broke asked, as Borilla walked around the car to meet him.

"Man, you know who that is, that's Lil' Shelia," Borilla said smiling.

"Man, that sho' is Lil' Shelia," Broke said with a wide grin on his face. He stared at the four feet, nine inches of ass and breasts that were bouncing beside Borilla in the car. Lil' Shelia reminded Broke of young Jada Pickett, with lots more ass and breast.

"She ain't little no mo," Borilla said, smiling broadly.

"Heeeeeyyyyy Broke," Lil' Shelia said as she emerged from the car with another girl that was sitting in the backseat.

"What's up Lil' Shelia" Broke said as Lil' Shelia and her friend approached him and Borilla.

Lil' Shelia had a nasty walk on her short frame. She walked as if she was stepping around broken glass, stepping cautiously side-to-side in a twisting motion like she was tip toeing around the broken glass to keep from cutting her feet.

"Girl, you sho' done grown out, I mean up," Broke said laughing. "You still a midget, but at least now you're a grown midget."

"Forget you Broke," Lil' Shelia said laughing as she hit him playfully on the arm.

"Borilla, I don't see why you laughing she said. You wan' laughing last night."

"Uh oh!" Broke said. "What happen last night?"

"Hmmph," Lil' Shelia said. "Ask Bo."

"What happen Bo," Broke asked laughing at Borilla who was smiling with all teeth showing. Broke felt good being around friends as he laughed along with Borilla and Lil' Shelia.

"Man, come on" Borilla said as he headed for the weight pile. Lil'

Shelia ran and jumped on Borilla's back with her arms around his neck as she wrapped her little legs around his waist.

"Tell him what happen." Lil' Shelia said as she rode Borilla piggy back into the yard.

Broke was left along with the other girl whom he didn't recognize. "Hey," he said suddenly, as if seeing the girl for the first time. Broke noticed that the woman was very beautiful with sable dark skin. Her body was a statue of perfection.

The girl was absolute in her beauty. Her skin was flawless and so tight and smooth that it looked like a stretch fabric of smooth silk had been molded to her every curve. Broke was flabbergasted by the startling beauty of the seemly shy girl.

"Hey Broke," the girl spoke softly.

The familiarity in her voice caused Broke to question her if she knew him after speaking. "Boy, I'm Sherry," the girl said as she walked away to join Lil' Shelia and Borilla in the yard. "Lil' Shelia ain't the only one that grew out," she said, while looking back over her shoulder. "Some of us didn't just grow out, we also grew up," she said before turning her head, knowing that Broke was staring after her.

"Damn!" Broke said in surprise. "Man, what they feeding these girls out here?" he asked loudly as recognition of who Sherry was hit him. "Man, why didn't y'all tell me that was Sherry," Broke asked as he walked into the yard and joined the others.

Borilla was spotting weights for Lil' Shelia who was lying on the weight bench. Lil' Shelia was laughing. "Man, I thought you knew that was Sherry," Borilla said, also laughing.

"He should've known," Lil' Shelia said, "as much as she used to chase him around when she was little."

"I didn't chase nobody around," the embarrassed Sherry said from the porch where she was sitting.

Broke remembered Sherry as the preacher's daughter. She was a skinny, dark-skinned, and nappy head fifteen year old when he left. Sherry had always been nervous around Broke. Everyone use to tease him about her having a crush on him. Being that she was fifteen when he left, Broke figured that she was now either eighteen or nineteen.

"Yes you did," Lil' Shelia said laughing at Sherry. "I remember."

"Shut up Lil' Shelia," Sherry said. "I'm ready to go," Sherry turned her head away from the trio at the weight pile.

"I thought you wanted to lift weights," Lil' Shelia said laughing. Lil' Shelia knew that Sherry still had a crush on Broke and had only used weightlifting as an excuse to come see him.

"I did, but I'm ready to go." Sherry said. Sherry was sitting with her back on one of the porch beams with one leg hanging off the porch onto the ground. Sherry looked like a black goddess to Broke. He had to fight to keep his composure as he tried not to stare at the black beauty. Sherry was also trying to ignore her attraction to Broke.

She was also having a hard time denying what she was feeling and had always felt when it came to Broke. There had never been anyone else for her but Broke. She had thought of him every day during his incarceration. She had written him numerous letters that she never mailed. When Broke's mother died, Sherry made sure to send him fifty dollars a month in prison. She had sent the money under the name of Aunt Della with the return address on her letters being a P.O. Box. Sherry had even answered Broke letters when he would write back to the fictitious Aunt Della that she had created. Sherry knew it was her destiny to be with Broke. She knew this because her heart told her so and this she believed.

"Girl, stop tripping," Lil' Shelia said as she joined Sherry on the porch and hugged her. Broke and Borilla lifted weights side by side. Sherry and Lil' Shelia sat on the porch in the comfort of the shade provided by the giant shade tree that shaded most of the front yard.

"You know you still going for Broke," Lil' Shelia teased Sherry, laughing at her own play on words.

This caused Sherry to smile. "Uh huh I might be going for Broke, but can't nobody keep it bo-rilla than you. Talking about me."

"That is so corny," Lil' Shelia said.

Borilla and Broke were taking a break from lifting weights and smoking a blunt on Borilla's car. "Man, I thought Uncle Raymond would've been don' sold this old heap," Broke patted the hood of the old Chevy, as he stood off the car and kicked the bumper.

"Man! this a classic," Borilla said proudly as he took a long drag from the blunt and exhaled the smoke into the air before blowing it out loudly. "I just got the motor rebuilt on this bad boy. I'm about to get it painted, soon as I get my money right."

"Shit man," Broke said, "you could've bought a new car for as much as you done spent fixing this one."

"Man, what I need a new car for," Borilla said. "Ain't nothing but turn rows I travel." Shit, if I had a new car, ain't no way in the hell! I'll be out here in all this dust." Broke and Borilla were laughing when Lil' Shelia shouted out to them from the porch.

"Broke, I'm thirsty," she said. "What you got in there to drink."

"It's some beer and Kool-Aid in the refrigerator," Broke answered.

"Man, you got beer in the house and ain't offered your cousin none." Borilla slid off the car and headed for the house behind Lil' Shelia and Sherry who were already entering the house as he and Broke made their way across the yard.

"Yo, Bo. Come here, I want to show you something." Broke led

Borilla into the bedroom once they entered the house. Broke couldn't help staring at Sherry, as he and Borilla passed her and Lil' Shelia in the kitchen. Even though Sherry was very much a woman, he couldn't help thinking of her as the little preacher's daughter. He had already decided that because of the close family ties between their parents that he wouldn't pursue his growing interest in the now beautiful woman.

"Grab me a beer," Borilla told Lil' Shelia as they passed.

Broke shut the bedroom door and unwrapped an old refurbished sniper rifle that he took out the closet and laid on the bed.

"I guess dad had this bad boy renewed," Broke said.

"No shit!" Borilla lifted the rifle and aimed it out the window. He peered through the scope as if he was zooming in on a target. The rifle was a sniper's rifle that Broke's father had shipped home from Vietnam. "Man I can still remember when your father showed us how to use this bad boy," Borilla said.

"Shit man, you never could hit nothing," Broke took the rifle.

"What about that time I hit that deer at a thousand yards," Borilla said.

"Negro please," Broke said as he moved the rifle sideways, back and forth as if following a target while staring through the scope. "If I remember correctly, it was a hundred yards, and you shot the deer broadside with a Winchester." Both men laughed as Broke wrapped the rifle up and put it back away. The rifle brought back fond memories of his father who had trained him how to use and care for the rifle. He had also trained Broke on how to survive in the woods and the military procedures of being a sniper. His father had been a Navy Seal. He had taught Broke everything the Navy had taught him. It was this training that had saved Broke's life during those first turbulent months in prison.

"Shit, can't neither one of us shoot now," Borilla said.

25

"Shit man, what you talking about," Broke said. "I can still shoot the eye out of a deer at a thousand yards."

"Yea, and if the cops catch you with a gun, they gone shoot you back into prison for about ten years. You do know the Fed's are taking all gun cases don't you," Borilla said more seriously.

"Yea I know," Broke said. "I'm cool. I'm still gone hunt though."

The foursome sat around in the house catching up on old times before Borilla suggested they ride into town. Broke hadn't been to town since coming home. His Aunt Vivian who had kept the house for him until his return had stocked the place with enough food to last a family of three for a month. After being deprived of good food for so long. Broke had been eating like a family of four and the food supply was getting low.

His white friend Billy who was the son of the farmer that sold Broke's father the land had left Broke the beer they were drinking. Billy had also been Broke's weed supplier before he went to jail. It had been Billy's weed that Broke had purchased for Fast Money on that ill-fated night he was arrested. Billy's sister had also found reason to visit on several occasions. Her reasons were more personal. She not only brought Broke weed that she stole from her husband, who was Billy's supplier, she also brought him the same sexual pleasures she first brought him as her young lover in the fields when Broke was left alone. Becky was five years older than Broke.

"I better follow y'all," Broke said. "I got to go to Pine Bluff anyway, so I might as well kill two birds with one stone and go after I leave town."

"You must've got your license," Borilla said, as he stood along with Sherry and Lil' Shelia who was clinging to his arm.

"I got them yesterday."

Broke retrieved the keys to his father's car off a hook on the wall. "It's

26

amazing what you can do over the Internet these days," he said. "I had them mailed to me."

They all gathered outside as Broke locked up the house and walked over to his father's car that was parked alongside the house. "Let's roll Borilla said as he headed towards his car."

"Where you going," Lil' Shelia asked Sherry. Sherry stood waiting to get in the car with her and Borilla.

"Where you think I'm going," Sherry responded.

"I thought you was riding with Broke?"

"I didn't come with Broke."

"Broke, can Sherry ride with you," Lil' Shelia ignored Sherry's remark and asked Broke the question.

"Girl shut up and get in the car," Sherry said. .

"If I wanted to ride with Broke, I know how to ask him."

"You want to ride with me Sherry?" Broke asked Sherry as he uncovered the car.

"Man!" Borilla said excitedly as he stared at the Cadillac after Broke removed the cover. "Boy, pop sho' kept that bad boy clean."

"You know pop," Broke said, "He would rather drive his tractor, then to drive this Caddy. You know this was his Sunday's car."

"I already know," Borilla said.

"So what's up Sherry? You want to ride with me or what Broke asked again?"

"All right Aunt Della, keep on playing games. You gone mess around and lose out," Lil' Shelia said laughing. "If you want to get broke off you bet not let Broke drive off."

"Forget you," Lil' Shelia, Sherry said before walking back into the yard to join Broke who was standing at the Cadillac.

Lil' Shelia knew that her mention of Aunt Della would get Broke's attention. She was laughing as she got into the car with Borilla and leaving Sherry to explain to Broke why she had called her Aunt Della.

"Who's Aunt Della?" Borilla asked Lil' Shelia as she scooted up under him in the car.

"Well I guess I can stop puzzling myself as to who Aunt Della is," Broke said to Sherry. "I done called every relative I know and don't nobody know an Aunt Della. We'll follow y'all." Broke shouted out to Borilla as he opened the passenger-side car door for Sherry.

"Damn cuz, you on some real gentleman type stuff," Borilla shouted out his car window as he cranked the car.

"Yea, and it's something he should learn," Lil' Shelia also shouted out the window.

"Girl you know you want a roughneck," Borilla said laughing.

"All right, roughneck. More like a turtleneck, the way you hid your head down there last night." Lil' Shelia rubbed between her legs.

"All right, you'll know the next time you put them little chicken legs around this turtleneck."

Lil' Shelia snuggled up closer to Borilla kissing him on the cheek. "Come on big baby, you know Lil' Mama just playing with her big daddy. You know can't nobody make this snapper snap like you."

"Bet not nobody be doing nothing to this snapper," Borilla said as he pulled off leaving a cloud of dust behind him.

"You ready Aunt Della," Broke waited until Borilla was far enough ahead for the dust to settle before pulling off behind him.

Sherry sat staring quietly out the passenger side window.

"So what made you send me money in prison?"

"I don't know," Sherry said, "maybe I wanted to."

"That still don't explain why you did it," Broke said as he steered the car around a hole in the dirt road.

"So, why did you want to," Broke asked again.

"Maybe, because I heard people needed money in jail."

"So why didn't you use your own name instead of Aunt Della."

"Duh! I did use my name, and I do have nieces and nephews, thank you. I never said I was your aunt."

Broke remembered that Reverend Della was Sherry's father but he wouldn't have guessed in a thousand years that it was her that had sent him money. "I guess you have a point, but it still don't explain why you sent it, but at least I know that you sent it, so thanks. Maybe someday I can pay you back. "

"Did I ask you to?" Sherry asked.

"I'm just saying," Broke said. "I don't want some young brother you got nose open coming around trying to beat me up because he say I owe you some money."

"I don't mess with young boys, thank you." Sherry said,

"Well, old boys then," Broke said.

"I don't mess with old boys, thank you," Sherry said.

29

"Well who do you mess with," Broke asked.

"Who have I always messed with?" Sherry asked as she stared at Broke.

"I don't know, "Broke said. "Who?"

"You," Sherry said as she turned her head and looked out across the open fields.

"Me," Broke asked.

"Yea, you." Sherry said as she stared at him again.

"Girl, how old are you?" Broke asked.

"I'm eighteen," Sherry said proudly.

"I'm twenty-one," Broke said.

"So, my daddy ten years older than my mama," Sherry said.

"Speaking of your daddy, how are your folks," Broke asked.

"Daddy's still preaching and mama still sitting in the front pew," Sherry said.

"You still go to church," Broke asked.

"On Sundays," Sherry answered.

"You ever go out and party?"

"For what, ain't nothing out there but trouble," Sherry said.

"What if I wanted to take you out?"

"That depends," Sherry said.

"On what," Broke asked.

"It just depends," Sherry said.

"Depends on what? I hate when women say stuff like that. It's gotta depend on something."

"I'm not a freak," Sherry said.

"Who said anything about you being a freak?" Broke stared at Sherry with a puzzled look.

"Nobody," Sherry said. "But I know how men do."

"How men do what."

"They like to take women out and show them on their arms like they done caught some freak, trying to impress their little friends. If I go out with a man, he's going to be my man, and not just somebody trying to show me off on his arms as his freak of the week. That's how women get reputations. Ain't but one man I ever wanted, and even he ain't gone touch me until I'm sure he loves me and I'm ready to be touched. And I'm not going to wait forever for him to make up his mind, so he better wise up and see the blessing God has placed before him. Because surely as the Lord giveth, He will taketh away."

Broke listened to Sherry and wondered what happened to the quiet and shy girl he once knew. He couldn't believe she had become so talkative and had such insight.

"You know, anything of God will be manifested in the light," Broke said.

"Yea, and anything done of man will come to zero," Sherry said. "Like the last red heifer that sent you to prison. So you just keep on going for broke and sneaking around with white women and see how that adds up."

Broke was surprised that Sherry knew about Billy's sister, Becky.

"Hmmph! I guess you thought didn't nobody know," Sherry said. "I use to see you and Becky in the field when you thought nobody was looking. I don't imagine she's had enough, since she's always sniffing around behind black men. You better hope her old crazy husband don't find out and catch you. They say he a member of the skinheads."

"Girl I don't mess with no Becky," Broke said. "And let me find out you were sneaking around spying on me when I was working."

"Humph!" Sherry said. "You wasn't always working, unless you talking about working your black tail up and down between that white girl's legs."

Broke couldn't help but laugh as he stared across at the beautiful black woman staring back at him with an angry pout on her face. He realized in that moment that he had found his mate.

Broke asked Sherry if she wanted to ride to Pine Bluff with him. "I got to check on something for my ex-cellmate. You remember Brick don't you. Borilla's uncle that killed Tacky from Pine Bluff back in the day."

"He still in prison," Sherry asked. "I was ten years old when that happen."

"Brick got life," Broke said. "He got to do at least fifteen years before he can be paroled. Anyway, he was my cellmate. He told me to pickup his son in Pine Bluff."

"I don't care," Sherry said. "Just make sure we're back before midnight."

"Why? You got a curfew."

"Nope, I'm just not going to spend the night with you."

"You just too darn smart," Broke said with a smile.

Michael Rogers

Chapter 6

Downtown Altheimer had changed a lot since Broke had last seen it before going off to prison. It wasn't the size of the small town that had changed. It was still a small town with a few building structures lining the highway that ran through the town. What had changed was the number of people now running in and out those building structures. The street was filled with cars and people moving about. Broke couldn't believe the number of people he saw moving about. What use to be a few older whites moving around or sitting out in front of the old building structures had now become hundreds of young black people and one or two white people? Broke didn't recognize any of the young tough looking men he saw hanging in front of the Jig Joint or standing around parked cars that lined the street.

"Who the hell is all these people," Broke asked Sherry as he pulled into an open bay car wash behind Borilla.

Lil' Shelia who loved attention couldn't wait to jump out the car. She put an extra swing in her hips as she walked over to Broke's car on the passenger side.

Lil' Shelia pulled open the passenger side door. "Let's go get some ice cream," she said to Sherry.

"Girl, I don't want no ice cream," Sherry said. "Set your Lil' hot butt down."

"Girl come on go with me to get some cream," Lil' Shelia tried to pull Sherry out the car. "Broke ain't gone leave you. Broke tell Sherry you ain't gon' leave her," Lil' Shelia was standing in the passenger door looking across the roof of the car at Broke with her head just barely visible. "Girl, come on go with me to get some ice cream" Lil' Shelia spoke in a strained voice as she pulled Sherry out the car before Broke could respond.

The men openly gawked at the two women as they walked across the street. Lil' Shelia was clearly enjoying the attention as she walked across the street like she was the Queen of Sheba blessing her subjects with her presence. Sherry who seemed embarrassed by all the attention had a frown on her face as men whooped and hollered after them.

"Man, who is all these young rude motherfuckers." Broke was speaking to Borilla who walked over to the stall where he was placing coins into the coin slot to wash his car.

"Man, you ain't seen nothing yet," Borilla said with his trademark smile on his face. "You outta see it at night."

***

Lil' Shelia and Sherry were waiting on the Dairy Queen parking lot for the traffic to clear so they could cross the street after getting their ice cream. Two men in a black Mercedes Benz that were about to pass them by on the highway, suddenly swooped onto the parking lot after seeing them standing alone. The driver door of the Benz open up and a dark skinned man exited the car.

"Say baby, let me holler at you," the driver said to Lil' Shelia.

"On't know you," Lil' Shelia cocked her head to the side and looked at the man as if he was crazy for addressing her.

"What about you sexy," the passenger asked Sherry as he leaned over in the car.

"I'm with someone," Sherry said politely.

"I'm with her," Lil' Shelia said to the other man.

"Awwww, it's that kind of party," the driver said.

Lil' Shelia didn't respond as she pulled Sherry by the arm into the street away from the men as the traffic broke.

"Man that black bitch fine," the passenger said as the driver got back into the car and steered it back into the street in pursuit of Lil' Shelia and Sherry. "I can make a grip off that bitch."

"I want that Lil' bitch," the driver said. "If that's who I think it is, I heard that Lil' bitch got some good pussy on her."

Lil' Shelia and Sherry were standing outside the car wash stalls waiting for Borilla and Broke to finish washing their cars. The black Mercedes pulled up fast behind them. This time, both men stepped out of the car.

The young men who had been standing around the car wash quickly rushed up to the car. "What's up Fast Money," they all spoke excitedly to the passenger.

Sherry was standing at the trunk of Broke's car when Fast Money approached her.

"Will you leave me alone," she asked. "I told you I'm with someone."

"Baby, whoever you with ain't nobody if it ain't me," Fast Money said. "A woman like you deserves the best. Thank God I found you in time. I can see from your little nasty attitude that you were about to become rotten from being on the ground around suckers for so long. Thank God I'm here. Now, what I'm gonna, got dammit shit! Nigger watch that damn water!" A sudden blast of water in the chest caused Fast Money to cuss loudly as he jumped back from Sherry. Fast Money was wiping down his shirt as he stared angrily at Broke with the wand in his hand.

"Oh, my bad," Broke said with a hard stare on his face. "I didn't see you standing there. It must be the sun or something, because it seems like you didn't see me either. Baby you wanna get in the car," Broke held the wand pointed towards the ground as Sherry walked past him and got back into the car.

Fast Money had regained his composure and now stood coolly before Broke as he rubbed his hands together. He had a cocky smile on his face as he stared at Broke with a smirk. Fast Money had no idea that Broke had been released from prison. This was not the same country boy he had sent to jail three years ago.

The young men who had been gathered around the car wash were now gathered around Fast Money. This bolstered Fast Money's confidence. Still, even though Fast Money was far from being a coward, he was no closer to being a fool. He cast a glance at the driver of the Mercedes.

The driver of the Mercedes was sitting with one leg out the car as he leaned into the car as if he had his hand on something beneath the seat. Broke didn't recognize the driver or any of the men who had gathered around Fast Money. He placed the car wash wand back into the holder after it shut off.

Borilla came around from the opposite end of the car wash stall and joined Broke at the trunk of his car. Lil' Shelia ran to Borilla's car and stuffed a razor in her bra and walked up behind Borilla.

"What's up Broke?" Borilla asked.

"Nigger gon' be dead broke you don't teach him who he fucking with," the driver of the Mercedes said threateningly. "What's up Fast Money?" The driver asked.

"What you want to be up trick!" Broke couldn't control his anger any longer as he stared in the face of the man that had cost him three years of his life in prison. The same man he held responsible for the lost of his mother and the reason he wasn't able to be there for her in her time of need. Broke thought of all the nights he had laid up in prison thinking about getting revenge against Fast Money. Killing Fast Money had been his motivation to keep going for the first two years in prison. It was Brick who was constantly in Broke's ear to let it go that had finally convinced him that killing Fast Money wouldn't bring back his parents or give him back the lost years in prison. Brick had said that the only thing Broke would accomplish by killing Fast Money would be a murder charge that would send him back to prison.

Broke thought he had put the past behind him. It seemed now that the past refused to die. That was, unless he killed it. And that's what Broke was thinking, as he prepared to do battle with whatever forces were prepared to line up against him.

The driver was about to step out the car when five men pulled up fast onto the parking lot in a pickup truck. Three big black men jumped out the back of the truck as the truck doors flew open simultaneously. What's up cuz the driver said as he got out the truck holding a pistol down beside his leg? The man on the passenger side also got out with his hand in his pocket. The three big men who had been riding in the back of the truck were all holding axe handles as they quickly walked over to join Broke and Borilla.

"Ain't nothing," Borilla said. "These Pine Bluff niggas don't know who they messing with."

"What up Broke?" the driver of the truck asked as he stared at Broke.

Broke recognized the men as three of Borilla's cousins and a couple of friends. He knew the situation was about to get out of hand and begin to think more rationally. His thoughts quickly became concerns for Sherry's safety. Sherry had gotten out the car and was standing with Lil' Shelia and Borilla next to Broke.

"It ain't shit cuz," Broke said. "I just didn't know the circus was in town."

"I hear you cuz," the driver said. "The circus stay in town these days," he said.

Fast Money walked over to the Mercedes. He was not afraid but with the money he was making off drugs in Altheimer he didn't want to blow up his spot. There was no need in stirring up the natives.

The youngsters were slowly backing up as Fast Money got into the car. They didn't want any trouble with the big cock strong country boys. They had already seen their work in the past. It was no secret that the men meant business.

"Yo Broke," Fast Money said with a smile on his face. "I'll tell Michelle that I saw you. Maybe we can get together sometime. You always did have that fire weed. By the way, thanks for patronizing my carwash," Fast Money spoke out the passenger window as the Mercedes slowly backed off the lot. "You always were a nickel and dime nigger," he said as the car pulled off the lot.

If not for Sherry's grip on Broke's hand, she was sure he would have attacked Fast Money. Broke's body tensed up as he stared angrily after Fast Money.

"Man, fuck that Pine Bluff ass nigga," Borilla said.

Lil' Shelia closed her razor and placed it in her pocket. "Whew! Man I thought I was gon' have to cut me a nigga," Lil' Shelia said as if exhausted.

This seemed to break the tension as the men all laughed. The five men who had arrived in the truck were responsible for another truckload of men who pulled onto the car wash lot after seeing them. It wasn't fifteen minutes before the lot was filled with locals who were talking loud and welcoming Broke home.

"Man I'm hungry than a mother," Borilla said after about thirty minutes of talk. "Let's go over to the Jig Joint and get somethin' to eat," he said to Broke.

"What's up with y'all," he asked his cousins who had arrived in the first truck.

"Man I'm fulla than a tick," the driver said."

"Shit, me too," the passenger said. The other men also declined

40

Borilla's invitation.

"What y'all getting into later," Big Earl the driver asked Broke.

"I got to go to Pine Bluff to pick up Brick's son," Broke said.

"Man, I ain't seen Lil' Brick in 'bout five years," Big Earl said.

"You wanna ride with me," Broke asked?

"Nawww man, I'm a let you and Bo take that trip. Y'all need to be careful though. You know them niggas from Pine Bluff."

"Man fuck them nigga's," Borilla said. Ain't neither one of them nigga's shit."

"I'm just saying, ol' big head boy, you can't sleep on these tricks out here."

"I hear you cuz," Broke said. "Bo, just talking. He ain't going nowhere no way. Me and Sherry just gon' run down there and pickup Lil' Brick and come on back."

Michael Rogers

Chapter 7

Broke was surprised at the expansion of the Jig Joint. It was no longer the one room club that it used to be. It was now a soul food restaurant and nightclub.

Lil' Shelia was in her element as she sashayed around the restaurant speaking to friends and frowning at foes.

"That Lil' woman something else," Sherry said.

"Girl set your lil' butt down," Borilla said as he pulled Lil' Shelia into his lap when she came back to the table.

"I can't help it if I'm bold, black, and beautiful," Lil' Shelia fluffed her hair as she tossed her head from side to side.

"Hmmph," Sherry said.

"Hater," Lil' Shelia said.

"Negro please," Sherry said before rolling her eyes at Lil' Shelia.

"Will y'all hush up! Lord Jesus," Borilla said, "can't take y'all nowhere."

"Man, who is all these new people in town?" Broke asked. "I haven't seen none of these people before."

"Man let me tell you." Borilla grabbed a piece of chicken out the basket of chicken that a young female waiter had placed on the table. He took a big bite off of a buffalo wing and chewed it down in two bites. Borilla finished the piece of chicken with another bite before he began to speak again.

"Man that's a long story with a short meaning," Borilla said as he wiped his mouth before reaching for another chicken leg.

"Dang! Bo, let somebody else eat," Lil' Shelia started at Borilla with her mouth open and a look of disgust on her face.

"Shit, in my family, you better get in where you fit in," Borilla said. "Mama never called for dinner twice. Once daddy got his plate, it was every man for himself."

Hmmph! Yo big head self must have been pretty quick," Lil' Shelia said. "Sho' don't look like you missed too many meals."

"You like it," Borilla said as he bit into another piece of chicken.

Lil' Shelia scooted the chair she had taken away from Borilla. "I got an image to uphold," she said."

"So what's up with all the new people," Broke was laughing along with Sherry.

"It's like the story of the man that brought in snakes to get rid of his mice problem and now he has a snake problem." Borilla was speaking between bites of chicken. "Right after you went to jail, old man Freeman decided he was going to run for mayor."

"Shit Freeman been running for mayor since I was a kid," Broke said.

"Yea and every time he ran, white folks would come all out the boondocks to make sure no nigger ever became mayor." Borilla was on his fifth piece of chicken as he spoke between bites. "That's when old black Freeman got the bright idea to bring in more black voters. He took twenty acres of his family farmland and turned it into a housing project for low-income families. He duped the city into helping him fund his project by presenting it as an initiative to create housing developments for low-income families that would be funded by the state and federal government under the new welfare reform initiatives. "Old man Freeman got the grant money to build his projects and then

44

went out and recruited every hoochie mama and gang banger he could find from Pine Bluff and moved them into the projects as Altheimer citizens. The only qualification they had to have was to be over eighteen and not have a felony record. To make a long story short, old man Freeman was elected Mayor of Altheimer in the next election, thanks to his newly registered citizens in addition with his old constituents. That's when all hell broke loose. White people downtown start selling their businesses and shit got real crazy. Old man Freeman was found hung a month after the elections and niggers start running around shooting and selling drugs like they were in the wild, wild west. Everybody say it was the skinheads who killed old man Freeman. They been hanging around on the outskirts of town every since the election, talking about reclaiming Altheimer for white folks

"Who's the mayor now?" Broke asked.

"Ain't no mayor," Borilla said. "They supposed to have a special election but the city council can't agree on nothing. The white minority of the city council won't meet with the black majority so they can have enough council members to form a quorum."

Broke had a look of surprise on his face as he stared at Borilla. "What nigga, I know politics," Borilla stuffed another piece of chicken in his mouth. "I don't see why all this shit a surprise to you anyway, you act like you been locked up in Zimbabwe." Borilla paused as he took a sip from his drink. "The shit been all over the news."

"Man, I didn't watch no news in prison. That shit was too depressing. The few times I did watch, I didn't hear nothing about all this. I do remember hearing about old man Freeman. Brick was trying to tell me something about Altheimer politics but I was half listening. Shit, I was too busy trying to survive in prison to be thinking about what was going on outside of prison."

"Mannnn, old man Freeman was a Beast!" Borilla exaggerated his words as he chewed on his tenth piece of chicken greedily. "He had mo' game than Parker Brothers. When them crackers sold all their businesses downtown, old man Freeman bought all of 'em through some Pine Bluff realtors."

"Boy you act like you ain't ate in days. I hate eating with yo' ol' greedy self." Lil' Shelia had a playful look of disgust on her face as she stared at Borilla.

Borilla ignored Lil' Shelia as he continued speaking in mumbling words above the smacking sounds he was making as he munched the chicken.

"Cuz, I'm telling you man, when them good kind white folks found out that old man Freeman owned downtown, them crackers made Ku Klux Klan robes out their bed sheets and called every skinhead cousin they knew. Crackers marched down Main Street in full regalia."

Broke almost choked on a piece of chicken as he stared hard at Borilla as if again surprised by his use of words.

Borilla took a sip from his soda. "Ahhhhhhhhhhhhhh," he said with a look of self-importance on his face. Everyone at the table was laughing along with several people that had been listening in on the conversation from adjoining tables.

"What," Borilla said. "Y'all act like a brother don't know how to speak proper English".

"Boy shut your big head up," Lil' Shelia popped Borilla playfully upside the head as she stood up and pranced away from the table along with Sherry.

***

"You ready to go," Broke asked Sherry. He was standing at the table along with Borilla when Lil' Shelia and Sherry returned from the ladies' room.

"I'm ready when you ready," Sherry said.

46

"Let's ride," Broke said. "I want to get back before dark".

"Hmmph! Lil' Shelia said. "Look like you taking dark with you."

"Forget you, shrimp," Sherry said.

"My God," Borilla said exhaustedly in an authoritative voice."Will you too pleeeease act more civilize in public. Getting to where I don't want to take y'all anywhere."

"Boy hush your big head up," Lil' Shelia said. "You don't be talking about acting civilized when you running around naked in the bush trying to catch this monkey."

"Girl will you hush! Sherry had a shocked and embarrassed look on her face as she stared around to see if anyone had heard Lil' Shelia's remark.

"What?" Lil' Shelia said with a smirk. "I can't help it if this snapper bring out the animal in men."

"I ain't talking to you," Sherry pushed her way in front of Broke in her efforts to avoid being seen with Lil' Shelia who was laughing behind her as they all exited the building together.

***

Broke drove slowly past the nondescript white building that served as the city jail. He had a puzzled look on his face as he stared at the building. A white patrol car sat out in front of the building.

"So who's the sheriff these days?" Broke asked Sherry.

"Ain't no sheriff," Sherry said nonchalantly.

"What? "

"Ain't no sheriff," Sherry said again.

Sherry was sitting with her feet curled up beneath her body with her back against the passenger side door. She was eating from the ice she had left from her drink.

"Then who's enforcing the law," Broke asked.

"What law," Sherry said, still with her nonchalant attitude.

"Come on girl, this is the twenty-first century you know, I don't care if this is some little country town. There gotta be someone to enforce law and order." Broke stared around for oncoming traffic before gunning the car onto the highway leading to Pine Bluff after exiting the excess road that ran through Altheimer and served as its' Main Street.

"This ain't the wild, wild west," Broke said once he was on the highway. He set the car on cruise control after reaching the desired speed as he stared across at Sherry.

"You got a lot of trust in that door, leaning on it like that," he said.

"You'll catch me," Sherry said as she dug around in the ice inside the cup with her straw. "They gonna elect a new sheriff when they elect a new mayor," she said.

"Hell, according to Borilla that might be never," Broke said.

"The State Troopers come through town off and on through the week," Sherry sucked more ice from the cup. "They have a trooper stationed in town on the weekend on Friday's and Saturday's. If all else fail," Broke waited as Sherry paused and sipped more ice from her cup, "we can always pray." Sherry giggled as she turned to escape Broke's stare by looking out the window.

"All right, Ms. Nonchalant," Broke said.

"What?" Sherry asked. "Ain't no sense worrying about what we can't control. We should try harder to control the things we worry about. Worry will kill you faster than anything else."

"Yea right," Broke said. Broke stared at Sherry until she smiled shyly and turned away.

"What," she asked again when she turned to face him and he was still staring.

"You too much, "Broke said.

Michael Rogers

Chapter 8

The ride to Pine Bluff was faster than usual; Broke attributed it to the conversation with Sherry and her pleasant company. He was completely mesmerized by Sherry. Not only was she beautiful, but she also had a great sense of humor.

Sherry was naive to many things pertaining to the streets but she had an abundance of knowledge and wisdom when it came to things pertaining to life in general.

Broke pulled into Pine Bluff with a feeling of nostalgia. He couldn't help but remember the last time he was there. He thought back to his father and the last time he saw him alive when he had visited with him on his deathbed. Pine Bluff was not much different than it was on his last trip.

Sherry sat in silence as she stared out the window at the historical black college of UAPB. She had made plans of attending the college in the fall. Now with Broke home from prison she was rethinking all plans that didn't in some way include him being by her side. Today had been the happiest day of Sherry's life. It was the most time she had ever spent with the only men she had ever wanted to spend time with. She could sense that Broke was beginning to feel her as well. Today was their beginning. Sherry was hoping that the end result would be a marriage of no end.

The deeper into Pine Bluff, Broke traveled the more worried the look on Sherry's face became. She had never been so deep into the heart of Pine Bluff. Her visits to town had always been to the business districts. Broke was traveling through neighborhoods that were filled with tough looking black men and boys that were hanging out in front of houses, leaning on cars, or standing in yards beneath shade trees drinking and smoking.

Broke pulled up into a fenced in two-story brick-housing projects on the Eastside of town. Sherry read the name of the projects on a large sign on one of the buildings. The name St. John's Housing Development struck fear into her as she thought back to all the horror stories she had heard about St. John's Projects over the years. Sherry was visibly shaken as Broke pulled up in front of one of the buildings.

Damn, just my luck, Broke was thinking. Building-D would be located in the middle of this bitch. Broke pulled up in front of Building-D and parked the car. It seemed that everyone and their mama were out and about as Broke stared around the two-story buildings that formed a semi-circle surrounding a parking lot filled with cars.

The place was alive with activity. Children were playing on what grass there was between project buildings or that which surrounded the parking lot. Men and boys of all ages were standing beneath stairways smoking and drinking beer. Young tough looking boys were running back and forth to the steady flow of cars that were driving through the parking lot.

The open sell of drugs was evident to Broke. Project moms were sitting in the shade or on stairway landing as if oblivious to what was going on around them. The mothers seemed only concerned for the young kids when they were constantly screaming at for occasionally wandering off the grass onto the parking lot amongst the flow of traffic.

"You're not scared are you?" Broke opened the car door as he smiled at Sherry.

"You're not leaving me out here by myself," Sherry said anxiously.

Broke couldn't tell if her remarks were a question or a statement. He laughed and told Sherry not to worry.

"Worry will kill you faster than anything else," he said."

Broke got out the car and walked around to the passenger side and open the door for Sherry.

"Damn! That nigger on some Jason Lyric type shit," a tough looking youngster said, drawing laughter from his friends as Broke held the door open for Sherry.

Broke pushed the automatic lock button on the passenger door and shut it behind him and Sherry.

Sherry clung to Broke's arm as they walked towards the group of boys. Broke was drawing hard stares from the men gathered around on the parking lot and the ten or more young men standing beneath the stairway landing of Building-D. He was also getting looks of approval from the assortment of women who were lounging around the building.

The boys looked to be in their early teens. The masks they wore on their faces complimented their urban fashions of sagging pants, slanted hats and do-rags. The boys fully accomplished the thuggish rugged look they were trying to portray. Broke was unaffected by their stares. Save the tough looks for white America he was thinking.

After surviving the killing fields of Cummins Prison Farm, Broke was not afraid of the tough man stares of the young wannabe bad guys. He knew that behind the stares were hearts of fear.

Broke had one concern as he walked up to the men. This concern was for the safety of Sherry. He didn't want one of the young lions to try and impress the lioness with a show of manhood.

Sherry felt like a piece of meat on a barbeque grill. It was this traditional scene of men standing around smoking and drinking while watching and waiting for the barbeque to cook that came to mind as Sherry felt a hundred eyes undressing her as men openly stared her up and down.

The laughter of his friends made the young lion more courageous. Some of the older men also laughed. This seemed to fuel the fire of the young lion.

"Yo' Jason, who you looking for?" the young lion asked Broke.

"Your mama," Broke said.

"Shhhhhhhhh,"

"Ooooooooooooo,"

"Dammmmmmmmm,"

"Mannnnn who this nigga?"

The boys beneath the landing uttered an assortment of murmurs and sighs. The young lion straighten out his posture as if ready to pounce on Broke. Broke felt Sherry tense up as she squeezed his hand she was holding.

"What you say nigga?" the young lion asked threateningly.

"I say I'm looking for your mama," Broke uttered the words without threat or with any anger in his voice. "And I'm not going to be too many more of them niggas," Broke said with more venom in his voice.

The young lion pulled his hat from over his eyes as if maybe Broke was missing the killer look that he was giving him. He was caught off guard by Broke's remarks. He knew now that he had to do something or his friends would ride him forever about the diss on his mama. ' The young lion was no coward, but he was no closer to being a fool. There was something about the quiet demeanor of the Zulu looking black man that set off alarm bells in his head. Even though he knew his friends would assist him he was not ready to rush the seemly unfazed man before him. That's why he lifted his hat so that the man could see his eyes. He wanted him to see the murderous look in his eyes. Hopefully this would warn him away.

"Nigga, you don't know where you're at," the young lion said as he took a threatening step in Broke's direction.

"Boy, sit your Lil' ass down!" a voice from atop the stairway landing said.

The young lion froze in his tracks at the sound of the woman's voice. He was glad that his mother had appeared on the landing and stopped him before it was too late and he would have had to tangle with the Zulu. It was one of the few times that he was glad to obey his mother's commands.

"I say sit yo' ass down!" the woman said again more sternly after the young lion stood his ground as if ready to attack Broke at any moment. Broke knew the posturing was only to impress those who were watching.

'You must be Broke," the woman on the landing asked.

The young lion patted his pockets before answering, "I got twenty dollars."

The boy stared dumbfounded as his mother, who along with Broke and Sherry laughed loudly at him causing him to wonder what he had said that was so funny.

"Boy, I'm not talking 'bout you," his mother said, still laughing.

"How you doing Verla," Broke asked, looking up at the woman as he and Sherry walked towards the stairway. "I see Lil' Brick just like his daddy, tough as nails and hard as hell."

"Lil' Brick' you don't know who that is," his mother asked the boy. "That's Broke," she said before he could answer. Verla had an impatient look on her face as she waited for recognition of Broke to register with her son. "The man on the picture with your father," she said, exaggerating her words. "Didn't your father tell you that Broke was coming by to pick you up this weekend?"

Lil' Brick soften the mug on his face into a wide smile as he reached out to take Broke's outstretched hand.

"What's up Lil' Brick," Broke said.

"What's up man," Lil' Brick said excitedly. "Why didn't you tell me who you was."

"I was just messing with you," Broke laughingly said.

"Hmmmph!, I wish you would've told me, Sherry said as they climbed the stairs behind Lil' Brick who was leading the way up to Verla's apartment.

Verla, who was standing in the doorway, stepped aside to allow Broke and Sherry to enter her apartment. Lil' Brick stood next to Verla as Broke led Sherry into the small apartment. Broke and Sherry took a seat on the sofa that Verla offered them. Broke spent the next thirty minutes telling Verla and Lil' Brick about his time in jail with Brick and how well Brick was doing. Verla listen and smiled when Broke would mention something Brick had said about her. Lil' Brick ate up the stories about his father. His chest swelled with pride to know that his father was holding his own in prison. There were several men in the projects who had done time with his father and who also spoke highly of him. These men would also look out for Lil' Brick in times of need or trouble.

His mother Verla was also known to shoot fast, and to cut even faster with the razor she kept in her bra. Lil' Brick was well protected within the pride of lions and lionesses that surrounded him in the projects. His only troubles came from the other cubs within the pride who were always competing with one another in acts of strength to see who would be the future rulers of the pride. Lil' Brick was amongst the top of those vying for future leadership roles in the concrete jungle known as St. John's projects. That's why his father had decided to send Lil' Brick to Altheimer to be with his relatives. He wanted Lil' Brick to be around men who could show him how to be a man. He knew that

Verla could only teach him so much before the man in him would refuse to listen and he begun to challenge her rule. Lil' Brick went to pack as Broke, Sherry and Verla continued their conversation.

"Girl, these black men gon' run me crazy," Verla was saying, "Shit, I feel like I'm, being stoned to death. I got Brick worrying me from in jail, a little brick worrying the hell out of me in my house, and I live in a concrete jungle where I'm surrounded by fools slinging rocks to rock heads up and down the street." Sherry and Broke were laughing as Verla shook her head and puffed her cigarette.

"Shit, I outta move to the country my damn self. I would move to Kansas City with my sister but I know Brick would have a damn fit. I'm trying to keep Lil' Brick close to him but shit's getting hard. These niggers out here so jealous, hell, they don't even want the picture of a man doing life in jail on the wall. Every time he call his son they wanna start some shit. Shit, last time I went, saw Brick, I had to almost kill an old nigga I was seeing. This fool gon' raise his hand like he gon' hit me when I come back from visit. I tried to cut that nigga eyes out. Then on top of all that, after I stop going to see Brick and got Lil' Brick running around here with his mouth poked out talking about he want to see his daddy, I catch this fool last week laid up in the car with another bitch cross the projects." Verla was talking in an animated fashion with her hands and head moving as fast as she was talking.

"Lil' Brick saved them fools that day," she said. "If he hadn't snatched my gun, hell, I'll probably be doing time. He still didn't keep me from putting my foot off up in their asses. I tried to break my foot off up in that bitch ass. Then, this ol' fool ass nigga gone try and pull me off her, talking 'bout that's enough. Man, I got my gun from Lil' Brick and pistol whipped that nigga until he looked like he had hills on his head." Vela was speaking even more excitedly as she told the story while slapping her big thighs with her hands and rocking back and forth like she was bowing.

"Hmmmmm, girl, I'm scared of you," Sherry said.

"Shit girl, I'm telling you, sometimes I feel like I'm the one in jail," Verla sipped from the cup off the table.

"That's the one thing Brick said he didn't want to do," Broke said. "Brick said he didn't want to lock you up with him. He said he wanted you to live your life."

"Shit, how I'm gon' live my life. Every time I look at that ol' big head boy of his I think about Brick."

"Brick said you were a stubborn woman."

"Who?" Verla almost choked on her drink.

Broke was laughing along with Sherry. "He said you was bullheaded and stubborn at times but you were a good woman and the right woman to raise his son. Brick said you was hard as him and probably more deadly. He say that's why he wan' worried about Lil' Brick being pushed around like no little punk. Not with you around."

Verla was laughing at Broke's words as she sipped from her drink. "Shit, he the one stubborn," she said. "That's why his ass in jail now. Ain't nobody more bullheaded and stubborn than him. If he hadn't been so bullheaded and stubborn he wouldn't-nah had to shoot Tacky. I told him not to be out there gambling with them fools." Verla sipped again from her drink. "Brick used to come down here all the time gambling with them niggers from the projects up against one of them buildings. I'll be up here waiting to go out and he'll be down there on his knees shooting dice. I told him them fools thought they were slick and would try to cheat him. I told him to stop gambling with them fools. But nawww, you can't tell his stubborn butt nothing. Then one night he caught Tacky switching dice on him and gon' slap him. Now, here he is twenty miles from home, in the projects, and he gon' slap a fool from the projects. Man, the whole projects got behind his ass. Then he gon' call me from a service station two miles up the road, talking about bring his car. Now, everybody mad at me for bringing him out here. I almost had to shoot a nigga just to get the car. Then two weeks later, Tacky fool ass go to Altheimer to a party and Brick shoot him. I tried to tell him to leave that shit along. But nawww, he too bullheaded to listen to me. Here I was with an eight-year-old son in the projects and he get locked up for life. Talking 'bout me being bullheaded. Hmmmph! I told him that shit was gon' happen if he kept gambling with them niggas. I'm still paying for that shit. That was Tacky's sister I caught that fool with in the car last week. She been hating on me every since Brick killed that fool. I done already had to kick her ass before and always over the same ol' shit, and that's all because of Brick and his bullhead."

"Well, when you go see him Sunday, tell him I said what's up," Broke said, changing the subject.

"Hell, I'm mad now," Verla said. "I might not even go see that fool," Verla said the words as if angrily reflecting on her circumstances and now blaming Brick for messing up her life.

"You know I done my whole bid without a visit," Broke said. "My mother couldn't drive and my father died while I was in the county jail. I could've had someone bring my mom but I didn't want her to see me locked up. She was sick a lot after my father died anyway and I didn't want her to have to travel all them miles. Anyway, I said all that to say this. When I use to watch Brick getting ready for his visits with you and Lil' Brick, I ain't never seen a man so happy. I swear, those were the happiest moments of his life."

Verla listened attentively to what Broke was saying. She said nothing as Broke spoke to her in a soothing and concerned voice.

"Men don't have much to be happy about in prison. Brick knows he fucked up. Still, you can't blame him for all that is wrong in your life. If you want to be loved, ain't no man gon' love you more than Brick. I know he sends you money and is probably a better father in prison to Lil' Brick than most of these fathers out here in the streets. I think your problem is that you still love Brick and can't find happiness without him because y'all never settled this issue. Your love was interrupted by the unfortunate events that led to his incarceration. Brick is still a good man and even in jail, is probably the best man for you at this time. He knows you have desires and want to have friends. Brick says he's cool with that. That's what he meant when he said he didn't want you to be locked up with him."

Verla had a look of concentration on her face that suggested that she was thinking about what about what Broke was saying.

"The problem I think you're having in your relationships with other men is that you're trying to give them love you don't have. All you really have is free time to share. Your heart still belongs to Brick as I can see by how excited you get when you talk about him and by how angry you get when you realize that you can't be with him and then you start to blame him for everything that's bad in your life. Brick needs you like you need him. Until you resolve this issue of love you have for him you should tell your new friends that they can only come second. It's not like you can't get your groove on but at the same time they must understand and respect the love you have for Brick as the father of your son."

Verla was about to respond to Broke when Lil' Brick entered the room dragging two suitcases and a glad bag filled with clothes and other items.

"Damn boy, you act like you leaving mama for good," Verla said. "Wait until I see your daddy Sunday. I'm-a tell him that you moved out."

***

Verla was standing outside the car speaking through the driver side window as Broke settled into his seat after walking around the car from holding the passenger door open for Sherry. Lil' Brick was seated in the back seat looking around the projects as if he was seeing it for the last time. He was smiling broadly and waving to friends.

"Well girl, I guess I'm-a let y'all go," Verla was saying to Sherry.

"Make sure Broke bring you back to see me sometimes."

"I will," Sherry said. "It was nice meeting you."

"Yea, you too," Verla said. "And you too, Broke. Even though I feel like I've been knowing you forever."

"I done heard so much about you from Brick, I feel like I know you too," Broke said. "Don't forget to tell Brick that I said what's up. Tell him I say to keep his head up. Tell him I haven't forgot about what we planned. I'm just trying to get myself together."

"I will" Verla said. "Boy don't you forget to call me," Verla said to Lil' Brick.

"I'm-a call," Lil' Brick said."

"And tell your aunt Clara to call me if she wants to go with me to see your daddy Sunday. Well, I guess I'm-a let y'all go," Verla stood away from the car. "Bye girl, and don't forget to call me sometimes," Verla said to Sherry.

"I will," Sherry said.

Broke waved bye one last time to Verla as he backed out onto the parking lot.

Verla waved before turning around and walking back towards her building. She stopped to speak with several women who were lounging outside of the building. Broke admired Verla for being a strong black woman despite her circumstances of life. Verla was still an attractive big boned woman. She wore her haircut short to her head like Anita Baker and had a body structure like Sheryl Lee Ralph.

Lil' Brick was happy to be getting away from Pine Bluff and the St. John's projects. He wasn't as happy about leaving Verla. Still, his was not a perfect world and for many reasons he was glad to escape it if only for a little while. He knew his mom would be all right without him. Lil' Brick waved bye to Verla and his friends as Broke steered the car away from his building.

Chapter 9

It was 10:00 PM when Broke made the turn-off from Hwy 79 onto the Altheimer exit. Lil' Brick and Broke had been freestyle battle rapping for the duration of the trip. Sherry had listened quietly with a content look on her face. Being with Broke was all that mattered to her. She had been in love with him for so long that it seemed he was part of her. For the first time in her life she felt complete. Sherry felt whole, and it didn't matter that Broke couldn't rap or that Lil' Brick could rap and that his raps were too vulgar. All that mattered to her was that she was with the man she loved. That was all that mattered.

"Damn!" Lil' Brick said as they entered Altheimer. There were cars of every size, shape, and color lining the street. Loud music was blaring from car stereos as young girls and boys gathered around the cars and along the street. The girls were half-naked and the boys wore the urban fashions of the stereotypical inner city hoodlum. "Man, I thought this was the country," Lil' Brick was staring around wide eyed at all the cars and people. "I see some people I know from Pine Bluff, look! There go Ray Ray, Pig, and Peanut. Man, I thought Lil' Joe was in jail. Let's get some ice cream," Lil' Brick said excitedly as they pulled in front of the Dairy Cream where traffic had slowed to a crawl.

Broke knew that Lil' Brick just wanted to be part of the scene. He thought of saying no but decided to stop and pulled onto the crowded lot. The parking lot was filled with cars that had people either sitting in them or standing around them on the hoods and trunks. Broke was lucky to find a spot. He parked the car and walked around to open the door for Sherry. Lil' Brick who was waiting anxiously in the backseat exited the car from the driver side door. The three of them were walking towards the Dairy Queen serving window with Lil' Brick doing his best thug impression walk. Broke held Sherry's hand as they walked slowly through the crowded lot. Lil' Brick felt like a celebrity when someone called his name from the crowd. He threw his arm up as a form of greeting as he continued walking with Broke and Sherry without turning to see who had called his name. The trio was approaching the Dairy Queen window when a black Chevy truck that was sitting high on oversized tires sped onto the lot causing everyone to move quickly out the way of being run over by the truck. Broke pulled Sherry to the side as the truck pulled up in front of him and parked.

"Man! Watch where the fuck you going," Broke said angrily.

The driver shut off the engine and the loud rock n' roll music blaring from the truck. There were four baldhead white men with tattoos all over their arms and bodies that were sitting in back of the truck. The men all jumped out the truck as if ready to attack Broke who stood with Sherry behind his back.

"What you say punk," the biggest of the white men said as he stared at Broke.

"I say watch where the fuck you going, cracker," Broke said defiantly.

The big burly, thirty something year old white man stared Broke up and down as he sized him up. Even with the backing of his friends he was unsure if he wanted to tangle with the big strong looking nigger. As he contemplated his thoughts, an even bigger white man that was the driver got out the truck.

"What you say nigger," the man spit tobacco at Broke's feet with a look of contempt on his face.

"I got your nigger, cracker," Broke eased Sherry over to Lil' Brick and prepared for battle.

"You want some of me, boy," the driver was the biggest of the men. He had a Nazi tattoo on his face and spider web tattoos on both elbows.

"Boy! You know they hanging niggers round here these days." The man stepped in front of his friends and stood ready for battle in front of Broke.

The parking lot was quiet as everyone turned off car stereos and became silent so they could listen to what was being said. The hanging of old man Freeman and the Ku Klux Klan marching through town had brought out old fears in the young blacks that many of them didn't even know existed. They had also seen the big white man who was arguing with Broke whoop two young black boys on the same parking lot just two weeks earlier.

The only difference then was that he had come with two more truckloads of white skinheads who were all armed with bats and chains.

"You niggers getting too tall round here," the white man said. "It's about time we chop some of you boys down."

"You picked the wrong tree, Paul Bunyan." Broke was fuming but showed no outward signs of anger. There was venom in his voice but he never raised it above the level of a even tone.

The driver turned red faced with anger as he approached Broke with his fist balled. I'm-a crush you nigger," he said as he cautiously circled Broke who was crouched in a boxing stance and waiting for him to come into reach.

"Crackers like you don't run nothing but your mouth and your women," Broke said. "And from what I hear, you ain't running nothing but your mouth. Why don't you take your wannabe Hitler-ass on back to your trailer park and practice being tough on some people you can scare."

"You got damn nigger!" The driver rushed Broke, swinging a wild punch at his head.

Broke easily sidestepped the blow and released a flurry of punches that landed with expert precision. The first blow was to the man's head and was followed by a right hook to the kidneys.

Broke continued to pummel the staggering man with blows to his body and head. He hit him so hard and fast that it seemed the only thing holding the man up where the uppercuts and hooks that wouldn't allow him to fall.

"Oomph! Oomph! Oomph! Oomph! Oomph!" was all heard as the big man grunted and groaned from each blow. His friends stood awestruck as they watched the complete annihilation of their friend. What must have seemed like a lifetime to the man being pummeled by the relentless punches of Broke had only lasted a matter of seconds. The barrage of punches from beginning to end hadn't lasted but ten seconds. In each of those seconds. Broke had hit the man on an average of three punches. This accumulated into a total of thirty punches to the head and body of the man with the last punch thrown being an uppercut that lifted the man off his feet and back into the arms of his friends. Broke had put everything he had into the punches to deter the other men from helping. He knew two of the men as friends of Billy. He also knew that they were cowards who were being pumped up by the other three men. Even as Broke had punished the driver he had kept his eyes on the two men he didn't know.

He was prepared for them if they had tried to help their friend. He had also noticed that Lil' Brick had taken a defensive stance between him and the other men. The men had made no attempt to enter the affray as they helplessly watched the beating of their comrade. Broke stood next to Lil' Brick as they watched the man friends try and revive him along with Billy's sister Becky who had jumped out the cab of the truck to aid and assist the men who were trying to revive her husband. Broke had known all along whom the man was and had recognized Becky in the cab of the truck. The parking lot had an eerie silence as all the oooooh's and ahhhhhhh's of a moment ago died down and the crowd of onlookers waited to see what would happen next.

"Man, he punished that big cracker," someone said.

"What-what-what hit me," another mockingly said.

Lil' Brick had a killer mug on his face as he stood next to Broke being pumped up by the words of the crowd. His fifteen years of project survival skills were on tap as he waited along with Broke for their adversaries to make a move.

The flashing lights of a state trooper vehicle interrupted the night as it sped onto the lot. A black state trooper emerged from the vehicle with one hand on his gun.

"Is there a problem here?" The trooper asked.

He gave Broke a hard stare before directing his attention to the group of skinheads that surrounded their fallen comrade in the back of the pickup truck. The beaten man was still groggy as he sat on the tailgate of the pickup with his head down while still trying to regain his senses.

"What's going on here?" The trooper asked as he walked over to the truck.

"Nothing officer," Becky said.

Becky didn't want Broke to get into any trouble. When she had realized that it was Broke that her husband was arguing with she had tried to straighten up her hair so she could look presentable to Broke. By the time she had finished touching up her face and hair the fight was over.

"What happen to him?" the state trooper asked. He cast another glance in Broke's direction before returning his attention back to the men at the truck.

"It ain't nothing officer," Becky said. My husband was clowning around and fell backwards into the truck as we pulled onto the lot."

"Uh huh, must've been a helluva fall. Make sure he don't fall around here again."

The trooper was staring hard at the various tattoos that covered the men. He wasn't fooled by Becky's remark and knew that there had been a fight. Being that from the look of things the skinhead had gotten the worse of the fight, the trooper decided not to pursue the matter. He had heard about the two truckloads of skinheads that had started trouble in town a couple of weeks earlier. Being a black man the trooper was silently proud that at least this time the skinheads had gotten what they deserved. He sensed that it was Broke who had done the beating. The trooper asked the skinheads to see their I.D. before walking back over to his car and getting on his radio. He was standing outside the car as he spoke to the dispatcher.

"Let's go," Broke said as he led Sherry to the car. They were followed by Lil' Brick who increased his swagger as he walked behind them. Broke was pulling off the lot when he saw the trooper approached the skinheads at the truck while unbuckling his holster.

He ordered the men to lean against the truck and spread their legs. Broke passed two more state trooper cars that were speeding in the direction of the Dairy Queen parking lot.

Sherry was still shaking as she sat quietly with her hands in her lap. She couldn't believe how calmly Broke was after what had happen. Lil' Brick was still in awe in the backseat as he stared back at the state trooper cars.

"They going to the Dairy Queen," Lil' Brick said excitedly. "Man them was some big ol' crackers," he sighed and said as he turned around in his seat and sat back as if exhausted. "I should've brought my gun. Shit, the projects ain't got shit on Altheimer."

"The gun ain't the answer to everything," Sherry said softly.

"Yeahhhh, but it'll sho' stop a lotta questions. Ain't that right Broke?" Lil' Brick asked Broke the question with great admiration in his voice.

"The greatest weapon you got is your mind," Broke answered. "You got to learn to control the power of the mind before you can control the

68

power of a gun. If not, you'll just end up shooting yourself or some fool because he stepped on your foot. Your daddy taught me that," Broke said. "He showed me how to think first and then he showed me how to use my hands as weapons when the need arose."

"My daddy showed you how to box," Lil' Brick's voice was filled with pride and admiration.

"You know ex-cons can't be around weapons don't you. Your daddy showed me the fundamentals of boxing for my protection and the protection of my woman." Broke cast a glance at Sherry. Sherry blushed at the words. She loved the fact that Broke had called her his woman.

"I had to teach myself how to use the fundamentals. Boxing ain't just about throwing punches. You must learn how to use strategy, which means you must learn how to think under pressure and not allow anger to cloud your judgment. That's what happen to that big cracker back at the Dairy Queen. I knew that what I said about him would insult his ego and anger him to the point of not thinking when he made his move. He was so mad that the only thing on his mind was crushing me. That's why he came in swinging so wildly. Because of his anger he either forgot or never considered that I would be hitting him back. That's what anger does. It blinds you by clouding your judgment. A boxer waits for the right opening to throw a punch. Even then you must know what kind of punch to throw. You must know when to jab or throw a cross, hook, uppercut, overhand or whatever to stop your opponent. All these are split second decisions and even while you're trying to decide what punch to throw you must also decide when and how to dodge the blows of your opponent."

Lil' Brick was sucking up every word of what Broke was saying. "I'll show you the fundamentals of boxing" Broke said. "It's you who must learn to think and use strategies. You can't be walking up to no man ready to fight without a strategy like you was about to do me today in the projects. Never be the aggressor, unless you must move quickly to keep your opponent from gaining an advantage like retrieving a weapon or you must move quickly as an aggressor because there's two or more and you're trying to eliminate one or two to even the odds when you know a fight is inevitable."

"For real though," Broke stared across at Sherry. "A good black woman by your side is better than a gun can ever be. Black women done saved more black men than guns or religion. When a man has a good woman at home he won't be out in the streets looking for trouble. If he listens to her, she'll keep him out of trouble."

"Shit, all the women I know be wanting to see a fight," Lil' Brick said. "Half the time it's them who start it."

"I said women, not girls," Broke said. "Them girls you talking about."

***

"Well, look like we're here," Broke stared across at Sherry as he pulled up in front of her house. Neither of them wanted the night to end. Sherry sat quietly as if she wanted to say something or was hoping that Broke would say something about the next time they would be together.

"It's eleven-thirty," Broke said, "Look like I beat the twelve o'clock curfew"

"Yea, look like it," Sherry said.

"What?" Broke asked as Sherry hesitated exiting the car. "You changed your mind about spending the night. You want me to wait until you get some night clothes."

"You'll be waiting 'til we get married," Sherry mumbled.

"Huh?" Broke asked.

"I didn't say nothing," Sherry had a sly smile on her face.

"Uh huh," Broke got out the car and walked around to Sherry's door.

"When you coming back," Sherry asked Broke as they stood on her porch.

"I'll probably stop by Saturday," Broke said.

"What's wrong with tomorrow?" Sherry asked.

"I'm going camping tomorrow," Broke said. "It's the one thing my father taught me that I love more than anything."

Broke saw a look of hurt come across Sherry's face.

"I guess some men would rather have a gun on their side than to have a good woman," Sherry said. "Bye Broke," Sherry said dejectedly as she placed her key into the door.

"What," Broke had a questioning look on his face. "You want to go with me?"

"Yea right," Sherry said. "I'm not going in no woods with you or nobody else."

"And here it is I thought you would follow me anywhere," Broke said.

"Not in no woods," Sherry said.

"I'll call you when I get back" Broke said.

Broke walked back to the car as if he had lost his best friend. Being with Sherry was like a breath of fresh air. He thought about canceling his camping trip and spending the time with her but decided against it.

Lil' Brick had moved into the front passenger seat when Broke got back into the car. "Man that's what I call fine," Lil' Brick said.

"Boy, what you know about fine. You probably haven't even had a girl yet," Broke pulled off laughing as Lil' Brick tried to convince him that he had a girlfriend and wasn't a virgin.

Broke was headed home after dropping Lil' Brick off at his grandmother's house. Lil' Brick was all smiles as his grandparents and cousins fussed over him like he was the prodigal son returning home.

Chapter 10

Broke was up early the next morning preparing for his camping trip. He loaded his camping equipment into his father's old pickup truck that he was planning to drive. Broke was heading out the house when he paused and thought of taking the sniper rifle. He decided against it after thinking about what Sherry had said about guns. Besides, Broke thought, it wasn't a hunting trip. He took his bow and arrows instead.

Broke drove out to his father's favorite camping sight. The trip was a twenty-minute drive that took him deep into the woods. The only accessible route to the sight was down turn rows beside open fields. Broke crossed the rickety bridge that was built by his and Billy's father above the ravine that led to the sight. There were few people who knew about the bridge. The only other route to the sight was a forty-minute drive through the woods from the adjoining town.

Broke couldn't help think about his father as he crossed the bridge. It was here at this site that his father had taught him how to survive in the woods. He had taught Broke how to kill with a gun, knife and his hands. Broke's father had taught him everything the Navy Seals had taught him.

There was a small stream that was a mile away from Broke's camp. He spent the day there fishing and enjoying the quiet solitude of being in the woods away from everything and everybody. The quiet serenity of the woods allowed him to reflect on his life. He thought about Sherry and was suddenly missing her. He wished now that he had brought his cell phone so he could call her. He hadn't because his father said that bringing cell phones to the woods would defeat the purpose of coming to the woods. He said that you came into the woods to escape civilization.

Broke cleaned the fish he had caught while still at the lake. He was heading back to his camp site to build a fire and fry the fish when he heard voices coming from across the woods off to his right. Broke listen closely. It was definitely voices that he heard. It sounded like someone was having some kind of party. Broke placed his fish on the ground and crept through the woods curious of whom the voices belonged.

He wondered if it was Billy or maybe Becky and some friends. They were the only people outside of himself that Broke knew used the sight. Broke crept to within twenty-five yards of the voices before he could see to whom they belonged. There was a group of men gathered in a clearing drinking and talking loudly. It didn't take Broke but a minute to realize that he had stumbled upon a meeting of skinheads. He recognized the two local skinheads Brad and Jason, who were present at the Dairy Queen the night before. Broke also recognized several other locals but did not know the majority of the men gathered in a circle around a large campfire. Broke could hear and see clearly what the men were saying and doing as he crept to within ten yards of the clearing and hid within the brush.

"Altheimer is a white man's town." A big ugly, pockmarked face, burly white man with tattoos all over his body was speaking to the crowd of men. "It was founded by white men for white women and children to live free of all the varmints that due to Northern Aggression and that nigger loving president are no longer in the chains of slavery where our good book says they so rightfully belong."

There were several whoops and hollers from the crowd of drunken men. "It's our job to take back our town from the nigger invasion that was started by that nigger Freeman. May god rest his nigger soul." The ugly man gave a knowing smile that caused the other men to laugh and shout even louder. He paused for effect before continuing his speech, "Now as you know, there's going to be a special election to elect a new mayor to replace our dead nigger friend. It's our sworn duty as white men to make sure this job goes to a white man. It's our job even if it means we must kill every nigger in that nigger village called Freeman town."

The crowd of onlookers erupted in applause and words of encouragement and support for their leader. Broke eyed the men carefully with one hand on his knife.

"It's time we send a message to these niggers. I hear there's talk in town that white men are cowards. I heard the niggers are starting to feel a little cocky after what happen last night. Now I know y'all heard about our brothers being arrested last night by that nigger trooper after an incident in town with a big nigger we'll definitely deal with later. I've done some checking and I think I got a lead on how to find this nigger. Thanks to him and that nigger cop, we may never see our brothers who were arrested on this side of the fence again. We all know of them being accused last year of some rodent killings in Sebastian County. Well it seems-that one of our own has turned state evidence. Unbeknownst to our brothers, murder warrants had been issued for their arrest and last night the nigger trooper executed those warrants. Now, I don't have to tell you what that mean." The speaker paused as he stared hard at the men. He cast a glance in Broke's direction that caused Broke to drop his head.

"We got to kill four rodents tonight to account for the two good men we lost. And why is that brothers?" the speaker asked loudly.

"Because one good brother is worth two worthless rodents," someone said.

"That's right brother, and why is that?" the speaker asked.

"Because rodents breed twice as fast as humans," a second voice said.

"That's right brother," the speaker said. "Now the first thing we got to do is get back our respect in town tonight. It seems the nigger cop arrived before our brother could retaliate on that cowardly nigger that swung on him when he wasn't looking. That's why tonight we're going back to town to show them niggers who's the boss. But first we're going to give two of our local brothers a chance to get some revenge for last night cowardly attack. Billy, bring out the rodent," the speaker said.

Broke stared hard to see if the Billy the speaker referred to was the Billy he knew. It was hard to distinguish at first but from what Broke could see the man didn't resemble his friend. Broke watched as the skinhead called Billy drugged a young black boy into the circle of men. Broke didn't recognize the boy but he could see that he was in his late teens and had been badly beaten.

The skinhead leader called for Jason and Brad to step forward. The crowd of men chanted loudly as the two men rushed the crumpled body of the black boy who was lying in a fetal position on the ground. They immediately begin to kick the boy in the head and body with the steel-toed boots they wore. The two skinheads stomped the helpless boy unmercifully as their comrades cheered them on... The men sounded like a group of killer apes as they chanted louder and louder.

Stomp! Stomp! Stomp! Stomp! Stomp! Stomp!

The chants drowned out the whimpering sounds of the helpless boy whose grunts and moans shook the soul of Broke. Broke wished now that he had brought his rifle. He wanted to kill. He had never felt so helpless in his life. He thought of rushing the men but knew that with only his knife, his chances of killing all the men were not of the greatest odds.

"Now that's how you kill a rodent," the leader spoke as he gave a final kick to the lifeless form of the dead boy.

"The stomping Chants had reached a feverish pitch as the leader stood over the dead boy holding his hands up for silence. He waited until the noise subsided before speaking.

"Thank you brothers, now as you know, our family is constantly growing. And tonight we want to welcome our newest family member. Now we all know what must be done before one can become a member of our great family."

The men grew loud again with whoops and hollers. Again, the leader held up his hands for silence. The leader waited for silence before signaling for a young boy who stood in the crowd. Broke recognized the young seventeen-year old boy as the brother of a dirt-poor cracker farmer he knew as Jake.

"Jake here has brought his little brother Stevie into our family. And after a successful hunt into the nigger jungle, little Stevie has proven his worth by ridding our society of one less rodent."

The brother of the young man presented a newspaper to the leader; Broke recognized the paper as a Pine Bluff Commercial.

"Let's see here," the leader said while posturing before his men.

"In today's paper if you'll turn to the dead nigger section, you'll see the headline. *23 Year Old Man Killed in Drive-By Shooting.* Now the article goes on to say something or the other about the growing gang violence in Pine Bluff. Well, it was a drive-by, and it was gang-related, but let's just say, we're not the gang they're looking for."

The men all laugh and stomped their feet in the dirt. The men stomped so hard that Broke could feel the vibrations of the ground beneath him.

"Stevie! Stevie! Stevie! Stevie! Stevie! Stevie! The young boy stood proudly before the men as they shouted his name. The leader again held up his hands for silence. He summoned another man forward. Broke didn't know the lanky man. The man said he was a witness to the extermination. He asked for Stevie to be accepted into the organization and for him to receive his mark of acceptance. The men all agreed in a symbolic vote.

The leader of the crew told three of the men to dispose of the dead boy's body that he referred to as a rodent on the ground. He then gave orders for the men to meet him in town later that night to show the niggers who still ran Altheimer.

77

Michael Rogers

Chapter 11

Broke crawled away from the men before standing and running back to his campsite. Broke was fuming as he loaded his equipment into the truck. Broke was not sure which route the skinheads would take out the woods. He carefully made his way through the woods with his lights off. Broke didn't know what he was going to do but he knew that he had to do something. He thought of getting some men together and waiting for the skinheads to arrive. He cancelled this thought and decided another course of action.

Broke parked the truck and jumped into the Cadillac after arriving home. Because time was of the essence, he never entered the house. He sped off in the Cadillac and never let off the gas until he reached town. Broke drove out to the highway and floored the Cadillac. He reached speeds of ninety miles an hour before turning around after driving ten miles towards Pine Bluff. He reversed his direction and again floored the Cadillac until he was surpassing ninety miles an hour in the opposite direction of Altheimer. He was five miles outside of Altheimer before he noticed flashing lights behind him. Broke pulled over to the side of the road and waited for the black state trooper to approach his vehicle. The trooper walked cautiously up to the driver side window with one hand on his holster. He instructed Broke to place his hands where he could see them. Broke placed his hands on the steering wheel; the trooper relaxed his hand on his gun after recognizing Broke from the Dairy Queen. He shined the light from his flashlight in Broke's face.

"Do you know how fast you were going?" The trooper pulled an ink pen from his pocket as he held the light on Broke.

"About ninety," Broke said.

"Ninety-five to be exact," the trooper said. "Are you in a hurry to get somewhere?" The trooper was flipping through his ticket booklet for the next blank page as he spoke to Broke.

"Look man," Broke stared up at the trooper as he spoke in a hesitant voice. "I was hoping you would be out here. There's something I think you should know."

The trooper eyed Broke suspiciously. Broke didn't seem like the type that would be playing around. Still, neither did he seem like the type that would be volunteering information.

"What's that?" The trooper asked.

"Look, once I tell you this, I'm out the equation." Broke stared hard at the trooper.

"Didn't I see you last night at the Dairy Queen? The trooper asked.

"Yea, that's why I knew you would be out here. My girl said you patrolled this area outside of town."

"You know there's a trooper stationed in town tonight don't you?" The trooper held his ticket book as if about to write a ticket as he clicked his pen.

"I don't know if I can trust the trooper in town. I don't have that much faith in white people right now." Broke said.

"All right son, what is this big news you got to tell me that's going to keep me from writing you this ticket."

Broke spent the next ten minutes explaining to the trooper what he had witness and what the skinheads were planning for later that night. He told the trooper to call the Pine Bluff police and ask about the drive-by. He also told him that he should asked the Pine Bluff police to come to Altheimer and arrest the two brothers Jake and Stevie.

Broke then gave the trooper the coordinates to the campsite. He suggested that the cops should also separate the locals Brad and Jason whom he knew as cowards from the others. Broke said he felt the two men would be willing to cooperate with the police once they were isolated from the other more hardcore skinheads that were propping them up.

The trooper listened to all Broke had to say with a questioning look on his face. Broke didn't seem like the type to be lying about something so serious. Still, this was an incredible story and he didn't want to put his job on the line based on some prank or wild accusations from a drunken or drug induced witness.

"Why don't we go back to the campsite and investigate your claims?" The trooper asked Broke to test his reactions.

"Look man!" Broke said angrily before sighing and lowering his voice. "I just got out the joint for some bullshit. I'm not risking no more than I've done right now. All you got to do is wait for the skinheads to come into town tonight and arrest them. Have the Pine Bluff cops take the two brothers and you take the locals Brad and Jason." Broke spoke with pauses in his voices, as if he was giving someone a recipe for baking a cake.

"I promise you, when you go to the site tomorrow you'll find enough evidence to stand up in any court in America. You'll also have the cooperation of the brothers Jake and Stevie along with Brad and Jason. These men are local cowards masquerading as skinheads just to belong to something." I know killers when I see them," Broke said with surety in his voice. "I recognized maybe three hardcore racist killers in the whole group. Once you separate the wannabes and cowards from under the influence of these men you'll have plenty witnesses to what happen in the woods tonight. I promise you," Broke said.

"All right son," the trooper said, still trying to read Broke. "I'm going to follow up on your story. If the skinheads show up tonight, we'll go from there. If not, I will be paying you a visit, Mr. Hudson."

Michael Rogers

Chapter 12

Boom! Boom! Boom! Boom! What the fuck! Broke rolled over in bed and reached for his knife underneath the pillow. He glanced at the sniper rifle propped up against the wall next to the bed. Boom! Boom! Boom! Broke jumped out of bed and walked into the living room holding his knife at the ready.

Cuz! Cuz! Cuz! Borilla was banging on the door while trying to peep through the window. Cuz! Cuz! Cuz!

Broke swung open the door just as Borilla was about to knock. "Man what is your problem" Broke asked sleepily as he left the door open and walked over to the couch and flopped down. "I thought you were the police."

"Man! I'm glad to see you" Borilla said excitedly. "I heard about you whooping that head. Man that's all everybody been talking about." Broke was laid out on the couch with his feet stretched to the floor staring at Borilla who was talking a mile a minute.

"Then last night three truckloads of heads come into town. Shit was about to go down!" Borilla was pacing the floor talking in an animated fashion as if he would burst with excitement. "Man every nigga in town was strapped. We was fentoo fuck up them heads. I'm talking about locals and Pine Bluff niggas. The only thing saved them heads was the police. Man, I ain't seen that many cops in my life! They even had Pine Bluff police. They took about five skinheads to jail."

"Who they take" Broke asked?

"Jake, Stevie, Brad, Jason and two more heads I didn't know" Borilla said. Man, it's a good thing them cops did show up. I'm tellin' you cuz. Shit was about to go down! Me and this big head was about to go toe-to-toe. I was gon' punish this cracker. I'm telling you cuz, shit was about to go down!

Broke listen to Borilla as he wiped the sleep from his eyes. "Man when they told me about you and that head, I like to had a fit. I been out here five times since that happen. It wasn't til' last night that I thought to ask Sherry where you was. I figured you would tell your baby." Borilla paused and gave a big smile. "I'm telling you cuz, I was going crazy. I thought them heads had got you. Man, I was gon' fuck up some shit. I'm talking about baby crackers and all. Don't nobody fuck with my cuz. Crackers lucky I wasn't there Thursday night. We-duh punished them crackers."

"Man what time is it?" Broke asked when Borilla paused long enough to catch his breath.

"Man, it's almost 12:00 O'clock" Borilla said. "The whole town being turned upside down with Feds and everything and you in here sleep,"

"What Feds?" Broke asked.

Borilla sighed loudly. "Man, you ain't heard nothing I said. I told you the whole town crawling with cops. I seen two carloads of Feds and about ten state trooper cars headed out to the drop back out in the woods. I like to shitted. I said damn I hope ain't nothing happen to my cuz out there in them woods. That's when I headed back over here. I don't know what went down in them woods but whatever it was it's gon' be on the news. It outta be on now." Borilla glanced at his watch.

Broke turned on the television and flipped through the channels. There was nothing on the news until later that evening. Broke and Borilla had spent the day working out and drinking. They were now relaxing before the television waiting for the six o'clock news.

There had been numerous news flashes about the body of a young black man being found in the woods on the outskirts of Altheimer. It was the leading story as the anchorman started off the newscast with details of the murder and the arrests of five white men that were alleged to be skinheads for the murder.

"Alleged my ass," Borilla said.

The anchor went on to say that the F.B.I was treating the murder as a hate crime and were expecting more arrests. Broke listened for further information about the drive-by shooting in Pine Bluff. He became angered when there was no mention of the shooting.

"What's up cuz? Borilla asked when Broke flicked off the television.

"Nothing," Broke said. "Them crackers full of shit."

The skinheads who Broke saw arrested were Jake, his brother Stevie who done the drive-by, Jason, and Brad who stomped the boy to death, and the final arrest was the witness to the drive-by shooting. Neither, the leader or any of the other men that Broke saw as hardcore were arrested. Broke knew that if the Feds had brought charges for the drive-by shooting the Feds could've also arrested the leader of the skinheads and possibly exposed the whole organization as one that was responsible for other drive-by's not only in Arkansas but in America as a whole. Maybe then, there could be peace between street gangs that oftentimes retaliated against their rivals or held old grudges because of drive-by shootings that were actually done by skinheads.

Broke was still angry an hour later as he and Borilla watched a TV special on Wayne Williams the alleged Atlanta child murderer. It was then that he understood why the Feds had refused to bring charges against the skinheads for the drive-by shooting. There were some who believed that Wayne Williams was innocent of the Atlanta murders. These people believed that Wayne Williams was a scapegoat who was used by the Feds to cover-up the Ku Klux Klan involvement in the murders of black children in Atlanta.

Despite evidence and testimony of Klan involvement in the Atlanta murders, the FBI never pursued the Klan. It's believed by some that the Feds prosecuted Wayne Williams to keep down racial tension.

Broke figured the Feds were doing the same thing in this case of the drive-by shooting. He figured the Feds didn't want it to get out that the skinheads were doing drive-by shootings of blacks as a form of initiations for new members. The whole country would be in an uproar. The fallout from such revelations could result in an all out race war if the black gang members sought to retaliate against the skinheads. Broke was sure that in the Feds opinions it was best that the black gang members kept blaming one another for the killings. Being that the five skinheads who were arrested would be convicted of a hate crime that could result in the death penalty for the murder of the black boy found buried in the woods, the Feds probably figured that justice had been served.

Broke was growing angrier by the moment. Still, he knew that there was nothing he could do to expose the skinhead's involvement in the drive-by without also exposing himself as a possible target for revenge by both the skinheads and Feds. To Broke, they were one in the same anyway.

"Damn cuz, come back from la, la, land Borilla said as he popped the cap on another beer that he had retrieved from the refrigerator.

"I'm cool," Broke said. "I was just thinking."

"Shit, I got to go," Borilla said suddenly. "I got to go and take Lil' Shelia to the beauty shop."

"Yea, you better get going," Broke laughed. "I would hate to see Lil' Shelia beat you down."

"Shit, I run this," Borilla said with his trademark smile. "I'm just gon' go and pick her up, I already got something lined up for tonight."

"All right," Broke said. "Mess around and somebody find you in the woods."

"I'm a pimp," Borilla said as he grabbed his keys. "You need to let me show you how to mack on Sherry."

Chapter 18

Broke and Sherry were looking for an apartment in Pine Bluff after enrolling at UAPB for the fall semester. Lil' Shelia who was not going to let Borilla out of her sight had also enrolled after Borilla who was back at full strength enrolled with Broke and Sherry. Broke purchased a brick duplex that was in close proximate to the campus. It was a nice investment and was much cheaper than paying dorm fees or renting an apartment. The duplex needed a little work but that would only raise the value of the house once Broke had completed the work. "Just a few walls and some drainage problems," Broke told Sherry as they looked over the house.

"I've already been through hell with you," Sherry said as she hugged Broke. "It don't matter where we live, as long as we live together."

Broke hired Borilla's uncle Jesse to fix up the house. He then furnished the house through an account that his father had with a black, furniture store named Yancy that was located across the expressway up the road from the college.

***

It was their last night in Altheimer and Broke had decided to show Sherry a good time at the Jig Joint along with Borilla and Shelia.

"Being that you're my man, I guess I can allow you to escort me out without people thinking I'm your freak of the week." Sherry teased Broke as he held the car door open for her to get out.

It was standing room only in the small one room club that was packed with people. Lil' Shelia had to use her club popularity and homegirl status to get them a table. It was Fat Teresa who had made room for them at her table where she sat with a tall lanky light skinned boy who catered to her like she was a queen.

"Girrrlll, who this young boy you got eating out your hand," Lil' Shelia leaned over and asked Fat Teresa when the boy went to use the bathroom.

"Shit girl, this that red snapper." Fat Shelia said laughing. "You better ask somebody. This shit make a nigger go oooweee! man."

"Girl you crazy." Lil' Shelia said laughing along with her former foe.

"Hey man, there go Big Earl-nem." Borilla was pointing towards the corner of the club off to the right of the bar. "Let's go holler at-em for a minute." Borilla stood and waited as Broke decided to join him.

"I'll be right back." Broke said to Sherry.

Broke and Borilla hadn't made it across the room before three Pine Bluff men approached their table. One of the men asked Sherry to dance. Sherry politely refused and said that she was with someone. The man who was obviously drunk didn't want to take no for an answer. He became insistent and tried to take the chair next to Sherry that Broke had left.

"Excuussseee me," Lil' Shelia said with a crazed look on her face. "But did anyone say you could sit there. My homegirl told you we were with someone."

"Shut up girl, before I put you in my pocket," the man said causing his friends to burst out laughing.

Lil' Shelia was about to respond when Fat Teresa stood up at the table. "Nigga, who yo' funny style ass talking too." Fat Teresa was moving around the table even as she spoke. Sherry stood up and got between her and the man.

"Come on Teresa. He ain't worth no trouble. We came out to have fun."

Broke who was watching the table from across the room almost broke into a run when he saw Sherry standing between Fat Teresa and the man. Borilla followed Broke through the crowd after seeing Broke's sudden move and then realizing what was happening.

The argument was becoming more heated between Fat Teresa and the man. The man pushed Sherry out the way causing her to stumble. Broke made it through the crowd just in time to catch Sherry as she stumbled into his arms. Broke was fuming with anger as he gently eased Sherry out the way. Fat Teresa and Lil' Shelia were now fighting with two of the men as the third one kept his hand in his pocket while watching the crowd. Broke after making sure Sherry was safe, walked over and with one punch, knocked the man out as the man attempted to pull whatever he had out his pocket. He then turned his attention to the man Lil' Shelia was hitting with a beer bottle across the head. Lil' Shelia was standing up on the table swinging down on the man's head with all the strength she had. Fat Teresa was going blow for blow with the other man until his knees buckled and he fell to the floor. The man who had been sitting at the table with Fat Teresa began stumping the man after forcing his way through the crowd.

Borilla grabbed the man Lil' Shelia was fighting and begin beating him down onto the floor. It was a chaotic scene before the bouncer came and pulled everyone apart. Being that the bouncers were Borilla's cousin? They didn't try to rough them up as they normally did to those that started trouble in the club.

They were picking the men up off the floor when Lil' Shelia pointed to a necklace that had fell out the shirt of one of the men.

"Bo, ain't that your necklace I gave you for Christmas."

"Hell yea, that's my necklace. I thought them punks looked familiar. That's them punks that robbed me."

The whole place seemed to grow silent. It was like they knew the place

137

was about to erupt. Big Earl was the first to go off. Even before Borilla could commence to kick the men Big Earl had already begin to beat them with a chair that he snatched up from the table. Borilla and his cousins stomped and beat the men until they were lying unconscious on the floor. It wasn't until Ray arrived and snatched them off the men that they stopped beating the helpless victims.

Borilla told Ray told that the men on the floor were the same men who had robbed him and left him for dead. Ray became incensed with anger. He arrested the men on drug and weapon charges. He would also make sure that the men who were all ex-felons on parole be held on parole violations. Ray fully intended to see that the men were prosecuted to the fullest extent of the law. He would also send word to his brother Brick to be on the lookout for the men when they arrived in prison.

***

The first month of school was uneventful. With all the homework, Broke didn't have much time for anything else. Broke had to get back into the mindset of being a student. Borilla, Lil' Shelia and Sherry were all enjoying the college experience. Sherry walked into the living room where Broke was trying to study. She was wearing bikini panties and a bra as she stood wide legged in front of Broke at the couch. As usual she got a standing ovation from Broke as he marveled at her perfectly sculptured body.

"Damn baby, why you do this to me?" Broke ran his hand up Sherry's leg.

"All work and no play makes Broke a dull boy," Sherry said. "I just thought you'll like to go for a ride before retiring for the night. You know can't nobody drive this car but you."

"Ain't you something," Broke said as he stood up off the couch. He followed Sherry into the bedroom with her lying back in his arms as he walked with her standing on his feet. As usual, the sex with Sherry was an award winning experience. Sherry was a very passionate lover. Her body had the warmest feel that Broke had ever experience. Every since that night when they had first Christian their apartment the two of them had been at it at least once a day. Sometimes they would lie in bed all day when they didn't have class exploring each other's body.

"Now can I finish my studying?"

"Yea, until I can catch my breath," Sherry said in a husky voice as she rolled over in bed and flipped through the TV channels with the remote. Broke stood and walked nakedly out of the room.

Broke finally finished with the last of the math homework. He gently removed Sherry's head from his lap where she had fallen asleep across the bed. Sherry looked so beautiful to Broke that he had to touch her. His soft caress caused her to awaken.

"Ummm," Sherry said with her eyes still closed. "Are you ready for round two?"

"I'm going to take a shower," Broke said.

Sherry said she would join him.

Broke had just finished adjusting the water temperature in the shower when Sherry entered the shower with him.

***

Lil' Shelia and Borilla were becoming quite popular on the campus. Borilla was trying out as a walk-on for the football team and Lil' Shelia with her sense of humor and outgoing personality was making friends easily. Lil' Brick spent lots of time at the duplex hanging out with either Broke or Borilla. Lil' Brick was showing great promise as a boxer under Broke's tutelage. Broke had also showed him a few knife fighting techniques. Brick who called weekly from prison had told Broke it was okay to teach Lil' Brick how to use a knife. Brick had also told Broke to keep a check on Lil' Brick and to make sure that he stayed in school.

Broke surprised Sherry on her nineteenth birthday with dinner and a movie. To cap the night off, he also took her to PJ's nightclub for a night of partying. PJ's was the most glamorous nightclub in town. It was ranked amongst the top of all the clubs in the country. PJ's was a popular spot for the college crowd. Lil' Shelia and Borilla were regulars in the club and were dancing on the lighted dance floor when Broke and Sherry arrived.

Sherry looked absolutely beautiful in the short black mini-dress she wore. The soft silky dress seemed to move with her body like it was part of her every curve. Broke had bought the dress and matching top for her as a birthday present. He had also bought her the white designer shoes, white pearl earrings and white pearl necklace that accented her neckline making Sherry the most stunning woman in the club.

Sherry wore her hair long in a Janet Jackson style. The gold chain around her ankle sparkled as she gracefully walked alongside Broke in the club. She was definitely not the little preacher's daughter tonight. With her statuette shape and flawless skin, Sherry was on every man's wish list as she held Broke's hand. Broke was dressed fashionably in a charcoal gray outfit. He wore his collar open with a gold chain glistening around his neck. Broke's muscular frame gave him a regal look as if he was a black king who was escorting his queen before their subjects. This is the royal impression that they gave as they walked through the club.

Borilla shouted when Broke and Sherry were passing their table. "What's up cuz," Borilla shouted.

Broke turned to see Borilla and Lil' Shelia who were seated at a table with another man and woman.

"What's up Bo," Broke shook Borilla's hand.

"Girl, you look like new money." Borilla said as he stood back and looked Sherry over. "What brings y'all out tonight?" Borilla asked with his trademark smile.

"Tonight's Sherry's birthday," Broke said.

"Oooooooooooooo girrrrlll, it sure is your birthday," Lil' Shelia who had joined them in the aisle was hugging Sherry while jumping up and down. "Why didn't you remind me?"

"Why didn't you remember?" Sherry asked. "I never forget yours."

"Yea, that's because it's in February, the shortest month of the year for the shortest person let you tell it," Lil' Shelia said. "Where y'all sitting at?" Lil' Shelia asked.

"I guess we're going to sit right here." Broke nodded to a table that had just became vacant next to Borilla and Lil' Shelia.

"Girrl, I can't believe I forgot your birthday." Lil' Shelia was upset with herself for forgetting her best friend and cousin's birthday. "We going shopping tomorrow."

Lil' Shelia turned to take her seat and bumped into Borilla who was standing in her way.

"Bo, move your big head self out my way. You the reason I forgot my homegirl's birthday."

"What I do? Borilla asked.

"Nothing, but kept me up all last night, trying to do something."

"I must've done something. I kept you up all night." Borilla said with a smile. Borilla hugged Lil' Shelia and pulled her down into his lap. "I'm a keep you up all night tonight too."

"Hmmph!" Lil' Shelia said. "Boy I'm not fooling with you."

"Who that is?" The girl sitting with Lil' Shelia and Borilla asked.

"Aw, that's my cousin Sherry and her husband, Broke. We grew out together. Tonight's her birthday."

The girl kept stealing glances at Broke throughout the night. Broke and Sherry were slow dancing to the song, I Will Do Anything by Jaheim. Sherry's eyes were closed as she leaned into Broke's chest. She had never been so happy. She felt like all the years of tears and pain were now worth the waiting. Broke held Sherry's chair out for her after returning to their table.

"I'll be right back." Broke kissed Sherry on the forehead. He walked casually through the club as if oblivious to the staring and glaring, eyes of those who watched him for reasons of envy, longing and admiration.

Lil' Shelia joined Sherry at her table. Sherry wasn't along but a moment before men began flocking to the table asking for a dance or conversation. Lil' Shelia pulled her chair up next to Sherry.

"Girl, these niggers like vultures. And the ho's ain't no better. Excuuuuseee me," Lil' Shelia said to a man who tried to lean over her to speak with Sherry. "No she don't want to dance. Can't you see me and my homegirl talking. Now gon' back over there with yo' friends. Bye. Bye." Lil' Shelia waved the man off with a flick of her hand.

The man gave her a stern look but said nothing as he tried to play down the embarrassing moment and strolled away. "Anyway, back to what I was saying. Girl these niggers in here like vultures. And the ho's ain't no better. Like that Lil' big titty ho' sitting at my table. Now here she is with her man and act like I don't know she been watching Broke all night. At first she was watching Borilla. Bo, no better. Every since that last heifer. He know the next time I'm gone. Look at her." Lil' Shelia nodded at the girl who had got up from the table and was now walking towards the bar. "I bet she gon' go and-try-and talk to Broke."

"Girl, I ain't worried about no woman. Sherry politely refused another request to dance as Lil' Shelia stared up at the man leaning across the table.

"Girl, he need to quit." Lil' Shelia said as she brushed off her shoulder. "Dripping that damn Jherri Curl juice all over my damn clothes. Look at him. Look like a damn frog. Gon' hop his happy ass over here like somebody want to dance with his ass. Girl, I'm telling you. These niggers crazy."

"Girl will you hush." Sherry couldn't help laughing as Lil' Shelia talked non-stop while staring around the club with a disgusted look on her face.

"Me and Broke, I mean Broke and I have been through too much for me to worry about some woman. And you know I'm not going nowhere. Plus I keep him satisfied. Ain't nothing like that black snapper Sherry said with a giggle of embarrassment."

"I know you didn't, I knnnnooooowww you didn't." Lil' Shelia stared at Sherry in shock and surprise.

"What?" Sherry said confidently. "You better ask someboby."

"Ask somebody hell, I'm-a tell somebody. I'm a tell your daddy. They always said the preacher daughters were the biggest freaks." Lil' Shelia was laughing loudly. "Ain't you something. I will say it's about time you got that thang oiled."

"Yea right," Sherry said.

"You must be doing something right," Lil' Shelia said. "I see you sporting them pearls."

"This my birthday present."

"They look good on you. I might have to borrow them bad boys sometimes."

143

***

Broke was leaving the bathroom when the woman he saw sitting with Lil' Shelia and Borilla walked up and slightly brushed into him. "Excuse me she said as she stared at Broke with lustful eyes."

"It's cool." Broke said.

"You having fun?" The woman asked.

"It's all right. Excuse me," Broke started to walk away.

"Well, if you ever get bored with the same ol' thing, just call Dorm-C on the yard and ask for Val. Everybody know me."

"I bet," Broke said as he walked away.

Broke walked over to the corner bar where three men and a woman sat with their backs to him at the bar. The men were speaking with a baldhead man behind the bar.

Broke stood at the end of the bar and called to the bartender. The men seated at the bar turned to face him. Fast Money gave a sly smile as he nudged the man who was with him at the car wash in Altheimer when they were confronted by Broke and the locals. Broke first thoughts were for Sherry's safety. He had found out recently that the men they had stomped out in Altheimer who had robbed Borilla were all on Fast Money's payroll. It was Fast Money's drugs they were selling the night of their arrest.

"Well, Well, Well," Fast Mony said slowly. "Look who's here, Michelle."

The woman at the bar turned to see Broke. Broke stared at the woman with a blank look in his eyes. To him, she didn't exist. To the woman, Broke was the most handsome man in the club. He looked regal and strong standing at the end of the bar. Her mouth dropped open in shocked surprise. Michelle had often wondered what had happened to

Broke. When she had first agreed to seduce and set him up as a fall guy for Fast Money, she didn't know that she would grow so fond of him. Broke was the only man that had ever treated her like a woman of worth. He had made her feel special at a time in her life when drugs were her only friend. Michelle had cried the night she watched from up the street as the cops had placed Broke in the patrol car. That was the last time she had seen Broke before seeing him again tonight. Broke felt nothing for Michelle. Even though she may have been beautiful to the world, she was ugly to him.

"What's up Mr. Broke, you can't say hello to your old friend.

Broke ignored Fast Money and asked the bartender for a daiquiri and slow gin fizz. Sherry walked over to Broke at the bar after leaving the bathroom. She hugged him around the waist. "What you order me." She asked. Sherry noticed the tense feel of Broke's body. "What's wrong?"

"Nothing to worry 'bout."

"You trying to get me drunk and take advantage of me. Huh!" Sherry who was already over her limit nibbled on Broke's ear.

Broke reached for his change and pocketed the money before kissing Sherry on her forehead. "Let's go," he said.

Michelle heart dropped in her chest as she stared at Broke with the beautiful woman on his arms. "So, Mr. Broke, ain't you gon' introduce your new lady friend to your old lady friend."

Sherry stared at Fast Money for the first time. She remembered him from the car wash and suddenly realized why Broke's body was so tense. Sherry also recognized Michelle. Sherry had seen Michelle on one other occasion in Altheimer. Michelle was with Fast Money when Borilla had told Sherry that she was the girl who had set Broke up and sent him to prison. Sherry was going to confront Michelle but was held back by Borilla and Lil' Shelia.

145

Broke had grown tired of Fast Money's mouth. The taunting was making him angrier by the minute. "Look here Mr. Fast Money. I'm not that same naive eighteen year old you set up as a fall guy three years ago. Don't think I can't touch you. Now if you really want to impress your friends you can show them how smart you are by leaving me the fuck alone." The men sitting at the bar with Fast Money raised up off their stools.

"All right fellows," the baldhead man behind the bar said. "Now you guys know I'm not gon' have no trouble in here, don't you." The man was staring at Fast Money as he spoke with one hand beneath the bar. Fast Money knew that PJ, who was the owner of the nightclub, kept a small baseball bat behind the bar. He was also known to use the bat without discretion if there was trouble in the club.

Broke was about to walk away when Fast Money told him that he would see him later.

"I hope so." Broke said.

PJ stared after Broke as he relaxed his hand on the bat. He liked the way Broke carried himself. Broke had shown no fear when Fast Money's crew had stood up as if they were about to make a move. PJ was almost sure that the only thing that kept Broke from attacking Fast Money first was the grip of the beautiful woman that clung to his arm.

"I'm a punish that Lil' punk." Fast Money took a sip from his drink. Michelle stared after Broke with longing eyes. She wished that she could correct her wrong. She wished that she could turn back the hands of time.

"Man, fuck that nigger," Fast Money's right hand man Benny said.

"I'll sure like to fuck that bitch," a short, premature balding, green eyed, man name Fat Man said. Fat Man who looked like he used to be handsome before drugs and alcohol, grabbed the seat of his pants. "That black bitch fine as all out doors."

146

"That's one of them corn fed ho's," Benny said.

"Bitch, ain't shit." Fast Money said with contempt in his voice. His jealousy was obvious to everyone but himself. "Square ass, broke ass ho. I wouldn't give the bitch a dime if she brought a whole cow home, I'll eat the meat, bury the bones, and tell the bitch to hunt her black ass on."

PJ stared at Fast Money from behind the bar. He never liked Fast Money. PJ was from the old school. He still played the game by old school rules. If you do the crime be man enough to do the time. If not for the money that Fast Money and his crew spent in the club trying to show off, he would have barred him from the club long time ago. PJ decided to burst Fast Money's bubble.

As owner of the most popular club in town, PJ had lasted so long in the business because he kept his nose to the street so he would know who was beefing with who. That way he could put extra security around the beefing parties after informing them that he was watching them.

"Damn, Fast Money," PJ said slowly. "If that's how you treat the men who stand up for you, I'll hate to be the one who cross you. Didn't youngblood right there do a three piece for you? Shit, from what I hear, he ought to be the one mad."

"Maybe you hearing wrong, or old age affecting your hearing," Fast Money spoke with an edge in his voice.

"Probably so," PJ said. "You know how the streets lie. It's a good thing too. I know some boys who done some time with youngster. I didn't know who he was until you called his name. It's hard to forget a name like Broke. As old as I am, that's the first nigger I ever heard named Broke. I remember him because ol' boy say a nigger name Broke who use to work for Fast Money was the best boxer in the prison system."

147

"Niggers ain't boxing no mo," Fast Money said, "Niggers shooting these days."

"I hear you." PJ said as he sat down at the bar. "I know you ain't worried no way, not with all this muscle you got around you." PJ stared at Benny and Fat Man with a pathetic look on his face. Neither man had a reputation for being tough.

PJ retrieved a bottle of cognac and poured some in a glass over ice. He handed the glass to Michelle. Michelle was sitting quietly with a blank look on her face stirring her straw around in the ice left over from her drink.

"Here you go baby. It's on the house. You look like you could use another drink."

If looks could kill, PJ would have died in his steps from the look Fast Money was giving him as he walked away. Michelle was about to reach for the drink when Fast Money's words caused her to pause.

"Bitch, leave that shit on the counter. Give this ho' another drink." Fast Money threw a twenty-dollar bill on the bar for the bartender.

"I'm ready to go." Michelle said softly.

Fast Money grabbed Michelle's arm with a firm grip as she stood off the stool,

"Bitch, sit your ass down!"

"Chill out Fast Money," Benny said as he stared around for PJ. He also cast a glance in the direction of the big bartender who stood when Fast Money grabbed Michelle's arm.

"Man, that's my song. I'm going to get me one of these ho's and dance." Fat Man was so afraid that he almost stumbled as he gave the lame excuse to distance himself from Fast Money in case PJ returned.

"Let go of me." Michelle tried to pull away from Fast Money.

"Bitch, I say sat your ass down." Fast Money tightened his grip on Michelle's arm.

"Let me go dammit," Michelle snatched her arm away from Fast Money's grip. She stood defiantly away from Fast Money as he stared at her with fire in his eyes.

Fast Money couldn't believe that Michelle was talking to him and acting like she was acting. He was about to slap her when PJ's voice froze him with his hand raised in the air. "Slow your roll, Fast Money." PJ's hand was again hid beneath the bar as he stared at Fast Money with a warning look on his face. Benny was so afraid that he was shaking.

He hoped that Fast Money didn't say or do something stupid to provoke PJ to use the bat. There were ten or more people sitting in tables in the area of the bar. They were all staring at Fast Money who began smiling.

"Man, fuck this ho." Fast Money reached into his pockets for his keys. "Let's roll, Benny."

"Yea man, fuck that bitch." Benny said after exhaling from holding his breath during the tense standoff.

***

Michelle sat in an obscure corner of the club. She watched Broke and Sherry for the rest of the night. She envied Sherry. The way Broke catered to her by holding out her chair or holding her in his arms were reminders of how Broke had once treated her. Michelle wished that she could explain to Broke why she had done what she done.

"I'm ready to go and unwrap my other present," Sherry nibbled on Broke's ear as they slow danced.

149

"What other present?" Broke asked.

"The one that's poking me between my legs." Sherry said. "Come on, let's go. I got a place you can hide it until the swelling go down."

"Ain't you something," Broke said.

"What's up cuz. Y'all 'bout to leave."

"Yea, we out." Broke said to Borilla as him and Sherry gathered their things in preparation to leave.

"Don't forget we going shopping tomorrow." Lil' Shelia said to Sherry. "And turn some music on with all that noise y'all be making all night."

"You just jealous." Sherry hugged Broke around the waist as she stuck her tongue out at Lil' Shelia.

"Girl please, you sound like a "Broke" record." Lil' Shelia started laughing as she leaned back in Borilla's arms at the table.

"Umm Hmm," Sherry said. "Well, at least we're not "Bo-rinnnngg, Bo-ring, get it, Sherry stuck her tongue out at Lil' Shelia as she turned to walk off with Broke.

Michelle stared after Broke and Sherry as they left the club. She was ready to leave as well but with Fast Money gone she no longer had a ride. She had refused numerous advances throughout the night from men who would have gladly taken her anywhere she wanted to go. Broke had raised the bar to high for the men in the club. Sherry decided to catch a cab and stepped outside underneath the canopy in front of the club to wait until one arrived. She was fortunate to have a cab waiting out front of the club.

The sexy redbone with her auburn colored hair cut short to her head caught the cab driver by surprise when she entered his cab. The cab driver wondered why someone so sexy and attractive would have to catch a cab. Surely she could have had any sucker in the club give her a ride home or wherever. He figured she was either visiting town, or got into a fight with her boyfriend, girlfriends or husband. The last possibility was that she felt she was too drunk to drive.

***

Broke placed his hand on Sherry's thighs as he pulled away from the nightclub. "I have to stop for gas," he said.

"Make it fast, I'm ready to go to bed," Sherry smiled and said.

"Yeah, me too," Broke faked a yawn.

"I wish you would fall asleep on me," Sherry snuggled up in Broke's arms.

Michael Rogers

Cream

Chapter 19

"Where to?" The driver asked.

"Chapel Village Apartments," Michelle said as she settled back into the backseat of the cab with her legs curled beneath her. The cab was very clean and had a nice smell. This surprised Michelle.

"So who made you mad?" The cab driver asked over the soft tune of reggae music playing across the car stereo.

"Do I look mad?" Michelle had a hint of frustration in her voice.

"Naw, not really, as a matter of fact, you don't. I just figured that someone as lovely as yourself wouldn't have to catch a cab from a nightclub. If so, the men in the club tonight must be on some other kind of time. But I could be wrong. Maybe you're just pretty on the outside."

"Just drive." Michelle said with a snap in her voice. "If I wanted to be bothered with idle chit chatter, I would have taken one of them rides you're talking about."

"I hear you," the driver said. "You know how some of us black men are. We think we have all the answers and that every woman wants us because we're so damn fly."

"Well, take it from me. We don't." Michelle said. "And can you please play something else on the radio."

"Oh yea, my bad. I forget at times, that just because I like Reggae, that it doesn't mean that everyone does. You seem more like the Destiny Child type anyway. How about a little Beyonce."

"Thank you." Michelle stared out the window of the cab.

"So you're a survivor, huh?"

"You mind stopping up the street at that convenience store so I can get me some cigarettes." Michelle ignored the driver's remark.

"I'm glad you mentioned that. I need some myself. Better get some gas too while I'm at it. I'll hate to run out of gas with Beyonce in the car."

The driver pulled onto the convenience store lot. He asked Michelle if she wanted him to bring her some cigarettes. Michelle handed him a twenty and settled back down in her seat. Michelle hadn't noticed Broke who was filling his gas tank across from the cab at the gas pumps. She only noticed him when she saw the cab driver embraced Broke in a brotherly hug like two long lost brothers who hadn't seen one another in a long time. Michelle wondered how the man knew Broke so well. She saw the driver place what she assumed to be Broke's phone number in his pocket. The driver returned to the cab with the same wide smile on his face that he had had when speaking with Broke.

"I'm sorry about the wait," he said as he handed Michelle her cigarettes. "I haven't seen my man in a while. That's my nigga right there. I didn't know my man had moved to town." The driver was speaking excitedly as Michelle sat wondering how he knew Broke so well.

"Where you know him from?" Michelle asked the question nonchalantly as if just making conversation.

"Oh, you don't wanna know."

"If I didn't, I wouldn't have asked."

"Well, Ms. Beyonce, if you must know. Me and my man done some time together courtesy of the state down at Cummings. We also used to box together. That's Broke. He was the best boxer in the whole prison system. We spent many nights trying to keep one another sane in that hellhole. Both of us were young when we went in and I guess the old heads thought we would be easy prey. Probably would've been if not for my man's old school homeboy name Brick. Old Head was a revolutionary, a George Jackson type motherfucker. If Brick hadn't taken us under his wings we'll probably both be dead or doing life right now. Cause we wan' going for the okey doke. We spent many hours learning about life under dude."

The driver got somberly quiet as he seemed to reflect on some deep dark thought that he wondered if he should reveal. "My man lost both parents while in prison. I remember when he lost his mother. He whooped five guards for trying to make him work after telling him they didn't give a damn about his mama. Now I know when you look at me, you see this debonair cab driver, but I have my demons. My man though. He's the most honest dude I ever met. Shouldn't-nah never even been in prison.

My man had to do three years. Some chick he loved set him up as a fall guy for this clown ass nigger named Fast Money. And I thought niggas were bad. It's women like that, who makes men like me single and heartless today."

"Can't nobody make you do nothing you don't want to do, and you should hear the woman side before you go jumping conclusions. Maybe she was naive and afraid or maybe she was in love with something that had a greater hold on her than your friend."

"I don't know the driver said." But whatever it was, it sure caused my man a helluva lot. All right, I've told you my story. Now what's yours."

"I don't have a story," Michelle said.

"Everybody has a story," the driver said, "Your's just might not be worth telling. My story is a love story. It's a romantic novel about a black man and his love for a big face chick called money."

"Is that right? Is that why you drive cabs? Michelle asked the question with her voice dripping with sarcasm.

"Not really," the driver said. "But you do meet some interesting people. Very interesting, if you know what I mean. Really, though, I just do this to keep out of trouble and to have an alibi in case something happens that fits my M.O. That way, if someone is robbed or killed, I'll have an alibi. By the way, I don't just drive cabs. I'm a man of many means. That's why they call me CREAM."

"Is that what your mother named you? Or is it just another ghetto street name you chose to give yourself street credibility."

"Naw baby, that's the way I live. People start calling me Cream after that Wu Tang song. You know the one. Cash Rules Everything Around Me."

"Yea I heard it," Michelle said as if unimpressed.

"So what's your name?" Cream stared at Michelle through the rearview mirror.

"MAAT," Michelle said.

"MAAT," Cream repeated the name. "Now, I know that's not a birth name. Awww, okay, you reclaiming your Egyptian heritage. You took your name after the MAAT system of righteous balance, peace and harmony."

"Hmmph, I think not, it stands for Money Ain't A Thing."

"Aw, okay, I see you got jokey, jokes. That's cool, I like a woman with a sense of humor. When you live like I live, sometimes you need to laugh. The way I live it seems I bring more pain than joy."

Michelle stared at the handsome driver. He didn't quite fit the mode of a cabdriver. Maybe if she had caught his cab on another, less stressful day, she wouldn't have been so sarcastic. Today, she had enough problems.

None bigger than the one standing in wait for her outside her apartment. Michelle sighed heavily as she stared at the angry Fast Money leaning on his car and waiting for her to arrive.

"It was nice meeting you, Cream. My name is Michelle." Michelle gathered her things. "I'm sorry for being rude. It's been a tough night."

Michael Rogers

Chapter 20

"Looks like you got company." Cream noticed Fast Money's black coupe that was parked in front of Michelle's apartment. Cream said nothing as he parked behind the Lexus.

"Well I guess this is goodbye." Michelle said.

"Yea, I guess it is." Michelle noticed a sudden edge in Cream's voice. She stared at him with a puzzled look on her face.

"So, how much I owe you?" she asked.

"Keep it." Cream said. "Maybe, you can buy a conscience."

"A what?" Michelle asked.

"Just keep the money." Cream sat up straight behind the steering wheel as he waited for Michelle to exit the car.

Fast Money stared angrily at Michelle. "Bitch, what took you so long! He was glaring at Michelle as he waited for her to walk over to him. I got people waiting all over town for me and yo' silly ass still out fucking around. I outta slap the shit out you. Silly ass bitch." Fast Money continued to glare at Michelle as he blew a blast of smoke from the cigarette he was smoking into her face.

"Ain't you got a key? Michelle asked the question in an agitated voice while trying to fan the cigarette smoke from her face.

"Bitch! You think if I had my damn key, I would be out here waiting for your dumb ass. Gimme the damn key!" Fast Money snatched Michelle's purse from her hand.

"Give me back my purse," Michelle snatched the purse back from Fast

Money.

"Slap!" Fast Money slapped Michelle to the ground and stood over her as she held her hand to her face while staring up at him. Fast Money kicked her in the side and called her a stupid ass bitch as he snatched the purse from her and dumped its' contents on the ground.

Cream was driving away slowly when he saw Fast Money slap the girl. He stopped the cab when he saw Fast Money kick her.

Cream was well aware of Fast Money. It hadn't taken him long to put two and two together and realize that Michelle was the girl who had set up his man Broke. He recognized her from the description that Broke had given him of her. Cream already knew of Fast Money's involvement with Broke's incarceration. When he saw him parked in front of Michelle's apartment he remembered the description Broke had given him of her. That's when he realized that the girl Broke had spoken of and the girl in the cab were one and same. Cream was about to pull away from the drama until Fast Money had kicked the girl.

He thought back to what the girl had said in the cab when he spoke bad about the girl who had betrayed Broke.

"Maybe she was naive or afraid," Cream thought back to the words as he stopped the cab and backed it up. Fast Money held his hand up to strike Michelle again as he kicked her for the fifth time.

"Bitch I'll kill you. Don't ever disrespect me again." Fast Money was poised to strike Michelle again when he noticed that Cream had returned and was getting out of the cab with his hand in his pocket.

Cream jumped out the cab and walked around to where Fast Money stood over Michelle. Benny and Slow, who was with Fast money, jumped out the Lexus and quickly walked over to the scene.

"What's up trick, you got a problem." Fast Money stared hard at Cream.

"Trick you know me." Cream said. "And I ain't gon' be too many more of them names. So you better check yourself. Now, the only problem we gon' have is if you hit my ho' again."

"Trick, this my ho'," Fast Money glared at Cream. He wasn't afraid of Cream but he didn't want any unnecessary trouble with him either. He knew of Cream and how Cream was holding it down in the Loop. He also knew that Cream had some serious players on his team. "You know the game." Fast Money said.

"Yea, I know the game, and if you know me, you know that I play by the rules. That's why I say we gon' have problems if you hit my ho' again. Bitch chose pimping on the way over. You know how it go. You can't leave a bag of goodies like this lying around in front of a brother like me. You know I got a sweet tooth. I only left her here for a minute to pack her things, while I ran to the store."

Michelle stared from Cream to Fast Money. She felt degraded as they treated her like she didn't exist or had a say in the matter of how she was treated.

"Baby, get up and go get your things. Unless you want to remain here with this wannabe hustler and sometime pimp."

Fast Money released his hold on Michelle and stepped from over her. Benny and Slow stood watching. They were waiting for Fast Money to give them the command to act.

"Nigga, one ho' ain't gon' break me. I'll have two more staying in this bitch tomorrow. Benny, you still got that bitch Jazz number. Aw shit, that's right, I forgot. Somebody killed that bitch for running off with this nigger here. I wonder what will happen to the next bitch that run off." Fast Money tossed Michelle's purse to the ground.

Michelle was uncertain of what to do. She slowly began to gather her things and place them back into her purse. It was true that she entertained Fast Money's out of town customers from time to time. She even housed large quantities of his drugs in the apartment. Still, she never considered herself a whore. Reality hit her hard as the two men traded ownership over her like she was a piece of property.

"Bitch get yo' shit and get yo' once a month blood dripping ass out of my apartment." Fast Money tossed the keys to the apartment to Benny. "Man, let this bitch in and watch her so she can get her shit. That shouldn't take long, being that everything in that motherfucker belongs to me. Including the clothes on this ho's back." Fast Money stared at Cream with a sneer. "I hope this nigger got something for the bitch to wear or her ass gon' leave here butt ass naked. Rule #33," Fast Money brazenly said. "Ho's can't leave with nothing but their wear and tear. A cookie pimp nigger like yourself probably wouldn't know this rule. It's a relatively new rule so young punks like yourself probably haven't heard of it yet."

"Clown ass nigga, who you think wrote the rule." Cream reached into the cab and popped the trunk from the glove compartment. He walked around to the trunk and pulled out a designer dress and a pair of designer shoes. Cream gave the items to Michelle and told her to hurry up so they could leave. Michelle took the clothes and walked fast into the apartment where Benny stood at the door. Michelle was in and out the house in ten minutes with a small bag of personal items in her hand. She was wearing the dress from the trunk. The dress fit her perfectly as did the shoes. Fast Money and his crew sat on the trunk of his car as Cream and Michelle were pulling away.

"You know," Cream stopped the cab and spoke out the window to Fast Money, "If certain people ever find out what happen to Jazz, the party responsible for her death might not want to be around. I would hate to see what might happen to those responsible for the death of such a fine black creature if they are ever found."

"If you find out who's looking for her killer, let me know." Fast Money stared hard at Cream. "I'll sure like to see the man who's bad enough to go after such a deranged nigga."

"You'll be the first to know," Cream pulled away from Fast Money and his crew while searching his CD case for a reggae cassette.

***

Michelle sat in the backseat of the cab with everything she owned in the bag beside her. She was a long way from Des Moines, Iowa. It was Fast Money who had talked her into leaving home. Michelle had first met him through some of her relatives that he knew back in Iowa. Fast Money had been running drugs out of Des Moines when Michelle first met him. That was five years ago. Michelle had moved to Pine Bluff with Fast Money after knowing him for only two months. Life had been downhill for her every since.

Michelle had no choice but to follow Fast Money orders. Fast Money who was heavy into smoking pre-mo's of crack cocaine mixed with marijuana had hooked Michelle on the habit. Not only had she become dependent on drugs, Michelle was also afraid of Fast Money. She had seen him abuse both women and men. Michelle had even witness Fast Money kill a man at a club in a small town in Iowa. She had also been witness to him shooting two other men on different occasions in little Rock where he also sold drugs.

Michelle had felt she had no choice but to seduce Broke the night Fast Money had pointed him out to her in the club. Fast Money had just caught a cocaine possession charge and was looking for a fall guy. He had chosen Broke as his victim when he saw the way Broke was eying Michelle down in the club. Michelle told Broke that Fast Money was her cousin. Once she gained Broke's trust, she used his stolen personal information to set up the house used for the bust in his name. Michelle had no intention of falling in love with Broke. It was Broke who helped her to kick her pre-mo habit. The short time they had spent together were the happiest moments she had spent in Pine Bluff.

Michelle had wanted to tell Broke about Fast Money's plans. She was just too afraid. She was afraid not only for herself but also for Broke. Fast Money had told her that if she warned Broke that he would kill him. Michelle thought about what Fast Money had said about the girl name Jazz. She vaguely remembered Jazz but didn't know that Fast Money had possibly killed her. Michelle suddenly became afraid as she stared through the rearview mirror at the handsome stranger that had saved her from Fast Money and whom she now depended on to protect her from him. Cream hadn't shown any fear of Fast Money but neither did Fast Money show any fear of Cream.

Michelle sat quietly in her own thoughts. Cream placed a reggae CD into the CD player. Michelle knew that this was Cream's way of saying that what she wanted no longer mattered.

Chapter 21

Cream drove quietly as he contemplated about what he had done and what he intended to do now that he had already done what he had done. He knew that Fast Money could be trouble. Cream had accomplished a lot since his release from prison two years ago. With the money he made selling drugs in prison Cream had come home with a mission. At twenty-four Cream was much wiser than his age. He was the only son of a church going mother and hustling father. Cream had the same high cheekbones as his father and the golden brown eyes of his mother. The dreads Cream had grown in prison now hung down to his shoulders. Cream was the classic pretty boy. He had the physique of a young Muhammad Ali. With his golden brown complexion and high cheekbones, Cream would put you in mind of a young Ali when Ali was known as Cassius Clay.

A handsome man with a quiet demeanor Cream was a true lady's man. Beneath the quiet demeanor rested a vicious mean streak. It was both his quiet demeanor and his viciousness that had attracted the two female prison employees who had become his sexual partners and drug couriers while Cream was in prison. Both women were fired for inappropriate behavior a month before his release. The two women now worked for Cream. Cream had been fortunate upon his release. True to his name it didn't take Cream long to find a new hustle once he was released from prison. Cream used the prison proceeds he had gained from selling drugs to purchase a cab company from an old friend of his father.

The business was located in the downtown area, of Pine Bluff, near the Pine Bluff City Jail. It was not the rundown cars or small cash flow, which had attracted Cream to the business. The real attraction of the business to Cream was the FCC license and freedom to roam indiscreetly in the cabs. The FCC license that he received to broadcast over his cab radios gave Cream the opportunity to set up a communication system that rival even the police department. Cream traded all the old cars of the former owner and bought five short body 98 Cadillac Seville like the one Broke drove. These were for his luxury line of service. He also bought four small Toyota's for delivering packages for his pickup and delivery service. Cream also added two pickups and two bob trucks to his delivery service fleet for picking up small appliances and furniture. The four traditional cabs he purchased he bought from a Little Rock cab company for $12,000.00. The other vehicles he had bought for $45,000.00 dollars plus trade-in values of his old cars. Cream had paid cash for all his purchases but had the dealers to carry the notes as if he was making payments to avoid the I.R.S.

With his cab company up and running, Cream's next purchase was a liquor store from an older white woman who had taken a fancy to him. The woman wanted to get out the business and offered to sell the business to Cream at a giveaway price. Cream had to buy the liquor store in his mother's name due to his criminal record. His next purchase was a private club in an area called the Loop. The Loop was located on the far end of the west side of Pine Bluff. Cream had been raised in the Loop. As a child Cream had always been the man in the Loop. Since coming home from prison, he was more the man now than he ever was in his younger days. Except now, Cream was no longer selling drugs.

Cream used the club as a cathouse. The women who used the club catered to the elites of town. Cream was making money hand over fist. He just didn't have anyone he could trust enough to give his heart.

Cream had fifteen girls and twenty men on his payroll. Stephanie and VJ had proven their loyalty to him as prison guards when they had hauled drugs and money for him in prison. Cream placed Stephanie over the cab company and VJ over the liquor store. Cream handled the girls who worked in the club.

Cream's right hand man was his ruthless homeboy, Skacehead. Skacehead and Cream had grown up fighting together for the top man spot in the Loop. Skacehead was quick tempered and violent. Cream had put Skacehead down with him because he figured it was easier to work with him rather then to have him as an enemy in the old hood. Scace as Cream called him was down for whatever and followed Cream's lead as long as he was kept at the top of the pecking order with respect for his opinions. Their bond of friendship was sealed because of the mutual respect they had for one another as standup men. Still, Cream had fought with Skacehead too much in the past to think that at some point in time they wouldn't have to fight again.

Cream felt his shirt pocket where he had placed Broke's cell phone number. His thoughts were interrupted when Michelle asked him where he was taken her. Cream stared through the rearview mirror at Michelle. He hadn't given much thought to where he was headed. He wished now he had never picked her up at PJ's. Cream only drove cabs at night. This allowed him to travel freely and to avoid the police attention he normally got whenever he drove his Range Rover or Corvette. He rarely took calls when driving the cab. He had only picked up Michelle because it was a busy night and he was helping out by dropping off a passenger at PJ's. Cream decided that Michelle could crash at his house until he decided what to do with her. He felt responsible for her now that he had gotten involved in her affairs.

Cream realized as he turned off Hazel Street onto Old Warren road where he lived that his destination had been decided long before he had given it any thought. Michelle sat back in the seat when Cream didn't answer her. She figured that at the time it didn't matter much anyway. Without any money or residence, she was all out of options. For the moment, her fate now rested in Cream's hands. Cream pulled into his driveway causing the sensor-controlled lights to illuminate the yard. The bright lights would have exposed anyone hiding in the darkness. The large ranch style brick house impressed Michelle. She had driven through the area on one other occasion in the past. She didn't know that black people lived amongst the affluent white professionals in the area, especially, black people, the likes of Cream.

Cream had bought the two hundred thousand dollar home from the same white woman who had sold him the liquor store. The liberal, northern white woman seemed to go out her way to thumb her nose at the prejudice of southern whites. Her husband had been from the south. When he died, she sold all her possessions and moved back up north. Because of her fascination for Cream, she felt that he would be the perfect candidate for revenge in her campaign to strike back at the southern prejudice that she had grown to hate. Her husband had been an influential banker and often entertained the town elites in their home. The same home she sold to Cream. The wife, Helen, would often hear her husband's friends speaking down about blacks. Being born of Jewish descent this never set well with Helen. She didn't see much difference between southern white prejudice towards blacks as she saw in the prejudice of Hitler towards Jews.

Helen had seen in Cream, all the things that white people hated about young black men. A young, strong, intelligent and handsome man, she knew that Cream would be perfect for her going away present to her white neighbors. Helen used her influence to insure that Cream's mother was able to purchase both the home and liquor store that she had sold to Cream. She could have made twice as much off the sale of the properties to the white friends of her former husband.

By way of Helen's revenge, Cream now owned one of the finest houses in one of the finest neighborhoods in Pine Bluff. His closest neighbors were a mile away. These neighbors had at first tried to scare him off with a burning cross and a rock thrown through the window. The rock had a racist note attached to it that told Cream to get out the neighborhood. Cream didn't know who was responsible for the note or the burning cross. It was for this reason that he had the sensor lights placed around his house. He also had Skacehead and some of his cronies to ride through the community one night from one end to the next and place AK-47 bullets along with family photos in the mailboxes of every family. That was the end of the white terror campaign against Cream. The whites along the road had thought they were dealing with an aging black woman. When they realized instead that they were dealing with her young ruthless son, the cowardice in them came out and they all crawled back into their holes. Those who could afford to move had already moved out the community. Now, thanks to Cream, there were several more black families along the road.

Helen had sold the house to Cream complete with expensive furnishings and decor. Michelle marveled at the spiral staircase and antique furnishings. "You can stay here until I figure out what I've gotten myself into," Cream said. Cream sat on the couch and reached for the telephone. He called the cab company and nightclub to check on things and to inform the staff that he was in for the night.

"Come on," Cream said in a voice void of emotions.

Michelle who was sitting quietly in a chair against the wall slowly rose from the chair. She followed Cream up the spiral staircase.

"You can use this room," Cream pointed to one of four bedrooms and told Michelle it was hers before walking back down stairs.

Michelle walked into the bedroom and stood in center floor for five minutes before sighing and taking off her clothing. She walked down the hall to the bathroom to shower. Michelle emerged twenty minutes later from the bathroom. Cream was coming up the stairs as Michelle was walking back into the bedroom wrapped in a towel. Her naturally curly hair was wet atop her head and covered her face as she dried it with another towel.

Cream paused for a second and took in the beauty of the sexy light-skinned woman that put him in mind of a darker version of Alicia Keys.

Michelle was startled by Cream's presence. There hadn't been more than ten words spoken between them since the incident with Fast Money.

"There's some clothes in the closet that should fit you." Cream took one last look at Michelle before walking into his bedroom.

Michelle found the closet to be filled with clothes. The dresser drawer and every other drawer in the room were filled, with clothes as well. Amazingly all the clothes were her size. Cream was on the telephone when Michelle walked down the stairs the next morning. From his expression upon seeing her, she could tell that the conversation was about her.

Broke was on the phone speaking with Cream. Cream had called to tell him about the incident with Fast Money and Michelle being at his house. If Broke had any problem at all with Michelle being there, Broke knew that Cream would put her out immediately. Broke told Cream that he was no longer angry with Michelle. He realized long time ago that Fast Money had pressured her into doing what she had done. If not for Sherry being his soul mate, Broke had not ruled out the possibility that him and Michelle may have resumed their relationship. Broke told Cream that Michelle could be like a condemned dog that he had rescued from an animal shelter or a snake he had picked up in the cold. Like the condemned dog, out of gratitude, she may be his best friend and protector. Or, like the snake, if he ever forgot how to rub her, and she's rubbed the wrong way, she may just bite and poison him. Or, Broke had said, she may be like the eagle you find with the broken wing. You may nurture her back to good health, but once she's well, and you come to like her company, she may up and fly away because she likes her freedom. As for me, I've been blessed with an angel, and I'm not mad at nobody, because it took all of what I've been through to appreciate what I have today. "It's destiny," Broke said.

"Shit, what about me. You don't think I need an angel." Cream said.

"She might be your angel." Broke said. "Just remember that the devil has angels too, we just call them demons."

"Man is that what them fools teaching y'all in college." Now, I got to figure out rather I'm going to need an exorcist or an animal trainer." Cream was laughing loudly.

He was still laughing when Michelle had walked down the stairs. "Well, either my dog, snake or demon done woke up," Cream said. "I got to go and figure out rather I'm going to need an exorcist or an animal trainer."

"Get at me later." Broke hung up the phone as Sherry laid her head in his lap.

"Who was that?" Sherry asked.

"That was Cream. The guy from the gas station last night who I was telling you about that I met in prison."

"Well, I hope your friend Cream don't get Creamed. You know what they say."

"What's that?"

"A leopard can't change its' stripes."

"That might be true, but that don't mean you can't change the leopard."

"Oh you just full of wisdom this morning, huh." Sherry straddled Broke on the couch still wearing just her panties and bra. "Let's see if you can answer this love call. Sherry took off her bra and tossed it before kissing Broke and moaning softly.

"I thought you and Lil' Shelia were going shopping." Broke said between kisses.

"We are," Sherry said as she unbuckled his pants. "But first, I got to please my husband."

"Is that right?" Broke asked.

"Uh huh," Sherry pulled Broke up from the couch by the arm. "This won't take long," she said.

"That's what you think," Broke allowed Sherry to pull him into the bedroom. As always, he was willing to go.

Chapter 22

Lil' Brick tossed a rock in the ditch as he held the hand of his girlfriend Kay Kay. He was walking Kay Kay home. Kay Kay lived with her mother two blocks down from the projects. Neither Lil' Brick or Kay Kay paid any attention to the brown unmarked Malibu that slowly trailed behind them.

The man driving the Malibu was admiring the young developing shape of the sixteen-year-old girl walking with the thug-looking boy. He figured she was a project girl. A hood rat as they were called. The fat man driving the car was wedged behind the seat of the Malibu. He was breathing shallow breaths as he watched with his mouth open as if hypnotized by the swaying hips of the girl. "Mmmmmm, just like I like them." The man moaned as he whispered to himself while rubbing between his legs. Young, tender and fresh, just ripe for picking he was thinking. His last one had been fourteen years old and still a virgin. That was rare, very few virgins made it past the age of twelve in these parts.

As a cop for thirty years, the man was now going through young daughters of the women who had been traded to him when they were young. Mothers of the young girl like the one he was watching were always in need. They either needed an old fine fixed, a warrant stopped, charges dropped, or in some cases, drugs were traded that he had taken off some young punk like the one walking with the girl. These mothers who he would do favors for, would in turn, do favors for him. Such favors like sending their young daughters to clean up his house. Not the house where he lived with his dogs in White Hall. They came to clean the drug house he had purchased at a police auction that was located two blocks away from the projects. The mothers knew before hand what was expected of their daughters. Many didn't care. Those that did care preferred to act ignorant of what they knew was happening. The money he gave the girls to buy their silence the mothers would sometimes take.

In an ironic twist, the mothers would become the enemy of the girls for taking their money, and he would become their best friend for giving them the money. The young girls eventually begin to seek him out and would even bring friends along with them on their visits in hopes of making more money for themselves for bringing a friend. The cop figured that nothing really mattered to the young project girls. Most had already experienced more sexual abuse, either from male family members, mother's boyfriends, or consensual sex with young boys, by the age of twelve, than most women would see in a lifetime. That's what the cop believed. That's why he acted with total disregard for the feelings of the young girls he chose for his deviate sexual pleasures.

***

Lil' Brick became nervously aware of the car behind them. He pulled Kay Kay behind him and waited for the car to pass. The cop pulled up beside them after being noticed.

"What's your name son?" The cop twisted in his seat as he spoke in an authoritative manner.

"Lil' Brick." Lil' Brick stood defiantly.

"I got a report of a missing person," the cop lied. "Someone's mother is worried about them not coming home last night."

"What's that got to do with me?" Lil' Brick asked the question with sarcasm in his voice.

"It depends on if this is the girl I'm looking for. What's your name sugar?"

"My name is Kay Kay," Kay Kay answered quickly, trying to be helpful.

"Kay Kay," the cop repeated her name. "Is your mama named Karen?"

174

"My mama name Kat, there she go right there." The cop looked to where Kay Kay was pointing to a woman in a yard up the street.

A big black Amazon of a woman was standing with her hands on her hips staring at them from the yard.

"Do y'all know Tricia?" the cop asked.

"Nope."

"Nope." Lil' Brick and Kay Kay both answered nope as they began to walk away.

The cop pulled away slowly but not before catching another eye full of the fat bottom and shiny black legs of the young girl. He cast a glance at the girl's mother who glared at him as he passed her by.

Kat was tending to the hedge bush in her yard. Kat worked hard for her money. She took pride in the fact that she was not on any government assistance and that she didn't have to live in the projects. She wasn't afraid of no man and had heard rumors about the cop that lived in the house up the streets from the projects. She swore that if she ever caught him with her daughter she was going to let some air out of his fat perverted ass.

"What that fool want?" Kat asked Kay Kay and Lil' Brick.

"He say he looking for some girl name Tricia," Kay Kay said.

"Uh Huh, the next time his fat ass want to talk to you, tell him I say talk to me. Fat ass perverted bitch. I wish I would catch his fat ass trying to mess with you."

"Don't worry, I know 'bout that punk." Lil' Brick said assuredly.

The detective thought about the young tender, tight body of the black girl, it was something about her that got him going. He wanted to see the pain in her eyes when he penetrated her in that tight butthole. It

175

was always the ones that he couldn't have that he wanted the most. And just like always he would somehow find a way to satisfy his lust. The longer the wait the better the pleasure. He just hated the wait. But he swore that when the time came he was gonna punish the little bitch.

The detective increased his speed as a call for assistance came over his radio. His thoughts were still on the girl. He knew that the route to success would not be through the mother. That was out the question. He figured his best route would be through the young thug. He wondered how much the girl loved the boy. He wondered if her love was so strong that she would be willing to clean his house as a favor to get the young punk out of jail on possession of drug charges. We'll just have to see won't we. The detective smiled to himself as a plan formed in his mind. He could already hear the young girl screaming beneath him as he began to place a call on his cell phone.

Chapter 23

Cream sat at the kitchen table going over his books after checking the receipts from the night before. VJ was fixing sandwiches as Stephanie worked the calculator.

This was the scene that Michelle walked in on when she walked downstairs after taking an afternoon nap. VJ and Stephanie paused from their tasks, and stared at Cream.

Cream hadn't noticed Michelle walk down the stairs. It was the sudden silence of VJ and Stephanie that caused him to look up. Cream followed the eyes of the two women to where Michelle was standing at the bottom of the stairs. Michelle stood as if unsure whether she should proceed further into the room.

"Cream, why didn't you say you had company." VJ went back to cutting cheese for the sandwiches she was preparing. "Would you like a turkey sandwich?" VJ smiled at Michelle.

"Yea, fix her a sandwich," Cream said. He knew Michelle was probably hungry, being that she hadn't eaten since he had picked her up the night before.

"Ain't no sense in being shy." Stephanie smiled at Michelle as she rung up receipts. "I'm Stephanie and that's VJ." VJ smiled and waved.

"Nice to meet you," Michelle spoke softly as she entered the room.

"Shit girl, you haven't met us yet. We still don't know your name." VJ said.

"It's Michelle." Michelle said.

"Well come on Michelle and let me fix you a sandwich. I'm 'a fix you one of them slap your mama sandwiches. Come on over here and have a seat," VJ pulled a chair out for Michelle at the table.

Michelle was reluctant to take the chair at first. It was the warm smiles on the two plain-looking women's faces that put her at ease. Michelle could tell the invitation and the smiles were genuine as she walked over to the table. Both VJ and Stephanie looked to be in their early thirties. They were neither ugly nor attractive. They were somewhere in between. It was their warm personalities that made them beautiful.

"It's about time this knucklehead brought something home with him outside of a cold."

Cream who was still wearing his pajamas and robe picked up his ledger and told VJ who had made the remark to bring his sandwich into the living room. "I can't work around all this yapping."

Both VJ and Stephanie begin to laugh. "Don't mind Groucho Marx, his bark is worse than his bite," Stephanie said.

VJ and Stephanie no longer had a sexual relationship with Cream. They hadn't been sexually involved since his release from prison. They now treated him like their younger brother. They were fiercely loyal to him and though they were both involved with men in their own age bracket, there was nothing that came before their duties to Cream. Cream had always taken good care of them. They in turn took good care of him. Both women were hard working and honest. There was no jealousy or envy as they sat with Michelle and talked for thirty minutes on a range of subjects. Though the topic of conversation took many directions, neither woman asked Michelle anything that would be considered personal.

Michelle sat curled up in the love seat after the women had left. "You need me to do anything?" She asked Cream.

"Naw, I'm cool." Cream never lifted his head from the paper he was reading.

"Look Cream," Michelle said, "I know you mad at me for what I done to Broke. But, you don't know the whole story. Like I told you, I didn't want to hurt Broke." Michelle spoke as if she had to get what she was saying off her chest. "I wanted to tell Broke once I got to know him. The reason I didn't was because Fast Money threatened to kill him if I did. I've seen Fast Money do some things that I won't say. I was scared for Broke. I didn't want to see him hurt. You may not believe me but I did care for Broke. I was young and naive. We all make mistakes."

Cream lowered his paper and stared across at Michelle. "Look," he said, "until I can figure out whether you're a dog, snake or eagle, I really don't know how to treat you."

"Fuck you Cream," Michelle said the words softly with tears in her eyes. "I may not be perfect but I'm not a damn animal."

Michelle stood up from the love seat. "I got feelings just like everybody else. And if you think I'm going to be another one of your damn whores you can forget it. I'm not proud of everything I've done in the past but it's not too late to turn my life around. I may not be shit to you but I'm still something to somebody."

Cream remained silent as he stared up at Michelle. Michelle stood wringing her hands as tears ran down her face. She hated the fact that Cream looked down on her because of her past. There was a part of her that wished she could correct her wrongs and live out her existence with Cream. Instead, Michelle hated him for hating her.

"You don't have to worry about me being in your way much longer. I called my mother and she said I can come home whenever I want. I've been thinking about leaving anyway. My mother says it's better to start over then to keep getting run over. So, you can stop looking at me all crazy. I'll be out your way next week. I should have everything together by then. So if there's anything you would like for me to do in the meantime you can feel free to ask. You don't have to worry about me getting the wrong impression and thinking that you care."

Michelle turned to walk away. Cream asked her to hold up. "You're right," Cream said. "Everybody do make mistakes. But when have you known anyone to solve their mistakes by running away from the problem."

"I'm not running away." Michelle said. "I'm running from a bad situation to a better opportunity. I just turned twenty-three last month. When I first met Fast Money I was eighteen. Fast Money was thirty-five. Coming from a place like Iowa, I thought he was the shit. It took me a couple of years to realize that he was some shit. By that time I was hooked on pre-mo's and had seen him shoot two men and kill another. I've just been going through the motion for the last few years. I'm not naive anymore and I'm not making excuses for my actions. Fast Money asked me to entertain a few of his out of town friends. I showed them a good time and a couple of them that I thought were cool, I admit I did sleep with them. But I'm not a whore. Not like you think. The men I was with I made that choice."

Cream listened attentively to Michelle as she cleansed her soul. "Fast Money mostly asked me to sit on his product and on occasion maybe to hold some money. Hell, for all I know, I was going to be the next fall guy. Which reminds me, I got to take my name off the lease of that apartment and utilities before I leave next week."

Cream listened to Michelle with a noncommittal look on his face. Michelle had the attitude of one who had been worried about something of great importance and had just gotten the word that everything was going to be all right. Like someone who had just taken the AIDS test and received negative results after years of at-risk sex. Cream knew that Michelle felt alive again after being liberated from Fast Money. Fast Money had taken the life out of her. Now that he was gone, her face had taken on a new glow of life. A new glow that made her even more beautiful. Even though Michelle had nothing, she now had everything. With her new attitude there was nothing or no one that could break her spirits. Cream didn't like the mushy feeling he was getting from looking up at the beautiful woman with tears on her face who had just poured out her heart to him. He remembered what happened the last time he became emotional over a woman.

"I got to make some rounds." Cream stood off the sofa and laid down the paper. "I'll be back in a couple of hours."

Michelle stared nervously at Cream. "Thanks Cream," she said softly. "I'm sorry. Tell Broke I never meant to hurt him."

"You can tell him yourself." Cream pointed to Broke's telephone number on the coffee table. Cream dressed and was out the house twenty minutes later. Michelle watched as he drove off in his Corvette. Michelle wished now that she hadn't been so rude to him when he had first picked her up in the cab. Even though she had thought he was handsome she had also viewed him as an annoying cab driver.

Michelle didn't want to see anything happen to Cream. She had never seen anyone stand up against Fast Money who wasn't shot or killed. If not for nosey neighbors peeping out their windows, who knows what would've happened at her apartment. Fast Money was a cautious and patient killer. He also had killers on his payroll in Nashville. Michelle had only seen them once. She prayed to God, for both her and Cream's sake, that she never saw them again.

Michael Rogers

Chapter 24

Cream didn't think much about Michelle as he drove to his club. The smooth reggae sounds of One Way featuring Jacob Killer Miller mellowed him out during the twenty-minute drive. Cream liked hanging around the club on Saturday afternoons.

Skacehead would be there with a few rollers along with the girls. Cream who wasn't fond of crowds, chose this time to socialize with the homies from the hood. He didn't want them to think that he was getting uppity. When brothers thought you were getting too uppity they would usually find some way to bring you down. Skacehead as usual was doing all the talking when Cream walked into the club. Cream entered the poolroom where dominoes, spades and pool game were being played.

"There my nigga go! Skacehead shouted excitedly when Cream walked into the room.

Cream smiled and shook hands with Scacehead. Scacehead was a stoutly built, red-faced man of twenty-three. He was handsome in a rugged way and reminded Cream of a younger version of the character Dirty Red in the movie the Five Heartbeats.

"Man tell these fools how much money we won off Sonny three weeks ago at the dice game." Skacehead leaned on his pool-stick as he waited for Cream to reply. "I ain't gon' say nothing," he said, "man these niggers gon' tell me we didn't win twenty-thousand dollars." Scacehead never gave Cream a chance to answer.

"Aw, naw, nigga, bet's off," Lee Lee, a dark-skinned man with his front teeth protruding from his mouth, said laughing. "How you gon' ask him and then tell him at the same time?"

"Bet's off my ass." Skacehead said. "Nigga you better have my five dollars when I come back." Skacehead laid his pool-stick on the table and steered Cream away from the crowd of men after Cream had said his hellos. A short, thick, fat bottom brown-skinned girl called Poochie made it her business to come up and hug Cream.

"Call me later," Poochie put on her most seductive look as she whispered in Cream's ear.

"Poochie, move yo' big ass out the way." Skacehead pulled Cream away from Poochie. "Man this motherfucker was off the chain last night. I had to send Lee Lee over to the liquor store this morning to get enough stuff to make it through tonight." Skacehead was drinking from a bottle of beer as he spoke excitedly while telling Cream about the club business of the night before.

"Shit didn't get out of hand did it?" Cream asked.

"Nigga please. You must've forgot who the fuck I am. Niggas know better than to clown up in here. Niggas know, not only will I kick their ass in the club, but I'm gone also send them young killers around to kick their ass the next day. It was cool though," Skacehead said as he calmed down. "Me and Lee Lee held it down."

"How the girls do?" Cream asked.

"Shit man, you know, ho' traffic is mo' traffic. That's what got things popping. Niggas in and out of here looking for girls. Then, while they wait their turn, you got freelance ho's who trying to pay light bills in here trying to catch. On top of that, you got good job-having niggas hanging around who trying to pay them bills. And then you got the squares who just come out to party and to be part of the crowd. I'm telling you, shit's been popping. And then you got Scace in the place chasing garters and lace. So you know shit gone go down."

Cream laughed along with his old friend and sometime nemesis. "Hey yo' man, I meant to ask you. I'm glad I thought about it. What's up with you and that nigga Fast Money. I thought I was gon' have to bust

184

that nigga head last night. He come in the club about one o'clock with five or six niggas talking loud and saying nothing. So I tell the nigga to chill out and shut the fuck up."

Cream watched as Skacehead became angry as if he was still talking to Fast Money. Skacehead was use to Cream telling him not to over-react and to keep the peace. "Look man, I'm not gon' be trying to pacify these niggas. You know how I get down. Niggers like Fast Money don't want to do nothing but start shit. I just let them niggas know that if any shit gon' be started then I'm the biggest asshole in the house. And when shit start flowing, ain't no stopping it until it's over."

"What he say when you told him to chill?"

"What else the nigga gon' do? He shut the fuck up. He mumbled some shit 'bout you getting in his business and said some shit like he was looking for you. So, I tell the nigga that if he had beef with you that he might as well bring the whole cow, cause I'm damn sho' gon' want some. Nigger got quiet after that. Next thing I know he all up in Poochie's ear. It wan' nothing though. Nigga just talking. I just don't want you to get caught slipping around that nigga. Nigga don't want none for real though. Niggas know I got them young killers round me. Young niggas eating good, and fucking good. Niggas can't wait to put in work to earn their keep. Look at that black ass nigga Lee Lee." Skacehead was laughing and pointing at his main man. "Even that nigga getting pussy and having money. You can't tell that nigga he ain't the shit. Standing over there in that Tom Landry ass hat looking like a black walrus. That nigga kill a brick, somebody try and shut down his gravy train. Fast Money just don't know how close he came last night."

I had to tell Lee Lee not to cut that fool. I'm telling you man, all you got to do is call. I'm telling you, motherfuckers don't won't none." Skacehead jumped up from the stool at the bar where he and Cream were sitting. "Come on, let me school you in some pool," he said as he led the way back into the poolroom.

Cream hung around the club a couple of hours before asking Skacehead if he wanted to ride out by the motel.

"Yea, let me get my hat." Skacehead disappeared into the back before returning fixing a Kango style hat over his head. Lee Lee had a look of disappointment on his face when he saw that Cream had driven his two-seater Corvette.

"Yo Roundhead," Skacehead called the big roundhead black man behind the bar. "You and Lee Lee hold the club down until I come back." Lee Lee's chest swelled with pride as Skacehead announced him second in command loud enough for everyone in the club to hear. "Let's roll." Skacehead followed Cream out to the car.

"No weapons." Cream said.

"Nigga, I am a weapon." Skacehead said as he got into the car.

***

The motel that Cream had referred to was a roadside motel that Cream had bought from an Indian family that moved away. Cream had renovated the twelve-unit motel and turned it into a plush haven for the girls who worked out the club. The way things worked were simple. Cream allowed the girls to use the club to meet clients. His benefit was that he had twelve beautiful women soliciting men in his club. The girls worked the club like they were just out for a good time. If a man wanted to hook up with one of the girls, they never mentioned money as a fee for hooking up. The girls would simply suggest that the client rent a room at the motel so they could be alone. The client already knew that the price of the room at one hundred and twenty-five dollars an hour was also the cost for the girl. The "No Vacancy" sign was always lit at the motel and only the girls were allowed to rent rooms. Cream would give the girls fifty dollars of what they made off each time they rented a room. He also allowed the girls to use the rooms as residence. With twelve girls using the rooms at a minimum of fifteen times each week, Cream made over thirteen thousand dollars per week as his take off the rooms.

Two prison buddies and brothers, Poky and Sleepy, ran the motel and acted as security for the girls. Both brothers were no nonsense ex-felons who were not the type to ask someone to do something twice. The killer eyes of Poky and the sneaky look of Sleepy were usually enough to warn most people away.

There were those like Fast Money and the cops who labeled Cream a pimp because he managed the girls. Cream didn't think of himself as a pimp. The women who worked with him were independent contractors who could leave anytime they chose. He didn't allow women with children to work with him and he had a waiting list of other girls who wanted to work the club. He would allow these freelance operators to work the rooms during the time of month when the regular girls couldn't perform because of women problems. Cream made sure that he kept proper books of all his business endeavors. He knew that all Uncle Sugar wanted was his proper cut in taxes. That's why he hired the best accountant he could find during tax time. He didn't want any problems with the government.

Cream and Skacehead sat around for over an hour in the Soul Bowl kicking the shit as they called the laughing and conversation they had with Poky and Sleepy. The Soul Bowl was a soul food restaurant across the street from the Cream Land Motel. Cream had helped Skacehead buy the property and Sleepy who had been a cook in prison managed the Soul Bowl for Skacehead. The girls were mostly asleep while Cream was there, with exception of a few who were already up and entertaining regulars.

"Man, let's ride out on the North side by Townsend Park. I need to holler at that nigger Kirk about some money," Skacehead said once they were in the car.

"Man, I know you ain't fucking with that crazy ass nigga." Cream pulled off the Soul Bowl lot laughing at Skacehead.

187

"Naw man, nigga owe me fifty dollars I lent him last week. He supposed to brought it by the crib yesterday and I ain't seen the nigga. Nigga know not to fuck with my money."

"Man you been looking for a reason to whoop that nigga ever since you found out he was fucking with Willie Jean. Face it man, you fucked up. You fucked that off. How you gon' sleep with a woman's mother and then whoop her for catching you and expect the woman to come back. You know damn well Kirk ain't got no fifty dollars. Kirk ain't had fifty dollars since he got out of jail a year ago."

Cream was saying all these things in a jovial manner because he knew how sensitive Skacehead was when it came to Willie Jean the woman he loved and lost because he had had sex with her drunken mother. "Here nigger, Kirk told me to give you this fifty dollars." Cream was laughing as he held fifty dollars out to Skacehead.

Skacehead couldn't help but laugh after Cream had pulled his card. He tossed the money back to Cream. "Nigga, Willie Jean still got you whooped." Cream put the money back in his shirt pocket.

"Nigga, look who's talking." Skacehead said laughing. "Yo' pretty ass ain't had a woman in your house since Penny left. Talking 'bout somebody got me whooped. Hell, I bet you still got her things in the closet." Skacehead was laughing loud at Cream as he poked fun back at him about his own woman troubles.

The mention of Penny brought back painful memories of her to Cream. Cream had met Penny while passing through McGhee Arkansas after coming from a funeral. He traveled back and forth to see her for a few months before moving her to Pine Bluff to live with him. Penny was a beautiful and shy country girl. She was at first impressed with Cream in the classic good girl loves bad boy type of way. Cream also loved her because she reminded him so much of his mother. Cream was happy in love for the first time in his life. That is until one day he came home and found a note on the bed from Penny.

The note simply said that Penny was leaving. It seemed that Cream had met Penny during a breakup with her childhood sweetheart and soul mate. He lost her back to him when the boyfriend got his number from Penny's mother and began to call her when Cream was out and about. Penny had written in the note that she couldn't face Cream and had made her decision based on the fact that she missed her parents country living, and the realization that she still loved her childhood sweetheart. That was six months ago.

Cream had not had a steady woman since that time. With his emotions placed on ice, Cream, now only brought women to his house for hours at a time. Michelle had been the only woman to spend the night since Penny.

"Look at you nigga. Just the mention of Penny and you zoned out like a zombie. Talking 'bout me being whooped. Shit, you got whooped with an extension cord, hot wheel track, and braided switches all together."

Cream couldn't help but laugh as he was kidded by his old friend. Skacehead was enjoying the moment and had to be told by Cream to let up on him after Cream told him that he had won the argument.

"You got that," Cream said. "But at least I'm man enough to admit I got whoop. You still in denial. Willie Jean still got your nose open. Wide open," Cream said with finality.

"Man, I got more ho's than Santa Claus, if I saw that rotten bitch crawling across the desert, I'll give her a glass of sand and a peanut butter sandwich." Skacehead laugh loudly at his own words before suddenly ending his laugh and changing the subject.

"Yo man, speaking of bitches, what's up with you and that ol' fat-booty bitch, Poochie?"

"Ain't nothing," Cream said. "She been trying to holler but I'm not interested."

"I don't trust that ho'," Skacehead said. "She always bouncing her big ass around ease dropping and shit. Then like I told you, I saw the bitch last night, all up in Fast Money's ear. You better watch that ho'."

***

Cream and Skacehead made it back to the club an hour later after stopping by Cream's liquor store to pick up a few more cases of whiskey. Lee Lee jumped off the bar stool and stood smiling from ear to ear like a happy puppy that was glad his master was home. "Nigga what you smiling so happy about." Skacehead smiled and gave Lee Lee some dap by hitting their fists together.

"What's been going on?" he asked as he stared around the spacious club. House of Cream, as the club was called, was top-notch. The decor was black and white with battery-operated colored mini-lights on each table. The club's name House Of Cream was in lights and ran the length of the wall above the bar. The club had an expensive atmosphere and was clean and spotless as usual.

"Ain't shit happen," Lee Lee said with the smile still on his face.

Some of the girls who worked with Cream in the club came up to see him. They were all fussing over him and jockeying for position to say something.

"Cream will you please tell Sleepy that just because we eat free that that don't mean he can eat free," a wide-hip, wide-mouth girl named Annett was saying to Cream.

"And tell Poky that just because his name Poky don't mean he can be trying to poke something every night," the young light skinned girl name Sylvia pumped her hips to indicate her meaning as she laughed along with the other girls.

"Yea, and just because they call Sleepy, Sleepy, don't mean we want to sleep with him. And sho' ain't nobody trying to sleep with no Poky. That nigga ruint," Annette said.

"Ooooooooo girrrlll, that nigga is ruint," Sylvia bucked her eyes as she held one hand over her mouth as if shocked by something she was seeing. "I'm telling you girl. Ain't no way I'll fuck with Poky. Shit you need two pussies for that nigger. One of them double-decker pussy's with one stacked on top of the other."

The girls were laughing as they clowned Pokey and Sleepy while standing around Cream at the bar.

"Why do you women use condoms?" Cream stared at the girls after asking the question.

"You use them for protection," a tall dark-skinned Tara Banks look alike named Jackie said.

"That's right," Cream said. "And you shouldn't have sex without them. Now even though you don't receive the same sexual stimulation when using a condom you wouldn't have sex without them out of fear for your health."

The girls all stared quizzically at Cream. "Cream what the hell that got to do with what we talking about?" Rah Rah a big Amazon of a woman asked.

"It's simple," Cream said. "Poky and Sleepy are like condoms. They're there for your protection and you should never have sex without protection. Now these brothers are not your typical latex or sheep skin type condoms. These brothers are roughneck condoms that won't bust under pressure. These condoms provide the kind of protection you women need in the world today. Instead of whining and complaining about the loss of sexual stimulation from use of the condoms, you should be more thankful for the protection that they provide. Think about that next time Poky want to poke or Sleepy want to sleep. I got to go." Cream stood off the bar stool as the girls stood silent for the moment.

"Forget Sleepy and Poky. When Cream gon' want to cream?" Jackie blew a seductive kiss and winked her eye at Cream.

Cream smiled at her before turning his head and staring around for Skacehead. "I got to go," Cream said again.

"There go Scacehead over there." Cream followed Sylvia's pointing finger to where Skacehead was standing with Lee Lee and some more guys.

"I'm out," Cream told Skacehead after walking over to him.

"All right bro, I got this. Skacehead gave Cream some dap. "I'll call you later tonight and let you know what's up."

Cream gave Lee Lee and Roundhead some dap and left the club.

Skacehead walked out with Cream and stood talking with him as Roundhead and Lee Lee unloaded the liquor from Roundhead's car.

Cream pulled off the lot and headed south. The road leading from the club ran north and south. The expressway was to the north and to the south was 13th Street. 13th Street ran the length of Pine Bluff from east to west.

Cream liked taking 13th Street as opposed to riding the expressway. The scenic route of black neighborhoods and people was more appealing to his sense of adventure. It was a twenty-minute drive from the Loop to Cream's house. He arrived home and walked into the house to the smell of food cooking in the kitchen. The smell of fried chicken reminded him that he hadn't eaten anything since the turkey sandwich VJ had prepared for him earlier that morning.

Chapter 25

Michelle was busy in the kitchen wearing an apron made of a towel wrapped around her waist. She wore a loose fitting dress and a blouse that she had taken from the female clothing in the closet of the room she was staying.

"You said make myself a home," Michelle wiped her hands on the towel around her waist before tending to some potatoes on the stove. "I hope you don't mind. I just thought maybe you'll want something to eat. I saw the chicken in the freezer and figured I'll cook it. It's the least I can do. Since I can't pay you for being so hospitable. Maybe it'll help you figure out what kind of animal I am. A dog, snake or eagle." Michelle said the last words with a smile.

"Naw, it's cool," Cream stomach growled loudly.

"Don't be embarrassed. My food has that kind of effect on people. It'll be ready by the time you wash up."

Cream ate four pieces of chicken and a half skillet of potatoes smothered in onion. Smothered potatoes were his favorite dish. He also had four biscuits. Cream didn't know if he was that hungry or rather Michelle's cooking was just that good. The last time he had eaten a home cooked meal in his home was with Penny. Penny's cooking was good but it seemed that Michelle had her beat. At least when it came to chicken and smothered potatoes. "I see you like good cooking." Michelle gathered up the dishes after Cream finished eating.

"Or, I was hungry." Cream sipped some soda from his glass.

"Yea right. Anyway, somebody called you earlier. I didn't want to answer your phone so you should have some messages on your answering machine."

"That's my business phone," Cream said, Whoever called probably called me on my cell. I'll check and see if I have any messages."

"You call Broke?" Cream waited for Michelle, who was rinsing out the dishes, to answer.

"I called." Michelle said in a soft voice. "I spoke with his girlfriend first, because I didn't want to be disrespectful or for her to get the wrong impression."

"And?" Cream asked impatiently as Michelle paused while dumping leftover bones from the chicken off the plates into the trash. "What she say?"

"She was real cool. We talked for awhile and then she let me talk to Broke."

"Sssssssss," Cream blew an impatient breath of air as he waited for Michelle who had started cleaning off the stove to begin again.

"What Broke have to say?"

"He called me a low-down, trifling, no-good bitch and said he would kill me if he ever saw me again."

Cream sat in shocked silence. That didn't sound like the Broke he knew.

Michelle smiled and told him she was only kidding. "Broke said that he forgave me long time ago. He say he knew that Fast Money made me do what I done. When I told him everything else, it only confirmed what he said he already knew."

"I see you got jokey jokes." Cream stood up from the table. "And here I was thinking you was a singer like Beyonce. What else can you do?"

"Hmmph, wouldn't you like to know." Michelle went back to cleaning dishes.

Cream walked out the kitchen but not before staring long and hard at the sexy redbone woman with the thick legs that were oiled and shiny all the way up to her apple bottom that was filling out the loose dress that she wore. "That dress fits you nice." Cream said.

"I got it out the closet. I hope you don't mind."

"Wear whatever you want. I don't think the person I bought them for will be coming back anytime soon. If ever." Cream said

"Well, just because the flower goes bad don't mean you should throw out the vase. You just empty the water with a good cry and then you pick another flower and place it in the empty vase."

"Is that right?"

"It sounds good." Michelle said. At least that's what my mama told me when I called home. She don't know I've been living in the desert and my only flower was a cactus bush."

"Well maybe the next one will be a rose." Cream said.

"Or," Michelle said with a pause, "It might be one of them damn flowers that blooms every seven years, what's the name of that flower?" she asked Cream who had a puzzled look on his face. "You know the one," she said. "The one that blooms every seven years and let out a horrible dead body smell that can't nobody stand and then goes away for seven more years."

"I don't know." Cream said. "But it sounds like a lot of black men I know."

Michael Rogers

Chapter 26

Fast Money sat quietly listening to the fat cop detective on the phone. The detective was on Fast Money's payroll. The cop wanted Fast Money to do him a favor. It was a simple request and Fast Money had agreed to it in return for a future favor. Fast Money called Benny after getting off the phone with the detective. He then walked back into the bedroom to finish what he had started with the big booty girl name Poochie who was lying across his bed.

Benny spotted the young man that the cop had described to Fast Money. He pulled up beside the young thug-looking boy who was walking with a young girl.

"What's up?" Benny leaned across the car seat and spoke through the passenger side window to the boy."

"What's up?" the boy said as he pulled his girl behind him.

"Ain't you Verla's son?" Benny asked the boy.

"What's up man?" Lil' Brick asked in an agitated voice.

"Chill out youngster." Benny said, trying to calm Lil' Brick. "I just want you to give this to Verla." Benny held out a black bag across the seat.

"Give it to her yourself." Lil'Brick turned to walk away.

"Man, I'm not trying to go into no projects." Benny was becoming frustrated himself. He couldn't see why the boy just didn't take the damn bag.

"What is it?" Lil' Brick asked. They were only blocks away from the projects.

"Ask your mama when you give it to her." Benny said irritably. He was sick of all the drama over a damn bag.

"Give it here. I'll take it to her." Kay Kay reached into the car and took the bag. She was tired of being held up by the man and was ready to go.

Lil' Brick was about to object but only sighed. He didn't want Kay Kay to start fussing again as she had been before the car approached. Lil' Brick stared hard at the man in the car, but held his tongue and said nothing to Kay Kay as she put the package in her pocket.

Benny who was ready to leave pulled off quickly after giving Kay Kay the bag. His instructions from Fast Money were to give the boy the bag to give to his mama. He figured that as long as the mama got the bag then everything was cool. His mission was accomplished.

Kay Kay patted the bag in her pocket as she and Lil' Brick reversed themselves and began to walk back towards the projects to take it to Verla. They were a couple hundred yards from the projects when two police cars swooped down on them and blocked them in from the front and back. Lil' Brick pulled Kay Kay behind him as he stood defiantly.

The unmarked Malibu that the fat cop from the other day was driving also joined the two squad cars. The fat cop got out of his car and joined the patrol officers who were already out their cars and detaining Lil' Brick and Kay Kay.

"Why y'all stopping us? Lil' Brick asked the fat cop.

The fat cop walked over to him and Kay Kay. "We got a complaint that someone was selling drugs out here that fit your description."

"Man I don't sell no damn drugs. You got me fucked up." Lil' Brick tried to walk away with Kay Kay.

The fat detective suddenly grabbed Lil' Brick and roughly spun him around and leaned him against one of the squad cars. "We'll just have to see about that. Won't we?" The cop commenced to searching Lil' Brick.

"Man what you looking for!" Lil' Brick tried to twist away as the cop searched him thoroughly between his legs around his balls.

"You must be some kind of punk." Lil' Brick was fuming as the cop roughly handled him against the car.

The cop was still searching Lil' Brick when Verla came running up from the projects after being informed about the situation by one of the other kids from the projects.

"Why you searching my son?! Let my son go. What the fuck wrong with y'all?! My son ain't done shit," Verla was being told to step back by the patrolmen as she tried to get to Lil' Brick.

"Stand back, ma'am."

"Lil' Brick, why they searching you?"

"I don't know mama. They talking 'bout somebody look like me was out here selling dope." Lil' Brick sounded every bit like a fifteen year old as he spoke in a strained voice to Verla. The fat cop held Lil' Brick sprawled across the trunk of the squad car with a firm grip on the back of his head.

"My son don't sell no damn dope!" Verla screamed loudly. "Let my son go!"

A small crowd had gathered including Kay Kay's mom Kat. The fat cop didn't like all the attention. He figured the young punk must have somehow tossed the package that Benny was supposed to have given him. With the scene getting out of hand he released Lil' Brick and backed away from him.

"All right," the detective said. "Back it up." He stared around the crowd as if looking for other suspects. "If I have to come back out here because of citizen's complaints of people selling drugs, somebody's going to jail."

"What the fuck you think we are motherfucker?" Verla glared back at the cop who seemed to be directing his remarks at her. "Just because we live in the projects don't mean we ain't got no damn rights."

The detective signaled for the other cops in a gesture of retreat. "Somebody needs to protect these young girls from your fat ass." Verla mumbled the words as she led Lil' Brick away from the cop by the hand.

The two patrolmen stared after Verla before casting glances at one another and then the detective.

The detective angrily moved in Verla's direction. "If you say one more word, I'm going to arrest you for inciting a riot, obstruction of justice, disturbing the peace and whatever else I can think of between here in the station. Now I said clear it out!"

"Fuck you." Verla said defiantly before turning and walking over to where Kay Kay and Kat stood off to the side of the road.

The crowd dispersed as fast as it had gathered once the cops had left. The detective was two blocks away when he saw Kay Kay hand Verla the black package out her pocket that he was searching for on Lil' Brick. 'Dumb motherfucker,' the cop thought. This fool gave the package to the girl instead of the boy. The cop hit the steering wheel angrily. He never thought to search the girl. He figured he would have had to call a female officer anyway. He thought for a moment about going back and arresting Verla for the package. He quickly dismissed this thought and decided that there were other young girls for him to pursue. He wouldn't get the chance to see the pain in those eyes after all. 'That'll just make it harder on the next one,' he thought as he turned off the street.

***

"What's this shit?" Verla asked as she took the package from Kay Kay.

"I don't know. Some man in a black car told Lil' Brick to give it to you. Lil' Brick wouldn't take it and I was ready to go, so I put it in my pocket to bring to you. That's where we were going when the police came." Kay Kay spoke fast as Verla opened up the bag.

Verla stared at Kat. "What man gave you this package?"

"I don't know him. Some man in a BMW," Lil' Brick said. "That's why I didn't take it, I start to say something to Kay Kay but didn't want to hear her mouth, cause I know she was all ready mad 'bout something somebody said that I done that I didn't do."

"Hmmph," Kay Kay turned her nose up and rolled her eyes at Lil' Brick.

"Look at this shit Kat," Verla held out her hand, and showed Kat some white rocks that she had poured into her hand out the bag. Kat looked at the rocks and stared back at Verla.

"Ain't that crack?" Verla asked.

"Shit girl, hell I don't know."

"That's what it look like," Verla said.

"Let me see," Lil' Brick picked up one of the rocks out of Verla's hand. "That is crack," he said excitedly.

"Uh huh, and how the hell you know?" Verla gave Lil' Brick a questioning look.

"Mama, I'm from the projects. I seen that stuff before."

"Uh Huh, that's all you better be don' done, is seen it. Give me that shit." Verla took the rock from Lil' Brick. "Your daddy suppose to call in a minute. I'm a ask him what it is."

"How daddy gon' know and he in jail? He can't see it through the phone."

"Boy, I know that. He'll still know what to do. You must think I'm crazy. Bring your Lil' butt on." Verla led the way as the four of them walked towards the projects.

***

Broke and Cream were sitting in Verla's apartment inspecting the white rocks.

Brick had called Broke and told him what had happened. Broke had asked Cream to ride with him because Cream knew more about drugs. Cream confirmed that the rocks were crack.

"It seems like someone was trying to set Lil' Brick up." Cream handed the drugs back to Verla.

"I bet it was that fat-ass cop," Verla took the drugs and laid them on the table.

"It probably was that fool. But why he want to set up Lil' Brick?" Kat asked.

"On' know," Verla responded with a puzzled look on her face.

"That punk stopped us the other day," Lil' Brick spoke as if he had suddenly remembered a vital piece of information.

"What did he say?" Broke asked.

"He said he was looking for a missing girl," Kay Kay volunteered the added information.

"He up to something, don't worry, I'll find out. Lil' Brick, you need to be careful and don't let nobody slip nothing on you." Broke stood up off the sofa.

"Hell, he might've been looking for Kay Kay," Verla stared from Kat to Kay Kay.

Cream and Broke both stared questioningly at Verla.

"Man, that fat perverted fool been picking up young girls since I was a kid. It ain't no secret. That's why his fat ass bought that house round the block. They need to put his fat ass in jail," Verla spoke with anger in her voice. Her neice had been a victim of the fat cop.

"But why would he want to set up Lil' Brick if he wanted Kay Kay?" Kat tried to understand the connection.

"Hell, I don't know. I just know he's a fat pedophile-ass motherfucker. And so do everybody else, and the police won't do shit."

"Don't worry 'bout it." Broke placed his hand on Verla's shoulder. "We'll get to the bottom of it. Just let me know if y'all see that BMW again."

"What we gon' do with this?" Verla picked the rocks up off the table.

"Flush it," Cream said.

"Here Lil' Brick, flush this shit." Verla tossed the bag to Lil' Brick. Verla noticed how Lil' Brick stared at the drugs. "Gimme that shit. I'll flush it," she said. "Knowing yo' Lil' slick ass, you'll be trying to keep some."

***

Kat stared after Kay Kay as she walked ahead of her, Broke, and Cream as they left Verla's apartment. To her, Kay Kay was just a baby. Kat wasn't naive enough to think that Kay Kay was too young for sex. She had even warned her and Lil' Brick about practicing safe sex. Still, she had never thought about warning her daughter about the dangers of grown men, especially policemen, that might be interested in her young body.

Broke and Cream followed Verla's direction and rode by the detective's house around from the projects.

"Man, what you think?" Cream asked.

"Shit, I don't know. It'll all come out in the wash," Broke said.

"I know some people that can check out that cop," Cream said, I'm a give them a call when I get home. Why don't you and Ms. Broke come out by the house a little later? We can go over what I learn and catch up on some old times. We haven't had a chance to kick it since we left prison."

"We might do that. Let me see what Sherry got up. What's up on Michelle?" Broke stared across at Cream. "She still there?"

"Yeah, she still there. She say she talked to you."

"Yea, she called." Broke said.

"Shit man, if it's a problem, like I told you, I can get ol' girl a room or something. We go too far back for some chick to come between us. She supposed to be leaving sometime soon anyway. If it ain't cool, we can just get together then."

"Naw man, it's cool. It ain't no problem. Who you think it was in that BMW?" Broke asked.

"I don't know," Cream said. "Pine Bluff's not that big. He'll pop up."

Cream dropped Broke off at home after giving him direction to his house. Broke had called Sherry on his cell phone and they had agreed to come over around nine later that night. Sherry was waiting in the doorway for Broke.

"How Lil' Brick doing?" She asked as she hugged Broke around the waist and placed her head on his chest.

Broke held Sherry around the shoulder as he walked hugged up with her to the couch.

"He's cool. Some cop tried to set him up."

"Why?" Sherry asked.

"I don't know," Broke said. "That's what we trying to find out." Broke kissed Sherry on the forehead. "Come on," he said.

"Not that."

Broke tossed a pillow in Sherry's lap. "Control your hormones," he said.

Sherry let out a playful sigh as she jumped up off the couch and followed Broke into the bedroom.

"What you looking at?" Sherry was oiling her legs on the bed. "Control your hormones," she said as Broke stared at her. "Where Cream stay at?" Sherry pulled on her pants as Broke patted on some cologne.

"Out on Old Warren Road," Broke said.

"Oooo, that's way out there," Sherry said.

"How you know?" Broke had a surprised look on his face.

"I told you, we be riding." Sherry said as she stood off the bed and placed on her blouse. "Lil' Shelia ain't been here but a minute and knows every hole in town."

Michael Rogers

Chapter 27

Michelle was in the shower and didn't hear Cream enter the house when he returned home. She was towel drying her hair as she walked nakedly back to her room.

Cream was coming up the stairs and gasped when he saw her. Michelle shrieked and dashed into the bedroom when she first noticed Cream. Cream was surprised at his reaction to Michelle's sexy body. She was absolutely beautiful. Her flawless body jiggled as she tried to cover herself before dashing into the room. It was this fleeting glance of her as she tried to escape his prying eyes that had Cream still mesmerized as he stood at the bottom of the stairs. "Damn, boy you slipping." Cream said to himself as he walked up the stairs.

Cream stood outside of Michelle's bedroom door and knocked.

"Yes," Michelle said.

"We gon' have company in about thirty minutes." Cream never bothered to open the door to the room.

"We," Michelle asked.

"Yea, Broke and Sherry gon' stop by for a minute. Cream walked across the hall without waiting for a reply from Michelle.

Michelle was still dressing when she heard Broke's voice downstairs coming from the living room. She was nervous. Michelle was still contemplating on what to do when someone knocked on the door.

"Yes," Michelle said softly. "Come in."

Sherry walked into the room. There was an awkward moment of silence as both women sized one another up after speaking.

"You coming downstairs?" Sherry asked.

"Yes, I'll be there in a minute," Michelle said.

Sherry was curled up in Broke's arms on the loveseat when Michelle walked down the stairs with measured steps.

"Hey Broke," Michelle said softly as if intimidated by Broke's stare.

"What's up, Michelle," Broke spoke as he rubbed Sherry's shoulder.

"I guess you met Sherry."

"Yea, we met."

"I hear you going back to Iowa," Broke said.

"Yea, I think it's time," Michelle said as she took a seat in the empty chair.

"It'll probably be good for you," Broke said. "You still young."

The ringing of Cream's cell phone interrupted the strained conversation. Cream spoke into the phone.

"All right man, cool," Cream hung up the phone and placed it on the table as he stared across at Broke.

"My man say that cop's name is Jones. Say he's a detective."

"Sound like that fool who arrested me," Broke said.

Michelle dropped her eyes as Sherry cast a glance in her direction.

"My man say he don't know who was driving the Black BMW but say he'll have a line on it fo' in the morning." Michelle raised her head and stared across at Cream. She knew that Benny drove a black BMW.

"Who you looking for in a black BMW?" she asked.

"Somebody in a black BMW tried to set up Lil' Brick," Broke said.

Michelle had a puzzled look on her face.

"Lil' Brick is the son of a guy we know in prison." Cream said. "Somebody in a black BMW gave Lil' Brick's girlfriend some dope after Lil' Brick wouldn't take it to give to his mother. The cops stopped them a few minutes later and searched Lil' Brick but didn't search the girl. Other than that, he'd be in jail."

"Benny got a black BMW," Michelle offered the information.

Broke gave a questioning look to Cream.

"That's Fast Money's flunky," Cream said.

"That's who it is then. But why would that fool try and set up Lil' Brick?" Broke tried to find a connection as he pondered the thought. "Hell, I betcha Lil' Brick don't even know that fool."

"I could find out." Michelle sat up in her chair. She was hoping there was something she could do to help. She was willing to do anything she could to show Broke and Cream that she could be trusted. "I can call him and have him meet me somewhere and see what he say. He was always trying to hit on me."

"Naw, that won't be necessary," Cream said. "I know that fool, you won't have to meet him. Just call him and see if you can get him to come to the Cream Land Motel. Tell him to go to the Soul Bowl cafe across the street. I'll take it from there. That's if you can get him to come."

"Hmmph," Michelle had a confident look on her face as she picked up Cream's cell phone and walked into the kitchen. She didn't want to create any ill feelings or bad memories by seducing Benny in front of those in the room. Benny answered the phone after the second ring. It didn't take Michelle long to convince him to meet her. To further convince him, Michelle asked Benny to stop by her old apartment and pick up the dress she had worn to PJ's the last night he saw her.

Cream called Sleepy at the restaurant and told him about the setup. He told Sleepy to send Benny to room 8 when he arrived.

***

Fast Money was furious after speaking with the detective on the phone. He angrily punched in Benny's number to see why he didn't give the boy the drugs as instructed.

Benny check the caller I.D. on his phone and decided not to answer once he saw it was Fast Money calling. He didn't want Fast Money to spoil his plans with Michelle. He had waited a long time for this day. He wasn't about to let Fast Money send him on some errand and miss out on the opportunity to finally satisfy his lust for Michelle. It took Benny thirty minutes to reach the motel after stopping by the apartment to pick up the dress she wanted. He walked into the Soul Bowl with an arrogant swagger as if he owned the place.

"What's up my man," Sleepy stared across the counter at Benny. "What can I do for you?"

"Let me get a coke," Benny said as he stared across the street at the motel.

Sleepy retrieved a coke from the cooler and handed it to Benny. The wall phone rung as he was handing Benny the coke. Sleepy answered the phone before giving Benny his change from the five he had given him.

"Are you Benny?" He asked. He stared hard at Benny.

"What's up?" Benny asked.

"Michelle just called from across the street. She say bring her a plate of ribs to room 8." Sleepy turned and began fixing the plate of barbeque without waiting for Benny to reply. "That's twenty dollars."

"Damn homey, you must've killed one helluva cow." Benny fished a twenty-dollar bill out of his pocket and tossed it on the counter in an arrogant manner.

"Yeah," Sleepy said with a drawl. "Bitch jump over the moon and landed right down on top my grill."

Benny paid for the dinner and another coke that Sleepy added to the order. He walked across the street balancing the order. He approached the door of room 8 and tapped lightly. Benny stared nervously over his shoulder when Poky walked up behind him at the door. He was about to say something to Poky when the door opened.

"What's up Benny?" Cream had an edge in his voice that complimented the look on his face.

Benny almost dropped the barbecue as he backed into Poky who prodded him with the bat he had in his hand. "What's up," he said.

"You tell us," Poky said. He took the ribs and coke out of Benny's hand. "Thanks for the dinner." Poky shoved Benny inside the room. He took a seat in a chair next to the door and began eating from the plate.

"Man, what's this shit?" Benny tried to show some toughness in his words but his shaking body told another story.

'Slap!' Cream slapped Benny hard upside the head. Benny gave out a painful cry as he dropped to one knee holding his face.

"Man, what's up?" Benny stared up at Cream with fear in his eyes. He was more afraid than angry. He wrestled with the thought of fighting back. He quickly lost this battle to the fear factor of more pain. A small man of medium build Benny had already sized up the three men in the room. They were all bigger and stronger than him; couple this with his cowardice, and the men in the room were like giants to him. Benny felt his best chance was to try and talk his way out of whatever it was he had gotten himself into.

211

"Nigga shut yo' bitch ass up, until I tell you to talk." Cream glared down at Benny. He had his hand raised to hit him again as Benny coward beneath him. "Nigga, why you try and set up my nephew?" Cream grabbed Benny by the collar.

"Brother, I don't know what you talkin' about," Benny spoke in a whimpering voice. He hoped that his use of the word brother would have some effect and help his situation.

"Bitch! You think it's a game?" Cream hit Benny with his fist causing Benny to scream out as he fell flat to the floor. "Niggah, why you give my nephew that package of dope?"

Benny realized that Cream was talking about the boy that Fast Money had asked him to give a package. Benny held his jaw with one hand as he raised up on one knee. He held his other hand up as a signal for Cream not to hit him again. "Hold up man. You talking about that kid out by the projects. Man, I don't know that boy. Fast Money asked me to give the boy a package to give his mom. I didn't even know what was in the package. Anyway man, little dude wouldn't even take the package. So I gave it to the girl he was with."

Poky raised up from the table as he sucked the meat off the bone of a piece of barbecue. His mouth was covered in barbecue sauce as well as his hands. Poky walked over to where Benny was kneeling on the floor. He bent over and wiped his hands clean on Benny's silk shirt. Benny stared with contempt at Poky but said nothing as he sucked in his breath. Fear gripped him as he stared up into the evil eyes of Poky. Poky licked the bone in his mouth before tossing it on Benny.

"Look here playa. You best start answering my man. And if he don't like the answers you give him, I'm gon' knock those pretty gold teeth down your faggot-ass throat. You got me playa?" Poky's threatening tone of voice was made even more frightening by his southern drawl.

Benny began to plead as he tried to reason with the men. "Man I don't know shit. I already told you, Fast Money asked me to give the boy a

212

package to give his momma. That's all I know."

"How did you know what kid to give the package to?" Broke asked the question as he stood off the bed.

"Fast Money told me," Benny said trembling. "He told me exactly what the boy would have on from head to toe."

"Who's the cop," Broke asked.

"What cop?" Benny asked.

"The cop that gave you the damn drugs."

The punch that followed the words came so fast that Benny never saw it coming. The next thing he remembered was waking up as Poky poured the ice from the cup he was drinking into his face. Poky was glaring down at him.

"Nigga, the next time I hit you, you won't be waking up no time soon. Now I done told you to answer my man's questions. Now, he asked you, who the cop that gave you the drugs?"

Benny was trying to focus as he shook his head from side to side. His eyes had watered over from the blow Poky had given him. His whole head hurt as if he had been hit by a truck. Benny was having trouble breathing as he rested on his elbows face down on the floor.

"It was detective Jones." The last thing Benny had wanted to do was to mention the cop on Fast Money's payroll. Not only was the cop a killer but he also had other killer cops that worked for him. Couple this with the fact that they were all police with the right to kill at will and this was enough for Benny to try and keep them out the conversation. The lick upside the head was enough to make him change his thought process. It hadn't taken but a second for him to make up his mind.

"Why the fuck a cop want to set up a kid?" Cream was sitting on the bed when he asked the question.

"The detective likes young girls." Benny felt the cat was already out the bag about the detective. He was now concerned for his own safety. He sat up on the floor. "Sometime, women on dope will trade Fast Money their daughters for drugs, or he might give them some money to sleep with the detective and some mo' police."

"That still don't explain why he would try and set up Lil' Brick." Broke was growing angrier by the minute. He listened attentively as Benny spilled his guts about Fast Money procuring young girls for the perverted pleasures of the fat detective and his pedophile cop friends.

"Some girls will trade sex to get their boyfriends out of jail. I guess the detective figured if he arrested the boy, he could trade the boy for the girl. That's the only thing I can figure." Benny stood up off the floor. "What's up man, I told you everything I know." Benny stared at the door to indicate he wanted to leave.

Broke nodded towards Poky who was blocking Benny's path to the door. Poky was about to step aside when Cream spoke from the bed. "Hold up." Cream stood off the bed.

"Which one of Fast Money's houses do he use as a stash house?"

"Nigga, you crazy! You trying to get me killed."

Poky leaned in close and whispered into Benny's ear. "Youngblood, the danger you're in is much greater than the danger you face. If I was you, I'll worry mo' about the right now, because tomorrow ain't promised."

Benny stared into the killer eyes of Poky. Benny was surely afraid of the big swollen head black man. It was like Poky could see right through him and into his coward heart. "I told you man. Fast Money got crooked cops on his payroll. They supply him with confiscated drugs from the evidence room. He don't tell me nothing." Benny stared around at the men in the room. "Hell, why don't you ask Michelle? That bitch knows more about his operation than me. I just make drops and provide muscle."

The men stared from one to the other before bursting out laughing at Benny who stood visibly shaking and talking about providing muscle for Fast Money. Poky prodded Benny with more questions until Cream was satisfied and told him to allow Benny to leave.

***

Benny walked quickly to his car. He was already thinking about getting revenge on the three men for humiliating him. He also swore he would kill Michelle for setting him up. He was putting his key in the ignition of the car when Sleepy walked up to the driver side door. Sleepy pecked on the window and startled Benny. Benny turned to see him kneeling down at the door and peering through the window at him. Benny pressed the power button and let the window down. Sleepy placed his right elbow on the windowsill with his left hand hidden from view.

"What's on your mind?" Sleepy asked the question nonchalantly.

"What?" Benny asked.

"Well just in case you're thinking about coming back. Take this as a reminder of what you'll find when you get here."

'Pow!' Sleepy fired into the car with the pistol he had hidden in his left hand. He shot Benny with no more emotions than someone that was swatting at a fly.

"Owww!" Benny let out a piercing scream as he stared down at the blood gushing from his leg. The bullet had torn into his leg above the kneecap. It felt like someone had suddenly shoved a hot poker through his leg. Benny was terrified as he held his leg in shock.

"Now get the fuck off my property nigga, if I see you again I'll kill you." Sleepy said the words with no more emotions than he had shown when he had shot Benny in the leg.

***

215

Cream and Broke drove out to the projects after leaving the Cream Land Motel. Kat and Verla listened as Cream explained to them what they had learned.

"I knew it." Verla said. "I told you that fat pervert was after Kay Kay."

Kat was so angry that she wanted to report the incident to the police department in the form of a citizen complaint. Broke told them that there were more cops involved. He said that until they knew who all the players were that they should wait.

"Just keep an eye on Kay Kay and Lil' Brick until we can bring this pedophile down."

***

Piss Mo called and told Fast Money that Benny had been shot.

"What?" Fast Money asked in surprise.

"Yea man, he in the hospital." Piss Mo spoke fast into the phone.

Benny had called Piss Mo after not being able to reach Fast Money. Piss Mo was Fast Money's eyes and ears. He had tracked Fast Money down at Poochie's house.

"What happen?" Fast Money asked.

"I don't know," Piss Mo said. "Benny told me that someone tried to rob him out west. He say when he wouldn't give them his car, the nigga shot him in the leg."

Fast Money hung up the telephone after speaking with Piss Mo. He punched in a number and asked to speak to Grizzle Hound. Grizzle Hound was his hired gun. Whatever it was that went down with Benny, Fast Money knew that Grizzle Hound would find out. Grizzle Hound was the alias name of Donnie Barnes. Donnie B, as he was sometimes called, was a west side legend. He was feared all over town

216

for his ruthlessness. Even as a crack addict, Donnie B. was still feared. It was out of fear of him that drug dealers would give him free drugs, in hopes that he wouldn't rob them or one of their workers.

Fast Money spoke into the phone with Donnie B. It was Fast Money that had named him Grizzle Hound after Donnie B had bit a plug out the chest of a man he was fighting one night.

Fast Money gave Donnie B the information he had and told him to check out Benny's story. If the story checked out to be true, Fast Money knew that Donnie B would settle the score with the guilty party. Fast Money also told Donnie B to track down Michelle.

Poochie was lying next to Fast Money as he made his calls and gave his orders over the phone. Fast Money was about to mount Poochie again when his phone rang.

"Damn," Fast Money said as he rolled off Poochie and snatched his phone off the dresser. "I should've left this motherfucker off." His mannerism changed when he recognized the voice of Detective Jones. The detective was calling Fast Money to inform him that the deal they had planned for Friday was good to go.

Poochie listened with a strained ear as Fast Money told the detective that he would meet him on Friday at the Port of Pine Bluff as planned.

Fast Money was more relaxed after getting off the phone. He had been waiting for over a month for the lab report to come back on the five kilos of cocaine. The drugs had been confiscated by the detective in a drug raid from a rival dealer of Fast Money. Fast Money who was supposed to have purchased the drugs from the California dealer had tipped off the cops about the drug transaction. Poochie had also played a role in the setup.

Fast Money had used her to get next to the dealer and to find out where he kept his drugs.

Fast Money's first intent was to rob the man. In the end, because of other debts he had to pay, he had decided to kill two birds with one stone. By setting up the dealer for the police, Fast Money was able to satisfy his cop friends with a drug bust and also rid himself of his competition at the same time. In the end, he would buy the drugs back at ten thousand dollars less per kilo form the crooked cops once the drugs had cleared the mandatory lab tests. The cops would replace the real drugs with fake drugs in similar packaging for trial purposes.

"Oh yea, about that other thing, I'm sorry 'bout that. I got something else for you though." Fast Money smiled as he spoke into the phone. "I'll have her mother drop her off later to clean up your place."

Poochie spread her legs for Fast Money as he got back into bed. Fast Money finished with her and got out of bed. He stretched and yawned before leaving the room. Poochie rolled over and wrapped herself up in the bedspread. Fast Money walked back into the room and told her that he had something for her to do and to get dressed.

Fast Money was intent on finding Michelle. Not only had she dissed him, he realized that she knew too much about his operation to allow her to roam freely. He couldn't have her have a sudden change of heart and feel it was necessary to cleanse her soul by telling all she knew in confession to her new man or to the police. That's why he had Poochie hanging around the House of Cream night club. He figured that eventually she would gain a lead on Michelle's whereabouts from someone in the club. He also had Grizzle Hound on standby to move at a moment's notice if she was ever found.

***

Scacehead eyed Poochie coolly when she entered the club. "I don't trust that bitch," he said to himself. Scacehead felt that Poochie had been hanging around too much as of late. It wasn't just the hanging around that troubled Scacehead. One of the girls had told him that Poochie was asking a lot of questions about Cream and Michelle.

"I knew it," Scacehead said after speaking with Lee Lee. Lee Lee had come in after Poochie and told him that Poochie had just left from lying up with Fast Money.

Scacehead placed a call to Cream. Cream and Broke were in route to pick up some Chinese food when his cell phone rang.

"What's up, Scace?" Cream spoke into the phone.

"Yo man, I told you that bitch Poochie was up to something. I told you I didn't trust that ho."

Cream stared with a puzzled look at Broke. "What's up?" he asked again. "What she do?"

"Bitch working for Fast Money," Scacehead spoke fast with anger in his voice.

Cream could tell from the way he spoke that Scacehead was about to do something violent. "Hold on man, chill out," Cream said. "What the bitch do?"

"Man, bitch 'round here asking all kind of questions about you and Michelle. So, I tell Lee Lee to watch the bitch. And you know that nigga gon' go beyond the call of duty. Anyway, Lee Lee go by the bitch house and say Fast Money was there for over an hour. He say the bitch been lying up with Fast Money all the time she been round here asking questions. Now the bitch back in here asking questions about Michelle again. I'm fixin' to break my foot off in this ho' ass."

"Hold on Scace," Cream knew that Scacehead was serious. "Be cool til' I get there. I'm on my way." Cream hung up the phone. He told Broke what Scacehead had said.

"Maybe she knows something we can use," Broke said.

"Yea, that's what I was thinking," Cream said as he punched a number into his phone.

***

Sherry and Michelle realized after an hour of talking that they had a lot in common. They were both young and had many of the same aspirations in life. Both women kept staring nervously at the door in anticipation of Broke and Cream's arrival.

"Broke is a good man," Michelle was saying when she saw the worried look on Sherry's face.

"Girl, I been knowing that since I was twelve years old," Sherry answered.

"Damn girl, you do got it bad don't you?" Michelle laughed along with Sherry.

"Yea, and like I haven't seen the way you be looking at Cream. I ain't the only one got it bad," Sherry said. "I'm just not afraid to admit mine."

"Cream's too complex for me," Michelle said. "He's a lot like Broke, but with a much darker side. The night I met him I saw him back Fast Money down when Fast Money was hitting me. They were talking some ol' pimp stuff, but for real, for real, I saw fear in Fast Money's eyes. It wasn't there for long, but it was there. That's how I know that Cream has a dark side."

"Cream and Broke ain't that much different," Sherry said. "Cream just more street. I don't think he's selling drugs but he will put his hands in the dirt to take out what's his. Broke on the other hand will put his hands in the dirt only to protect that which he loves. That's why I say they're not much different, because they both will do what's necessary to get the dirt off the things they love. I've seen Broke when he's angry. I've seen what he can do and I've seen what he has done. That's why I don't worry as much about Broke as I do about what Broke may do to someone if provoked that might cause him to go back to jail. If I lost Broke back to the prison system for any reason, I don't know."

"Come on girl," Michelle interrupted Sherry as she reached over and grabbed her hand. "Ain't nothing gon' happen to Broke. Like you said, it's the other people we better worry 'bout."

Sherry almost jumped out her seat when she heard Cream keys unlocking the front door. The door open with Cream leading the way while trying to balance the bags of food and drinks in his hands. Broke was doing a similar balancing act with the bags he carried in his arms. Sherry stood and met Broke with a kiss as she relieved him of some of his packages. Broke kissed Sherry on the forehead as she snuggled up in his free arm and walked with him to the dining room table.

"You act like I been gone forever," Broke said as he placed his bags on the table.

"Define forever," Sherry said.

Cream sat at the table and dialed a number, into his phone after placing his bags on the table along with Broke's. "I hope you like Chinese food," he said to Michelle who had helped him with the bags and was now emptying the contents upon the table along with Sherry.

"What y'all trying to do, feed an army. Who gon' eat all this food?" Sherry asked.

"Well, we didn't know exactly what everybody wanted," Cream said. "So we got a little bit of everything."

"I see," Sherry said.

"What's this," Michelle had a frown on her face as she sniffed the contents of one of the bags.

"Hmmph!, Girl I don't know what that is, look like a cat foot," Sherry said with a frown on her own face.

It wasn't long before all the food was gone, including the unknown substance.

221

"It's a good thing we brought enough for an army," Cream said with a smile. "Anything less and the troops wouldn't have enough strength to fight."

"Look like somebody was hungry," Broke said.

"Yea, look like it," Sherry said to Broke. "Make people think I can't cook as much as you ate. And still eating, look at you, cat food all over your mouth." Sherry kissed Broke as she leaned over him to clean up the mess of empty packages and excess food.

"Yo, Broke, Cream said as he stood up from the table, "I'm a follow up on what we were talking about. You know how Scace is."

"You want me to ride with you?" Broke stared at Sherry as he asked the question.

"Naw man, I done kept you away from Sherry long enough already. I'll call you if I get a lead. Ain't no sense in making Sherry worry no more 'n she has already."

Broke hugged Sherry close. "This one gone worry no matter what."

"I'm not the only one who worry." Sherry cast a glance at Michelle.

"We all have our reasons to worry about one thing or another," Cream said. "But it's a rare and beautiful thing to find someone to love and appreciate you."

Michelle was busy cleaning as Broke, Sherry and Cream prepared to leave.

"You want me to help you clean up before we go?" Sherry asked.

"This ain't nothing," Michelle said. "It's nothing to worry about," Michelle placed emphasis on the word worry as she slammed some trash into one of the bags. "I can handle it," Michelle said. "I'll see you later." Michelle continued to clean the leftover food and packages off the table.

Sherry noticed the edge in Michelle's voice and knew that she was directing her remarks at Cream. "Well, I'll see you later then," Sherry said as she walked out the kitchen wrapped up in Broke's arms.

Cream called Scacehead and told him he was on his way. Then he called Sleepy and Poky and told them to get the room ready.

Michael Rogers

Chapter 28

Poochie was still nosing around the, club hoping to hear something she could report back to Fast Money about Michelle's whereabouts. Thanks to Fast Money she was paid up on all her bills and even-had money in the bank. Her car would be out the shop on Friday and she was sporting a new outfit that Fast Money had given to her out of his closet the night before. There was not much she wouldn't do for Fast Money at this moment. She was trying to prove her worth to him. Though she would have preferred to be with Cream, Poochie was not the type of woman to wait for a man to make up his mind about her. There were many men in pursuit of her. Cream's lack of interest in her was an insult to her ego. Poochie was not one to find fault in herself, so therefore, she surmised that something had to be wrong with Cream. Why else wouldn't he want to be with a dime like her? Her wide hips, properly positioned on a bowlegged frame, had men falling head-over-heels for her. With an attractive face to go with her bootylicious body, Poochie was built for comfort.

Poochie finished her drink at the bar and thanked Sylvia who had bought it for her. Sylvia licked her lips seductively as she stared at Poochie. It was no secret that Sylvia preferred women to men.

"So what's up," Sylvia asked Poochie.

"Ain't nothing," Poochie said. I'm just trying to stay sucker free and ahead of the game." Poochie knew that Sylvia was attracted to her. Even though she was strictly on men, she was flirting with Sylvia in hopes to use Sylvia's attraction to her advantage.

"Do you know that girl name Michelle that use to work for Fast Money?" Poochie asked the question casually as she sipped from her drink.

"Yea, I know Shell," Sylvia said. "She staying at the Cream Land."

Poochie eyes lit up as she stared across the bar at Sylvia. "She do?" Poochie almost shouted the question before collecting herself and toning down her voice. "When she move over there?"

"Cream brought her over there the other night. What's up?" Sylvia asked suddenly. "Why you looking for Shell?"

Sylvia's question caught Poochie by surprise. "I was just asking," Poochie said.

"I use to kick it with her, and I haven't seen her in a while. What's up with you? You gon' be around later?" Poochie tried to change the subject away from Michelle now that she had the information she needed. "I might come back and holler at you later if you gon' be around."

"I'll be here," Sylvia said. "If you looking for Michelle she in room 8 at Cream Land. You want me to call her?"

"Naw, that's all right, I'll holler at her later. Just tell her I said what's up. She know my number."

***

Poochie hung around for a few more minutes before disappearing out the club when Sylvia walked into the poolroom. She hurriedly exited the club and sped away in her car. Poochie called Fast Money and told him what Sylvia had said. Fast Money told her to go by the motel and check to make sure the information was valid. He told Poochie to call him when she knew for sure. Poochie drove over to the motel and parked in front of room 8. She walked up to the door and knocked softly.

The door opened slowly. Poochie stared up at a baldhead man who answered the door before trying to peep around him into the room.

"What's up?" Poky asked as he blocked Poochie's view into the room.

"Is Michelle here?" Poochie asked the question in an agitated voice.

"She's in the bathroom." Poky openly stared at Poochie's shapely body causing her to feel uncomfortable.

Poky stepped aside to allow Poochie to enter the room. "You coming in or what?"

Poochie paused reluctantly as she stared around the room. If not for her wanting so desperately to please Fast Money, she would have never entered the room. Instead, she stepped cautiously in.

Poky locked the door behind her causing alarm bells to go off in Poochie's head.

"Where Michelle at?" Poochie said in an even more agitated voice.

"Why you looking for Michelle?" Poky asked the question as he stared at the gap between Poochie's legs.

"Because I am. Who is you?" Poochie asked the question as she stared up at Poky with a look of contempt. She could sense that Poky was not a trick waiting for Michelle as she had first thought upon entering the room.

"Look man, tell Michelle, Poochie out here or move so I can leave. I don't know you and I didn't come out here to play no twenty questions with you." Poochie had an attitude as she stood glaring up at Poky with her hands on her hips.

"Naw, what you gon' do is shut the fuck up with that Lil' smart ass mouth and start telling me why you looking for Michelle. That's what you gon' do."

The way Poky spoke to her caused Poochie to become even angrier. "Man you don't scare me! I ain't telling you shit! You better move your ass out my way. You got me fucked up," Poochie tried to make her way past Poky to the door.

"Bitch! You think it's a game, huh?" Poky picked Poochie up in a bear hug from behind. He slung her on the bed where she bounced high and landed with a plop.

"Nigga!" Poochie was fuming with anger as she gathered herself in preparation to fight. She was too angry to be afraid. She reached for her purse that had landed on the floor. Her eyes followed the path of her purse to where Sleepy was emerging from the bathroom zipping up his pants. It was then Poochie begun to fear.

Poky walked towards Poochie as Sleepy entered the room. Poochie managed to stand before Poky grabbed her and tossed her back onto the bed. Poochie was kicking and cussing as Sleepy and Poky secured her in the bed by grabbing her arms. Poky pulled some handcuffs out his pocket as they flipped Poochie onto her stomach. Him and Sleepy wrestled with the struggling girl as Poky secured her hands to the bedposts with her arms outstretched.

Poochie was cussing and foaming out the mouth as the men secured her until she was spread-eagle across the bed on her stomach with her head hanging off the foot of the bed.

Poky ran his hands across the fat mounds of Poochie's butt cheeks. "Damn, this a big ol' butt." Sleepy pulled her head up while kneeling on one knee at the foot of the bed.

"Get your got damn hands off me!" Poochie was screaming at Poky who was rubbing her butt like he was rubbing a crystal ball.

"It's not your ass you better be worried about," Sleepy said. He twisted Poochie's head by the hair causing her to stare up at him with a strained and painful look on her face. What Poochie saw in the eyes of Sleepy caused her to shiver in fright. His black eyes were cold and mean as he glared down at her with a scowl.

"My man wanna know why Fast Money got you snooping around asking about Michelle," Poky asked the question while still holding Poochie's head up by the hair and forcing her to stare into his eyes.

Poochie gave a defeated look at the mention of Fast Money's name. "Fast Money ain't got me doing nothing."

"Yea, and I'm Smokey the Bear." Sleepy nodded at Poky who sat on the bed with Poochie.

Poky pulled a knife out his pants and flicked it open. He then lifted the short dress Poochie wore above her waist. Sleepy held Poochie firm by the head as she spit and cussed at Poky who had cut away her thong and left her exposed and at his mercy. Sleepy dropped her head and stood. He pulled off his belt as Poochie stared up at him with a look of fright on her face. She swore to call the police if they touched her.

"I don't work for no damn Fast Money. I don't know what y'all talking about. Let me up, dammit. I swear you bet not touch me." Poochie was trying to sound tough while pleading all the while in hopes she could convince the men that she was telling the truth.

Whack!

"Owwwww!"

Whack!

"Owwwwww!" Poochie screamed loudly as the heavy leather belt came down hard across her butt and thighs.

Whack!

"Stop got dammit! I ain't playing with y'all!"

Whack! Whack! Whack!

"Stop got dammit, motherfucker, let me off this damn bed."

Whack! Whack! Sleepy swung the belt harder and harder until Poochie had welt marks across her backside.

"Why Fast Money looking for Michelle."

Whack!

"Huh! Why he looking for Michelle!"

Whack! Whack!

"Huh! Huh! Ain't gon' keep asking you."

Poochie was screaming and crying as the big belt landed again and again across her butt and thighs. "He say he just want to talk to her." Poochie couldn't take anymore. She dropped her head before lifting it again to stare up pleadingly at Sleepy. Protecting Fast Money was not worth the pain and humiliation she was going through.

Poky stood off the bed. He was in an excited state after watching Sleepy spank Poochie's fat butt and seeing it jiggle with each swing of the belt.

"Man this ho ain't gon' tell us nothing by you hitting her on her big ass with no belt. Shit every man don' ever fucked this bitch done probably spanked this big ass. I know what'll make her talk. I know how to make her tell us everything we want to know." Poochie had a frighten look on her face as she stared up at Poky who was stepping out his pants.

"I told you I don't know nothing." Poochie stared at Sleepy with a pleading look on her face. She was hoping he would do something to stop the evil eyed man who was undressing before her. Poochie followed Poky with her eyes until he walked out of her view somewhere behind her.

Sleepy showed her no concern as he grabbed her roughly by the hair and twisted her head until she stared painfully up at him.

"Now, I'm gon' ask you one more time what Fast Money is up too. If you don't give me the answers I want to hear, I'm a turn my man loose on you. Now, what do Fast Money want with Michelle?"

Sleepy twisted Poochie's head until she could see Poky stroking what had to be the biggest penis on a man that she had ever seen in her life. Poky looked like he was stroking a third arm as he stared at her spread wide in bed. Poochie eyes grew wide in fear of what he was about to do.

"When I put this monster in her ass, she gon' tell us everything she ever done. She gone tell us our history since the beginning of time." Poky had a devious smile on his face as he climbed into bed between Poochie's legs.

"I'm-a hit you like Ice Cube," Poky smiled wickedly at Poochie. "No Vaseline."

The thought of Poky forcing the mule tool into her bowels, quickly made up Poochie's mind. "I don't know what Fast Money want with that girl. All I know is that he told me that if I heard anything to call him or some dude name Grizzle Hound that he got looking for her." Poochie spoke so fast that Sleepy had to ask her to slow down.

"What else he up too?" Sleepy asked, "Whose the cop he got on his payroll and where do he keep his drugs and money."

"Man, I don't know shit about no cops and money." Poochie felt Poky's hands on her butt as he began to rub her.

"I heard him tell some cop to meet him at the port on Friday." Poochie stared up at Sleepy who nodded at Poky. "I think it's a drug deal. I heard Fast Money say something about some drugs. I don't know shit else."

Sleepy nodded to Poky who gave a long sigh as he palmed Poochie's butt one last time before getting out of bed. Poky had just got out of bed with Poochie and was putting on his clothes when the motel room

231

door opened and Cream walked into the room.

"What the hell?" Cream stared as if shocked to see Poochie strapped across the bed. "Man what the fuck y'all doing. Let that woman up." Cream spoke in an angry voice as he stared hard at Poky and Sleepy. "I asked y'all to talk to the damn girl. You niggas crazy. Get them damn cuffs off that woman. Poochie, you all right."

Poochie stared up at Cream with a look of relief on her face. The look was quickly replaced with one of anger as she was freed from her cuffs. Poochie snatched her dress down to cover her body as she begin to cuss.

"Hell naw I'm not all right! I'm fitn'to call the police on these motherfuckers. Black motherfuckers kidnapped and was fitn'to rape me." Poochie had fire in her eyes as she stared back and forth from Poky to Sleepy. "I don't know who these fools think I am." Poochie continued to call Poky and Sleepy every name she could think of as she angrily fixed her clothes.

Neither Sleepy or Poky showed any concern to what Poochie was saying. Cream told the two men to step outside so he could speak with Poochie alone. Poochie was still fuming as Cream sat on the bed beside her and stared at her with a serious look.

"Ain't nobody ever treated me like that," Poochie said.

Cream sighed loudly before scolding Poochie in a stern voice. "Bitch please. Save that shit. You whores think it's a game. While you round here crying because somebody done felt your ass, you lucky to be alive. People done already died in this beef and now just because some nigga give you a new outfit and a few dollars you want to join the feast. Ain't nobody hurt you. So I'm not trying to hear all that sob story shit."

Poochie stared at Cream with a shocked and surprised look. She had never seen Cream act this way before. The fear that she had earlier begin to creep back into her as she listened to Cream without saying a

232

word.

"Niggas don't care no more about killing whores these days than killing niggas," Cream said. "The only reason you're still alive is because I like you enough to let you live. Now it's up to you how much longer you can enjoy this privilege. I got too much at stake for you to be talking 'bout running to the cops over nothing."

"They didn't have to do me like that," Poochie said in a whining voice.

"Look-a-here Poochie." Cream's spoke in a soothing voice. "Fast Money is going down one way or another. Now I know you're a get-it girl and still trying to get it while the getting is good. Ain't no sense in you getting caught up in Fast Money's troubles. Now I already got my suspicions about Fast Money in the disappearing of one of my girls. If something happen to Michelle, I'm not going to ask no more questions. Everything around Fast Money will be eliminated. Everything and everybody." Cream stared hard at Poochie to drive home his point. "There's an African proverb that says, *'when the eagle eats the snake, it eats everything in the snake's belly'*."

Cream reached into his pocket and pulled out a wad of money. He peeled off two thousand dollars and handed the money to Poochie. "It's not too late for you to join a winning team," he said. "This should hold you over until the eagle has had its' fill of snake. When the snake is gone you can work with the girls in the club. Until then, I want you to be my eyes and ears in the snake's pit."

Poochie took the money and folded it away. She stared at Cream and thanked him for the money and opportunity. "Be careful," she said. "This snake you're after, got handlers with badges."

Cream stood off the bed. "Don't worry about me," he said as he handed Poochie a card with his number on it. "I been dealing with snakes all my life," he said. "I've been bit so many times by snakes like Fast Money, that I'm immune to their bite." Cream left Poochie on the bed and told her to call him if she heard anything.

"Thanks Cream," Poochie said as he walked out the door.

***

Broke and Cream rode out to the port early the next morning. They were scoping the layout after Poochie called and told Cream what time Fast Money would be meeting the cop. Broke and Cream were trying to figure what angle they could use to trap the men. Broke told Cream that he thought he had a plan that would work.

"What is it?" Cream asked.

"We're going to give Fast Money a taste of his own medicine," Broke said with a sly smile on his face. Cream drove as Broke explained.

Cream dropped Broke off at home where Sherry was waiting for him to take her to her father's church in Altheimer. Cream was trying to dial home on his cell phone as he drove away from Broke's house. "Damn" Cream said as he tossed the cell phone into the passenger seat. "I forgot to charge up that damn battery," he was thinking as he headed for home.

He wondered what Michelle was doing, 'Probable cooking' he thought. He had to admit, Michelle was a hell of a cook. He was going to miss her meals when she was gone back to Iowa, he dreaded the thought. He knew that her delicious meals were the least things he would miss about Michelle.

Cream and Michelle were still like strangers after weeks of living together. An occasional smile or witty remark passed as conversation between them. Michelle had heard that Fast Money had someone looking for her. Cream warned her that she wouldn't be safe in Iowa because Fast Money had Iowa ties. He told her that she was safer in Pine Bluff. She agreed and decided to stay. Although, in her heart, she knew that fear was not her only reason for staying.

Chapter 29

Scacehead was shooting pool with Lee Lee when Lee Lee suddenly placed his pool stick on the table and said he'd be right back.

"Unk unk nigga, shoot your shot," Scacehead said.

"Man I got to go pee," Lee Lee said as he walked fast towards the bathroom.

"Nigga you better, hurry yo' ass up. You gon pay me my five dollars if you don't make this shot." Scacehead leaned on his stick as he sipped from his beer.

Lee Lee walked into the bathroom while fumbling with his zipper. The flushing of a toilet drowned out the opening of the door and Lee Lee's entrance. Lee Lee stood next to one of the bathroom stalls taking a leak. His ears perked up when he heard someone in the stall next to the urinal mention the name Michelle and Cream's house. Lee Lee finished quickly and rushed out the bathroom without washing his hands. The occupant in the stall hung up his cell phone without knowledge that Lee Lee had been listening in on his conversation. He hung up his phone cautiously when he heard the bathroom door close. He thought Lee Lee was entering instead of exiting.

The caller was Piss Mo and, true to his name, he had been taking another one of the many pisses that due to his being shot in the bladder he had to take on an hourly basis. Piss Mo had overheard Scacehead telling Lee Lee that Cream was probably at home with that fine ass redbone name Michelle. Piss Mo knew his boss Fast Money was looking for Michelle and had went into the bathroom stall to call and inform him to her whereabouts.

Piss Mo had also heard Lee Lee bragging about Cream's badass house.

He said it was located on Old Warren Road. He'd heard enough to pinpoint the location. He also passed this information to his boss.

He was stepping out the stall when Lee Lee, Scacehead, and Roundhead all stepped into the bathroom. Without warning, Piss Mo was crumbled to the floor with three punches from Roundhead. Piss Mo was stilled dazed when Lee Lee asked him about the call he had overheard him make. Piss Mo was about to lie but was only able to mutter the words "I wasn't" before Lee Lee kicked him in the chest and knocked him back into the stall with his back against the toilet.

"Nigga, I'm a ask you one time who you was talking too." The look on Scacehead's face was enough to convince Piss Mo to tell the truth. He knew that Scacehead was unmerciful and cruel when he became violent. Piss Mo who was bleeding out the nose, told Scacehead that he had called Fast Money and the nature of the call.

Scacehead rushed out the bathroom and tried to call Cream on the phone behind the bar. He became frustrated and cussed loudly after trying several times to call Cream without an answer to his calls. "Watch this fool Roundhead," Scacehead said as him and Lee Lee rushed out to his car.

**

Grizzle Hound crept cautiously up to Cream's house. His car was parked up the street from Cream off to the side of the road. Fast Money had given him the location along with the promise of nine thousand dollars to kill both Cream and Michelle. For that amount of money Grizzle Hound would have done a whole family, even if it was his own. He crept along the side of the house where he was concealed by hedge bushes.

Grizzle Hound smiled a wicked smile of satisfaction after finding an unlocked window. He eased the window up and climbed into the house with his gun drawn.

**

Michelle rolled over groggily in bed after being awakened by the ringing of the telephone. The phone had been ringing constantly for over thirty minutes. Being that she was a guest in Cream's house and the phone was in his bedroom, Michelle didn't want to answer the phone. Cream hadn't given her any indication that she was anymore than a houseguest.

Being that no one knew she was staying at Cream's, Michelle figured the call had nothing to do with her and decided to let the answering machine record the calls. Cream could return the calls when he got home or Michelle figured that the callers would call his cell phone. Either way it go, Michelle wasn't about to answer Cream's telephone.

Grizzle Hound stumbled over a small table beneath the window of the room he had entered. It was this noise that caught Michelle's attention as she sat up in bed. It sounded like something had dropped to the floor. Michelle figured it was Cream. She eased out of bed and walked over to the mirror on the wall. She wanted to fix her hair and face before Cream saw her.

Grizzle Hound had already checked downstairs and was now moving cautiously up the stairway with his gun drawn in search of Michelle. Michelle walked out her room just as Cream was entering the house. She paused in fright at the top of the stairs as she stared at Grizzle Hound with the gun in his hand. Grizzle Hound was half way up the stairs when Cream entered the house and saw him on the stairway. Cream rushed into the house as Grizzle Hound ran and grabbed Michelle who was standing as if in shock at the top of the stairs.

"Come here bitch!" Grizzle Hound grabbed the frighten woman around the neck as he placed the gun barrel up to her head. Michelle had never been so frighten. Her lips trembled as tears poured down her face. Her eyes were transfixed on Cream as he stood at the bottom of the stairs, moving cautiously towards them.

"Don't move nigga. I'll blow this bitch head off. Get your pretty ass back down them stairs. Move!" Grizzle Hound forced Michelle's head to the side as he pressed the gun hard against her temple. Cream slowly backed back down the stairs without taking his eyes off Grizzle Hound.

"Come on Hound. You know me. Let the girl go and let's talk like men. You know how I get down nigga. I got a safe full of money, right over there. I know who sent you. Whatever he's paying you nigga, I'll double. Take the money and we can forget this shit ever happen. If not nigga, ain't nothing he paying you gone keep me from finding yo' ass."

Grizzle Hound laughed at Cream. He walked slowly down the stairs with Michelle still sobbing as he half dragged her and half carried her in front of him. His first intention was to shoot Cream when he reached the bottom of the stairs. He was now thinking about the money Cream said he had in the safe.

"Let's see the money pretty boy." Grizzle Hound motioned towards the safe with his gun as Cream backed away from him as he descended the stairs. Cream was trying to buy time as he figured out his next move. He knew that Grizzle Hound was going to kill both him and Michelle if he didn't do something. There was no other way for this to end.

"I told you it's in my safe on the wall. Let the girl go and you can have it all."

"Nigga, let me see the money first, and then we can talk about the girl. And don't try nothing stupid. Or, you will be the first one to die. Then I'm gon' have me some fun with your little friend before I bust a cap in her ass."

Cream opened up the safe and allowed Grizzle Hound to see the stacks of money. He held his hand on the door so he could slam it shut if Grizzle Hound didn't release Michelle.

"You see the money, now let the girl go or I'll shut the door."

Grizzle Hound smiled as he pushed Michelle away from him towards Cream. "All right nigga, take the bitch. Now throw me the money out the safe or I'm-a bust a cap in her ass right where she stand."

Cream pulled out the stacks of money and tossed them to the floor at Grizzle Hound's feet.

"Hurry up nigga, I ain't got all day. And don't try no stupid shit." Grizzle Hound held the gun pointed at Michelle as he knelt to pick up the money.

"Ain't nothing like being paid twice to do one job. And to think that your dumb ass thought I'll let you live. Nigga you slipping." Grizzle Hound pointed the gun at Cream who stood defiantly staring at him with a fierce look of anger.

"Just don't you slip nigga," Cream said. "You know this won't end with me. And when you get to the hell we're going to, I'll be there waiting for you."

"Tough talk for a weak nigga who's about to die. Who you trying to impress? Must be the bitch, because you know nigga, whenever I get to hell, I'm-a still be the hound. All right pretty boy, Fast Money sends his regards."

Grizzle Hound stuffed the last of the money into his trousers before standing and pointing the gun at Cream's head. Michelle stared at Cream with tears still pouring down her face. She knew now after hearing Fast Money's name that it was her fault the man was there and that it was her that the man had come to kill.

"No!" Michelle pushed Cream out the way as Grizzle Hound pulled the trigger on the gun.

Pow! The gun sounded off loudly. The bullet grazed Cream before hitting the wall behind them. Michelle and Cream both fell to the floor where they laid looking up at Grizzle Hound who had a smile on his face as he prepared to fire again.

"Who gone save you this time pretty boy?" Grizzle Hound pointed the gun at Cream's head as Cream covered Michelle with his body on the floor. *"Pow!"* He pulled the trigger on the gun. It was at this moment that Lee Lee come flying through the air and grabbed his gun hand.

Lee Lee landed into Grizzle Hound with a flying body tackle. The crash caused Grizzle Hound to shoot into the floor besides Cream and Michelle before tumbling to the floor with Lee Lee atop him. Scacehead who had rushed into the room behind Lee Lee stomped the gun out of Grizzle Hound's hand. Grizzle Hound tried to fight back but was no match for the brutal whooping that Scacehead and Lee Lee put on him as they stomped him on the floor until he was unconscious.

Cream stood up and pulled Michelle up along with him. "You all right?" Cream asked Michelle. Michelle nodded her head to indicate she was fine. She couldn't believe that they were still alive. She was trembling in Cream's arms as he spoke soothingly to her telling her it was all right now as he held her tightly against his body. Cream's soothing words calmed Michelle as she sobbed against his chest.

Scacehead was breathing hard as he walked over to Cream. "Man, answer your damn phone. I been trying to call you for thirty minutes. I'm glad we got here in time."

"Shit man, my battery down."

"Hell, you ain't got no batteries on your house phone. What's wrong with it."

"I heard the phone ringing," Michelle said.

"Why didn't you answer it?" Cream asked.

"I didn't want to answer your phone."

"Well, it's a good thing you left the door open."

"Naw, it's a good thing you stopped by," Cream said as he walked over and closed the front door.

"Man, me and Lee Lee drove like a bat out of hell trying to get here. Lee Lee caught that nigga Piss Mo in the bathroom at the club talking to Fast Money on the phone. He told us Fast Money had this nigga," Scacehead kicked Grizzle Hound hard in the side causing him to grunt from the pain, "right here out looking for Michelle. He say he told him that Michelle was over here. That's why I was trying to call and warn you. Me and Lee Lee drove over here after not getting an answer. I thought ol' boy had you cuz."

"Shit he would've if it hadn't been for Michelle pushing me out the way of the first shot and then Lee Lee flying through the air and saving me from the second shot."

"I told you, I had them young killers on the payroll." Scacehead slapped hands with Lee Lee who was beaming from the praise.

Lee Lee smacked Grizzle Hound upside the head with the gun he was holding on him after Grizzle Hound moved on the floor. "Be still nigga, man what we gon' do with this fool?" Lee Lee asked.

"One thing for certain, we can't let him go." Cream said. "Call Sleepy and Poky and tell them to come over. They'll know what to do."

Scacehead pulled out his cell phone and made the call as Cream had suggested. "What about that nigga Piss Mo," he asked as he waited for someone to pick up on the other end of the phone call.

"Turn him over to them young wolves you always talking about. You say you got them young killers on the payroll. Just make sure he's not found before Friday. I got something planned for that nigga Fast Money. I don't want that nigga to spook him into hiding."

"I got that nigga," Scacehead said. "Don't even trip."

"Don't kill the nigga," Cream said. "He told you what you wanted to know, just lay him up for a while. Nigga ain't no threat."

241

Poky and Sleepy arrived thirty minutes later. They carried Grizzle Hound bound by his hands and feet and loaded him into their service van. Poky wanted to finish Fast Money as well but Cream told him that he would take care of that himself.

Cream told Michelle to pack her some clothing after everyone had left. He wanted to move her to a safer place until he finished his business with Fast Money. He told her he was going to place her in a room at the Hilton for a few days.

Michelle reminded Cream that she was going back to Iowa and that she could use the money he paid for the room as bus fare for home.

Cream told her it was probably best if she didn't go back to Iowa until Fast Money was dealt with. "Remember, you did meet him in Iowa," Cream said. "I'm sure he still has eyes looking for you there as well as here."

It was true that Cream was worried about Michelle's safety. It was also true that when she pushed him out of the way of Grizzle Hound's bullet, she had done so without regards for her own safety. This unselfish act of love had bonded Cream with her. Cream figured that if she was willing to take a bullet for him, he had to explore the deeper reason as to why. He couldn't deny his own attraction to Michelle. He also liked having her around. If things went according to plan with Fast Money on Friday, he might ask her to stay.

"Well, since I'm responsible for this mess, let me clean it up before we leave." Michelle walked over and picked up the spilled food bags that Cream had dropped when he entered the house and saw Grizzle Hound, "Tacos," Michelle said, "My favorite."

"I thought you might be hungry," Cream said. He had overheard Michelle tell Sherry how much she loved tacos. Cream knelt to help Michelle. She stared affectionately at him. He smiled warmly back. They both found what they were looking for. Cream could no longer deny his love for her. He took her face in his hands and his kiss took her breath away.

Michael Rogers

Chapter 30

The Port of Pine Bluff was located on the far east end of town. It was a scenic park surrounded by water to one side and open fields on the other. There was one way in and one way out. Four guys were playing basketball on the ball court to the right of the park's entrance. Two cars were parked side by side in front of one of the pavilions at the far end of the park.

FM got out of one of the cars and walked over to the other car where two occupants sat in the front seat. FM carried a black bag in his right hand. The fat cop and his partner who FM was meeting, paid little attention to the two boats sitting fifty yards out from them in the water. Their thoughts were on the money in the bag that FM carried in his hand. FM entered the car and passed the bag he was carrying over the car seat to the fat cop. He then proceeded to inspect the contents of a black bag that was sitting in the backseat of the car where he was seated.

"This cool," FM said as he closed the bag. "I'm out," he said as he reached for the door. "I'll probably have something for you a little later," he told the fat cop. "Meat so rare it might even bleed." FM got out the car and quickly walked back over to his own car.

FM drove off with the two cops trailing him through the park. There was a levy that ran along the exit of the park along the road that led back to the populated area of town. FM had made the turn alongside the levy when a bevy of state troopers and other official cars came speeding down behind him and the two cops from atop the levy. There were cop cars blocking the road ahead of FM causing him to slow his car as he tried to find an exit around the cop cars. With cops behind him and before him, FM knew it was over. He stared across at the five kilos of cocaine that was sitting in the seat next to him.

FMs first thoughts were that the fat detective had set him up. He had already made up his mind that he was not going down alone. Detective Jones stared at his partner as if his partner had answers to the questions in his head. Such questions as to why were they surrounded by cops and did FM set them up. He flipped the switch on the emergency lights as he drove behind FM with the other cop cars trailing. FM pulled over to the side of the road after realizing there was no escape. The fat detective quickly exited his car before any of the other cops. He moved with the speed of a much thinner and much younger man. His partner was on his heels as they both raced up to FM's car one to each side. Both cops had their guns drawn as they screamed at FM through the passenger and driver side windows. "Don't move! Don't move!" Both cops screamed at FM with their guns pointed at him in the car.

"You fat motherfucker." FM cussed at the fat detective as he stared at him in anger. He was sure now that the detective had set him up. "I'm not going down alone." FM said. "Your fat ass going down with me. You can," FM never got a chance to finish his last sentence. Both cops shot him in the chest.

"He got a gun!" *Pow! Pow! Pow!* FM's body jerked violently as the bullets tore into his chest and exited his body into the car seat. He was dead even before he slumped forward where he rested with his head leaning against the steering wheel as his lifeblood poured from his body.

"He had a gun," the fat detective told the first of the FBI agents who rushed upon the scene. "He was going for a gun, the detective said again as he fought to catch his breath. "It's underneath his leg." The gun that FM always kept underneath his leg when driving was clearly visible on the car seat beneath him.

"We were executing a reverse sting operation," the detective said. "We didn't know that you guys had been notified. If you'll check the black bag in the suspect's car, you'll find five kilos of cocaine we used in the sting. You'll also find the fifty thousand dollars we received for the buy in the car." The fat detective spoke authoritatively as if he was running the investigation instead of being investigated.

The two FBI men huddled up with the local authorities in discussion. It was agreed by all that without FM there was no way they could prove the detectives were lying.

The officers in the boat had no recording of actual conversation between FM and the detectives. They only had pictures of them making what the detectives could say was the transactions of a reverse drug sting operation.

The Fed's decided not to pursue tampering with evidence charges as well. The agents felt that these charges were not worth pursuing based on the fact that the drugs were recovered as part of a sting operation.

It was decided that it was best to drop the investigation against the detective and to pursue the charges against FM as a convicted felon who was apprehended by the joint efforts of the local and federal authorities. Detective Jones was not worried in the least about no internal investigation. As a decorated veteran at the end of his career his only thought was that he wouldn't get to bust the cherry of the young virgin that FM had promised him.

***

Broke called the state trooper who he had provided the details about the meet between FM and the detectives. The state trooper told him that no charges would be filed against the detectives. Broke became angered when the trooper told him that the bust would go down as a joint effort between the local task force and FBI to combat drugs in the Pine Bluff community. He explained everything to Broke before thanking him for his help and promising Broke that the Feds would still uphold their end of the bargain that they had made with him.

"Here we go again," Broke said angrily. "First you let a skinhead off for a drive-by shooting because you didn't want to stir up racial tension. Now you gonna pen a medal on and give praise to a pedophile cop who shot and murdered his accomplice to keep him quiet about their drug dealing. Just because it's good publicity and shows joint efforts between law enforcement agencies during this post 911 era. Ain't that some shit!" Broke slammed down the phone.

"What's up?" Cream asked.

"NAACP," Broke said, "Negros Ain't Acting like Colored People." He told Cream what the trooper had told him. "Might want to call Poochie," he said, "Let her know what's up."

Cream sighed heavily and pulled out his cell phone.

***

Fast Money was livid with anger. His eyes blazed as he paced back and forth across the floor. The gun in his hand made a statement all of its' own. There's a rat in this bitch," Fast Money spat out the words.

"Fast Money, you tripping," a caramel skin girl name Honey exhaled the marijuana smoke she had inhaled from the blunt in her hand.

"Bitch!" The girl jumped as Fast Money directed his anger at her. "Did I ask your dyke ass to speak. If I say a motherfucker telling, a motherfucker telling." Fast Money turned his steel gaze slowly in a sweeping motion. The other four men in the room all froze under the stare. The two brothers Theotis and Mitchell stood next to Maurice and Benny.

Benny stared nervously towards the door. He was thinking about his chances of making it out the door before Fast Money could stop him. Benny was for sure that Fast Money had discovered his betrayal. He knew that Fast Money had eyes everywhere. Benny figured that someone must have told Fast Money about his visit to the Cream Land Motel. Fast Money's gaze rested on Benny.

"Where Fat Man at?" Benny asked the question to buy some time. Fat Man was Fast Money's driver and most trusted member of his team.

"Dead," Fast Money said without emotion. "It was supposed to be me. I sent Fat Man to make a run and the Feds were waiting for him at the drop. Detective Jones killed him to protect his own ass. You can hear the official version on tonight's news broadcast. Somebody in this

248

bitch dropped a dime, right now, this is the only thing that matters to me." Fast Money stared hard at his crew.

"Maybe the Feds were after the crooked cops," Benny said. He felt more relaxed now that he knew he was off the hook. The last place in the world he wanted to be was on Fast Money's bad side. Benny had a hard time distinguishing at times who was the biggest devil between Fast Money and Satan.

"Thought about that," Fast Money said, "eliminated that as a possibility."

"Maybe your new spy bitch playing both sides," Honey said with an edge in her voice. Honey didn't like being yelled at. Not even by Fast Money. If it had been one of the other men in the room she would have either shot or stabbed them for disrespecting her.

Fast Money stared at Honey. Honey expected him to snap at her again. Fast Money was thinking back to the call he had received from Detective Jones about the drop. He remembered that he had taken the call in the presence of Poochie.

"Go find that bitch and bring her here." Fast Money gave the order. Honey was the first to move towards the door. "You stay here," Fast Money told her. Honey stood in place as the others quickly rushed out the room. Fast Money walked over to her. "You might be right about this bitch. I would love to send her conniving ass on a trip to the country to see our friend."

"I'll love to go with her." Honey said. "I'm sure Moe would love to see what I would do to that fat bitch."

"I'm sure you would love it too," Fast Money said. "With your devilish ass." Fast Money unzipped his pants. Honey quickly dropped the shorts she was wearing. She was naked beneath them. "Leave the fuck me boots on," Fast Money said.

***

Poochie was running scared after receiving a call from Cream that Fast Money had escaped the trap set for him. Her car was idling out front of her house. Poochie was walking fast to the car when she spotted a black SUV rounding the curve a couple of blocks up from her house.

"There that bitch go!" Theotis shouted the obvious to Bennie who was driving the SUV. "Damn that bitch got a big ass on her" Theotis said excitedly. He was more interested in catching Poochie for his own lustful purposes than he was for Fast Money. The way Poochie's ass bounced in the tight shorts she wore had Theotis fantasizing about tying her up and making her his sex slave.

Benny blew the horn and sped up the SUV. "Bitch trying to run, he said.

"Man, catch the bitch!" Theotis screamed. Poochie was speeding away in her car. Benny sped up after her. Poochie never let off the gas as she rounded the block leading out the subdivision where she lived. Benny couldn't catch her in time before Poochie could make it across the busy intersection up the road from the subdivision. Benny was stopped by the red light at the intersection. Theotis was pissed.

"Man you can't drive worth a shit," Theotis said," and what the fuck you blow the horn at the bitch for, you knew she was going to run. Theotis watched as Poochie's car disappeared into traffic. The thought of fucking her in her big ass would take much longer to vanish from his mind. "Knew I should've drove," he said pouting in his seat.

Broke and Cream were in route to Poochie's house when she called and told them about the chase. Cream gave her an address to a house he owned in Little Rock. He told her he would have the neighbor to give her the key. You can stay there until we resolve this situation." Cream hung up the phone and stared at Broke.

Probably need to call Sleepy and Poky," Broke said, "tell them to be on the lookout for cops and robbers."

"What we need to do is kill this nigga." Cream said. "I feel like I'm walking around with a gun to my head."

I'm sure he feels the same way." Broke said. "Only difference is that his hand is on the trigger. He know that it will be suicide to show his face. Fast Money ain't no coward but he ain't no closer to being a fool. He'll go into hiding for a while now that he knows Grizzle Hound is out the picture. He know we're watching and waiting to checkmate his every move. The game is far from over but in the end we'll win."

"We better," Cream said. This game is to the death. And I'm much too

250

fly to die. Both men laughed. So what's up on Brick?" Cream asked. "I'm tired of seeing my man in a cage."

"Only weak men want to want to see a lion in a cage," Broke said. "It makes them feel safe to roam freely and to do the things they couldn't do if the lion was free. But now the lion is loose. Brick should be home next week. These good kind white folk have no idea of the hell they're about to unleashed upon themselves."

"Dig that." Cream said laughing.

Michael Rogers

BRICK

Chapter 31

James Franklin, A.K.A Brick, was still finding it hard to believe that he was a free man. It had been two weeks since his release from prison. The day his name had been called to pack his belonging had begun as just another day. Brick had had no idea that he was going home. It was now two weeks later and he was just beginning to feel free. It was all because of Broke that Brick had been granted parole. The Feds credited Brick for Broke's assistance in the Fast Money sting. Cream and Broke had also purchased a home for Brick and his family, it had been the happiest day of Verla's life when Brick and Lil' Brick first brought her to the house and told her it was theirs. She had been equally happy when Brick had first arrived in the projects at her front door on his day of release. Things were looking up for Brick as he contemplated his future. Thanks to his many years in Arkansas prisons, he was not a stranger in Pine Bluff. He was well known by former prison buddies and their families who he had met during weekly visits. Brick traveled back and forth to Altheimer on a daily basis to visit with his family but he had no desire to move back to Altheimer.

Pine Bluff was now his home. With the money he had hustled up on in prison, he was living comfortably in his new house with his wife and child. Still, Brick was a restless man on a mission for justice. He was not satisfied with living the quiet life. He had studied too long and too hard in prison to come home and forget all that he had learned.

Brick had old scores to settle. He hadn't forgotten the cop who had tried to set up Lil' Brick. He crept silently along the side of the fat pedophile cop's house. The darkness concealed him as he stayed close to the ground dressed in all black. The cop's house was next to a wooded area from which Brick had stalked his prey. He had waited in the thickets of the woods for over an hour for the young girl he had seen enter the cops house to leave. The girl looked to be in her early teens with unkempt hair as she hopped off the porch and waved bye to the cop who was standing in the doorway.

"Tell your mama I say thanks for the food and for letting you help me around the house." The cop said the words for the benefit of anyone who might have been listening. He stared after the girl before shutting the door. He had a satisfied look of accomplishment on his face. The fat cop was still smiling to himself when he walked back into his bedroom and removed a video tape from the hidden camera in the closet. He took the secretly recorded tape of him and the girl into the living room and placed it into the DVD before walking into the kitchen to retrieve a beer from the refrigerator. He walked back into the living room drinking his beer as he took a seat in his favorite chair after pressing play on the DVD.

The fat cop was busy rubbing between his legs when a six three Herculean figure of a black man dressed in black appeared before him. The cop choked on his beer as he stared up in fright at the figure. He tried to say something but only panic escaped his lips. By the time his survival extinct kicked in it was too late. He reached for his gun to no avail. The figure was upon him. The knife in the figure's hand landed with a soft thud in his outstretched arm. A pitiful cry escaped the cops lips as he screamed out in pain. He began to panic as he stared at the blood gushing from the wound in his arm. The knife looked odd sticking out both sides of his arm as the figure pulled another knife from his waist and waved it in the cop's face.

"Who are your friends?" Brick held the tip of the knife inside the nostril of the fat cop. He flicked the blade and blood poured from the cop's nose where the blade had cut it in half up to his eye. The cop let out another pitiful wail of pain. "Who are your crooked cop friends?" Even as Brick asked the question, he never gave the cop a chance to answer before cutting him again across the forehead. He was enjoying torturing the cop. He stared across at the TV screen and saw him peeing on the little girl who had left the house earlier. This scene enraged Brick to the point that he couldn't stop himself as he began to slice the cops face and body. The fat cop screamed in pain as he fell back on the sofa kicking and shaking. Brick left him to suffer as he walked around the house and gathered every flammable liquid he could find. He proceeded to pour the liquids all over the house and over the fat cop who was going into shock on the sofa. Brick removed the DVD from the player, retrieved others from the bedroom closet and walked towards the back door pouring the flammable liquid along his path.

"An eye for an eye, and a tooth for a tooth," Brick said as he tossed a match to the liquid. He ran off into the woods clutching the DVDs he found in the closet, along with twenty thousand dollars he had found beneath the bed, in a bag he carried. Brick would view the DVDs in his private room when he got home. He made still photos of all the cops who were on the discs. He was incensed with anger after watching the abuse of numerous young black girls at the hands of pedophile cops who had sworn to protect and serve them. Brick swore he would bring them all to his brand of justice. He had spent many years in prison with nothing but this thought in mind. Now that he was free he swore that no longer would black people suffer at the hands of crooked cops who operated above the law. He swore to make any cop who crossed the line of cop and robber pay for crossing that line. The time was over that cops could rape, rob, and kill black people without fear of consequences. Detective Jones was just the first. There would be many others. Brick swore to this.

***

The young girl who had been with the cop earlier had forgotten her necklace and returned. The cop had given her the gold necklace. She banged on the cops door and called his name. She turned the doorknob and found it unlocked. She entered the house and found the cop covered in blood. The house was on fire. She screamed for help as she dragged the cop slowly towards the front door.

Michael Rogers

Chapter 32

Broke read the morning paper as Sherry dressed for church. "It seems like someone tried to kill that fat cop last night," he told Sherry as she walked past him.

"Really?" Sherry asked.

"Yep, say somebody attacked him and tried to burn him up in his house."

"Ummph," Sherry said.

A knock on the door interrupted their conversation as Sherry walked to see who was knocking. She walked back into the room a few minutes later along with Cream, Michelle, Borilla, and Lil' Shelia.

"Man what you doing?" Borilla asked. "I thought we were going fishing."

"I'm ready," Broke said. "I just got to get my shoes."

"Man, fish gon' be through biting by the time we get there."

"What's up Cream?" Broke stood and shook Cream's hand.

"My daddy say if you fish on Sunday, the only thing you gon' catch is the devil." Sherry said.

"Not if your woman is in church praying for you." Cream said.

"Yea right," Michelle said. "Sherry you ready?" Michelle walked into the bedroom where Lil' Shelia and Sherry were both busy prepping in front of the mirror.

Michelle and Sherry had grown close since Michelle had decided to stay in Pine Bluff with Cream. Michelle's unselfish act to save Cream's life had washed away her sins of the past. When Cream had told Broke about her actions, it was Broke who had helped Cream to convince Michelle to stay in Pine Bluff.

The three women walked out the bedroom a few minutes later. Sherry walked over and kissed Broke. "We're fixing to go," Sherry said as she pulled her keys from her purse.

Cream squeezed Michelle's hand as she said bye to him in his ear. She winked at Cream as she turned to walk away. Though Cream and Michelle were not prone to showing public affection, they were very affectionate in the privacy of their own home. They had already bed wrestled twice this morning before getting out of bed. Their passion for one another could not be denied. Whenever it flowed, they let it run freely until both parties were exhausted and satisfied.

"Borilla, give me some money to put in church," Lil' Shelia sat on Borilla's lap with her arms around his neck.

"You already got some money," Borilla said.

"I'm talking about for you." Lil' Shelia said.

"You act like God don't know we together," Borilla said. "If He don't know, you better tell Him. The way you be bouncing up and down on me every night calling His name."

"Get thee behind me Satan." Lil' Shelia gave the sign of the cross as she got off Borilla and followed Sherry and Michelle out the door.

***

It was later that evening and everyone was gathered at Broke's family home in Altheimer. Brick and Lil' Brick had also joined them along with Verla. The four women were deep-frying the fish the men had caught earlier in the day. Lil' Brick was exploring the woods behind the house with one of his cousins. Bricks brother Ray pulled up in his patrol car after the fish were through cooking. Everyone sat around eating and joking underneath the big shade tree.

"Man, I still can't get over you being no sheriff," Brick said to Ray between bites of food.

"Hell, me either," Ray said. "It ain't much to it anyway," Ray said as he poured hot sauce over another piece of fish. "Shit, you know me, I been knocking niggas out all my life. The only difference is that, now when I knock them out, it's all legal and I get paid to do it. Plus, now I can knock out Crackers too, now that's the fun part."

"All right, don't think that badge makes you bullet proof." Brick stood to get another piece of fish. "These youngsters these days got more guns than the Pine Bluff arsenal."

"Man when you know me to be scared of a young punk with a gun? Don't get it twisted," Ray said. "It's still Ray day and it's gon' be Ray way. These Lil' punks know me. Those that don't, they better ask somebody."

"I hear you big brother," Brick said, "If it gets too rough you know who to call."

"Who?" Ray asked.

"Your little brother, that's who." Brick said.

"Man why would I call you," Ray said. "When I can make one phone call and have every trooper in the state here in less than an hour. Just make sho' you stay out of trouble. I got this." Ray bit into his fish. "Did Borilla tell you what Clara said," Ray asked Brick as he chewed the fish.

"Naw, Borilla ain't told me nothing." Brick said.

"Boy!" Ray screamed at Borilla who was lifting weights with Lil'

Shelia. "Why you didn't tell your uncle what your mama told you."

"I forgot," Borilla said from the weight pile.

"That boy act like he on dope." Ray said. "I outta arrest his ass. Anyway, Clara said she want y'all to stop by and pick up some things she got for Lil' Brick. Speaking of stopping by, I almost forgot. I got to go by the Mayor's house." Ray stood to leave.

"Take this plate to mama and daddy," Sherry stood off Broke's lap and picked up a plate of fish off the picnic table that she had prepared for her parents.

"Man, break out the dominoes," Brick said after Ray had left. "Let me punish you two brothers like I use to do back in the joint."

"Shit, when was this?" Cream said as he followed Brick and Broke over to the picnic table where Broke was busy cleaning a section off for their use. "Hell, if I still remember correctly, you still owe me your chicken for another month."

"And you owe me the cake." Broke said.

***

"Damn man," Brick stood and shook Broke and Cream's hands as they sat around relaxing after the domino games. "If somebody would've told me a few weeks ago that I'll be a free man, I never would've believed it. I don't know how to thank you brothers. Who would've thunk that the three of us would be able to actually live out some of those dreams we talked about while in that hell hole of a prison? I owe you cats my life. I don't know how I'm going to repay you."

"Man don't go getting soft," Cream said. "Without you, it's a whole lot of brothers who wouldn't have made it out that hell hole. Shit we owe you our lives."

"That's for real," Broke said. "What we got to do now is to continue to live. We got to do some of those things we talked about while in prison. We got to take back our streets. We here now. It's time to move."

"I'm already on top of that," Brick said.

Michael Rogers

Chapter 33

Brick was smiling as he sat behind the desk in his office of the non-profit organization he had started. Finally, his Prisoner Assist Program Association (P.A.P.A) was up and running. This was after six weeks of wrangling with city and state officials over proper paper work and other issues. It was created to assist black prisoners and their families. The P.A.P.A program was a mentoring program that also provided supplies and services to inmates and their families. Brick had designed the program in prison in hopes of one day setting it up as a community service upon his release. Broke and Cream had helped him design the program.

Brick had twenty ex-felons working with him in the program. These were handpicked men who had been mentored by Brick in prison. These men had proven themselves in prison to be hard and thorough. The men of P.A.P.A were street wise and militant. They were of a different breed than the men around them. In prison, Brick had watched the men he selected develop into strong soldiers who were dedicated to the cause of black liberation. In prison, there were no secrets. Some men became weaker and succumbed to their weaker desires. Some men became stronger and preyed on the weaknesses of others. Brick chose his men from the breed of men who became protectors of the weak and the strongest of the strong. He had chosen the men of P.A.P.A from the best of the men he knew. He didn't choose men simply because they were strong and violent. He chose men that were strong and intelligent, men who wouldn't hesitate to meet violence with violence, but only when necessary. Men who would fight and die for what they believed to be a worthy cause. Brick chose men that not only could give orders but were also able to take orders and make the proper adjustments in times of crisis when the orders were compromised.

The two men sitting in front of Brick were of this breed. Rabbit was short, black and stocky with fat jaws and a Mr. Potato head. Stone was as hard as his name. He was all muscle with a stone mask for a face. Stone earned his name because he never smiled or showed emotion. When he did smile, as he was doing now while shaking Brick's hand, his smile was more like a sneer that appeared at the corners of his lips. Rabbit had been a former high school football star. Brick had placed him in charge of P.A.P.A's athletic program. Stone was Rabbit's assistant and the two of them were there to discuss the athletic program.

P.A.P.A had just closed a deal to purchase a former school that was now being converted into a learning center. The school came complete with a gymnasium that had been refurbished, thanks to the money Brick had liberated from the crooked cop the night of his attack. A winter basketball league was being formed consisting of three age groups. Brick had invested heavily in the gym to prepare for the upcoming season. He figured that the gym would serve a twofold purpose. It would give young people a place to go to combat idle time that often led them into trouble and it would also serve as a community center for community gathering.

P.A.P.A had many goals. These goals were not just to reach and teach the children of black prisoners but to also educate the community as a whole. P.A.P.A was created to be a force in the overall community. Brick knew that if P.A.P.A was going to be a viable force within the black community, then therefore, P.A. P. A had to be a force within itself. That's why Brick had chosen the men he'd chosen. P.A.P.A was not a militant organization, neither was it a turn the other cheek organization. Brick knew that if he expected change in the black youth he was trying to reach, he would have to be able to protect them from those around them that might mistake this change as signs of weakness. Brick felt that a gunfighter could only lie down his guns when those around him knew that he was protected by others with guns.

It was not Brick's intention for P.A.P.A to change the world. He knew that the gangs wouldn't lie down their guns. He knew that the drugs would always be there. Brick recognized and respected these forces of evil within the black community. He respected their rights to exist. Being that the church taught that God gave everyone freedom of choice in life, Brick didn't feel it was his right to interfere with the choices that some men and women made. He was not trying to be God and change everyone to his idea of right. Brick felt it was his job to protect those who had already made the right choices or those who wanted to do right but were too afraid to try. These he considered as civilians. Because Brick felt that the police force was not doing its job of protecting the civilians in the war torn black communities, P.A.P.A was also created as an alternative force to protect the civilian population. Brick swore to protect the civilian population from the occupying forces of cops and robbers who would, at times, step across the lines of choices that separated the two sides.

Such was the case with the crooked cop who he had attacked weeks earlier. Such would be the case of the cops he had targeted for later that evening. Even though Brick trusted his alliance of ex-felons who worked with him at P.A.P.A, he would not involve them in his private war. The heat generated from the last cop's attempted murder had just died down enough for him to feel safe enough to attack again. The next two cops on his list were partners. Both were white men and crooked to the core. Not only were they on numerous videos abusing young black girls, they were also known to brutalize and shakedown young black drug dealers on the corners.

***

James Coke was a big white cop with white hair. His partner was a tall skinny white cop name Ethan Taylor. Brick followed the two cops on a Friday night. He had already witnessed them shake down two drug dealers and pickup a young girl. Brick hid behind one of the wrecked cars at the salvage yard where the cops had parked their squad car with the young girl in back. Brick waited for thirty minutes for the girl to leave.

The salvage yard where the cops were parked was located on the west side of Pine Bluff. It was located three blocks off Blake Street, which was the main road that traveled north and south through the black community. It was lined with pawnshops, cleaners, convenience stores and other assorted businesses. The black community was located to each side of Blake Street for miles. To the west was the Loop and to the east was the heart of west side Pine Bluff.

The salvage yard where the cops were parked was owned by a white man who had once killed a black man for trespassing on the salvage yard premises. Because the owner was in cahoots with the police, he was once allowed to line wrecked cars up and down the streets around the salvage yard, those living in the neighborhood would have their cars towed from their yards if the cars were not in running condition and didn't have tags.

Brick waited for the young girl who appeared to be in her early teens to leave. He crept silently up behind the two cops who were standing at the back of their squad car. Both cops were naked of their guns as they fixed their clothing. The tall lanky cop name Ethan had his back to Brick as he told his partner of how he had only given the young girl half of what he had promise to give her. Both men were laughing when all of a sudden a startled expression came across the older cops face.

The look of sheer horror that came across his partner's face caused the younger cop to stop speaking in mid-sentence. He instinctively reached for his gun as he turned to face whatever evil it was that was causing the horrid look on his partner's face. In a fit of terror, the older cop was fearfully trying to back up over the trunk of the squad car.

The younger cop also fell back against the squad car with his hands behind him as he turned to see the Herculean figure of a menacing looking black man approaching with a saw-off shotgun pointed at them. Both cops were shaking in fear.

Brick made the cops lie down on their stomachs with their hands behind their heads. The cops had at first tried to threaten Brick with warnings of what would happen to him if he done anything to them as cops. This pseudo act of bravado lasted for about a minute. That's when Brick told the cops that they were no more cop material than their crooked cop friend that he had tried to burn up in his house. This is when the two cops begin to plead for their lives. They knew that if Brick was responsible for the attack on their friend, that they were about to die.

Brick said nothing as he walked up to the lanky cop and knocked him unconscious to the ground with the butt of the gun. His partner begin to plead more earnestly before being hit upside of his own head and knocked unconscious to the ground besides his partner. Both cops were lying face down in the dirt. Brick kneeled over them with a Bowie knife in his hand that he had removed from the sheath on his side.

***

A salvage yard worker found the cop bodies the next morning. Both cops had been castrated with their organs stuffed into the mouth of their partner. The cops had bled to death during the night as their fellow officers were searching frantically for them all over town.

Pine Bluff was a city under siege after the latest cop murders. With three Pine Bluff police officers killed in a two-month period, an all out investigation had begun. Both police and press were following every lead. With few clues and with no one taking responsibility for the murders, the case was drawing national attention. The FBI was now spearheading the investigation.

The Mayor of Pine Bluff was on the stomp asking for more police funding to hire and train more officers. He portrayed the dead cops as heroes who died in the line of duty. He said the cop killings were the results of an inadequately funded police force that was battling on the frontline of the war against drugs and gang violence. Brick who had followed the Mayor's politics while in prison had never liked the mayor or his politics. Even though he hated all politicians, he particularly hated the Mayor.

A tall graceful FBI agent studied the evidence gathered and sent to her of the cop killings. Agent Scott was one of the FBI s best profilers. Her profile of the killer was that of a black male, late thirties, muscular...probably from lifting prison weights which would make him an ex-con out for revenge against cops who may have either wronged him or someone he loved. Agent Scott's profile of the killer also concluded that he was not remorseful in his acts of violence.

Agent Scott's supervisors considered her uncanny ability to profile suspects as a gift rather than something she had achieved through the benefit of FBI training. To say her skills came from the benefit of FBI training would also suggest that Agent Scott was twice as smart as her white male counter-parts who had received the same training but was nowhere near her level of expertise.

Agent Scott's profile of the cop killers also led her to believe that the cops were dirty. She was sure the killings had something to do with the cops off duty extracurricular activities. Agent Scott wasn't buying the official report that the cops who were killed at the salvage yard were there to meet with an informant. If so, and the police knew this, why then did they search all night looking for the two cops. There was no evidence of a major case the cops were working. Something wasn't right. Agent Scott closed the cop files before her. She was more interested in the file of the Asian drug dealer she picked up off the table and opened.

Agent Scott stared at the picture of the young Asian drug dealer at the top of the folder. She had been in pursuit of the dealer for the last six months. If not for her being undercover on the Asian drug dealer's case, Agent Scott would have had to take a more active role in the cop killing case. As it was now, she was simply offering profile and technical assistance to the agents in charge of the case.

Due to the growing frustration of her superiors, Agent Scott knew that she had to arrest the Asian drug dealer sooner than later. If not, her superiors had threatened to pull the plug on the case. A worried look came across the beautiful face of Agent Scott. Agent Scott was worried about the possibility of the Asian drug dealer being allowed to remain free to sell his poison in the black community with impunity.

Agent Scott had another thought that frightened her. She didn't want to believe that she was capable of such thoughts and surely not capable of doing what the thoughts suggested she do. She figured it was just the stress clouding her judgment. Yet in her heart she knew that she was fully capable of carrying out the thoughts in her mind. Agent Scott would not allow the drug dealer to escape. If all else failed and her superiors decided to pull her off the case, Agent Scott knew that she was fully capable of killing the Asian drug dealer.

***

Brick checked his watch to note the time. "Baby, what's up? You ready to go." Verla stared affectionately at Brick. "That's the third time you done checked your watch in the last ten minutes." Verla squeezed Brick's hand that was resting on her leg beneath the table.

The House of Cream was packed for amateur comedy night. Brick and Verla sat at a table with Broke, Sherry, Cream, Michelle, Borilla and BeBe. Bebe was a college friend of Lil' Sheila. The table was located in a roped-off section designated for M.A.M.A. AND P.A.P.A.'s executive staff. Lil' Sheila's chair next to Borilla was empty. She was about to take the stage as a contestant in the contest. M.A.M.A. was P.A.P.A.'s sister organization.

Lil' Shelia sashayed across the stage. She was ten minutes into her act and the crowd which had been hostile towards the other contestants, were loving her.

"Look like a star is born," Broke said.

"Hmmph, you mean a star was created." Sherry said. "Bo, how long Lil' Shelia been practicing her act. And don't tell me she haven't been practicing because I know better," Sherry said smiling.

"Don't make me lie cousin-in-law," Borilla was smiling from ear to ear. "She say she gon cut me off if I tell."

"Bo, I think you just told," Broke said.

"Well act like ya'll were surprised when she come back." Borilla was smiling his trademark smile of showing all thirty-two teeth.

Brick was having a great time and laughing harder than everyone at Lil' Sheila's raunchy brand of comedy.

Verla noticed that even though he was having a great time, Brick was still checking his watch every few minutes. He tried to do it casually but she noticed.

BeBe, who was watching Brick closely, also noticed and wondered why Brick was so concerned with the time. Brick seemed anxious to her. BeBe wondered why.

Brick leaned over and kissed Verla on the cheek. "I'll be back shortly," he said. "If I'm not back before the show is over, have Broke drive you home. Don't fall asleep on me." Brick kissed Verla again and smiled at her.

"Look who's talking," Verla returned Brick's smile.

"I should be back," Brick said as he stood. Brick told Broke and Cream to hold down the fort. "I got to make a run," he said. "Ladies," Brick smiled and nodded at the women around the table. "Be cool, Bo," he said before walking away.

BeBe studied Brick as he walked away. She wondered where he was going and why Verla was so nonchalant about it. BeBe had no idea of the bonds of love and trust that had been forged between the couples at the table. She didn't know of the trials and tribulation they had faced and weathered together. If so, she would have understood why Verla didn't question Brick's need to leave. She would know that the women's concern whenever their men left them for whatever reason were concerns of whether they would be able to return.

"I'm just saying," Lil' Shelia was saying on stage. "This shit is scientific. Bo talking about he want a house full of kids. I say, nigga, I thought you wanted to be a football player. Fuck you gone do with a daycare center cause I know you not talking 'bout me having no house full of kids. Bo out his fucking mind."

Lil' Sheila wore tight apple-bottom jeans that made her plump bottom shake as she sashayed across the stage. She was in complete control.

"Then Bo gon' ask me to marry him like that shit supposed to make it all right. I say, Bo, even if we do get married, the pussy still mine. Talking 'bout he want to make me a respectable woman. Fuck, he mean, gon' make me a respectable woman? I say, Bo, don't nobody give a damn about being respectable these days...motherfuckers marrying for benefits. Fuck respectability. Bush got shit fucked up for everybody. Even them smart-ass gay motherfuckers out of work. And you know shit fucked up when a gay person can't find a job."

"Bo talking 'bout making me a respectable woman. I say Bo, motherfuckers marrying for benefits these days. Why you think all these gay motherfuckers out there marching to get married? These motherfuckers want to be included on that damn company insurance policy. They want that damn tax credit on their income tax form. Most of all, these motherfuckers want that damn social security and other government shit owed there good dick-sucking or good pussy-eating ass in case their partner die. That's why these motherfuckers marching...don't give a damn about no respectability. Motherfuckers thinking about liability."

"Motherfuckers don't need license to love. Motherfuckers need license for them got damn benefits. Here this good pussy eating or good dick sucking ass gay person done sucked this nigga's dick or ate this bitch's pussy for the last ten years, man got to wear pampers because he done had all the grip fucked out his ass by some big dick motherfucker...bitch pussy looking like burnt pressed ham meat between her legs because of some raggedy mouth bitch sucking on it all night...done lived under the threat of A.I.D.S., been spit on by homophobics...treated like shit by Republicans who hate their ass and

271

shunned by family all because of love. Then after suffering all these years of abuse here this motherfucker come ten years later and say she like dick again...or this nigga say he want some pussy and this gripless asshole or deformed pussy motherfucker is kicked out the house without any benefits. That's why these motherfuckers out there marching. They want that gotdamn marriage license. A license to keep niggas from fucking over them. That gotdamn ownership license. Fuck respectability. It's about liability."

***

Brick waited patiently for the two bowling buddies to walk to their respective trucks. This would be his most daring attempt for revenge to date. Brick sat parked across the street from the bowling alley parking lot. The two men he was waiting for walked outside the building laughing with their fellow cop friends. The men all belonged to a bowling league. It appeared from their conversation that they had won tonight's games.

Brick pulled off slowly behind the two men. He had been watching them as targets for the last two weeks. It wasn't hard getting their bowling league schedule. Brick knew that the cop in the SUV would go left and the other target would go right. All Brick had to do was remain five hundred yards between the two targets and he would be fine. Brick picked up the small control box between his legs. The box had a toggle switch in the middle with two red lights to each side of the switch. All Brick had to do was to move the switch back and forth until both light were lit. This he done as he watched the cops turn in their respective directions for home. Brick moved the toggle switch back and forth. Two loud explosions rocked the earth around him. Both cop vehicles were blown to bits across the busy intersection. Brick checked his watch for the time. If he hurried he could make it back to the House of Cream within twenty minutes of his leaving.

***

Lil' Sheila was still on stage when Brick returned. The crowd had asked for an encore performance. Be Be watched Brick suspiciously as he took his seat back at the table.

"I'm telling you House of Cream, we fucked up and still getting fucked over. I'm all for gay rights because I understand that gay people are people too. We can't judge a person because of who they fuck. See, I know this shit is political. Politicians done created a voting bloc of gay people and now use them for their political agenda by championing gay causes like they care about gay people. Politicians don't care about shit but the rich people who put them in office. Gay people marching and shit talking 'bout gay rights when if we all had human rights we wouldn't need gay rights because everybody would have the right to fuck whoever they wanted to fuck. But I digress...Scacehead give me my damn check." Lil' Shelia ended her act to a standing ovation. Scacehead walked out on stage and presented her with a five hundred dollar check. Lil' Shelia studied the check in her hand.

"I want cash." Lil' Shelia said. "I saw your ass on the Five Heartbeats." She stared at Scacehead with a frown on her face.

The crowd roared in laughter. "What if this motherfucker bounce. Shit, I be at school from nine to five." The place went crazy as Lil' Shelia clowned Scacehead who resembled Dirty Red from the movie the Five Heartbeats. No one was laughing harder than Scacehead.

"Girl you got skills," Brick said when Lil' Shelia joined them at the table. Lil' Shelia sat on Borilla's knee and hugged him around the neck.

"I just hope God don't strike this table with lightning." Sherry said smiling.

"How you know God didn't put it on my heart to say," Lil' Shelia said. "Who else He gon' get to tell it like it is." Lil' Shelia stuck her tongue out at Sherry.

Be Be's phone beeped on the table. "I have to take this call," she said picking up the phone. Be Be stood from the table and walked off. "I have to run." She said after returning. "It was nice meeting you all." Be Be gathered her things in a hurried fashion.

"Well sister, don't be a stranger," Brick said. "M.A.M.A. and P.A.P.A. can use all the help we can get."

"I'm sure we'll meet again," Be Be said. "I learned a lot tonight. I'm sure I'll be snooping around trying to find out more."

"Just give us a call." Brick said.

***

"Baby, you see the paper?"

Verla tossed the morning paper onto Brick's desk at P.A.P.A. "All hell done broke loose," she said. "Two more cops were killed last night. These were blown up all over Harding Street. Every government agency you can name in town. Whoever doing these killings might want to cool it for a while." Verla smiled at Brick. Brick stared up at her from his desk." I made you some coffee." Verla placed a cup of coffee on Brick's desk.

"Thanks baby," Brick said. "You know I love you don't you." Brick stared deep into Verla's eyes.

"I love you more," Verla said. Verla smiled and walked out the room.

***

The agent ran her suspect's name through her FBI computer files of known criminals. She was not at all surprised by what she found. The suspect fit her profile to the letter. He had already killed once and had recently been released from prison for the murder. The attack on the first cop at his home had happened two weeks after the suspect's release. If the agent was right the suspect would definitely kill again. Even if he stopped killing cops, his killing days were far from over.

274

The suspect was what the agent called a transformed killer. His first kill may have been a simple act of violence. The suspect might not have meant to kill his first victim. Still, he was a killer at heart. He was transformed in prison to a Robin Hood type killer. He now killed for a cause that allowed him to feed his need to kill without regret or remorse.

The crooked cops were just the beginning. The agent thought of turning her files and notes over to her superiors. Something within her made her pause. Maybe she too felt the black community needed a protector. A Robin Hood to protect them from themselves and others. Others like the Asian drug dealer she was after. If not for the frustration and anger the agent felt from being unable to bring the drug dealer to justice and the lack of support she was receiving from her superiors, the agent probably wouldn't feel the need for a black Robin Hood to save the people. She probably wouldn't have the thoughts of killing the Asian drug dealer herself. If not for her new way of thinking, the agent would surely give her superiors her profile of the cop killer suspect. Instead, because of her new way of thinking, she gave them the profile of a white male, probably a former cop who was trying to protect the honor of the badge by ridding the force of cops he knew were dishonest but refused to break the blue code of silence to bring them to justice. He would rather kill them instead.

***

Detective Jones was back on the job. If not for the sudden need to take a dump, he would have been at his desk when the chief had summoned him. Detective Jones had delayed his retirement. There was no way he could afford to pay his rising medical bills if not for the health insurance policies of the Pine Bluff Police Dept. The chief had told Jones in so many words that he should retire. The FBI and other government agencies had been reviewing all case files handled by the drug task force that Jones once headed. They were asking lots of questions about questionable arrests and court convictions. Luckily, the Feds didn't really care about the cases. They were more interested in Jones than anything else. They were looking for vengeful suspects that the files might reveal.

"Jones!" the chief shouted for Jones who was in one of the bathroom stalls. Jones answered him with the flush of the toilet. "Wipe your ass and get down to the conference room," the chief barked the order. "Somebody want to see you. ASAP!" the chief said before walking out the bathroom.

Two federal agents were waiting for Jones when he walked into the conference room. The black agent nodded at a chair at the end of the conference room table. Neither agent bothered to speak. Detective Jones tried to appear calm. The hideous scars covering his face helped to hide the nervous fear that crept up his spine.

"Detective, do you have any idea why somebody is killing members of your former task force," the white agent sitting across from Jones asked.

"No sir, none at all." Jones' nervousness began to show. "I figure it to be some disgruntled criminal who was a victim of our success.

"That's what we thought at first," the agent said. "But when we reviewed your files, we didn't find any arrests of suspects who fit the profile of such a killer. Most of your arrest were low-level and questionable. We didn't find any that were major enough to warrant the death of four cops, not to mention the attack on you at your home. Is there something you're not telling us detective?" The agent paused and waited.

"No sir, nothing I can think of at the moment," Jones said.

"Detective," the agent paused again. "What would you say if we told you that we think you're a lying piece of shit." The agent spoke calmly with a noncommittal look on his face. Jones jumped up from his seat.

"I don't have to stand for this!" Jones shouted angrily.

"Sit your ass down!" the black agent stood quickly to confront Jones.

"We're not through talking to you. We got four dead cops, two of which were blown to hell all over Harding street by criminals using military grade weapons and you sat your lard ass here trying to jerk our chains. Now, for the most part, your task force arrests were a bunch of nickel and dime hustlers at best. These killings have nothing to do with your mediocre crime fighting efforts. Whatever you and your dead cop friends were into, you pissed off the wrong man, someone who is fully capable of declaring war on the Pine Bluff Police department and eliminating every son-of-a bitch who work here if you don't come clean and tell us what you and your friends were into outside of your police work." The black detective eyes bulged in his head as he stood shouting in Jone's face.

"Tell us detective," the white agent spoke. "Where do you and your friends take the little girls now that your playhouse has been burned to the ground? The agent fingered a file folder on the table. Jones heart skipped a beat. "Isn't that the real reason someone has declared war on you and your former task force. The reason four of your friends are dead and you look like you lost a fight to Edward Scissor-Hands." The agent spoke in his quiet manner of speaking.

"Are you serious," Jones found his voice. "If so sir, I have no idea of what you're talking about."

The loud crashing of a chair to the floor caused Jones to jump. The black agent had slammed the chair to the floor. "Listen here you fat piece of scarred shit. We know all about your little pedophile ring of cops. All about the little crack babies ya'll raped over the years in your little playhouse of horrors. The least of your charges right now is withholding evidence and obstructing of justice. If you have any information that can help us bring this killer to justice I suggest you start talking or I swear I'll bury your lard ass in the federal penitentiary for the rest of your miserable life." The agent glared at Jones in anger.

"Sir, I have no idea of what you're talking about," Jones stared evenly at the agent. "And from what I gather, neither do you. Now, I don't know where you got your information, but someone is seriously jerking your chains. For a couple of well dressed agents in nice suits, you're not as smart as the suits make you look. Now, if all you have are unsubstantiated allegations and wild hunches, I have nothing further to say to you without being in the presence of my lawyer." Jones turned and began to walk away. The agents let him leave. Jones gave a long sigh of relief once he was outside the conference room door. He was wondering how the feds knew as much as they did about him and his friends.

"What do you think," the white agent asked the black agent once Jones had left.

"I think our witness is telling the truth," the black agent said.

"Yeah, me too," the white agent agreed. "It's too bad he's a white racist who's about to stand trial for stomping a black kid to death."

"His words would never hold up against a decorated thirty year veteran like Jones." The black agent pulled out a cigarette.

"Yeah, tough break," the white agent said. "If only he had remembered his cop cousin telling him about fucking teenage black girls at Jones' house before the cousin was blown to hell all over Harding Street, he might have at least escaped the electric chair. They do still use the electric chair in Arkansas, don't they?" The white agent gathered his file folders.

"Shit, I hope so," the black agent said. "That bastard need to fry."

***

Detective Jones arrived at his home in Gould, Arkansas, still shaken by his encounter with the Feds. A shutter-of fear moved through his body as he thought back to his own near death experience. If not for the girl being assisted by neighbors to drag him out the house, he too would be dead. Detective Jones had spent weeks in the hospital recovering from his injuries, of which, both physical and mental, would never heal.

Detective Jones would forever wear the marks of the beast who tried to kill him. The doctors had been able to save his nose but there was nothing they could do about the scars left behind by the knife across his face and body. At least he had fared better than his friends. They were all dead. Killed by the same evil who had tried to kill him.

The dead cops were all on the videotapes secretly recorded by Jones. They didn't know about the tapes. Based on his knowledge of this privilege information, Jones knew that the killings were of a vengeful nature. He also knew there would be more killings.

Detective Jones thought of warning the other cops. It was a fleeting thought. He had a better idea instead. Jones wanted to kill the cop killer so bad that he decided to use his remaining cop friends on the videotapes as bait. A sinister smile came across the detective's face. The thought of killing his attacker was all he had left to smile about.

Jones stood to answer a knock on his door. He had purchased the home in Gould to get away from all the scrutiny of those who knew him in Pine Bluff. Gould was located twenty-seven miles south of Pine Bluff. Jones had purchased the home under an alias name.

His neighbor was an elderly white lady who was sympathetic to Jones because of his condition. The plump neighbor had a nice looking thirteen-year-old granddaughter. The granddaughter was supposed to clean Jones' house today. He figured it was her at the door. Jones smiled his crooked smile as he walked towards the door.

***

Detective Jones called two of the remaining cops who were members of the former drug task force. One he couldn't reach. It was the one who was with him the day at the Port when he had killed Fat Man to save his own ass. This cop was a relative of the mayor. He had ridden the good publicity from the drug bust at the Port to higher office. He wouldn't accept Jones' thirteen calls. The other cop was a source of worry for Jones. He had sent Jones voicemails about what to say in an upcoming sit-down with Feds. Jones knew that if the Feds spoke to the scared detective, he would tell them all he knew.

Jones set up a meet with the cop on Grider Field Road which was to the south of Pine Bluff on the outskirts town. He told the cop that they needed to talk but shouldn't talk over the phone because the Feds might be listening. The cop's paranoia played well into Jones' plans for the cop. "Can't trust these Feds," Jones chuckled and said. "They everywhere."

***

"Another cop killing," Verla said the words as she placed Brick's dinner on the table.

"What?" Brick asked surprised.

"I just heard it on the news," Verla said. "Say they found the body of a dead cop out on Grider Field road. Some kids found it in some woods while playing."

Brick bit off a piece of chicken as he tried to figure out what was happening. His first thoughts were that maybe he had a copycat killer. He also wondered if maybe it was an insurance scam by someone in the dead cop's family who may have had more use for his life insurance pay out than they did for the cop. When Brick opened the paper and saw a picture of the dead cop, he recognized him as one of his remaining targets from the videotapes. He now wondered if maybe Fast Money who had proven to be elusive had killed the cop as a possible weak link in his chain of dirty cops. Whatever the case, it really didn't matter to Brick. He was satisfied that the cop was dead. His only regret was that it wasn't him who had killed him.

***

The streets of Pine Bluff was hotter than the devil's bath water. Cops and media were everywhere. Brick had given the remaining cops a reprieve until the heat died down. Every police agency in America was

280

using the Pine Bluff cop killings as calls for more police funding. Of all the voices across America, none was louder than that of the Pine Bluff mayor. A republican with his own agenda, Brick watched the mayor in his latest press conference. The mayor was saying that all the cops belonged to an elite drug task force. He suggested that the cop killings were related to the great efforts of these cops to combat violent drug dealers.

Brick could see now that the Mayor was using the cop's deaths as a platform to attain a higher office. The Mayor had upgraded his appearance and was saying all the right things to align his fight with the greater fight for justice as prescribed by George Bush and his fight against terrorism around the world. The Mayor was to appear on two major talk shows in the upcoming weeks. As a republican Mayor, the Republican Party saw the mayor as a man on the rise within the Republican Party. He was now being groomed by the Republican Party to push their party's agenda to the people of Arkansas.

The Republican Party leaders had a fundraiser for the mayor in Little Rock. The Mayor also brought along the Pine Bluff police department's chief of detectives. The chief of detectives was also his brother-in-law. He was also identified and targeted by Brick from the sex tapes as the next cop up for termination.

Brick decided that he would kill two birds with one stone. It was too dangerous in the present climate for him to physically kill the cop. With so much heat still being generated by the other cop murders, Brick decided to send his final message in a way that would destroy all the other cops involved including the mayor. He refused to allow the Mayor to make a martyr of those pedophile cop and to ride the sympathy of the people into higher office. Brick was determined to bring not only the Mayor down, but to also bring down all the fake politicians that now gathered around the Mayor seeking press. Brick was determined to knock them all off their self-righteous pedestals.

Brick listened with disdain to the Mayor's speeches on eroding family values and the lost of morality in America. The mockingbird was singing loudly and Brick wanted him to be heard loud and clear before taking away his song. He waited until the sweet songs of political rhetoric were at their loudest in the air across the Arkansas media. Brick knew that a mockingbird was just another bird when you took away its song.

Brick made copies of all the sex videos and still images of the pedophile cops and little black girls they abused. He mailed these images to every media outlet in Arkansas. He also mailed copies to all major black organizations. It didn't take long for the feeding frenzy to begin. The FBI, who had also received copies, began to round up the remaining crooked cops as the national media converged once again on Pine Bluff with their cameras and questions. The Chief of Detective was arrested in the midst of a Republican Party fundraiser for the Mayor. The Mayor looked on helplessly as his brother-in-law was handcuffed by the FBI.

The NAACP also got involved with cries of civil rights violations. Big time lawyers filed lawsuits against the city of Pine Bluff on behalf of the girls identified on the videos. The Mayor was no longer the darling of the press. He was now being hounded with questions of police corruption. The Republican Party quickly distanced themselves from the Mayor. The mockingbird had lost his song. He was now just another bird. A Dodo Bird that would never fly any higher than his present office position and had little chance of being re-elected to that position once his term was up.

The end result would be the election of a black mayor in the next mayoral election. The chief of detectives and the other cops identified on the videos would all be sentenced to ten years or more in prison. The young girls would be paid compensation for damages received. Brick was satisfied with the results of his actions. He gave no further thought to the lives he had taken. If he had any regrets, it was that he wasn't able to get his hands on the other cops. Brick had not been a killer when he had first killed Tacky and went to prison for his murder. Now, taking lives came easy for him. Brick had been remorseful after killing Tacky. He hadn't considered the consequences of his actions.

Prison had taught him how to kill without remorse. He now planned his killings to avoid the consequences of his actions. The city of Pine Bluff had no idea of the force it had released from its prison. Brick had the revolutionary spirit of George Jackson and Huey Newton. His blackness was defined in the spirit of Marcus Garvey and Malcolm X. He had the love and dedication to his cause of Dr. King and Kwame Nkrumah. He could be as brutal as Shaka and as cunning as Hannibal. Brick was as hard as his name except when it came to Verla and Lil' Brick.

Michael Rogers

Chapter 34

Verla was smiling with both an inner and outer joy as she watched Lil'
Brick playing one-on-one basketball with Brick at the park across the
street from where they lived. Brick's muscular body flexed as he
crouched in a defensive stand while guarding Lil' Brick. Lil' Brick
tried to dribble the basketball past him. He faked right with the ball
causing Brick to stumble. He crossed Brick over before he could
recover and dribbled past him to the basket.

"Game!" Lil' Brick said excitedly. "Get your weight up!" He taunted
Brick as he walked around the court beating his chest.

"Run it back," Brick said smiling at his son. Lil' Brick was a miniature
version of his father with his mother's brown eyes.

"Lil' Brick, stop beating up on your daddy, and go to the store for
me," Verla was standing on the sideline after walking across the street
to the court.

"I'll whoop both of y'all put together," Brick said as he picked up the
basketball and shot a jumper.

"Yea right," Verla said. "You can't even whoop Lil' Brick. You know
you don't want none of me." Verla picked up the basketball and shot a
twenty feet jumper that swooshed through the hoop. "Swoosh," She
said as she held her shooting pose while shaking her hips. "You better
get your weight up talking 'bout messing with me."

"Woman please," Brick said, "Take it out."

"Gon' beat him mama," Lil' Brick said. "He can't go left and his
jumper is broke."

"Boy, I been letting you win, you'll know the next time you win a game." Brick picked his t-shirt up off the court and tossed it over his shoulder. "Come on Lil' Brick, let's go to the store for your mama. I need something to drink myself."

Brick and Lil' Brick were still talking basketball as they walked the two blocks up the street to the white-owned grocery store. It was a hot sunny day and neither of them had bothered to put on their t-shirts. Brick had meant to put on his shirt before entering the store but was so engaged in the conversation with Lil' Brick that he had forgotten to put on the shirt. He still had the shirt thrown across his shoulder when he entered the store.

"Hey! You can't come in here without a shirt." The white owner snapped at Brick as if he was a child. It took all Brick had to contain himself as he stared at the short fat white man who was glaring at him from one of the aisles with his hand on his hips.

Brick weighed the consequences and decided that now wasn't the time and he put on his T-Shirt after nodding for Lil' Brick to do the same. Brick walked over to the beer cooler as Lil' Brick went in search of flour for Verla. Lil' Brick was drawing hard stares from the owner as he walked up and down the aisles of the store sagging in the urban fashion style that gave him the appearance of a stereotypical gang banger.

"Y'all sell flour?" Lil' Brick asked the man who had spoken earlier after tiring of searching up and down the aisles. The man was standing next to a meat cooler talking to another white man in a white apron. A sawed off shotgun was clearly visible hanging on the wall behind the man in the apron.

"It's right there," the owner said in an agitated voice." He pointed to the next aisle over from Lil' Brick.

Lil' Brick was about to respond to the man's attitude before he caught Brick eyeing him from the cooler. Brick nodded at Lil' Brick in a keep cool gesture. Brick had become even more angered by the shotgun behind the counter; it was no secret to him why the men had the gun behind the counter.

The white woman working the cash register gave a fake smile as she thanked Brick after bagging the groceries and handing him his change. The owner was standing outside when Brick and Lil' Brick exited the store. Brick stared hard at the owner.

"Will you be open tomorrow?" Brick asked.

The owner didn't bother to answer. He nodded towards a sign over the front door of the store. The sign read "Open 9 AM - 9 PM, Seven Days A Week."

"I understand," Brick said with a drawl. "It's a question you really can't answer ain't it, because you never know."

The owner stared after Brick with a puzzled expression on his face. The full meaning of Brick's words didn't dawn on him until the owner was awakened out of his bed at 2:00 AM by the Pine Bluff Fire Department. His store was little more than ashes when the owner arrived on the scene. The owner walked around in the ashes with tears in his eyes. The store had been a fixture in the black community for twenty years. He had paid the college tuition of two sons thanks to the proceeds made from the store. With a third son about to begin college in the fall, he didn't know what he was going to do.

The owner was sure the cause of the fire was arson. The firemen at the scene told him that the fire appeared to be the result of faulty wiring. The owner was seething in anger as he thought back to the black man's words earlier that day. Brick's words played over and over in his head as he trampled through the rubble of what use to be his store. "Because you never know, because you never know, because you never know." These words kept running through the owners mind as he kicked what use to be his cash register.

Brick and Verla were lying in bed when Lil' Brick knocked on the bedroom door.

"Come in," Verla said as she covered herself.

"I'm fento to go." Lil' Brick said as he stood in the doorway clutching his school books.

"Did you eat?" Verla asked.

"Shoot, you can't miss that joker, talking about no eating. He gon' eat if he don't do nothing else." Brick rolled over in bed.

"Y'all hear about that grocery store catching fire."

"What store?" Verla asked Lil' Brick.

"That cracker store up the street." Lil' Brick said. "It was on the news. Say it burned all the way to the ground."

"I'll tell you the truth," Verla said after Lil' Brick shut the door. "Black folk can't have nothing."

"Shit girl, what you talking 'bout black folk." Brick sat up in bed as he spoke. "Them crackers didn't give a damn about you or no other black folk. That store been robbing black folk for twenty years. Cracker had a sawed-off shot gun behind the counter to show you how much he think of black folk."

"Hmmph! The way some of these bad-ass kids are today, I'll have a gun behind the counter too," Verla said as she laid across Brick's chest.

"Damn that cracker." Brick eased Verla off him as he prepared to get out of bed.

"Don't worry, his insurance company will buy him an even bigger store to take your money. That way, he can then send his grandkids off to college off your money, while he treat your kids like shit when they

288

come into his new store."

"I'm just saying baby," Verla snuggled up closer to Brick. She could see that he was becoming angry. The last thing in the world she wanted to do was to make him angry. She had something else in mind for them to do besides argue over some white man's store that she didn't really care about. Verla kissed Brick in his chest as she begin to rub him. Her body was on fire as it had been every night that the two of them had been together since his release. "Come on baby," Verla spoke in a hoarse voice. "I don't wanna argue 'bout no white man store."

Brick kissed Verla atop her head as he began to rise below the waist. "Maybe if the cracker reopens, he'll have a better attitude," he said before dropping the subject and kissing Verla.

Michael Rogers

LOUIS X

Chapter 35

Louis X spoke fervently to the group of young boys and girls gathered in his classroom at P.A.P.A. Louis X was formally from Chicago before catching a drug charge in Pine Bluff. He had served five years with Brick at both Cummins and Tucker maximum security prison. Louis X was also known as ScandaLouis before joining the Nation of Islam while in prison. As Scandalous, Louis X was a leader of the Arkansas chapter of the Gangster Disciples. He was also one of the prison leaders of the gang. While in prison, Louis X and Brick had done business together and had become good friends while at Tucker Max where Louis X had been sent for stabbing an inmate called Rat who had raped a brother of one of his friends. Brick had been sent to Tucker Max at the time for security reasons because the officers at Cummins felt he had too much influence over the other inmates. Brick had been shipped after a Cummins officer had been stabbed in a near riot situation after a cop beating of an inmate.

Brick and Louis X thought a lot alike. That's why Brick had sent for him. Louis X had a way with the youngsters. Brick had brought him onboard to run the youth development part of the P.A.P.A program. Louis X was more militant in his religious views than most Nation of Islam members. The Youth Development curriculum of P.A.P.A was geared towards raising the self-esteem of black youth ranging in ages of eight to sixteen. Louis X did not bite his tongue in trying to convey his message to the at-risk group of children who attended his classes. He knew there was not much he could say that the children in his class didn't hear on a daily basis.

"You young brothers and sisters are an endangered species," Louis X was saying. "You're little black babies being raised in playpens filled with deadly toys. Your parents are either gone from home, gone on drugs, gone on alcohol, or just don't know what to do to save you. The babysitters are either asleep in the other room or don't give a damn about you because you're not their children. The educational system is looking for reasons to fail you so that they can kick you out of their schools and back into the streets. Once back into the streets, the police label you as thugs and gang bangers. As uneducated black babies you eventually accept this role because it's the only role available for you that you think you can play."

Louis X picked up a newspaper and showed the picture of a local youth who had been killed in a drive-by shooting. "You join gangs and sell drugs to survive as black children in playpens of filth and degradation. This confirms in the minds of those who pushed you out into the streets that they were right about you all along."

Louis X spoke with hand gestures and eye contact that held the forty or more youngsters glued to their seats as they listened attentively to his every word. "It's you the next generation who must break the cycle and change the direction of our people."

"How many of you know what a spy is?" he asked.

Every hand in the room was raised.

"That's good," Louis X said. "A spy is a vital part of any nation. Spies are not snitchers who tell on their own people to help themselves. That's the kind of spy the police wants you to be. They want you to do their jobs for them. They want you to tell them everything that goes on in your homes and community. Well, that's not the kind of spy we want you to be. P.A.P.A needs spies to help us help our people. As spies for P.A.P.A, we need you to blend in with this society but to never lose your identity, or the purpose of your mission."

Louis X stared intently around the room. He paused to see if his words were having any affect on the young audience. Louis X was proud of the fact that, as always, the young men in attendance were eager to learn.

"We need you to go to your schools and learn all that the enemy is trying to teach you. Granted that most of what they're teaching you is irrelevant and that the history you learn is full of lies, you still must learn the lies so you can weigh it against your own truths of existence. P.A.P.A needs you to learn mathematics, science and chemistry so you can become our future doctors, scientists, and engineers. Only then can you help liberate our people. We need you to learn their English so you can become lawyers and judges. As spies for P.A.P.A it will be your job to make sure you gather this information from our enemies. You must remember always that your cause to help black people must be greater than your cause to help yourself. 'People First' must become not only your battle cry but your way of life."

"Now I know it's not easy growing up in broken homes but I want you to know that this can't break you. I know some of your mothers are on drugs or maybe alcohol. I know there's probably some knucklehead black man lying around doing nothing but whooping you or pissing you off and your mothers probably don't seem to care. I want you to know that the big brothers here at P.A.P.A, we are your fathers and your brothers. We will fight your battles for you. If you need help, please don't hesitate to call us."

Louis X stared at a young girl sitting on the front row. He smiled at her and told her that he loved her. "Many men will tell you this," he said, "but not all of them who say this will have your best interest in mind. Some men will say and do anything just to try and trick you into their bed. So, if any man pushes up on you, whether it's your mother's boyfriend, the preacher, teacher or anyone else who you don't want in your space, just let us know."

Louis X stared hard at two young men giggling. "You young brothers shouldn't feel so safe and secure around all men either. There's some sick brothers out there, and some of these brothers likes to prey on young black boys. I seen it in the prison I left and I know that most of these men are coming home. Don't think that these men, many of who

293

are already on the streets, won't try and push up on you just because you're a boy. As I said in the beginning, young black people, you're all on the endangered species list. Don't ever feel safe just because you're around your own. Some of our own are our greatest enemies. That's why P.A.P.A has created the hotline number I gave you. Don't hesitate to call that number whenever you have a problem; no matter how small. Remember, you are not alone anymore. P.A.P.A will always be by your side. Remember, that you are secrets agents for your people. So we need you to go to school every day and learn everything you can learn because the information you gather will be needed to help us defeat our enemies."

**

Brick was sitting with Cream and Broke when Louis X entered his office after his class was over. Broke and Cream both knew Louis X from prison and quickly got up to shake his hand.

"Man, what's up," Broke said smiling as he shook Louis X hand.

"Brother Broke, man how's life treating you," Louis X shook Broke's hand, returning his smile.

Cream, who was waiting to shake Louis X's hand after Broke, shook his hand with a soul shake. "What's up X," Cream said as the two men shook hands.

"You know me, brother Cream. Still trying to beat the system."

"Don't worry," Cream said. "Brothers gonna work it out."

"What about the sisters?" Verla asked the question as she entered the room carrying some food bags.

"Most definitely got to have the sisters," Cream said smiling at Verla.

"Let me hear it then," Verla said as she walked over and placed the food bags on Brick's desk.

"Especially sisters like you," Louis X said. "Ain't too many sisters can hold the reins of a young black man and guide him down the righteous path without a man's help. We need more sisters of your caliber."

"Well, I can't take all the credit," Verla said as she leaned over and kissed Brick. "This knucklehead may have been locked up, but he was always here in spirit."

"Yea, don't forget about financially," Brick said jokingly as he pulled a burger out one of the bags on his desk.

"Man, seeing all these food sacks, just reminded me how hungry I am," Louis X said as he pulled his keys out his pockets. "I think I'll go and get me a salad or something."

"Man, you better grab you one of them burgers," Brick said laughing. "I can't believe you still eating like a rabbit. We free now brother."

"Come on Brick, you know Brother X ain't gon' eat no flesh." Broke said, "Remember when he almost got us all shipped to Tucker Max just because one of the cooks at Cummins prepared the salad in a pork pan? I wonder if that dude ever learned to walk again," Broke jokingly said.

"Come on brothers, it wasn't that bad. All I done was slapped the dude around a little bit."

"A little bit, man, if I remember correctly, the dude was a leader of a rival gang and the only thing that kept things from jumping off was that you and the cat went head up after cooler heads prevailed."

"You mean, after somebody mailed him a picture of his dear mother shopping at the County Market with a bulls-eye drawn on her chest. I wonder who would do a thing like that," Louis X gave a knowing smile at Cream.

"I have no idea," Cream said. "I'm just glad it didn't come to that."

"Yea, me too." Louis X shook hands with everyone before leaving. He drove out to the mall of Pine Bluff to pick up some materials and food.

Chapter 36

Louis X was standing in line waiting to pay for his salad at one of the mall's delicatessens. He noticed one of the kids from his class sitting alone at one of the tables eating ice cream. Louis X paid for his salad and walked over to the kids table.

"Hey little Jimmy," the twelve year old boy's eyes lit up when he looked up and saw that it was Louis X speaking to him.

Lil' Jimmy was a small child for his age. He had big eyes and was so quiet in class that he would often go unnoticed. It was like the kid was afraid that if someone noticed him, he would be ridiculed or made to leave the room.

"Hey! Mr. Louis," Lil' Jimmy eyes lit up as he spoke to Louis X.

"What's up little man," Louis X returned the boy's smile as he patted him on the head. "Where's your mother?" Louis X asked the question as he stared around the delicatessen.

"She at work," Lil' Jimmy said, still smiling as he licked the ice cream cone in his hand.

"So who brought you here?" Louis X asked.

Lil' Jimmy looked up towards a black man who was approaching the table. Louis X followed Lil' Jimmy's eyes and his face immediately became twisted into an angry mask.

"Well, I'll be damn," a tall lanky black man with rat-like features said as he walked towards the table where Lil' Jimmy was sitting. "If it ain't Scandalouis X."

Louis X recognized the man immediately. It was the same man who he had once stabbed in prison. Everyone called the man Rat because of his rat-like features and his rat-like ways. Louis X didn't even pretend to like the man as he stared at him with a seething anger.

The rat-looking man had a devilish grin on his face as he reached for Lil' Jimmy's hand. "Come on Lil' Jimmy," he said. "Let me get you back to your mother before she begins to worry."

"Bye, Mr. Louis X," Lil' Jimmy said.

"All right Lil' Jimmy, I'll see you later," Louis X said. "Take care of yourself and don't forget what we talked about in class. If you have any trouble with anybody, don't hesitate to call the hotline number."

"All right, Mr. Scandalouis X, we'll see you around." The rat-looking man smiled over his shoulder at Louis X as he led Lil' Jimmy away by the hand.

"You can count on that," Louis X said.

***

Louis X was furious when he returned to P.A.P.A. "Man I should've killed that nigger in prison," Louis X said to Brick who was sitting behind his desk.

"It ain't like you didn't try," Brick said. "Don't worry about that fool."

"It ain't that fool I'm worried about," Louis X said. "I'm worried about Lil' Jimmy. I gotta roll man, I'll catch you later." Louis X was still fuming as he left Brick's office.

Brick stared after the small-statured, light-skinned man he knew as Louis X. Brick knew that behind the quiet demeanor and horn-rimmed glasses, was a man capable of both love and brutality. He also knew that it was love for that which he loved that brought out his most brutal nature. Brick had said nothing to try and stop Louis X as he threw up his hand and walked out the office. What went unsaid between the two men, was already known in their hearts.

Men like Rat could not be allowed to destroy what they were trying to build. The children were the future. It was P.A.P.A's goal to teach and protect them. Louis X was like Brick when it came to accepting his role as teacher and protector. Brick knew that Louis X would do whatever necessary to fulfill his duties.

***

Louis X was deeply concerned about Lil' Jimmy's absence the following day at class. Lil' Jimmy was usually one of the first to arrive. Louis X asked a couple of the other boys about Lil' Jimmy after class. The boys told him that they hadn't seen Lil' Jimmy.

It was a fat kid name Charles Jr. who told Louis X that Lil' Jimmy was in the hospital.

Louis X paid little attention to speed limits and red lights as he drove like a bat-out-of-hell in route to Jefferson Regional Medical Center to check on Lil' Jimmy. He couldn't help but think the worse; he was sure that Rat had something to do with whatever had happen to Lil' Jimmy.

Louis X rushed into the hospital upon his arrival. He stopped by the nurse's station on the children ward and was given Lil' Jimmy's room number.

The nurse on duty must've thought Louis X was a relative of Lil' Jimmy's. She told him that Lil' Jimmy had been treated for a fractured arm and bump on the head. She said the hospital was keeping him overnight for observation. Louis X figured that Lil' Jimmy had to be either on Medicaid or his parents had good job insurance. Otherwise, he was sure the hospital would have discharged him already.

Louis X walked into Lil' Jimmy's room holding a toy gift he had bought for him from the hospital gift shop. Lil' Jimmy was watching cartoons. A petite woman sat in a chair besides him at the bed. The woman was a quiet looking, brown-skinned woman with attentive eyes. She wore a Pizza Hut uniform complete with bib atop her braided hair.

Louis X assumed from the striking resemblance that the woman was Lil' Jimmy's mother.

Though she appeared to be in her early twenties, Louis X figured her to be in her late twenties because of Lil' Jimmy's age.

"Hello," Louis X spoke as he entered the room and closed the door behind him. The woman at the bed had a questioning look on her face as she stared up at Louis X. She was about to ask him who he was when Lil' Jimmy shouted out Louis X name.

"Hey Mr. Louis!" Lil' Jimmy said excitedly as he sat up in bed.

"Heeeeyyyy, Lil' Man, we missed you today." Louis X stood a few feet away from the bed with a smile on his face while staring at Lil' Jimmy. "Are you all right?"

"I broke my arm," Lil' Jimmy said as he held up his broken arm.

"I see," Louis X said. "The nurse told me you bumped your head too. Secret Agents got to be careful," Louis X said.

"I know," Lil' Jimmy said. "I was running."

"Lil' Jimmy, didn't I tell you to lie down and be still." The woman at the bed spoke in a motherly voice to Lil' Jimmy.

"How you doing ma'am, I hope it's all right that I stopped by to see Lil' Jimmy. My name is Louis X. I work at P.A.P.A. One of the other kids told me that Lil' Jimmy was in the hospital and I just wanted to check up on him. I hope it's all right with you."

"Nice to meet you, my name is Angie. I'm Lil' Jimmy's mother."

"Nice to meet you," Louis X extended his hand. "I brought Lil' Jimmy a toy, I hope you don't mind. I picked it up down stairs."

"It'll be fine." Angie said.

Louis X handed Lil' Jimmy the toy in his hand. "Now, you listen to your mother and be a good agent," he told Lil' Jimmy.

"I will." Lil' Jimmy said. He thanked Louis X for the toy as he propped himself up in bed in a sitting position and begin to tear away the plastic wrap from around the toy with his teeth.

Louis X visited with Lil' Jimmy for a while before asking Angie if he could speak with her outside in the hallway.

Angie turned and told Lil' Jimmy to stay in bed before standing. Angie was surprised by the demeanor of Louis X. Lil' Jimmy always spoke highly about Louis X when he came from his classes. Because of the way Lil' Jimmy spoke about him, Angie expected Louis X to be a giant-like figure. She never expected the short, Kufi-wearing man in the horn rimmed glasses. If she had met Louis X on the street, she would have expected him to be selling bean pies or Final Call newspapers. There was something about the little man that Angie trusted; that's why she hadn't objected when he asked her to accompany him into the hallway. The fact that he was taking time out for her son who attended his class at P.A.P.A with friends after school meant a lot to Angie as well.

"I know it's none of my business," Louis X said once they were in the hallway.

Angie stood with her back to the door of Lil' Jimmy's room.

"But as the coordinator of P.A.P.A's Youth Development Program, I'm deeply concerned about black children and especially those who attend my classes. Lil' Jimmy is one of my best and brightest students. The reason I wanted to speak with you is that I saw Lil' Jimmy in the mall the other day."

"He was probably with me," Angie said. "I have two jobs. One of them is in the mall."

"I understand," Louis X said. "But when I saw Lil' Jimmy, he was with someone I knew from prison."

Angie stared hard at Louis X with a puzzling look. "You were in prison?" She asked.

"I done five years," Louis X said. "I haven't always tried to live righteously," he said with a reassuring smile.

"How do you know Emmanuel?" Angie asked.

"Who's Emmanuel?" Louis X asked.

"The guy you saw Lil' Jimmy with at the mall."

"Oh, we call him Rat," Louis X said smiling, "I don't mean to be so personal, but is Rat, I mean Emmanuel, your man or something?" he asked.

"Or something," Angie said. "He's just somebody I know."

"Well, the reason for my concern, and please don't take this the wrong way, I'm not trying to get all up in your business. As I said, I like Lil' Jimmy and I feel you should know what I'm about to tell you. I served my last year at Tucker Max for stabbing Rat."

Angie had a surprised look on her face. She was still having a hard time believing that Louis X had been in prison. She surely didn't want to believe that he was capable of stabbing someone.

"The reason I stabbed him is because he had a reputation for raping young inmates who were weak. One day, he raped the brother of a friend of mine and I lost it, so I stabbed him. The other day when I saw him with Lil' Jimmy, it brought back those memories. Then when I heard that Lil' Jimmy was in the hospital, I couldn't help but think the worse. Like I said, I'm not trying to get in your business and I'm sure that you're woman enough for any man, but this guy Rat, he shouldn't be trusted around Lil' Jimmy, or any other kid. Some men in prison have sex with men because they're homosexuals; some because they have no discipline or control and just want to have sex with anyone or anything. Then you have the predators who just like to dominate others. Rat is of the breed that possesses the qualities of all the deviates in one. That's why I feel that, despite how much woman you may be, I don't think you should leave him alone with your son."

Angie turned and stared at the door to Lil' Jimmy's room before turning back to face Louis X. "When you saw Lil' Jimmy with Rat, or Emmanuel, in the mall, I was getting off work and he walked with him across the corridor to get an ice cream cone. Emmanuel is a janitor where I work and I could see them from my workstation. I don't just bring anyone around my son."

"Look, sister Angie, I'm sorry if I offended you," Louis X said apologetically. "But my concern was for Lil' Jimmy. I hope you understand. If every mother was as thoughtful as you, we wouldn't have to worry about the Rats of the world. But, you and I both know that some mothers are so desperate to have a good black man that they'll bring Freddie Kruger home if he had a job or was a baller. And we both know that there's some sick black men out there. To bring awareness to this problem, I also teach a class for single mothers on Monday's and Wednesday's at P.A.P.A. I would love to have you in attendance if you could stop by sometime. The classes are from six to eight in the evening."

"Maybe I can stop by on Wednesday," Angie said. "That's my off day from my second job at night." Angie popped the collar on her Pizza Hut uniform.

"So, which job has the good insurance," Louis X asked smiling.

Angie gave him a puzzled look. "Oh, I just figured that since Lil' Jimmy was getting such excellent care with an extra night stay, that somebody must have good insurance or Medicaid. And, since you're working two jobs, I figure it can't be Medicaid. Most hospitals will discharge uninsured black folk with their chest still open after open heart surgery."

"I know, that's the truth," Angie said. "Well, that'll be my day job with the insurance," she said smiling. The two of them were still laughing when a nurse walked up to the door carrying a tray with water and pills.

"Time for medicine," the nurse said. Louis X and Angie both stared at one another before sharing a private laugh at the nurse's expense as they followed the nurse into the room.

"Probably sugar pills." Louis X whispered into Angie's ear.

"I know," Angie said under her breath, "probably twenty dollars a pill."

Louis X hung around for another thirty minutes before saying that he had to go. He said goodbye to Lil' Jimmy and was about to say bye to Angie before she stood and followed him out the room.

"Well, I guess I'll see you Wednesday," Angie said. The look between Louis X and Angie was warm and friendly.

"I hope so," Louis X said.

***

Louis X had twenty-five women who attended his single parent class on Wednesday nights. The women done so for many reasons. The majority of them had children who attended P.A.P.A's many functions. Some were there because it was a requirement for free daycare offered to single parents by P.A.P.A. Louis X also had his admirers. These women were impressed with the words and presence of a strong, black man that spoke as eloquently as Louis X.

"All right sisters, let us assemble ourselves." Louis X adjusted some papers on his desk as the women begin to scramble to their chairs. The class was just settling down when the door opened and Angie walked into the room. Louis X gave a broad and genuine smile that did not go unnoticed by his other admirers in the room.

"Hello sister, I'm glad you could make it," Louis X walked over to Angie and ushered her to a chair that was normally reserved for special guests at the front of the room. Some of the women were not impressed by the special treatment that Angie was receiving.

Louis X handed Angie one of the pamphlets he had in his hand before walking around the room and distributing the pamphlets to the other women.

"The literature we're going to discuss tonight is probably the most important piece of psychological damaging information that you as black women will ever read. Now, last week I had the brothers of P.A.P.A apologize to you sisters for the past and present roles that black men have played in your abuse since our coming to America. We were men who allowed you to be raped by the so-called slave masters. We are men today who will run off and leave you to raise our children alone. We haven't protected your images and have allowed white women to steal your rightful positions as queens of the world. We have also allowed them to steal your beauty."

The women were all smiles as Louis X reminded them of last week's meeting and told them how beautiful they were. At last week's meeting, Louis X had had twenty men from P.A.P.A all dressed in tuxedos to present the women in the class with roses and a written apology for past and present actions of black men. Louis X finished passing out the literature and took his position in front of the class.

"Hold on brother, Louis," Vickie a big-breasted, dark-skinned woman said as she squirmed in her seat. "Where that Lil' Mike Mike at from last week? Shoot, don't tell me I wore my good perfume for nothing, hell I want me another apology and a back rub."

The other women start laughing as big Vickie continued squirming in her seat.

"Well sister Vickie, I'll see what I can do about that next week," Louis X said.

"Next week, hell, what about tonight? I'm ovulating."

The women all roared with laughter. "Girl, your eggs dried up thirty years ago, talking about you ovulating. Hell you must mean over eating." Gloria who was Vickie's best friend poked fun at her friend.

"Shoot woman, I don't know what you talking about. I read in the Ebony the other day that a woman don't lose the desire until she's near seventy years old. Ain't that right brother Louis?"

"I don't know sister," Louis X said. "Why don't we ask Ms. Carol?"

Ms. Carol was an eighty-five year old woman who always attended the meetings with her granddaughter. She used a walker and was stooped over in her chair when Louis X called her name.

"Ms. Carol, at what age do you think a woman begins to lose her sexual desire?" Louis X asked.

"Well child," Sister Carol said as she perked up with a smile. "I'm afraid you gon' have to ask somebody a little older than me."

The room exploded in laughter at the words of Sister Carol. The women were still laughing when Louis X held up his hand for silence.

"All right sisters," Louis X said smiling, "May I have your attention please." Louis X waited until the women were still and silent. "Now, as I was saying, the information contained in these pamphlets is very real. The pamphlet is called Let's Make A Slave. The infamous Willie Lynch speech is also included in the pamphlet. Now, rather this information was actually used by slave owners, to control slaves, I really can't say. Neither can our historians. In my personal opinion I do feel that if it wasn't used by all slave owners it was surely used by some."

The women were all scanning their pamphlets as they listened to Louis X. "Let's first discuss the Willie Lynch speech. It's on the last page of your pamphlet. Now, Willie Lynch, if you read his speech, was a wickedly wise old white devil. Willie said that his methods for controlling the slave if properly installed could last for up to three hundred years."

Louis X had the attention of every woman in the room as he paced the floor slapping the pamphlet in his right hand against the open palm of his left hand. "Minister Farrahkhan spoke about the Willie Lynch speech during the Million Man March. Since then the speech has been quoted on many occasions. The wickedly wise Willie Lynch taught that to control the slave you had to pit them one against the other by playing on their differences. Now, let's look at some of his methods and see if they sound familiar."

Louis X opened the pamphlet in his hand. "Willie Lynch said that the slave owners should use such differences as age, and color to create division amongst the slaves. Again, rather this is true or not, I don't know, but I do know that some of the problems detailed in this pamphlet do exist within our communities."

Louis X went on to discuss the Willie Lynch speech in length before moving on, to the Let's Make A Slave portion of the pamphlet. Now in this portion of the pamphlet, there's graphic references to the black woman and child. The writer says that in order to control the black slave population, you had to first break the black woman. He said you had to break the black woman like you would a horse. He says you must first break the black man in front of the black woman. You do this he says, by taking the strongest man slave and whipping him in front of the weaker and more submissive slaves and the black women. This he says will instill fear into the other slaves and make them more obedient.

Most importantly he says, it, will also make the black woman raise her children up to be obedient to their enslavers because of her love for her male child and the fear of what would happen to him if she raised him to be too strong. Once you break the black male, the writer says you can then breed him with the broken black woman. He goes on to say that once broken and bred together, the black woman and man will raise you ass-backward children."

Louis X paused for affect as he finished reading the pamphlet. "Sisters, as mothers, you hold the future in your hands," he said. "You must not be afraid to raise your children as strong black men and women. You must also begin to demand more of the black men you choose as your mates. You must stop choosing your mates based on the size of his penis and his sexual prowess. These things do not make a man. It only bears evidence that he's a male."

Louis X finished his lecture with a question and answer session. "Brother Louis," Big Vickie held up her hand.

"Yes Sister Vickie."

"What if your man, you know, got a big one, but he's a little slow in other areas. Can you forgive him for being slow, because he can make up for it in other areas. I mean, I'm down with the good man stuff, but I also like me some good other stuff too."

"Girl will you hush," Gloria said to Vickie as the other women all begin to laugh. "You know good and well that all your men come battery operated."

Louis X was saying his goodbyes to the last of the women when he was approached by Angie at the end of the line. "I was very impressed with your class," Angie said. "You seem to have quite a following and admirers I might add. I thought for a minute there that I was going to need protection."

"Well, I'm glad you enjoyed the class," Louis X said. I do hope you will join us again."

"I look forward to it," Angie said.

"You're not from around here are you?" Louis X asked as he walked Angie to her car.

"No, I'm originally from Chicago, my mother moved here with me when I was sixteen, following some male." Angie placed emphasis on the word male.

"Well, ain't that something," Louie X said. "Who would've thunk it, a fellow stepper, all the way down here in Arkansas."

"Are you from Chicago?" Angie asked.

"Southside finest," Louis X said. "That is, I was until I got arrested for introduction of narcotics into the Pine Bluff area of Arkansas."

"Wow, I got family all over Chicago," Angie said.

"Who knows, we might be kin," Louis X said.

"I hope not," Angie mumbled, almost to herself.

"I missed that, what you say?" Louis X asked.

"Oh, nothing, I got to go," Angie said changing the subject. "I got to go and pick up Lil' Jimmy before he run his father crazy."

"Speaking of Lil' Jimmy, how is my little soldier?" Louis X asked.

"Your little soldier been running around like crazy every since he left the hospital," Angie said. "He's over to his father right now."

"That's good," Louis X said. "Children need to spend time with their fathers."

"Well, he definitely does that."

"So I guess the two of you are cool then." Louis X held Angie's car

309

door open for her.

"Yea, we cool," Angie said. "At least now. I met Richard when I was young and impressionable. He was a few years older and I got in over my head. The first time we had sex he forced his way upon me. A month later, we had consensual sex and Lil' Jimmy was the result. It was also the end of our relationship. I had to go through my pregnancy alone because Richard didn't think the child was his. You know the story. We got DNA tests done after Lil' Jimmy was born and he's been a good father ever since."

"Well, at least he did come around." Louis X shut Angie's car door. "Some black men never do." He said.

***

Louis X hadn't been able to sleep since his encounter with Rat inside the mall. He knew it was just a matter of time before Rat raped some unsuspecting child. Louis X couldn't let that happen. Rat had to be stopped.

Louis X spotted his quarry and eased behind him in traffic. He had been tailing Rat for days. He followed behind Rat along the familiar route Rat took each day for home. Louis X was waiting for the right opportunity.

His moment arrived at an intersection where Rat was being held up by a red light. Louis X pulled up alongside Rat at the light. He rested the barrel of the pistol grip shotgun he brought for the occasion on the driver side windowsill.

Boom! Boom!

Louis X fired twice. The first shot struck Rat and caused him to turn. Rat stared in shock and pain at Louis X.

The second shot took away the pain and most of Rat's head. Louis X sped away before Rat's body slumped over the steering wheel.

Chapter 37

The men of P.A.P.A were playing their weekly pickup game of basketball in the gymnasium. Cream who was the best ball player on the court was doing his usual trash talking as he made a basket and ran back down court as a defender. He was knocked hard to the court by a blind side pick set by Brick.

"Foul!" Cream said loudly. "Man, that's a moving screen." He said.

"Naw, that's a brick wall." Brick said.

Lil' Brick inbounded the ball to Brick. Brick tossed the ball back to Lil' Brick in the corner. Lil' Brick made the twenty feet jumper and threw up a fist sign.

"Game," Brick said. "Get off the court. Next! I told you boy, you'll never beat the Brick Factory."

Broke and his squad took the court for the next game. The Brick Factory which was the name of Brick's squad held the court down all morning. It was 12:30 when the games ended and everyone was sprawled out around the bleachers exhausted.

Sherry and the other women brought in plates of barbecue for the men and begin to pass the plates around. Angie handed Louie X a fish plate with a smile. The two of them had come together. Everyone was sitting around enjoying their meals when Louis X stood up and asked for everyone's attention. The gym grew silent as Louis X took the court and begin to spread powder all over the court.

"Man, what brother Louis doing? Broke asked Cream who was sitting next to him.

"I don't know man, might be some kind of voodoo to make his game better."

"He gon' need more powder than that," Broke said laughing, "better get him some chicken feet to go along with that powder."

"All right brothers, and sisters," Louis X said. "Check this out. Now most of you know that I'm originally from Chicago. Now in Chicago, we got this thing we do that I'm going to hip you too. The other night after class I found out that sister Angie is also from Chicago. So what we propose is to bring a little of the windy city flavor to the dirty south. Hit it Angie."

Angie pushed the on button on a CD player and joined Louis X on the dance floor. The two of them begin to move smoothly like they were gliding on the floor to the sounds of R. Kelly's stepping song. Everyone applauded loudly when the couple finished dancing and took a bow.

"Man," Brick said excitedly. "Boy, I didn't know you could step. You got to show me that. I been wanting to learn how to step every since I first saw somebody do it, shoot, I done forgot now, boy you got to show me how to do that." Brick was rambling on as he jumped off the bleacher wiping his hands of rib juice and smiling broadly as he spoke to Louis X. Sherry and the other women were already in a line with Angie trying to eat off their rib tips while cupping their hands beneath the meat to keep the sauce from dripping on their clothes as Angie showed them how to step.

"Look-a-here," Louis X said. "When Angie and I were talking about it the other night, I figured we could use the gym to teach people how to step. See, stepping is not just a dance, it's also an exercise that we can use to enhance our wellness program here at P.A.P.A."

"That's a good idea, Cream said.

"See, I figured we could use the gym to teach people how to step. Once we teach them, Scacehead and Cream can then have steppers night on one of their slow nights at the club. We can raise money for P.A.P.A by charging a cover fee at the door and the club can make money off the bar and food it serves."

"Man, that's a helluva idea," Scacehead said. Once people learn how to step, you know they gon' wanna go and show off their moves."

"The thing is," Broke said, "that we got to define the movement so can't nobody else can steer it away from us once we popularize stepping in Pine Bluff."

"We can form stepper clubs," Verla said. "We can design and sell T-Shirts with P.A.P.A emblem on the back and a silhouette of a couple stepping on the front with something like Step Up above the silhouette image and the club name and phone number beneath."

"That's a good idea," Michelle said.

"The whole thing sounds good to me," Brick said. "Just make sure that I learn how to step."

"Daddy, I seen you dance." Lil' Brick said. "And you still doing the robot."

"Robot, boy you don't know nothing. Watch this;" Brick turned the music back up after turning it down. "Come on Vee, let's show these youngsters how it's done."

"What youngsters?" Verla asked. "You act like I'm old or something. Hell, I just turned twenty-one myself."

Brick and Verla were joined on the court by the rest of the crew as they all done their version of the step dance.

"It wouldn't take long for the P.A.P.A's Stepping Club to become over one hundred strong in membership. The stepping club was broken into four parts. Verla and Sherry formed a club called the High Steppers, Michelle and Angie formed the Stepping Wolves, Lil' Shelia and

BeBe formed the Stepping Lions. The Stepping Lions were mostly composed of college students and two college professors. Poochie and Sylvia, who were now a couple, formed the last group called the Hot Steppers.

The club had been divided into four separate clubs for recruiting purposes and to create dance competitions and competitiveness amongst the group members. It was Sherry's idea to divide the stepping club into four parts. She felt it would give the appearance that the movement was growing and would also serve well those people who wanted a choice in life. Each club had rehearsal time in the gyms. The House of Cream nightclub had steppers nights on Thursday nights at the club. Stepping nights were so popular at the club that it was standing room only. People came from all over to show their moves against the steppers of P.A.P.A. Louis X also invited step clubs from Chicago to come down and compete with the local steppers.

Lil' Shelia and BeBe were two of the best steppers in town. They held their own against the Chicago Steppers as well. BeBe was a tall, dark-skinned version of Whitney Houston. BeBe had a grace about herself that was inherited from her rich upbringing and prominent family. Lil' Sheila had met BeBe, whose birth name was Karen Scott, at cheerleading tryouts at UAPB. BeBe was a senior who had transferred to UAPB to complete her senior year. Her and Lil' Shelia had become friends at school. Because of their like scheduling, Lil' Shelia now spent as much time with BeBe as she did with Sherry.

MIKE MIKE

<u>Chapter 38</u>

Sherry was on her way to karate practice when Lil' Shelia and BeBe pulled up in front of the duplex. "Girl, what you up to?" Sherry asked Lil' Shelia.

Lil' Shelia was skipping up to the duplex as if in a hurry as BeBe waited in the car. "Shoot, I forgot my purse," Lil' Shelia said. "I'm fento go watch Borilla at football practice. Me and BeBe got cheerleading practice too."

"Well, I'll see you later," Sherry said. "I got practice myself, and it's not me and BeBe, it's BeBe and I."

"You and BeBe, where y'all going," Lil' Shelia said laughing as she unlocked the door and disappeared into the duplex.

"Hey BeBe, " Sherry spoke to BeBe as she walked out to her car.

"Hey Sherry," BeBe said, returning her smile. "Your little cousin about to run me crazy," BeBe said.

"Now, you know I know, don't you," Sherry said as she open her car door.

Mike Mike and Broke walked out the house as Sherry was backing out the driveway. Mike Mike's real name was Michael Rogers, Jr. Every one called him Mike Mike to distinguish him from other Mikes. Mike Mike looked a lot like the afro wearing Jim Kelly of the so-called blaxploitation films. He was tall and light skinned like Jim Kelly and even wore his hair in the afro style of the star. Mike Mike was of mixed heritage but never knew either parent. He had grown up in foster homes where his good looks were both a blessing and a curse. It was a blessing because the caretakers always treated him special because of his adorable looks. It was a curse because the special treatment always got him in trouble with the other kids. Mike Mike had to learn early how to protect himself and the things he was given. He also, learned how to use his looks to his advantage. He grew up using his charms and looks to disguise the contempt in his heart for most everyone he met. Mike Mike had once been so isolated from the world that he loved only himself. Everyone else was a hustle to him. It was his hustling ways that landed him in prison for two years. He would have gotten more time if not for the female judge taking a liking to him and showing him some leniency.

Mike Mike was arrested for shooting two men who had cheated him in a car deal. The prosecutor had been livid when the judge had sided with Mike Mike's lawyer and his plea for mercy. The lawyer detailed Mike Mike's troubled life as a young child growing up in foster homes. The prosecutor had called Mike Mike a monster and said that he did not deserve any leniency. Even though it was Mike Mike's first time being arrested, the prosecutor demanded further justice. Despite the fact that the two white men who Mike Mike had shot were now confined to wheelchairs, the judge still showed Mike Mike leniency based on the fact that the gun he had shot the men with, he had taken in a struggle from one of the men after being threaten by the man with the gun.

Mike Mike and Broke had met in prison. As with Cream the two of them had become close because of their ages and out of mutual respect for how they had carried themselves in prison. Being close with Broke had also brought Mike Mike under the tutelage of Brick. Mike Mike now worked as an administrator for P.A.P.A along with Broke after being summoned by Brick.

The two of them were relaxing at Broke's house drinking beer on one of their rare off days together on their conflicting schedules. BeBe eyes were glued to Mike Mike's as he and Broke walked over to

Broke's car. They both waved at BeBe as they got into Broke's car and again as they were pulling out the drive past her car.

Broke was steering his car onto the road when Lil' Shelia came hurrying out her side of the duplex. Lil' Shelia was walking fast towards BeBe's car before diverting her attention away from BeBe's car and walking fast towards Broke's car. She was waving frantically as she sashayed up to Broke's car telling him to wait up for a minute.

"Hey, Mike Mike, Broke I almost forgot to tell you. Bo' want you to stop by the school after practice. He gon' be on the football practice field."

"What's up?" Broke asked.

"Onknow," Lil' Shelia said.

"All right," Broke said. "bout what time they get through practicing."

"They outta be through about six," Lil' Shelia said.

"All right," Broke said again, "I'll shoot through there."

***

Borilla had made the UAPB football team after competing with a two-year starter for the defensive end position. Borilla had won the spot after the starter had gotten hurt during one of the team's practices. The starter was a Pine Bluff local and high school football legend. Borilla's troubles begin with the former starter and his friends after the starter had been cleared to play and the coach refused to give him back his starting spot over Borilla. Borilla was the hardest hitting defensive end the coach had ever seen. He played the game with total disregard for his own safety and even less regard for the safety of others. As an old school coach who prided himself on putting the best players on the field, there was no way the coach felt he could justify not giving Borilla the starting position.

Borilla had already had several verbal and one physical confrontation with Peanut the former starter. He had easily whipped the short stocky boy. The two of them had almost tangled again on another occasion when Peanut and two of his friends had cornered Borilla on the parking lot one day after school. The coach had intervened on that day but Lil' Shelia knew that another confrontation was imminent.

Lil' Shelia and BeBe were waiting around for Borilla after football practice. They were sitting at the end of the bleachers near the entrance to the playing field leading from the dressing room. Borilla was one of the last ones to leave the building. He came out with his gym bag over his shoulder. Borilla had more body mass and muscle thanks to the use of the USPB's gym and equipment.

"It's about time you brought your butt out," Lil' Shelia said.

"I thought you were already gone," Borilla said.

Lil' Shelia didn't want to tell Borilla that she had stayed around because she was worried about him and his troubles with Peanut and friends. If not for Borilla telling her not to tell Broke, she would have already told Broke what was going on after the first incidence. Borilla was afraid that Broke might go back to jail if there was any trouble so he didn't want him to get involved. Still, after seeing Peanut gathered up with some local toughs earlier in the day, Lil' Shelia was worried that the men would try and jump Borilla again. That's why she had lied when she told Broke that Borilla wanted him to meet with him after practice.

Lil' Shelia was holding Borilla's hand after taking one of his bags. "Boy what you got in this bag?" She asked.

"What?" It's too heavy for you," Borilla asked.

"Naw, it's funky." Lil' Shelia turned up her nose as if smelling something foul.

The trio walked out to the parking lot with BeBe and Lil' Shelia talking about their stepping club. Borilla was looking around cautiously. He had already been warned by a friend that Peanut and some of his friends were planning to jump him after practice.

Lil' Shelia squeezed Borilla's hand tightly as they approached the stadium parking lot and saw Peanut and three other boys standing behind Peanut's car. He had deliberately parked in front of Borilla's car.

Lil' Shelia had a worried look on her face as she squeezed Borilla's hand even tighter. "Here that punk come now," Lil' Shelia heard one of the men say. It was then she reached into her pocket and pulled out her razor.

BeBe, whose car was parked fifty feet away, stayed with Lil' Shelia and Borilla as they approached Borilla's car. The men were all mean mugging Borilla as they stood off Peanut's car.

"Who gon' save you now punk. The coach ain't here. I know you didn't think it was over." Peanut tossed his jacket into his car as Borilla removed his hand from Lil' Shelia and pushed her out of harm's way.

"Nutt, why don't you gon' and leave that stuff alone." BeBe pleaded with Peanut.

"I ain't leaving shit alone," Peanut said. "This punk been talking all that shit 'bout what he gon' do, let's see him back it up now."

"Whatever, punk!" Borilla nosed flexed wide as it always done when he was angry.

Lil' Shelia stood beside him with her razor in her hand prepared to do whatever she could to help her man.

BeBe stood next to Lil' Shelia, still trying to talk some sense into Peanut. After realizing that Peanut wasn't trying to be reasonable, BeBe tried to speak some sense into one of the other men.

"Bitch, fuck that shit!" One of the men said.

"Punk, who you calling bitch!" BeBe tossed her purse to the ground as she saw that reasoning was out the question and a battle was imminent.

The men rushed Borilla in a mob rush causing Lil'Shelia to stumble to the ground. A black infinity sped onto the parking lot as an all-out brawl broke out between Borilla and the men. Broke and Mike Mike jumped out of the car and rushed into the melee pulling bodies off the pile and hitting them as they tossed the men to the side.

Broke dropped one of the men with a hard right followed by a three piece to the head as the man fell to one knee. Mike Mike kicked a fat buck-tooth boy with a roundhouse kick that knocked him ten feet away from the battle. Broke grabbed another man and was pounding him as Borilla beat Peanut unmercifully while straddle his chest on the ground. BeBe and Lil' Shelia had moved away from the fighting scene after Broke and Mike Mike had arrived and got involved. One of the men was bleeding from a cut on his arm where Lil' Shelia had stabbed him with her razor. Mike Mike was using karate chops and kicks to the head and chest of the fourth man that had him gruntingly backing up as he tried to fall and escape the pounding. Broke had knocked one man out and was still pounding the other until he too fell to the pavement without moving.

BeBe watched in awe at the boxing skills of Broke and was even more impressed with the karate skills of Mike Mike. Peanut and his friends were all laid out on the parking lot moaning and groaning loudly in pain. Broke and Mike Mike waited for Borilla and the girls to leave before pulling off the lot themselves.

Sherry had a worried look on her face as she wiped some blood away from Broke's lip as he sat in the tub. She was afraid that he had hurt someone and that at any moment the cops would come storming through the door. Even after Broke had told her that everything was all right Sherry couldn't help worry. Broke asked for his cell phone and punched in some numbers.

"Baby, will you stop worrying," Broke said as he waited for the party he called to answer the phone.

"That's like telling me to stop breathing."

Mike Mike had told Broke that the men they fought were from Preston Pike.

Cream answered the phone and Broke told him about the incident and asked him to see if he could get a line on the men in case something happen to Borilla and he needed to find them.

**

Peanut and the men were on the corner later that evening just after dark. They were getting drunk and trying to recruit help from the other men gathered with them for revenge purposes. They already had several of the men committed to helping them. A rugged looking man name Ice, had offered to eliminate the problem on a permanent basis for the right amount of money.

The men were all talking bravado talk when Scacehead, Roundhead and Lee Lee all walked up. The three known killers all seem to walk up from out of nowhere as they stood before the men on the corner. Lee Lee held a long barrel 44 Magnum along his leg. Roundhead had his hand on the pistol butt of a 357 Magnum in his waist. Scacehead patted the nine millimeter in his waistband as he walked up to Peanut. Everyone on the corner was standing in stunned silence.

"What's up Scace," Ice who a minute ago had offered to eliminate Peanut's problem, asked with a toothpick in his mouth."

"Ain't shit," Scacehead said. "That's what I'm trying to find out." What's up Peanut," Scacehead said with an edge in his voice. Scacehead stared hard at the men who had been with Peanut earlier during the incident with Borilla. He knew them from their wounds.

"Which one of y'all was the ones who jumped on my peeps over at

UAPB today."

The men who hadn't been involved in the incident backed away from Peanut and the other men. They all knew that Scacehead had a quick temper and wouldn't hesitate to shoot someone if provoked. Ice had also changed sides and was now standing next to Scacehead.

Scacehead stared hard at Peanut. "Nigga, you got a problem with my peeps,"

Scacehead had a scowl on his face as he stood nose to nose with Peanut. "Man, I didn't know them were your people." Peanut had a look of fear on his face.

"Little punk-ass, football-playing-ass nigga, why you think I haven't already bust a cap in your Lil' bitch ass. If I even thought you knew them were my peeps, I would've already dropped your faggot ass."

Scacehead's lips trembled as they always done when he was on the verge of exploding. Peanut had seen the look many times. He couldn't help but flinch as Scacehead suddenly jabbed his finger in Peanut's face and poked him on the nose.

"I'm-a give you punks a pass this time," Scacehead said. It won't be no next time."

There was no more talk of revenge by the men after Scacehead left. Ice and another man walked off with him, Lee Lee and Roundhead. The rest of the men went back to drinking with a new sense of purpose. They were now toasting the fact that Scacehead was not in a violent mood and no one had gotten shot.

Chapter 39

BeBe was half listening to the freckled face college professor with receding hairline. Her mind was not on his lecture about computer technology but rather on the mission that had brought her to Pine Bluff in the first place. As an F.B.I, agent for the last five years, BeBe was well suited for the role of a college student, thanks to her youthful appearance. Though she was only twenty-nine, she still looked every bit of twenty-one or less, depending on her attire. BeBe was following an elaborate drug operation that was the brainchild of an Asian college student. The thug who went by the name of Cass to his associates was also known as Cassius Lee to his college professors.

Cassius Lee was a young looking thirty-year-old Asian man of Japanese origin. He was originally from California and it was there that he had developed his elaborate drug distribution scheme. Now in his eighth year of college, the Asian drug dealer had attended a different Historic Black College Universities in each of his eight years of college.

Cassius Lee traveled across the country moving cocaine while attending the different colleges of his tuition. He would never spend more than one year at the same college before moving on to the next. With some drug usage already prevalent on college campuses, Cassius Lee would increase the market upon his arrival by flooding the campus with cheap, high quality drugs. What Cassius Lee left behind in his wake were once promising young black college students who were now failing classes and also victims of substance abuse.

BeBe had been tipped off about Cassius Lee by one of his former associates after her arrest. She had been assigned to Cassius Lee's case after doing a profile on him and discovering his method of operation. After months of following him, she was no closer to catching him now, than she was when she had first started the chase. With her informant in prison awaiting a time cut to testify against Cassius Lee, the pressure was on BeBe by her superiors to bring him to justice or drop the case.

This was easier said than done. BeBe had found that getting an indictment against Cassius Lee was not easy. It seemed that his college classes were paying off in more ways than one. Not only was he a popular student with the instructors, he was also a shrewd business man who knew his way around the law.

BeBe hadn't been able to figure out Cassius Lee's method of moving drugs or his methods of laundering his money from the drug proceeds. Cassius Lee was at the top of his class. He was cordial, and had perfect attendance at every school he had attended. With majors completed in psychology and business management, Cassius Lee was now working on his third major in the computer technology field.

BeBe had managed to have herself placed in the two classes Cassius Lee was taking at UAPB for the fall semester. BeBe knew that she had to catch him soon. When she had first presented his profile to her superiors, she thought they would be enthusiastic about bringing down his operation. She was surprised when they had not been enthused and had delayed her pursuit of the case for over six months by assigning her to other assignments. It was this delay that had allowed Cassius Lee to clean house and to escape from her grasp after his associate was arrested.

BeBe at first thought that the post 911 era had something to do with the lack of interest that her superiors had shown her. She felt that with their focus on terrorism that maybe the war on drugs was no longer a priority. She never thought that racism had anything to do with their decisions. She never stopped to consider that because Cassius Lee was an Asian man who was selling drugs to black college students that the FBI just didn't think of this as a high priority case. BeBe was smart, but being raised in an upper-middle class household had not prepared her for the institutional and sometimes blatant racism of America.

***

Sherry was tired and sore after karate practice. She had been attending the class on Tuesday's and Thursday's for over a month since September. The class was being taught by a young Asian student. The student was a master in Tae Kwon Do and Sherry had learned a lot over the two-month period in the class. She had first read about the free class on the school bulletin board. Sherry walked sore and tired away from the small downtown building where the karate class was held.

The tight sweats hugged her body as she walked out to her car. Men couldn't help but stare. For a moment, Sherry thought that she might have to use her newly acquired skills. She still hadn't gotten use to all the attention and rudeness of Pine Bluff boys and men. It seemed at times that some of them had never seen a woman. This unwanted attention was partially the reason that she had decided to take the karate class. Lil' Shelia had lasted a week in the class before dropping out. "Shit girl, that's why I carry my knife," Lil' Shelia had said when she had quit. "I do enough kicking in bed trying to get away from Bo. I don't have the stamina for this shit." Sherry smiled to herself as she thought about Lil' Shelia's remarks while backing away from the building.

Broke was standing outside with Brick and Cream when Sherry made it home. "You ready to practice," Broke asked.

"Ummph Ummph, I'm too tired tonight," Sherry said. "Cassius Lee tried to kill us tonight." Sherry normally practiced with Broke and Mike Mike in the back yard most evenings. Mike Mike was just as good if not better than Cassius Lee. Broke was good but his focus was more on his boxing than karate. He also showed Sherry some knife moves. Broke had jokingly told Sherry that he was training her to be an assassin for the cause. The truth was, because Sherry was still naive to many things in the world, Broke was worried about her safety when he was not around. Sherry kissed Broke and spoke to Cream and Brick before walking into the house.

"Stay focused," Brick smilingly said to Broke.

Broke smiled after turning away from watching Sherry walk towards the house. "Got to keep my eye on the prize," he said.

"We also got to figure out where all these new young smokers coming from. Shit getting out of hand when I see four young college sisters from UAPB trying to sell their tails on Main street. Then I see another three or four of them hanging out around the projects. That don't include the young cats that I've been seeing riding looking for dope in hot areas. We got to be observant of this type shit."

Brick took a sip of his drink as he paused. "P.A.P.A got to protect the future," he said. "I don't know what the hell is going on, but I'm telling you, I be paying attention to everything. Brother Louis X also brought it to my attention the other day after his class. He say he been seeing the same thing."

"Shit man, I been noticing shit myself," Cream said. "I thought it was just me."

"Well, I haven't been in town long enough to know one smoker from another," Broke said. "I do know that there's a lot of drug activity on the campus."

"These new smokers, I'm talking about," Brick said. "Whatever going on, I want the brothers to keep their ears to the streets so we can find out."

Chapter 40

Cassius Lee ushered the last of the students out the building after their Tae Kwon Do lessons. He pulled the blinds tight and secured the door before walking into an office located at the back of the building. Cassius Lee opened up a safe that he had located behind a picture on the wall. He pulled two large wads of cash out a desk drawer and tossed them into the safe. There were similar wads of cash stacked up to the top inside the safe. Things were going better in Pine Bluff than Cassius Lee had first thought they would. Cassius Lee was having no problems moving his product. He was even thinking of extending his stay. Pine Bluff was a small town with a big city disease, and Cassius Lee was just another germ plaguing the people. If he followed his normal routine, Cassius Lee only had three kilos left to sell in Pine Bluff before it was time to shut down shop. He would have accomplished his goals.

Cassius Lee was working on his third major. He already had two and enough money to last him a lifetime thanks to black colleges. In this sense, he was graceful for the black college experience.

Cassius Lee's father had told him long ago that black people were the key to Asian success in America. He had told him that black people were mostly consumers who would rather buy from stores, shops and other businesses ran by those from outside of their communities and race rather than to buy from one another. He told him that blacks were like children that had to be fed. Cassius Lee had taken his father's advice. He had done as he suggested and set up shop within the black community. He just didn't use the traditional methods.

Cassius Lee gave no thought to the young lives that he destroyed. To him black people were like the food you ate to survive. Just like the beefeaters had no love for the cows they ate and the lions had no love for the gazelles, neither did Cassius Lee have any love for those who he ate off of to survive. He lived by the creed of survival of the fittest.

***

BeBe was sure that Cassius Lee was keeping his drugs inside the karate school.

The profile that she had of him showed that he opened up a karate school wherever he attended college. BeBe figured that Cassius Lee would set up free karate schools for students and transfer his drugs to the schools prior to his arrival on the college campuses that he attended. Even though this was her theory, BeBe was no closer today to finding out how Cassius Lee's operation worked as she was when she first began her investigation. She was sure she was missing something. She just couldn't put her finger on it. BeBe sighed loudly as she put away her notes on Cassius Lee and went to bed.

BeBe and Lil' Shelia were sitting with Sherry the next day talking about the karate class. Lil' Shelia jumped after being startled by BeBe who suddenly jumped to her feet after something Sherry said caught her attention.

"Oooooo, that's it," BeBe said as she gathered her books. "I got to go."

"What's up?" Lil' Shelia asked.

"I'll tell you later," BeBe said before rushing out the house.

BeBe rushed home and logged on her computer. Sherry's words were still echoing in her head as she logged onto the FBI database. The words that had little meaning to Sherry and Lil' Shelia, had lots of meaning to BeBe. Sherry had said that she hated sparring with two of Cassius Lee's students because they were too skilled. It seems like they done took karate before Sherry had said. Sherry had referred to the two students as Samson and DeLil'ah.

BeBe figured that these two had to be the missing pieces to her puzzle.

Being that Cassius Lee never sold drugs directly, BeBe figured that he had to be using someone he could trust who knew how to move large quantities of drugs in small pieces. BeBe knew Samson and DeLil'ah from seeing them around the college campus. Even though they were in their first semester, the two of them were very popular on campus.

BeBe ran the names DeLil'ah Jones and Samson Thomas as she knew the students through the computer. She was trying to see if they had records. There were no profiles or criminal records of Samson and DeLil'ah. BeBe then went online to see what colleges that the two had attended. She then crossed referenced these colleges with those that were attended by Cassius Lee.

BeBe snapped her fingers when she saw that they had all attended the same colleges over the course of the last eight years. In all cases either DeLil'ah or Samson had arrive earlier than Cassius Lee. BeBe figured that DeLil'ah or Samson would arrive early to scout the next location and to set up the drug operation for Cassius Lee. BeBe also checked the opening dates of the Karate schools at each location. As she figured, Samson or DeLil'ah had rented the building for the schools before Cassius Lee's arrival. BeBe was sure as she sipped from a cup of tea that she had her connection. Now, all she had to do was prove it to her superiors. Maybe then she could buy more time. That's if she couldn't bring the case to a close within the next few weeks.

***

BeBe had been on Samson and DeLil'ah for weeks of extended time and her superiors were not impressed by her progressed. The additional period of time they had given her to solve the case after her findings was at its end. She only had two more weeks before she would be reassigned to another case. That's why BeBe had no choice but to confide in Sherry in hopes that she could provide her with some information about the karate school. BeBe felt she needed the additional eyes of Sherry if she had any chance of solving the case.

Sherry was shocked to find out that BeBe was an FBI agent. She was even more shocked to learn that Cassius Lee, Samson, and DeLil'ah were the suspects that she was pursuing. Sherry told BeBe that she would have to first speak with Broke before she could assist her.

"Broke and I don't have secrets," Sherry said. "I wouldn't feel comfortable doing something like this without telling him first. This could be dangerous for him and I."

BeBe's reluctantly agreed to Sherry's demands. A meeting was setup at Cream's house for later that evening. Broke had told BeBe about Brick's suspicion concerning the recent increase of young crack addicts in Pine Bluff. He had told her that they were already working on resolving the issue and that they should all meet to discuss the best course of action. BeBe had agreed and the meeting was planned for Cream's house at seven that evening.

Broke, Mike Mike, Cream, Louis X and Brick were all present at the meeting. Sherry, Michelle, Verla and BeBe were also present; BeBe had just finished explaining what she knew about Cassius Lee's operation. Brick was fuming in anger as she confirmed his suspicions. He was already thinking of how he was going to kill Cassius Lee after the meeting was over. Brick couldn't help thinking about all the promising young black minds that the Asian drug dealer had destroyed.

Cream called Scacehead and asked him if he had a line on either Samson or DeLil'ah. Scacehead told him he'll make some calls and call him back.

"What's up Scace," Cream asked as he spoke into his phone, thirty minutes later.

"Nigga call himself Samson, Scacehead said. "He pumping drugs into the backwoods through Backwood's Billy."

"What about the girl?" Cream asked.

"Bitch a dyke," Scacehead said. "Poochie say she almost had to cut the

330

bitch last week over your girl Sylvia. Say the bitch strung out over Sylvia."

"No shit," Cream said.

"No shit," Scacehead said. "Nigga, you know I keep my ears to the streets. If a rat poot the cat gon' tell me what kind of cheese he had for dinner."

"Why you think I called you," Cream said. "Yo! Yo!, Hold up," Cream stopped Scacehead before he could hang up the phone.

"What's up?" Scacehead asked."

"Who's the man?" Cream asked.

"Shit nigga, I am." Scacehead said braggingly.

"Naw man," Cream laughed. I'm talking 'bout in the relationship between Sylvia and DeLil'ah."

"Aww shit man, both of 'em ho's," Scacehead said laughing. "Man you know Sylvia don't give a damn about a man or woman. Whatever going on between them ho's, Sylvia the one in control."

"All right man, I'll get back at you." Cream hung up the phone and turned to Brick and explained what was said.

"That's it then," Brick said, as he formulated a new plan in his head. He decided to forego killing Cassius Lee for the moment but only if the plan worked.

"The dyke is the key to bring this punk down," Brick said. "This what we gon' do."

BeBe sat and listen as the four men took control of her operation and devised a plan of action. She knew she would be fired if her superiors knew what she was doing.

Brick told Mike Mike to join the karate school so Sherry wouldn't have to be involved. He told Cream to have Sylvia to pick DeLil'ah's brain to see if DeLil'ah had access to drugs.

"Tell her to backdoor the question so the dyke won't think she's prying but to let it slip out like she's looking for some weight. Me and Broke, Broke and I," Brick corrected his grammar after Verla stared at him. Verla had been on Brick about speaking more properly being that he was the spokesman for P.A.P.A.

"Anyway," Brick said after sighing. "Broke and I will act like Sylvia's cousins who's looking for some drugs."

BeBe spoke up for the first time since the men had taken over the conversation.

"Why don't I have an agent act like her cousin," she said. That way after a couple of buys, even if she won't take him to Cassius Lee to buy, we can bust her and lean on her to cooperate."

Brick was reluctant at first, but finally agreed that BeBe had a good plan. Mike Mike joined the karate class the next day. BeBe also joined as his girlfriend. BeBe who was also a black belt held back her skills, as did Mike Mike. There was nothing out the ordinary during class for the first few days. The only suspicious thing BeBe and Mike Mike saw was one day when DeLil'ah disappeared into the back office with Cassius Lee after class. She had reemerged a few minutes later and left the building. BeBe figured that DeLil'ah must have picked up the four ounces that she had promised Sylvia she could get for her.

***

Sylvia who took pride in her ability to control both men and women had had little trouble getting DeLil'ah to voluntarily and willingly score some drugs for her. The two of them were in bed with DeLil'ah between Sylvia's legs. DeLil'ah had been obsessed with Sylvia since their first night together. Sylvia was using DeLil'ah for her pleasure between her legs when Cream called her on the phone as had been their plan. Sylvia took the call like she was speaking with her cousin who had just arrived in town. She pushed DeLil'ah away from her as she hung up the phone and got out of bed.

"What's up baby?" DeLil'ah asked.

"Nothing," Sylvia said. "I got to take care something for my cousin." Sylvia picked up the phone and made a mock drug call to Scacehead.

"Yo, my cousin just called," Sylvia spoke into, the phone. "Nigga, why you sell the shit. Damn! man. That's why I don't like to fuck with you. You told me you was gon' hold on to the shit. I told you he was coming."

Sylvia walked around the room with the phone to her ear. She spoke with an agitated voice into the receiver as if she was angry.

"I already told you, he wanted four zones. Man, I can't believe you sold the shit. Now what I'm gonna tell my cousin. I done had that boy drive all the way down here from Little Rock, thinking you had something. And you talking 'bout you done sold the shit. Bye boy, I got to go. Shit it's too late to call him back. He just called me. He's already in town. Umm Hmmm, yea I know. Yea, umm humm, bye."

"Damn! Sylvia said as she hung up the phone. Sylvia sat on the side of the bed. DeLil'ah begin to nibble on her neck and rub her back.

"Bitch, move." Sylvia said agitatedly. "I ain't in the mood for that shit."

The slightly overweight, Missy Elliot looking, DeLil'ah had a dejected look on her face. Sylvia stood off the bed. "You got to go," she unaffectionately said to DeLil'ah. It was then that DeLil'ah told Sylvia that she could help her.

***

BeBe's fellow FBI agent masquerading as Sylvia's cousin's had now bought six ounces of powder from DeLil'ah in the last four days. He had also had her bring him three ounces of crack cocaine. BeBe suggested the crack amount because it would trigger a higher penalty in Federal prison than the powder amount. She figured that with DeLil'ah facing twenty years as opposed to five years, that she might be more willing to talk.

It was this reality that DeLil'ah was facing when the agent flashed his badge and arrested her on possession and distribution charges. DeLil'ah wasted little time deciding whether or not to become an FBI informant.

BeBe led the FBI raid on the karate school the night of DeLil'ah's arrest. BeBe found two kilos and two hundred thousand dollars in the safe and behind some wall paneling of the back office. Indictments had already been issued for both Samson and Cassius Lee. Samson was found dead of a broken neck four days later. BeBe figured Cassius Lee had killed Samson to eliminate him as another potential witness against him.

Without proof or evidence, BeBe knew her case against Cassius Lee had taken a serious turn for the worse. Being that the karate school had been rented in Samson's name; all the evidence found in the building could be denied ownership by Cassius Lee.

Her case now hinged on the testimony of DeLil'ah.

***

BeBe was furious after being summoned to the Federal Court by the prosecutor's office a few days after Samson's death. As a courtesy, the prosecutor had called her to inform her that Cassius Lee's lawyer had been in contact with them.

The prosecutor was an aging white man and wasn't really interested in prosecuting an Asian citizen for selling drugs to blacks. As a former card-carrying Klan and present day conservative the walrus looking white man still held dear to his views of old.

That's why he liked his job as federal prosecutor. Thanks to the war on drugs and the conspiracy laws use to prosecute drug offenders, he used his position to railroad blacks into federal prison every chance he got. The schemes that federal prosecutors used in federal courts that allowed them to convict and have black men sentence to decades in prison, it was better to prosecutors with their own racist agendas than hanging niggers from trees.

BeBe stormed out the prosecutor's office after their meeting. She was furious and stomped down the hall with a glum look on her face. The prosecutor had told BeBe that because the building was rented to Samson Thomas and because Samson Thomas was dead, it would be difficult to prove that the drugs that were found in the building belonged to Cassius Lee. He also said that DeLil'ah's testimony didn't guarantee a conviction. The prosecutor also said that there was nothing substantial about the three students all attending the same colleges at the same periods of time over the years. He made mention of Cassius Lee's outstanding academic and attendance records. For these and other reasons, the prosecutor had agreed to lessen Cassius Lee's charges to misprison of a felony.

BeBe was furious because the most time that Cassius Lee could receive for this charge was three years in prison. Misprison of a felony simply stated that a defendant knew about a crime but hadn't reported it to the authorities. BeBe had asked the prosecutor what he would do about DeLil'ah. The prosecutor said he would offer her five years if she copped a plea. BeBe then argued that DeLil'ah had already copped a plea and had agreed to testify against Cassius Lee as her supplier. She had also reminded him about her other informant already in prison who also waiting to testify against Cassius Lee.

"Well, I just don't think that this is enough." The prosecutor had said. He said that DeLil'ah had to be held responsible for what he called a substantial amount of drugs that she had sold to an undercover officer. "As for your other witness, I have reason to question her credibility."

The prosecutor had an arrogant smile on his face when BeBe had stormed out his office. He had the same crooked smile on his face when he told her that she had done an outstanding job and asked her if she would like to be the arresting officer to place the handcuffs on Cassius Lee when his lawyer surrendered him to the federal marshals the next morning on the court house steps. The prosecutor had then stood to shake BeBe's hand.

His smile was still present as BeBe stormed out his office after refusing to shake his hand.

BeBe was still furious as she related to Mike Mike what the prosecutor had said.

The two of them were cuddled up in Mike Mike's bed. They had been dating since the day they had joined the karate class as a couple. After play dating for deceptive purposes the two of them realized that they had a lot in common and decided to pursue their mutual interests.

Mike Mike called Brick and told him what BeBe had said. Brick was pissed when he called Broke. Broke was cool and calmly told Brick not to worry and to just chill.

Brick swore vengeance on Cassius Lee and it took Broke most of an hour to calm him down.

***

Cassius Lee arrived at the courthouse building at approximately 9:00 AM the next morning. He was dressed fashionably in a black Sean Jean outfit. He stepped out of a black Benz accompanied by an Asian female. He was also accompanied by his slick, high priced, deal making lawyer. Cassius Lee took a deep breath of air and blew it out arrogantly as he smiled up at BeBe who was standing at the top of the courthouse steps.

It had already been decided that he would be released on bond after his arraignment. Cassius Lee smiled at BeBe as he brushed imaginary lent off his shirtsleeve. He waited as his lawyer leaned over into the car to retrieve his briefcase off the car seat.

The lawyer slammed the car door shut and turned to join Cassius Lee and the Asian female who stood next to him. A loud scream and look of panic came across the Asian woman's face. The smile on Cassius Lee's face suddenly disappeared and became a twisted mask of pain and fear. Blood spurted from his chest, as he grunted from the first of two bullets that slammed into his body. The first bullet hit him in the heart and lifted him three feet into the air. The second bullet landed an inch above the first. Either bullet would have killed him. Cassius Lee was dead before he hit the ground as his pretty Sean Jean suit became a bloody mess of crimson red. All that could be heard was the screaming of the Asian woman. The lawyer was cowering on the ground besides the car with his briefcase over his head as if to protect himself. BeBe reached for her gun as she ran off the courthouse steps and wrapped her arms around the Asian woman. BeBe guided the woman to the ground and covered her with her body as she held her gun in the direction from which the shots were fired. The shots had come from the top of a downtown building from over a thousand yards away.

Michael Rogers

Chapter 41

The Feds were furious about the death of Cassius Lee. It had been over a week and all they had was motive. BeBe told her superiors that she had reliable sources who told her that Cassius Lee had been killed by his Asian suppliers. She said he was killed by his suppliers because they thought that Cassius Lee was about to make a deal with the Feds. Her superiors accepted BeBe's theory. In truth, BeBe didn't know who had killed Cassius Lee. She had no idea who could make such a shot under the wind conditions of that fatal morning.

BeBe did have a theory of who had killed Cassius Lee. Her theory was that Cassius Lee had been killed as a result of four angry black men who she had recently met. One of which she had fallen in love with. Mike Mike was the only one she had told about Cassius Lee's arrival time at the courthouse. Still, she didn't know which of the men were capable of making such a shot as had been made. Her profile of the men didn't reveal no extraordinary shooting skills. It simply revealed that they were all dangerous ex-felons who had all done time together in the Arkansas prison system. When BeBe done a more extensive profile of the P.A.P.A organization, she was both shocked and alarmed at what she found. P.A.P.A was comprised of twenty ex-felons. All of them were harden and profiled as highly dangerous. Each man had served time with James Franklin, A.K.A. Brick, who was the founder of the organization.

There was a strong possibility that P.A.P.A was no more than a black militant organization being disguised as a non-profit organization, If BeBe had discovered this profile a few months ago, she would have alerted her superiors. Instead, BeBe kept the information to herself. P.A.P.A. and its' operatives would become her own secret agency. Her own little death squad who she would feed bits of information on those she felt were a threat to the welfare of the black community.

Being around the men and women of P.A.P.A had opened BeBe's eyes to a new reality. She was no longer the naive female FBI agent. She no longer felt that racism which was once the bedrock of the FBI under J. Edgar Hoover, was a thing of past. She knew now that nothing had changed within the department. Not even the name of the department building. If any changes had been made, BeBe figured now that the changes had only been made for the worse. The Co-InTel Pro that had been created under Hoover in the 1960's to spy on black leaders and organization to prevent the rise of a black messiah was still alive and well. Its' focus had not changed. Except to become more broad and sinister.

The Patriot Act passed after 911 was simply the Co-InTel Program at a higher level. The Anti-terrorist Bill and all anti-gang legislation were designed to prevent the rise of black messiahs. BeBe learned that the FBI's greatest fear was that some young black leader amongst the rank of gang members would rise up and unite the black street organizations across America. The rapper Tupac was assassinated because he had the charisma to be such a leader. His death was well planned and carefully executed by those who were afraid that he would become more revolutionary than violent in his words and deeds.

BeBe had learned a lot from the men of P.A.P.A. Everything that she learned was backed up by evidence and research. The men of P.A.P.A were very diligent in their own research. With the combined efforts, of BeBe's research they were now in possession of information that the government would kill to prevent from being exposed.

The knowledge BeBe had attain and her love for Mike Mike had created a serious conflict of interest within her and the FBI. She had at first thought of quitting the bureau but was encourage too stay by Mike Mike and Brick.

"It's not that we don't need law enforcement officials," Brick had said; "because we do, we just don't need any more like the kind we already got."

Brick told BeBe that there was nothing wrong with law enforcement officials as long as they understood their roles. He told her to always remember that the black voice of protest against the wrongs that she saw perpetrated against black people must be higher than the blue wall of silence that was put up to hide those wrongs.

For movie viewing day at P.A.P.A, Brick showed the movie the Spook That Sat By The Door. This movie about a black C.I.A agent who was using the C.I.A for his own deceptive purposes to plan a black revolution became BeBe's favorite movie of all time. It also gave her a blueprint to follow in her new role as FBI agent for the people. The letters FBI that she wore so proudly emblazoned on her uniform and other attire now took on new meaning to BeBe. To her the letters now stood for Free Black Individual and also for Following Black Instincts. BeBe loved to call herself FBI in reference to her new titles when speaking with her superiors or other individuals. The joke was on them as she would stand before them with a broad smile on her face declaring her loyalty to the FBI. Brick told BeBe that by redefining the letters on her back she had successfully redefined her role in the black struggle. BeBe was transferred to Washington DC a week before Thanksgiving. She returned for P.A.P.A's first annual Thanks-For-Giving Dinner.

**

Lil' Sheila had the audience in stitches laughing at her jokes. The House of Cream was packed for her Thursday night performance. "Say what you wanna say," Lil' Shelia said. "But I'm not with that rich nigga athlete marrying some broke white nanny or shoe sales person. You never hear about no rich white man marrying some poor black bitch name Lakisha from the projects. Ain't none of that Pretty Woman shit happening in the hood. That's some made for TV shit. Black men are the only ones dumb enough to do this shit in real life. These dumb motherfuckers think any ol' white bitch will do. Just as long as she's white. Big dick nigga done ruint poor Lil' JoAnn's pussy from the hood. Leave her broke, big pussy-ass soon as he get that football contract. Here JoAnn is with a deformed pussy trying to find a good man while some white nanny lying up with Raheem's ass in a damn mansion feeding his black ass grapes. Fuck that." Lil' Shelia said to laughter. "That shit ain't love. That's a damn investment. A got damn white bitch's career plan to marry some dumbass unsuspecting black athlete who like to collect trophies and see her ass as the ultimate prize."

"See House of Cream I'm all for poor whites and poor blacks falling in love. This shit I can agree with. See, Becky gon' have to give up some shit if she want to date Nutt black ass from the hood. Becky gon' have to make some got damn sacrifices. She want to date niggas she got to do some nigga shit. Bring Becky's ass to the hood and Big Mama got something for her ass to do. Give Becky ass a bowl of peas. Here gal, shell these peas...fuck you mean you don't know how, Ki Ki show that gal how to shell them peas. Here pick these greens, clean these chitterlings. You want to fuck niggas you got to do some nigga shit. Ain't no got damn Mr. Belvedere. Fuck you mean you cold...Keshia open up that oven door so this child can warm up. Central heat and what, no honey we don't have that, Ray Ray where that blanket at go under that door. Yeah honey, I know the shower is broke and the water is cold in the tub. Ki Ki show that girl how to heat some bath water on the stove in them pots under the sink. The hot water tank don't work child. Naw honey you got to sweep the rug, ain't no damn vacuum cleaner. Go sit in the living room you hot, we got some air in there. Ki Ki get your own baby...Keisha you and Becky take these clothes down to the laundry mat." Lil' Shelia had the place roaring in laughter.

"See black folk in the hood we not prejudice. White bitch want to fuck niggas and live in the hood she more than welcome. Come on bitch and share in our misery. Black folk welcome Becky's ass with open arms. Be helping her hide from her dad and shit when he come looking for her ass with little brother Ted riding in that damn station wagon with the wood grain paneling on the side. Becky hiding behind houses and shit. Niggas be on the lookout telling her where to run and hide. Becky one of us now, even Big Mama helping to hide this good helper bitch and lying to her daddy. Big Mama never told a lie in her life. But let Becky's daddy ask her if she's seen Becky good helper ass and watch and see don't Big Mama stretch the damn truth. Everybody love poor little Becky. But Becky's ass in for a rude awakening she want to date a nigga from the hood.

'Bout the only relief this bitch get from helping Big Mama is not having to walk the got damn dog. Dog got to go outside and shit, he know to have his ass back in five minutes. He lucky to be in the house in the first damn place. Let this motherfucker out the house and he be outside straining like a motherfucker trying to shit, knowing his ass might not get back inside. Be waiting at the door like a got damn cat burglar. Sneaking his ass in when the door open, curled all up against the damn door trying to become one with the door hoping Big Mama don't see his ass with his tail all between his legs trying to find a corner to hide. Mutt be quieter than a motherfucker hiding his ass in a corner praying Big Mama don't notice him. If you make eye contact with him he be looking like one of them damn dogs on those abused dog commercials. Begging with his eyes for you to be quiet. Becky who's use to her dog being inside the house at home don't know no better and start to call the dog name. Here kilo, here kilo, I got a bone for you. Dog be like...shut up bitch. Staring up at Ray Ray hoping he'll tell the bitch to be quiet. Man who this white ho calling my name. She gon' fuck around and let Big Mama see me. Next thing you know Big Mama screaming at Ray Ray to get that damn dog out of her house. Dog be outside madder than a motherfucker at Becky telling the other dogs how she fucked him around." Lil' Shelia took a sip of her drink.

"Dog be outside madder than a motherfucker. Man I was in that bitch for a damn hour, til this white bitch kept calling out my damn name, made Big Mama see me. Then you got that smart Lassie motherfucker outside trying to explain what happened to the dog. See man, white folk let their dogs stay in the house. My cousin live with this white family in White Hall. This bitch be kissing them all in the mouth and shit. Be eating that high protein dog food. Man you ought to see this bitch. Bitch teeth whiter than a motherfucker. Got the shiniest coat I ever seen. Crackers be taking her for walks and picking *up her shit* in bags when she shit. I use to live like that back in the day when I had my own TV show. Back when Collies were the shit. Motherfuckers

343

don't fuck with light skinned dogs no more. Niggas want them black as Dobermans and Rottweilers. Done left our ass out in the cold tied up to a damn tree. Got damn piece of plywood propped up at one end with a stick supposed to be our dog house. Bitch colder than a motherfucker. I should call PETA on these niggas. Lassie madder than a motherfucker."

Then you got the Pit Bull jumping into the conversation. Man PETA ain't shit. PETA don't give a damn about a dog in the hood. I called them motherfuckers the other day and told them about this nigga had me fighting bitches in the woods. Got me dragging 'round a got damn tractor chain trying to make me strong. Make my ass swim ten miles a day talking about it'll give me stamina. Bitch almost bit my ear off the other day in a fight. And then when I did whoop the bitch and had her down I couldn't even fuck the bitch because this nigga done cut my nuts off talking 'bout it'll slow down my aggression. I called PETA and they ain't done shit. I should start biting niggas in the ass. Let them see how it feels."

Lil' Shelia had the club roaring in laughter. "Dogs be outside madder than a motherfucker she said. "Now I'm not saying this shit is right. It's just how we treat a dog in the hood. Becky want to hang out with black folk she got to know this shit. "Then you got them Rin Tin Tin, Run Joe Run, German Shepherd motherfuckers adding their two cents in on the conversation. Be like man, I'm going to a shelter. It's cold as fuck out here. Least the shelter got heat and food. I might get adopted by a white family. I'm sick of this nigga shit. Sick of got damn collard greens, rice, potatoes and got damn beans. And then they gon' throw that shit on the ground like we dogs and shit. Motherfucking chicken bones ain't got no damn meat. Vet say I got high blood pressure now from eating all this nigga shit. How the fuck I'm gon' bite somebody with my teeth all rotten and shit. You right Lassie, we ought to call PETA on these niggas."

That's how we treat dogs in the hood. I'm not saying the shit is right but that's just how it goes. Hell, if it's any consolation to the dogs, niggas don't treat each other no better. Becky learn this shit real quicky like. Two months after living around niggas Becky eating chitterlings and wearing hoochie mama clothes. Done forgot all about little brother Ted and her swimming pool at home. Becky ass swimming in the got damn street after a good rain just like every other nigga in the hood. She one of us now and I can appreciate Becky for sacrificing all she had because she fell in love with Nutt ol' broke ass and followed him to the hood. Love is the key to happiness. So when you find it no matter where you find it you should cherish it as a gift from God. Just don't be fooled like these fool ass rich niggas who marry poor white women who wouldn't even look at their ass when they were broke. That shit ain't love. Them got damn business deals. Thank you House of Cream." Lil' Shelia ended her act to a standing ovation.

***

Brick and Verla were asleep after Lil' Sheila's show. Brick rolled over in bed to answer his cell phone. He also checked the time on the bedside clock. It was after 1:00 AM. Brick wondered who would be calling so late.

"Hello," Brick spoke into the phone. "Hey Be Be, what's up." He said.

"Hey Brick, sorry about calling so late." Be Be said. "But there's something I think you should know."

"About what?" Brick sat up in bed.

'The one that got away," Be Be said. "He was spotted in Gould by a tipster to our hotline. He's scheduled to be picked up in about four hours. The agency wants to make the arrest. Publicity reasons and grandstanding by the agent in charge of the investigation. His flight from D.C. won't arrive for about three hours. That gives you at least four hours, because of prep time after his arrival, to finish what you started. Write this address down." Be Be waited until Brick got a pen and paper. "Tell everyone I said hello," Be Be was about to click off.

"Wait." Brick stopped her. "How did you know it was me?" He asked.

"You fit my profile," Be Be said. "I didn't know for sure it was you until now, "Be Be said, "you just told me." Be careful." Be Be hung up the phone.

"What Be Be want?" Verla who had awaken asked.

"I got to take care of something," Brick said. "If something happens and I don't return, I want you to find someone else worthy of your love." Brick stood off the bed to dress.

"Baby what's wrong," Verla jumped out of bed and rushed to Brick. Tears were in her eyes.

"Vee, you know I can't lie to you, and I don't like keeping secrets from you. Neither can I tell you something that might jeopardize your own freedom. Just know that I love you and that I would never betray our trust. Everything I do is for this cause I believe in and you know it. I'm not the man I was when I first went to prison. I've always regretted killing Tacky. Since then I've killed others. Those I don't regret. If I die in my line of duty, just know that I died fighting for a cause I believed in enough to die for. I love you baby." Brick kissed Verla before releasing her from his embrace to dress.

Verla couldn't stop crying as she watched Brick dress and leave. It was not her place to try and stop him, only to love him and to support his mission. Verla knew that Brick was not the same man of years past. This only made her love him more. Verla knew Brick now as a man. Not the male who had left her eight years earlier. Men built communities and destroyed all that got in the way of their efforts. Men knew how to love and respect the black woman as their strongest ally and companion in their fight. To love a real man was a blessing many women would never know. Verla considered the women of M and P in the same veins as Coretta Scott King, Betty Shabazz, and Myrlie Evers. These were all strong black women who loved men who lived under the constant threats of death. Men who would eventually die fighting for the causes of black liberation. Verla knew that the women of M and P would have to face their challenges of love as these strong and brave black women had done as their examples in how to love real black men. In life and death they would have to stand strong for their men. Yet, unlike the sisters of old, Verla also knew that the women of M and P had to fight with their men in a new way of fighting away from the cameras and lights of the media. These were violent times and called for violent measures at times. Sisters had to be prepared to fight both for and with their loves. Not against other women but against the forces of evil that the men they loved were fighting against to protect them and their children. Verla was all in and ready to fight. Brick would just have to understand the actions she was about to take.

***

Brick didn't know if Be Be had went back to her roots as an agent and was setting a trap for him. He trusted that she was still loyal to the cause. Brick stared at the address Be Be had given him and compared it to the address on the house in front of him. They were the same. He crept up to the small wood frame house located on a side road in the small town of Gould.

Brick tried several windows before finding one that was open. He crept into the house careful not to make a sound. Brick continued to creep upon entering the house. He was in a crouching stance moving cautiously through the house. He passed a room with an open door and peeped inside. The light was dim in the room. Brick could see a bulk of a man lying beneath the covers of a bed. He crept up to the side of the bed and peered down at the sleeping figure. Brick recognized the scarred face of the man he was hunting. He wanted the man to look him in his eyes when he killed him. Brick raised his leg and stomped the man hard across the leg. The man grunted in pain as he turned in bed to see Brick standing over him. A terrified look came across his face.

"Remember me?" Brick asked. He raised his weapon to kill the man.

"Boom!" The gun blast was loud in the room. The smell of gun smoke filled the air after the thunderous blast.

Michael Rogers

"Got'cha!"

The gun blast knocked Brick back against the dresser across from the bed. He broke his fall with his good arm. The other arm was helplessly attached to his wounded shoulder. Blood gushed from the wound above Brick's chest where the bullet from the cop's gun had entered. Brick leaned back against the dresser to keep from falling.

"Got'cha you good too," the cop said. "I thought that might be you breaking and entering. I'm going to enjoy killing you." The cop stood out of Brick's reach. "Gonna kill you nice and slow."

The scars across the cops face looked even more hideous as the cop's face became an angry mask. "Before I kill you, why don't you buy yourself some time by telling me who you are and why you decided to start killing cops. Surely it wasn't over a few crack babies you saw on videotape doing what they do best. Hell, half the girls you saw on those tapes were seasoned veterans by the time I got to them. I wouldn't's exactly call them kids. You know what I mean."

"Even if you kill me, you're still finished," Brick said. "You're just as dead as your cop buddies." Brick was trying to distract the cop as he gripped a hairbrush he had taken off the dresser in his hand to throw. He hoped to be able to reach the cop if he tried to dodge the brush.

"Maybe so," the cop said, "but not before you." The cop smiled a wicked smile as he raised the gun to fire at Brick's head.

Brick knew it was now or never. He flung the brush at the cop. His momentum caused him to lose his balance. Boom! The second blast of gunfire seemed much louder than the first. Brick stumbled against the wall and stared at the cop. The cop's smile turned into a twisted mask of pain. He dropped his gun and slowly crumpled to the floor with a look of shock and surprise on his face. The bullet that killed him had struck him in the heart. The cop was dead before he hit the floor.

"Can you make it?" Broke asked Brick as he walked over to assist him.

348

"I got no choice." Brick said.

"Here, press this against the wound to stop the bleeding." Broke handed Brick a towel he took off a chair. "Look like it went straight through," he said. It's not as bad as it looks. You go ahead. Verla is outside waiting for you. I need to sanitize this house, your DNA is all over the place. I'll be right behind you."

***

A nurse was waiting for Brick's arrival at the M and P clinic. She cleaned and wrapped Brick's shoulder and hooked him up to an I.V. machine. Brick had passed out due to loss of blood by the time he arrived. The nurse said he would be dead if not for his conditioning. Verla was sitting next to Brick at his bedside when he awakened.

"I called Be Be back," Verla answered the question in Brick's eyes. She finally told me what she suspected and what she had told you. I called Broke and told him that I had a bad feeling. So we used the address I got from Be Be to find you. We wasn't going to interfere. It wasn't until after you didn't come out for a while that Broke decided to go inside the house. Baby, I know I shouldn't have disobeyed you but I also knew that if I didn't I wouldn't see you again. Maybe that was selfish of me, thinking about my own loss, but I love you and I'll rather die beside you because I know I can't live after you. Not this time. Not after this love." Verla began to cry as Brick reached over and took her hand. He was too weak to speak but his eyes told Verla everything he wanted her to know. Everything he wanted her to hear. Verla knew how much Brick loved and appreciated her as he squeezed her hand in his.

***

The Feds arrived thirty minutes after Broke had left the house. The house was in flames. By the time the fire department could put it out the house was ashes. The agent in charge was furious. He knew the cop killer had struck again. The killer or killers were very thorough.

349

They were also determined and disciplined. Worst of all they were still free. Someone had tipped them off about the cop's location and pending arrest. The agent didn't know who, but he swore to find the party responsible if it was the last thing he done on earth.

CLEAN

Chapter 42

The men of P.A.P.A were all in attendance for the community gathering to give thanks to the people who made P.A.P.A work.

P.A.P.A's Thanks-For-Giving day had nothing to do with Pilgrims or Puritans except to show them as the hypocrites they were in history. The Thanks-For-Giving Day was celebrated on the Thanksgiving Holiday because the day was already set aside for black people to be off work. P.A.P.A didn't have any problems with being off on government holidays. After four hundred years of free labor in America, P.A.P.A felt that any off day was a day to be celebrated. The men of P.A.P.A just didn't celebrate the days in honor of why they were given. P.A.P.A celebrated American holidays in honor of its' own black heroes and heroines.

The men of P.A.P.A had established their own propaganda division. The propaganda department was headed by Henry (Glean) Guy. Henry or Clean as he was more commonly referred to by his friends was a student of the teachings of Marcus Garvey. The Honorable Marcus Garvey taught that all negative propaganda against black people had to be challenged and defeated. Henry also held to this opinion. This is what he taught the young men and women who attended his class.

Clean stood at the blackboard with his back to the thirty or more students who attended his evening class. He was writing slogans from the black power era on the blackboard as he continued speaking to the youth. The young men in his class were all paying close attention to Clean whom they all admired and respected.

"What are some of the greatest tools of the white propagandist today."

Clean turned and stared from face to face of the young toughs sitting on the gym bleachers.

"Come on brothers, we been through this already."

"The educational system, a young light skinned brother said."

"Good answer," Clean said. "The American educational system is nothing more than a propaganda machine. It's institutional propaganda that's being forced into the impressionable young minds of black children. Take your school text books for instance. These books are filled with images of supposedly great white men doing great white things. This is propaganda on the institutional level."

"Who discovered America?" Clean waited for an answer.

"Columbus," someone said.

"According to your history books," Clean said. "That's propaganda, how can a man discover something that was already there and never lost in the first place, and what about the people who were already here. Ben Franklin discovered electricity with a kite and a key, Abe Lincoln never told a lie or was it George Washington, no, I think it was George Washington who chopped down the cherry tree. Regardless of who done what, there's nothing that any of these men done that would qualify them before God as worthy. George Washington was a slave owner, Abe Lincoln said that blacks were not equal to whites and wanted to send blacks back to Africa, Thomas Jefferson also owned slaves, but in your history books, these are all great men. This is white supremacy propaganda. Despite the fact that the black Egyptians gave the world mathematics, science, agriculture, architecture, medicine and domestication of animals, in your school history books these people are never shown as black people. Egypt is not shown as being in Africa and every depiction you see of ancient Egyptians today are in the images of white people. The only mention of black people in your school history books are of black people as slaves in America or as alleged cannibals in Africa. This is propaganda

352

at the institutional level. Propaganda at the institutional level is used to establish in our minds the idea of white supremacy, and if we allow white supremacy to exist within our minds we also establish the concept within ourselves of black inferiority.

Clean paced the gym floor while slapping the palm of his left hand with the ruler he held in his right hand.

"White propaganda is the overpriced artwork you see being sold for millions of dollars that were created or designed by deranged white men who were not respected during their own times but now being taught to you as being geniuses. As geniuses today, their artwork and sculptures are being sold for millions of dollars for the benefit of establishing white art as the highest form of art. The Queen of England is kept on her throne to show a white monarch and to validate the lies you read about in your history books of great white kings and queens. Such fabled myths as King Author and his so-called Knights of the Roundtable, Robin Hood, and others. It's all propaganda," Clean said, "and it must be defeated."

"Propaganda is the greatest tools of war. And believe me young brothers, we're at war. This war is the war of the races. And you must choose sides. As young black men when you don't choose to side with your people, you have in fact chosen to side with your enemy. You then become the propaganda they use to destroy our nation."

"How so?" Clean stared hard at the boys, "how are you used in this war of propaganda?"

Clean singled out several boys, "Richard, Pete, J.J, nobody knows huh. Look around you at the men sitting next to you, when you go home today, look around your communities. The way we live and act are the greatest form of propaganda to support the alleged inferiority of black people in the world today. Our inferior conditions and stereotypical behavior as thugs and drug dealers make it easy for the white propagandist to suggest that we are what the images suggest, uncivilized and backwards people. Let us remember that we are in a race war. Let us remember that white people first brought us here as slaves in chains. Let us remember that we were labeled as beasts of burden. Let us not forget that our women were raped and our people were hung to establish white supremacy here in America. Let us not forget that our people of Africa were labeled as savages and cannibals and that Africa was raped of its' resources to establish white supremacy around the world."

Clean took a seat as he continued speaking. "The condition of our people around the world is used to continue the lie of white supremacy by showing our people in inferior conditions. These conditions are used by the propagandist to excite white people. The propagandist uses these images to keep white people in constant fear of the big black beast killing them in their sleep. This fear of the black man as told by Sister Francis Cress Welsing, in her book the Isis Papers, is because the white man knows that the black man can breed him out of existence. That's because our genes are stronger and anytime the two races mix the offspring from this mixing will be a black child. If we as black and whites were allowed to mix freely in America, the end result would be an all black or Arab looking people. The white propagandist knows this and it's his job to insure that the mixing of races never happens. That's why the white supremacist uses propaganda to keep the races fighting amongst one another. It's all about his survival. When we live down to the low-expectations of the propagandist, we help him in his cause.

Clean stood again as he begin to speak more fervently. "As black boys in the stereotypical images of thugs and gangbangers the propagandist uses your images against you. He criminalizes your images so that when you are arrested and brought before white jurors, these jurors are quick to convict you in kangaroo courts of law. You are then sentenced as thugs to unjust prison sentences. As young black men in prison, the propagandist will no longer have to worry about you producing little black babies who will compete with his little white children for future rule of the world. With you in jail or dead, the propagandist has accomplished his objective. He has stopped you from reproducing. He has controlled the growth of the black population."

"With you neutralized he now concentrates on your woman. By destroying the black male, the black woman and child must then turn to him the white man for assistance. In efforts to paint himself as a loving and caring person, he gives her a house in the projects. He provides her with food. He mis-educate her and her child. This reinforces within his own mind that he is a good person and that black people are an inferior species who he must attend to as the white man's burden."

"So young brothers, do you see now how propaganda is used in the world around you. Propaganda is used in every war to raise the morale of one group and to hopefully lower the morale of the opposition. I need you to be aware of how propaganda works. Study the TV shows you love to watch so much. Study the news, but most importantly young brothers, study thyself. Our greatest weapon against the propaganda machines of America is the weapon of change. We must change ourselves and our inferior conditions. By doing this we take away the things, our enemy uses to justify the mistreatment of our people in America and around the world. So brothers in closing, I say to you, if you really want to be in a gang, join the gain called black people. If you really want to fight, fight as a soldier in the race war that's been waging for hundreds of years. I'm not impressed because you can pull a trigger and kill each other. The propagandist we face has killed millions by effective use of propaganda that incites us to kill ourselves."

Clean held up his fist in a black power salute, get-em up" he said. All the young men threw up the black power salute. "I thank you brothers for coming and I want you young brothers to remember that the future of black people tomorrow will depend on your actions today. Next week we'll address the N-Word and its' use as a form of propaganda."

Clean was tidying up his papers when Doretha walked into the gym. He threw up his hand in a form of wave greeting. Doretha waved back at him as she stood waiting for her son. Eddie Jr., jumped off the bleachers and said bye to the five or more boys who were still sitting with him. "Bye, Mr. Guy," he said as he rushed cross the floor to where his mother was standing. The two of them walked out together after waving a final goodbye to Clean as they left the building.

Doretha was glad that Eddie Jr., who was the spitting image of his father and who also had his father's temper, had someone like Mr. Guy to mentor him and to help channel some of his aggression. Doretha was having a hard time trying to juggle her career as a registered nurse and keep Eddie Jr., out of trouble. Her live in boyfriend was of little or no help. As a matter of fact, he was also part of the problem. He was also the reason for Doretha's recent hair and weight loss. That's why Doretha wore the scarf around her head. At thirty-five with strong African features, Doretha was still a very attractive woman. Because of her wide nose, full lips and sable dark skin, many people mistook her for being from Africa. Doretha could still remember growing up as a child when the word ugly was most commonly used to describe her features. Nappy head, black and ugly were words she still despised today.

***

Eddie Jr., who was thirteen was still talking excitedly. He had been talking since they first entered the car. "Look Mama," Eddie Jr. said as he held up a necklace. The necklace was made of a black leather strap with a leather medallion that read: Black Is Still Beautiful. "Mr. Guy, say this is propaganda," Eddie Jr. said. "He gave all of us a necklace. This is what mine's say."

"That's nice," Doretha held the medallion part of the necklace in her hand and read it aloud.

"This yours," Eddie Jr. said as he held out another similar styled necklace to Doretha.

Doretha read the inscription on the necklace. "A Nation Can Rise No Higher Than Its Women." Beneath the quote was the name Elijah Muhammad.

"Hmmph," Doretha said after she finished reading the inscription. "I know that's right. Tell Mr. Guy I said thanks." Doretha hung the necklace around her neck.

***

Doretha's live-in boyfriend, Eric, was hanging up the telephone when Doretha and Eddie, Jr. entered the house. Good, he was thinking to himself. This bitch finally back, now I can go and meet this little freak, Belinda. Belinda was interning as a registered nurse at the hospital where Doretha worked. She had been coming on to Eric every since he had first met her at the hospital.

Eric was light-skinned and tall. He loved to dress and was a notorious womanizer. Eric had been a player back in his younger days when light-skin and so-called good hair was still the standard of beauty. His college days had been spent breaking both the hearts and bank accounts of young women of all ethnic groups. Now, at forty-seven years of age, slightly overweight, without the so-called good hair and the drop in value of light-skinned men, Eric was not the man he used to be. He now depended on his dress and charm to win him the hearts of women. Eric always joked that Wesley Snipes, when he stabbed Christopher Williams in the hand in the movie New Jack City, and called him a pretty motherfucker, had taken away his shine as a light-skin brother. As a former Disc Jockey, and now present day Program Manager for the local 1340 AM Radio Station, Eric still had many women in pursuit of him thanks to his position and charm.

Doretha was Eric's cash-cow. She had come at a time when he was deep in debt and about to be kicked out of his apartment. Being the conniving womanizer that he was, it hadn't taken Eric long to spot the vulnerability of Doretha. At the time, Doretha was raising her eight-year-old son alone after losing her man to prison, Eric met her during a Just Say No benefit concert that his radio station was sponsoring to raise awareness about the dangers of drugs.

Eric was introduced to Doretha by the mother of one of Eddie Jr's friends. That was five years and hundreds of lies ago. Eric, who had a preference for light-skinned women, was not really attracted to Doretha. The biggest benefit of him being with her was that Doretha was financially secure as a Registered Nurse. Doretha's salary as an RN was double the measly salary of Eric's as a Program Director for an AM radio station.

Eric found that Doretha was also a gold mine when it came to meeting other women. He had met more women by being around Doretha during hospital functions than he had met during most of his years of D-jaying. It was at the hospital's Halloween party that Eric had met the petite, light-skinned girl named Belinda who he was going and visit.

Eric kissed Doretha on her cheek after greeting her at the door. "What's up little man," he said to Eddie Jr. "What's that on your neck?"

It's a medallion," Eddie Jr. said excitedly. "Mr. Guy gave it to me." Eddie Jr. held the necklace up for Eric to see and for him to read the words written on the medallion.

"Yea, that's cool," Eric said before turning to Doretha. "I see you got one too." Eric held the medallion portion of Doretha's necklace in his hand and read the inscription aloud. "Hmmph," he said. "Elijah Muhammad, ain't that the one called himself the prophet of them black Muslims." Eric said the words without interest as he turned to leave without waiting for a reply from Doretha.

"Where you going?" Doretha asked.

"I got to run-off to the station for a minute," Eric said.

Eric was out the door before Doretha could say anything else in response.

***

It took longer for Eric to reach Belinda's house than it did for him to

358

finish his business with her inside the house. The fifteen-minute ride getting to her apartment was ten minutes longer than the ride between her legs. Eric rolled over exhaustedly as the twenty-year-old woman stared at him disappointedly.

"I know you didn't," Belinda snapped. She was still in the heat of passion and couldn't believe that Eric had finished. Belinda cussed Eric and asked him was he serious.

"About what," Eric asked.

"About being finished." Belinda had an angry look on her face.

"Yea baby, I told you I got to get back home," Eric said.

Belinda was still fuming when she walked Eric to the door ten minutes later after he had washed up and dressed.

"I'll see you tomorrow." Eric said.

"Naw, you won't, as a matter of fact. You can forget this address, you gon' stay home and take care of your business." Belinda slammed the door in Eric's face after mumbling something dissatisfactory about his sexual performance.

"Eric smiled to himself as he walked away with a contented look on his face. "Bitch got to learn to get her's first," he said to himself with a chuckle.

***

Doretha sat on her bed staring at a picture in her hands of Eddie Jr's father. Eddie Sr. was a strong, chiseled face black man. The picture that had been taken two weeks after Eddie Jr. was born. He held Eddie Jr. in his hand as he smiled from ear to ear. It was approximately one year later that Eddie Sr. had been killed after being stopped on a routine traffic stop that had escalated into a police officer also being shot and killed.

Witnesses to the shooting had testified that the cops were roughing up Eddie Sr. because he had questioned them about the routine stop. One of the cops had called Eddie Sr. a nigger after forcing Eddie Sr.'s head down on the hood of the car. The quick temper of Eddie Sr., and his despise of the word nigger, had made him use his great strength to fling the cop who was pushing his head down on the hood of the car to the ground.

The cop had reacted by pulling his gun as he landed on his back. The cop fired a round from his gun that struck Eddie Sr. who stood over him with a menacing look on his face. Eddie Sr. charged the cop on the ground after being shot and had managed to take away the cop's gun. He stood holding the gun on the fallen cop when the second cop who had come up from behind Eddie Sr., shot him in the back.

Being shot in the back caused Eddie Sr.'s finger to jerk the trigger of the gun in his hand and he accidently shot the cop on the ground in the head. Eddie Sr. was shot six times by the second cop after firing, the fatal shot into the first cop.

Thanks to his conditioning, Eddie Sr. would survive the gunshot wounds. If not for eyewitnesses who testified in his behalf, Eddie Sr. would have received the death penalty for his crime. Instead, because of eyewitnesses and circumstances surrounding the case, Eddie Sr., escaped the death penalty and was sentenced to life in prison.

In a strange twist of fate, because of blood loss from his gunshot wounds, Eddie Sr., had technically received the death penalty when he was given an A.I.D.S tainted blood transfusion by the hospital.

Doretha was certain that the hospital had purposely given Eddie Sr., the tainted blood. Eddie Sr. married Doretha in prison. He wanted her to be the beneficiary to whatever claims he was awarded in his negligence lawsuit against the hospital.

After seven years of wrangling, the hospital settled out of court with Doretha for two million dollars. Eddie Sr., was killed in prison a year later. He was killed by another inmate after Eddie Sr. allegedly tried to rape a female prison guard.

Michael Rogers

Chapter 43

Brick stared after Clean as Clean drove away from P.A.P.A. Brick had a smile on his face as he thought about Clean and how they met. It didn't seem like Clean had aged a day since they first met in prison years ago. Clean had been tried and convicted as an accessory in the murder of two bank tellers and had been facing life in prison without the possibility of parole at the time. Because Clean had been the driver and never entered the bank, he had been spared the death penalty that his two co-defendants had received. Clean had already served seven years of his prison sentence, before Brick was incarcerated. Clean had spent his first five years at Tucker Maximum security prison. He was then shipped to Cummins prison where he had been for two years before Brick's arrival. Clean was Brick's first cellmate. It was Clean who had taken Brick under his wings upon Brick's arrival. Clean had helped Brick adjust to prison during his first year. He shared with him his books on the black experience and taught him all that he knew on the subject. Brick moved out of Clean's cell to have his own cell a year later. Eddie Sr. became Clean's cellmate after Brick.

Brick, Clean, and Broke were the only people outside of the female officer and Cream, that knew what really happen during the alleged rape attempt of the female officer by Eddie Sr. The whole thing was setup by Eddie Sr., to help free Clean from prison.

Eddie Sr., knew that he was dying and that he wouldn't last another year in prison.

Eddie Sr., who had been watching Clean as his cellmate had seen qualities in Clean that, he liked. As a standup man himself, Eddie Sr. saw a lot of himself in Clean. It was for this reason that he wanted to give Clean a second chance at life.

Eddie Sr., told Brick about his plans. Brick was skeptical about the success of the plans but had agreed to help Eddie Sr. Brick enlisted Cream and Broke to help. He knew that Cream had several female officers on his payroll. He also knew that Broke was a thinker and could help him in the planning of what Eddie Sr. had suggested. Cream used a girl name Earline to help them with their plans.

The plan was for Earline to place herself in a compromising position while performing her official duty. Eddie Sr., had then snatched the screaming Earline around the neck and placed a knife to her throat as he drug her off to a secluded area. The area he drug her into was an enclosed area where Clean was working. The other cops all came running to assist the screaming Earline only to find that they had been barricaded out the room by Eddie Sr. Clean, who had been cleaning out a room in back of the area had come to Earline's assistance when he heard her screaming.

Clean ran and pulled Eddie Sr., off the screaming woman. Eddie Sr., had his pants around his ankles and was positioning himself to enter Earline when Clean dove on him.

Clean and Eddie Sr., struggled over the knife in Eddie Sr.'s hand. Eddie Sr., waited until the other officers had broken through the barricade and ran into the room before faking a fall and falling on his own knife.

Earline was naked and still screaming hysterically as the cops covered her body and rushed her out the room. Clean was thrown to the floor and roughly handcuffed as Eddie Sr., lay dying in his own blood on the floor next to him. "Goodbye old friend." Clean whispered to Eddie Sr., as the cops snatched him up in handcuffs and carried him out the room.

Thanks to Earline's testimony and her showing of gratitude for Clean's unselfish act to save her life, Clean had had his sentence reduced from life without parole to life in prison. Under Arkansas's rules of parole, Clean was made eligible for parole after serving a minimum of fifteen years of his sentence. After finishing his fifteen year sentence, Clean was granted parole by the parole board thanks to letters of recommendation to the parole board from Earline and other officials. Clean was released from prison six months after Brick.

Earline was also compensated in a negligence lawsuit. She received two hundred thousand dollars in a settlement and was promoted to a lifetime job on the administrative level with the Arkansas Dept. of Correction. Earline was now a contributing member to P.A.P.A'S sister organization called M.A.M.A.

Henry (Clean) Guy reported to P.A.P.A upon his release. The debt he owed Eddie Sr., was one of life. He swore he would repay this debt even if it took his life. Eddie Sr., had asked Clean to look after Doretha and Eddie Jr. He told Clean that Doretha was a good woman who deserved a righteous brother. He told him that he wanted his son to be raised in the knowledge of self. This was all he asked of Clean.

Clean first met Doretha once when she had come to pickup Eddie Jr., from P.A.P.A. Doretha knew about Clean's involvement in the death of Eddie Sr., but she didn't know that the death was staged. Doretha felt that Clean's unselfish act to save a black woman from being rape was done more so out of love and respect for the black woman than for any hate that he may have had for Eddie Sr.

There was something about Clean that Doretha admired. Clean was not handsome in the traditional sense. He looked more like Booker T. Washington than Denzel Washington. Neither did Clean have the traditional ex-con physique that ex-con's developed from years of weight pile workouts. Clean was as his name suggested, "Clean". Clean was always starched and pressed. He carried himself with pride and dignity and was always polite. Clean had an aura or self-assurance that made him look more handsome than his physical features. Behind it all was an intelligent and deadly man who had sworn his allegiance to Brick and the P.A.P.A. organization.

Michael Rogers

Chapter 44

Eddie Jr., stood ready to fight as three members of the Baby Killers jumped out a car. The Baby Killers were one of the fastest growing gangs in the Pine Bluff area. It had been formed by a local tough who went by the name of Baby G. All the gang members used the word Baby followed by their first initial as their street name. If two or more members had the same first initial, they would then follow their initial with a number beginning with one and counting upward based on their entry into the gang.

Eddie Jr., was visiting his cousin Pearl who still lived in the old neighborhood where he had grown up. Doretha had moved out the neighborhood after receiving her settlement. Doretha had offered to buy her oldest sister Delois a home in the affluent neighborhood where she lived. Delois had refused to move. Eddie Jr., was walking from the store with Delois' daughter Pearl when a carload of boys begin to whistle at Pearl from the car as the car had cruised slowly beside them. Delois and Doretha were sitting on Delois' porch watching when the boys had all bolted from the car and surrounded Eddie Jr., and Pearl.

"Bitch, you hear me calling you." A fat crooked hat-wearing boy got in Pearl's face. Pearl knew the boy as Greg who lived in the neighborhood. Greg went by the name of Baby 3G since joining the Baby Killer gang. Greg had added more swagger to his walk and had become more disrespectful because of his gang status.

Greg had recently been released from prison for shooting a man two years earlier. Eddie Jr. was five years younger than Greg. The two of them use to play together as neighbors in the old neighborhood when they were younger.

"Chill out Greg," Eddie Jr., said.

"What, Lil' Nigga, who you telling to chill." Greg had a scowl on his face as he glared hard at Eddie Jr.

"Don't call me nigga," Eddie Jr., said as he remembered the speech that Clean had given them at P.A.P.A., the night before.

"Nigga, I'll call you whatever the fuck I want." Greg was about to say something else before the words were stuffed back into his mouth by the fist of Eddie Jr. The sudden blow to the nose startled the larger boy as he stared in surprised shock at Eddie Jr. The other boys also starred in shock surprise.

Greg quickly recovered from the blow and cussed loudly as he began to swing wildly at Eddie Jr. Eddie Jr., was fighting back along with Pearl as they stood up to Greg and the other boys who had all join Greg when he begin to swing at Eddie Jr. Eddie Jr. and Pearl held their own against the boys until Doretha and Delois ran up to the scene.

Delois who was big and stout snatched Pearl away from the fight and pulled Pearl behind her. Doretha struggled with the boys before managing to pull Eddie Jr. away as well.

"Stop this shit!" Delois screamed as she tried to keep the boys away who were still trying to get at Pearl and Greg. Delois was calling Greg by his name as she shuffled her big body between him and Eddie Jr., while continually pushing him away.

"Stop Greg! I mean stop, got dammit! What the hell wrong with y'all?"

A small crowd of people had gathered in support of Delois who was well liked and respected in the neighborhood. Delois finally manage to stop the fighting and stood breathing hard before the boys.

"I'm-a kill that Lil' nigger." Greg said.

"Boy, gon' home, you ain't gon' do nothing," Delois said.

"You watch bitch, I bet I be back," Greg angrily said.

"Lil' punk, who you calling bitch." Doretha and Pearl had to hold Delois back as she tried to get to Greg.

"Watch bitch, I bet I be back," Greg said as he and his crew loaded into the car.

One of the boys leaned out the passenger side window of the car and threw gang signs with his hands. "This BK bitch," he said. "We'll be back."

"What y'all out here fighting for," Delois was still breathing hard as she asked the question of Pearl and Eddie Jr.

"We were walking back from the store when Greg n' em pulled up behind us talking crazy. Greg was trying to show out on somebody, calling me bitches and ho's." Pearl was recounting the story as the four of them walked towards Delois' house. "Eddie Jr., told Greg to chill out and Greg called him a nigga and they start fighting. That's when them other boys start hitting Eddie Jr., and I start helping him."

Doretha was still shaking as she called Eric and told him what had happen. Eric told her to call the police when Doretha asked him to come over to Delois' house. Eric claimed that he was working on a program for the radio station. He said he couldn't come because he had to finish the project and would see them when they got home.

"Boy I'm not leaving my sister," Doretha almost screamed into the phone. "What if they come back?" She asked.

"Take her with you," Eric suggested.

Doretha knew that Delois wasn't going to leave her home. Neither would Doretha leave Delois alone in case the young gangbangers returned. Doretha wished now, more than ever that she could get Delois to leave the old neighborhood and move closer to her.

Eric hung up the phone with Doretha as the radio station secretary resumed her position on her knees between his legs. He was not about to leave the station and miss out on the skills of Juicy Jaws. He was also scared to death of the young thugs who were involved in gang activity. Eric had seen up close and personal, the ignorance of these thugs. He had been run off from a woman's house he was dating by her young gang banging son and his friends. The boys had shot up his car when he had said something that one of them didn't like. This incident prompted him to do a radio show on gang activity in the Pine Bluff area. The show featured two rival gangs in a dialogue session about the possibility of a truce between the gangs. The show ended in violence when a fight broke out and one of the boys was stabbed during the altercation. That had been enough for Eric. He wanted nothing else to do with gangs. He hoped the police locked up all the little gangster bastards. Eric gave no further thought to Doretha or gangs as he laid back in his chair with Juicy Jaws between his legs.

Chapter 45

Doretha sat with Delois and their two children in Delois kitchen. The kitchen was located at the back of the old family home. The house was not much different than Doretha remembered it as a child. Doretha stared out the back window at the levy that ran behind the house. Her and Doretha had walked many miles up and down the levy that ran for two miles to the north of the old neighborhood. The levy separated the neighborhood from a lake that ran the length of the neighbor hood and on down to the Port of Pine Bluff. The neighborhood known as Potlitka had not changed much over the years. The houses were not as pretty as Doretha remembered, but the memories that each house brought to mind would last forever. Each house had its' own story to tell. These were the homes of old friends who Doretha and Delois use to visit as children. Potlitka was a small neighborhood. It was only six blocks long and three blocks wide. A small beer tavern and liquor store were the only business outlets in the neighborhood. There use to be a neighborhood grocery store but it was closed down after the owner was knocked over the head and robbed. Mr. Bill, as Doretha remembered him, had been a fixture in the community for over thirty years.

Mr. Bill was the first victim of a new mentality that swept through Potlitka during the eighties. This mentality was one of drugs and gang violence that erupted like a plague on the once quiet and peaceful community. These elements arrived at a time when the elders of the community who once held the community together were dying off. The children of these elders, had now, either took over the family homes like Doretha, or sold off the property to people outside of the community.

Without the glue of the elders or the cohesiveness of old friends, Potlitka had fallen victim to drugs as crack cocaine emerged on the scene. The once quiet and peaceful community was now a rundown community that was filled with the same social ills as larger communities all over America. What had started off as local youngsters making a few extra dollars off the misery of Potlitka addicts, had quickly evolved into a wide open market that now drew addicts, dealers, and gangsters from all over Pine Bluff. The small beer tavern called the Sunset Strip was now one of the hottest clubs in Pine Bluff from Thursday's through Saturday's.

Doretha's parents had died in the nineties. Delois was the last of a dying breed of Potlitka faithful who refused to leave what Doretha called their tribal land. Of all the holdouts, Delois was one of the few who was not hooked on alcohol from hanging around the neighborhood liquor store or addicted to drugs after becoming addicted during the craze of crack cocaine.

Eddie Jr., handed Doretha back her cell phone after she had allowed him to use it to make a call. He could see the fear in his mother's eyes. It was like they were being held hostage in his aunt Delois' house because his aunt refused to leave. When Doetha had suggested that they call the cops, Delois had told them there was no reason. As a woman of faith, her Bible was her weapon. She said she wasn't afraid of idle threats and wan' no young hoodlums gon' make her leave her home.

Chapter 46

Eddie Jr., wished his aunt's bible had a gun hidden in it when Pearl suddenly screamed and come running through the house. "Mama! Mama! Lock the doors! They coming! They coming from over the levy!"

Pearl ran frantically through the house checking windows and doors to insure they were locked. Doretha looked up in fright as she saw ten or more boys creeping across the levy behind the house with bandannas across their faces. The boys had guns in their hands as they creped over the levy as if they were hunters who were stalking a prey.

"Call the police! Call the police!" Delois screamed at Pearl who stood shaking like a leaf.

"Now she wants to call the police," Doretha thought as she grabbed Eddie Jr., by the arm and pulled him into the interior of the house.

They were all cowered on the floor besides the bed in Delois' bedroom as Pearl called 911 and asked for assistance. Pearl was still on the phone when the first of the shots ranged out.

"Pow! Pow! Pow! Pow!" Gunshots resounded off the house as Eddie Jr., tried to cover the women with his body beside the bed.

"Pow! Pow! Pow! Pow! "The women shouted with each gunshot as they all begin to cry and pray to God for their safety.

The gunshots finally ceased to the sounds of screeching tires, running feet and the sounds of men voices. It wasn't long before the sounds of running feet and someone shouting out orders were the only sounds that could be heard coming from outside of the house.

"That's P.A.P.A.!" Eddie Jr. said excitedly as he jumped up off the women.

Doretha at first thought Eddie Jr. was speaking about his dead father.

"That's P.A.P.A.!" Eddie Jr., said again. "I called the hotline number!"

"Boy, get back here!" Doretha screamed after Eddie Jr., as he bolted out the room.

Doretha ran after Eddie Jr., who ran into the living room and unlocked the front door.

"Boy, don't open that door!" Doretha was screaming as Eddie Jr., flung open the door.

Eddie Jr., burst out the door with Doretha screaming at him. Doretha followed Eddie Jr., outside to the sight of Clean, Brick and Broke giving orders to twenty or more men. The men were in foot pursuit of the boys who were now running with their guns stuck in their waists while trying to escape the angry black men.

Brick and Broke were furious as they stared at the damage the bullets had done to Doretha's house. Clean was so angry that the vein across his forehead looked like a vine running across his face. Clean hugged Eddie Jr., like Eddie Jr., was his long lost son before walking over to Doretha to see if she was all right. The veins on his forehead was still thick across his brow as he listened to Doretha explain what had happen.

Poky walked up on the porch of the house as Delois and Pearl exited the house. Poky stared affectionately at the big boned Delois. Delois was still shaking as she hugged Pearl in her arms.

The cops arrived a few minutes later after everything was back under control. The men of P.A.P.A were positioned on every corner of the neighborhood and along the levy. They were now fifty strong in number. The first cops on the scene had called for more backup after seeing the men of P.A.P.A.

"Who are all these men?" One of the cops asked.

"We're the neighborhood watch," Clean said.

"What you gon' do bout' them shooting up my house," Delois pointed to the numerous bullet holes in the house walls.

The cop who had spoken, inspected the holes, and asked Delois if she knew who had fired the shots.

"It was them damn Baby Killers," Delois shouted.

"Do you know any of them by name?" The cops were looking around Delois' house as if they suspected she was selling drugs or involved in some other kind of criminal activity.

"Why are you searching my things? Get out my house!" Delois ran two of the cops out her house who were looking through her personal property.

"Ma'am, why were these men shooting at your house?" the cop who seemed to be in charged asked Delois.

"I don't know." Delois said angrily. Delois didn't want to mention the earlier altercation between Eddie Jr. and the boys.

A detective soon arrived on the scene. The detective seemed more concerned about the black men standing on the comers and levy than he was with the men who had shot up Delois' house.

"Who are these men?" he asked as he stared around.

"Neighborhood watch," Poky mockingly replied.

"Who are you?" the cop asked Poky.

"I'm here to see 'bout my friend," Poky said.

The cop walked out the house to his car and got on his radio to call for more assistance.

Broke signaled to Brick who was on the corner. Brick spoke into his walkie-talkie and when the detective emerged back from his car, the men of P.A.P.A had all disappeared with exception of Clean and Poky.

"Where did they go?" The detective asked one of the uniformed cops who were standing around one of the many police cars now surrounding Delois' house.

"I don't know," the cop said. "They were there a second ago."

The cops left after getting no help from Delois, who felt like she was being treated more like a suspect than victim.

The detective left Delois' house with one thought on his mind. He was wondering and determined to find out, what organized force of disciplined black men could arrive at the scene of a distress call in such large numbers, before the first officers arrived.

This was a question he was sure to answer.

Clean and Poky sat with Delois and Doretha for over an hour. Despite Doretha's pleading and the encouragement of Clean, Delois still refused to leave her home.

"It ain't right for a woman to be forced to leave her home by a group of young thugs," Poky said. "These young men don't have no respect today. If Ms. Delois don't want to leave her house, she shouldn't have to leave, and we shouldn't ask her to leave. I've guarded stuff for the government as a soldier that was far less valuable than a mother and child. I'll see to Ms. Delois and her child being safe. That's if she don't mind me camping out on her porch tonight."

"That'll be all right," Delois said. "I can't ask you to do that, I wouldn't want to keep you away from your family."

"The only family I got is my brother Sleepy," Poky said. "Believe me, camping out on your porch will be a welcome relief from his ol' stinky feet."

Delois agreed to allow Poky to protect her. She told him that he didn't have to sleep on the porch but could use a couch she had in her den.

Pearl snickered along with Eddie Jr. who nudged her in her side. It was obvious to everyone that Delois and Poky had a mutual attraction for one another.

"Well, I better be going," Clean said as he stood off the couch.

Doretha also stood and said that her and Eddie Jr. had to be going as well.

Eddie Jr. asked if Pearl could spend the night at their house. Delois said that would probably be best in case the boys did return.

Clean walked Doretha to her car. He shut the car door behind her and stood back as she seated herself behind the steering wheel of the car.

"Thanks for everything," Doretha said. "I've never been so scared in my life."

"That's understandable," Clean said. "I'm just glad we got here in time."

"Speaking of getting here in time, how did you arrive so fast? Doretha was staring up at Clean out the driver side window.

"Well," Clean said. When Eddie Jr., made the distress call to P.A.P.A's hotline, Brick and I were already in the downtown area. As for the other men, they' re always on duty like firemen. They're ready to drop whatever they're doing and report to the scene whenever the distress signal goes out. Being that so many brothers responded, I guess they were all in the area."

"Well, I'm glad they were, and thank you again," Doretha said as she started her car.

***

Clean drove over to the East End division of one of P.A.P.A.'s headquarters that was housed in one of Cream's sub stations for his cab company. Cream had six mini- stations for his cabs throughout the city. The mini-stations were set up to help his cabs reach any locations in the least possible time. The substations were created to cut down on gas, wear and tear of cabs and faster pickup. Whenever drivers dropped off a customer and their car became empty, the cab drivers would wait for their next call at the nearest substation to where their cars became free of passengers. The mini-stations were also headquarters for P.A.P.A. men on duty.

P.A.P.A kept five men on duty at each station at all time. This allowed P.A.P.A. to assist those that supported P.A.P.A whenever they needed assistance. The men traveled in cabs that were purchased by P.A.P.A. for their use. The cabs were outfitted with radios and placed under the auspices of Cream's cab company.

P.A.P.A. was growing fast as an organization. It now included a women's division that was headed by Michelle, Verla, Angie and Sherry. This division was called Minority Assistance and Management Agency (M.A.M.A.). The goals of M.A.M.A. were to assist black women in finding jobs, men, and getting government assistance. The women of M.A.M.A., acted as mentors to young black girls. M.A.M.A. believed and taught that it was black women who determined the fate of black people. M.A.M.A. taught that before black men would change that black women had to demand the change. With Verla as its leader, the women of M.A.M.A. were just as determined as the men of P.A.P.A. and sometimes more sinister.

Doretha was impressed with Clean and the men of P.A.P.A. She

378

questioned Eddie Jr., more about the organization on the ride home. Eddie Jr.'s eyes lit up as he explained to Doretha what he knew about P.A.P.A. He was especially excited when he spoke of Clean and the class Clean taught at P.A.P.A.

Michael Rogers

Chapter 47

Eric was sitting on the couch in his robe watching television when Doretha and the children walked into the house. He placed a spoon of ice cream in his mouth as he stared up at Doretha from the couch.

"Y'all all right?" Eric asked the question nonchalantly as he ate another spoon filled with ice cream. Doretha walked past Eric without speaking. Eddie Jr., and Pearl both bolted for Eddie Jr.'s room.

"Like you give a damn," Doretha angrily threw her keys on a table. The sight of Eric sitting snug and comfortable while watching television and eating ice cream on her couch had driven Doretha's temper to the boiling point. The nerve of this two timing bastard, Doretha was thinking. Here me and my son being shot at by gang bangers and he sitting his ass at home eating ice cream. That's it, she said to herself.

Doretha was not the fool Eric thought she was. She always knew about his infidelity and lying ways. She had tolerated it because she had bought into the myth of there being few good black men. After witnessing what she had witness today, Doretha knew the myth was a lie. Seeing those strong black men take charge of their community had excited something in her for the first time since Eddie Sr. had went to jail. She also saw how impressed Eddie Jr., was when he spoke of the men of P.A.P.A. Eddie Jr., never spoke highly of Eric. He would only say that Eric was cool. Even then he never said Eric was cool in the way that suggested that he liked him. It was more in a way of saying that if Doretha was happy then he was happy.

"What you mean I don't give a damn," Eric said. "What the hell could I do?"

"You could've cared instead of sitting here stuffing your damn face with ice cream. You could've called to see if everything was all right."

"Call for what, woman, I knew you was blowing everything out of proportion.."

"Out of proportion!" Doretha almost screamed the words. "I guess you think gangbangers shooting up my sister's house while we lay crying beside the bed is out of proportion! The only thing out of proportion around here is us. I want you out of here tomorrow." Doretha stared angrily at Eric as he sat with a dumbfounded look on his face.

"Woman, stop tripping," Eric said. "How the hell I know them Lil' punks were going to shoot up your sister's house." Eric had raised up off the couch and followed Doretha into the bedroom.

"It's not just that." Doretha said with quiet anger. "I'm tired of people calling my house all time of night and hanging up in my face. I'm tired of you lying to me and coming in here smelling like some other woman. I ain't no fool. Don't forget, I wash your clothes. I know what dried secretion look like. I am a nurse."

"Baby stop tripping and let's talk," Eric was whining as he tried to charm Doretha.

"I'm through talking," Doretha said. "It's been over a long time. I'm just making it official. You can save the charm for the little hot intern who's running around the hospital talking about you and her. Better yet, save it for Juicy Jaws down at the station who I heard you bragging about to one of your Lil' DJ friends on the phone. I want you out tomorrow. I mean it."

Doretha snatched some nightclothes out her dresser drawer and stormed out the bedroom. Eric stared after Doretha with his mouth open. Doretha had never looked so beautiful to him. What he saw tonight as he looked at Doretha was not the dark skinned woman who he took for granted but the big house, fancy car, expensive clothes and everything else she done for him disappearing into thin air. Eric hoped that Doretha would calm down so he could talk some sense into her.

He had no place to go if she carried out her threats to put him out.

Doretha was up early the next morning fixing breakfast. She was dressed in jeans and t-shirt when Eric walked into the kitchen. Eric at first thought that he had been given a reprieve. That is until he saw his bags packed by the living room door. Doretha was like a stranger to him. She asked him if he wanted breakfast as she poured some juice in Eddie Jr.'s glass.

"Naw, I'm cool," Eric said coolly. He was grateful when Doretha handed him a thousand dollar check. He only had a couple of hundred in his checking account. Eric loaded his things in his old car that he hadn't driven in months. He had to boost the battery to get the car started. The tags had expired on the car since he drove it last. With the luck Eric was having, he was not surprised when a cop pulled him over two blocks from the house and gave him a ticket for expired tags. Eric drove over to a friend's house name Melvin. Melvin agreed to let Eric live with him until he got back on his feet.

***

"Man, I can't believe you let all that money get away," Melvin said as Eric unpacked.

"Shit man, you know me," Eric said. "I got ho's making way more money than a nurse. Shit, nurses come a dime a dozen. I got this little intern name Belinda that's about to be a nurse."

"Shit man, I'm not talking 'bout no nurse." Melvin walked into the room and sat on the bed. He laughed when he realized that Eric didn't know how much Doretha was truly worth. "I'm talking about that two million dollar settlement homegirl got from that lawsuit she won against the hospital."

"What settlement Eric asked?"

Melvin laughed in Eric's face as he called him a clown before telling him about Doretha and the lawsuit she had won against the hospital.

***

Doretha was laughing to herself as she hung up the telephone. She was laughing at Eric who had just called her. Eric had at first begged her to take him back before ranting and raving about Doretha not being honest with him concerning her wealth.

"You got two million dollars and you give me a funky ass thousand dollar check after all I've done for you."

Doretha couldn't help but laugh when Eric had said that they had a common law marriage and that he was entitled to some of her wealth. He told her that he was entitled to alimony and that he would see her in court. "You can have your little funky ass thousand dollars," Eric had said.

"Well, if that's how you feel, I'll call the bank and have them stop the check, and I'll see you in court," Doretha said.

"Payback's a mother," was the last thing Eric had said before hanging up the phone.

Doretha was still laughing when Eddie Jr., called her into the living room where him and Pearl were watching television. The urgency in his voice caused her to hurry.

"What is it Eddie Jr.," Doretha asked as she walked into the room.

"Look." Eddie Jr., said.

Doretha turned her attention to the television where Eddie Jr., was pointing. Two reporters were reporting the news in front of a burning house. The reporters were reporting that the burning house belonged to a local gang member by the name of Greg Long. Greg Long was the leader of the Baby Killer gang. The house was reported as being a popular hangout for gang members. The reporter said that the house had been shot up and burned the night before. Three gang members had been shot and Greg Long had been reported kidnapped by his fellow gang members.

According to the police, Greg Long had been kidnapped by men in hoods who had stormed into the house and shot his fellow gang members. The men had then sat the house on fire before disappearing into the night with Baby G.

Doretha couldn't help but wonder if the men of P.A.P.A were responsible for the kidnapping and arson. She wondered if Clean was all right and if he had anything to do with the shooting of the gang members.

Doretha called Delois and asked Delois if she was watching the news. Delois told her that she had seen the broadcast the night before. She said that she was glad that someone had burned the little gangbangers out. Poky was still at Delois' house and Doretha asked Delois to ask him had he seen Clean. There was a pause on the line before Delois told Doretha that Poky said that Clean was speaking to a group of young men at P.A.P.A. Doretha gave a sigh of relief. She was glad that Clean was all right. She walked back into her room and said a silent prayer for Clean and the men of P.A.P.A.

Michael Rogers

Chapter 48

It had been a long night for Baby G. He was still shaking after being snatched out of his bed in the middle of the night. He had watched three of his men get shot in the legs after being pistol whipped and stomped. His home had been torched and Baby G had been taken to a wooded area and tied to a tree. It was there that he had been threaten and beaten by the hooded men. The men had told him that they would kill him if he ever gave the orders to have his Lil' punk ass gang shoot up another civilian household.

Baby G was sure that the hooded men meant business. The way the men had raided his house had made a believer out of him. The men had raided his home with military precision. Baby G sensed that the men were disciplined killers. A well dressed, sharp-looking man who had shot Baby K in the leg had shot him with the ease and concern of someone who was shooting a can off a log. He had shot Baby L in the same manner. Before shooting the boys, the man had taken three bullets out the six shot revolver. In a game of Russian roulette the man had spun the cylinder of the gun and placed the gun to the head of Baby 3G. He fired the gun twice on empty chambers before removing the gun from Baby 3G's head and telling him that it was his lucky night. Baby 3G had pissed himself as he cried and pleaded for his life. The man slapped him upside the head with the gun as he stood from over him. "You're not that damn lucky," the man had said before shooting Baby 3G in the leg. The man had then shot Baby L who had been cowering on the floor and pleading for his life.

Baby G was drug from the house and taken into a wooded area out in the Loop. He had been left in the woods after being beaten and threatened in the same game of Russian roulette. Baby G had never been so afraid in his life. As leader of the Baby Killers, he had been in numerous shootouts and fights. He was far from being a coward, but he was no closer to being a fool.

Baby G had managed to find his way out the woods and was picked up on the highway by an old man in a pickup truck. The man dropped Baby G off at his mother's house. Baby G was still there after showering and changing clothes. He was speaking to his lieutenant, Baby 2K, on the telephone. Baby 2K told him that it was Baby 3G who had given the order to raid the woman's house. Baby G told Baby 2K to call a meeting of all the members. He wanted to see every member of the Baby Killers at the park in one hour. Baby G would make damn sure that no one would ever give another order to shoot up a home without his approval. The last thing in the world Baby G wanted was for them hooded men to visit him again. He was sure that he wouldn't survive a second visit.

***

"Guess what House of Cream," Lil' Shelia asked the question of her audience. "Y'all know my man is one of the best football players in the country. Well, guess what. Today, he asked me to marry him." Lil' Shelia waited until the applause died down.

"That's what I done," Lil' Shelia said. "I applauded this niggas decision to finally do something right. See, my girl Sherry and Broke got married before they moved in together. Sherry's my cousin and her dad is a preacher so he married them before we moved to Pine Bluff. I been dating Borilla since high school. He was my first and will probably be my last so when he asked me to marry him I cried. And just like always, this big head nigga found a way to fuck up something good. I'm all happy and shit about to cry and then Bo dumbass gon' go and ask me one of the dumbest questions I ever heard. Had me wondering if I wanted to marry his dumb ass. Guess what he asked me House of Cream." Lil' Shelia paused as she stared down at Borilla with a frown on her face.

"This dumb motherfucker asked me if I thought he should go pro after this season. Now here he is the number one defensive end prospect in the country and this dumb motherfucker ask me if I thank he should go pro. Now, ain't that the dumbest shit you ever heard. I say Bo, what the fuck you mean do I think you should go pro. What the fuck else you gone do. You ain't academically qualified to do nothing Bo but to be a Physical Education teacher. I say Bo, P.E. stand for poor employment. I say grant it Bo you could get a job as a P.E. teacher, tell me what stupid motherfucker gone give you a five million dollar signing bonus to teach a bunch of hardhead ass kids how to do jumping jacks. I say, and what about your mama Bo."

"I say Bo your mama still hanging clothes out on a got damn clothesline tied between two pecan trees. And it ain't because Mama Clara care about no damn environment or her clothes being fresh. Not with all that damn sap getting on her clothes.

Got your daddy Ray walking 'round here smelling like a damn pecan pie and you gon' ask me should you go pro. I say Bo yo' mama need a dam washing machine. Let that be the reason. It don't make no damn sense for your four year old nephews to have kung fu grips from ringing out got damn clothes. Shook one of them motherfuckers hand the other day and he damn near broke my wrist and you gon' ask me should you go pro."

"I say, plus Bo, your daddy Ray need a got damn real boat. He can't keep fishing in that raggedy ass aluminum piece of shit he took us fishing in last week. Here I am looking for a life jacket in this piece of shit and come to find out Ray got the life jackets tied around the damn boat to keep it afloat. I say not only do you need to go pro Bo, you need to take your ass down to Bass Pro and get your daddy a damn boat. If you don't whenever you do go pro you gon' fuck around and be missing Ray in that damn green room. Ray riding 'round in the damn Arkansas river with all its' swirling water in that damn sardine can he call a boat. Engine the size of a damn trolling motor. A one horse powered piece of shit and that horse is a got damn Shetland pony. And this nigga gon' ask me if I think he should go pro."

"See, I hate it House of Cream when black folk be running around echoing that white folk shit about athletes should stay in school and get their education. I mean, don't get me wrong. We at M and P are all

389

for education. But when you got a dumb motherfucker who can dunk a basketball with his got damn feet who think that taking the SAT test mean he has to take it on Saturday why the hell you want him to stay in school. If he ain't learn shit all these years it's too late. Let his ass go play some mindless sport and make millions so he can marry him a white bitch. We got enough dumb motherfuckers in the hood. Spread these niggas around. He can always hire him an educated motherfucker. Got damn mama living in Sugar Ditch Mississippi or fucked up on drugs and this good jumping motherfucker the only thing between Lil' sister selling her ass on the corner or going to college so she can be somebody and they telling this nigga to stay in school so the school can get rich. This dumb motherfucker end up back in the hood because he blow out his knee or he date rape the wrong bitch and cracker can't cover it up so they kick his ass out of school. Nigger come back to the hood as a sexual predator and still dumb as fuck and mad at everybody. Gon' have another Sugh Knight on our hands."

I told Bo something that made his mind up real quick. Talking 'bout do I think he should go pro. I say Bo, one of us going pro. Either you is or I am. So either you can make millions lying motherfuckers down on the football field or I can make us thousands lying motherfuckers down in my bed. That shit made his mind up real quick. Bo don't want me to put this good pussy on the market. Not his favorite got damn dish. I'll be like a super Wal-Mart if I put this pussy on the market. Have ho's filing anti-trust lawsuits against my ass for monopolizing the pussy selling industry. Have this pussy open all night...three holes no waiting. Have a got damn family plan. Kids over eighteen get in for half price. Have Bo black ass at the bedroom door handing out condoms and Viagra. Gon' ask me if I think he should go pro. You got damn right I think you should go pro. Why the hell you think I been with your dumb ass all these years. I knew you could do something other than eat a pussy. Every night eat, eat, eat, fuck, fuck, fuck, suck, suck, suck, all because Bo got damn testosterone high from lifting all them damn weights and he need to fuck something. All in my booty and shit with his ol' freaky self. Talking 'bout baby relax and it'll go in. I say nigga let me see you stick a coke can up your asshole...and how the hell you know how to take a dick up the ass...telling me to

390

relax my ass muscles. Gon' tell me he saw it on a porn tape. Every night Bo coming to bed with some new shit for me to do. That's it baby, hold it open. Just like that Fluffy. He like his pussy doggy style. Talking 'bout he a Rottweiler. Calling me Flufffy and shit. Got me barking in bed. Arf! Arf! Arf!" Lil' Shelia stuck her tongue out at Borilla. The crowd was going crazy with laughter.

"Here I am House of Cream, four feet eleven inches tall and because of Bo I got the pussy of a seven feet bitch, and this nigga gon ask me if he should go pro. Bo out his damn mind. Look at him. That's my man and I betcha his dick harder than any nigga in the house. With his ol' freaky self. You damn right you better go pro." Lil' Shelia kept the crowd laughing as she clowned Borilla across the stage for near an hour before ending her act.

***

Fast Money was in Nashville, Tennessee. This was home. It had been months since his last visit. Fast Money wasn't sure who had tried to set him up in Pine Bluff. He only knew that Poochie had been involved. Based on his information, and Cream's way with women, Fast Money was sure even without proof that Cream and Broke were somehow involved.

Fast Money had left Pine Bluff the same day that Grizzle Hound's body had been found in a shallow grave with two bullet holes in the back of his head. Grizzle Hound's death was a rude awakening for Fast Money. He didn't think the Grizzle Hound could be killed. Fast Money knew after Grizzle Hound's body was found that he too was in clear and present danger.

That's why Fast Money was in Nashville. It wasn't that he was afraid. Fast Money knew no fear. He was far from being a coward, but he was no closer to being a fool. He knew that he had to meet force with force. He also knew that the forces he had in Pine Bluff were not enough for the danger he faced.

***

Fast Money was the only son of a ruthless hustler and pimp father named Big Money. Nashville with Minnie Pearl, Hee Haw and country music, was far from being country. Black natives called their city Cashville Ten-a-key. Nashville was one of the most violent and crime ridden cities in America. Fast Money was born into this city and the hustler lifestyle to a whore named Dee Dee and her pimp, Big Money. Dee Dee was an unfit mother who didn't give a damn about nothing in life but from where she would get her next high. Fast Money had watched both his mother and father stab, shoot or stomp both men and women who dared to get in the way of their money or high.

Fast Money grew up fast. By the age of sixteen he had seen more cities than a Greyhound bus driver. He was home-schooled by hookers who would rather spend time teaching him to read and write as opposed to lying beneath sweaty johns.

Fast Money had only loved once in life. He had fell in love with the fifteen year old daughter of one of his teachers. The love affair ended abruptly when Big Money walked in on them in bed one day. Big Money told Fast Money he was fucking his sister then ordered him out of the room with the girl. Big Money then sent a big black brute of a man into the room. Fast Money knew the man as a Nashville, police officer.

Fast Money confronted Big Money when he could hear his sister calling his name for help. He could also hear the brute who was raping her laughing behind the closed door. Big Money slapped Fast Money to the floor. He told him that nothing mattered to him but his money. Not him, his mother or the bitch child of one of his whores.

Fast Money couldn't face his sister again after that day. The cop who was on Big Money's payroll made frequent visits to the house. He never left before forcing his way on the girl. Fast Money abided his time. He waited patiently for two months before he got his revenge. The cop liked to drink crushed ice over gin before going into the girl's room. Fast Money filled the ice tray with broken glass from a fluorescent light he had broken. He made sure to grind the glass up so fine that the cop wouldn't detect it in his drink. Fast Money had no idea that on the day he was getting his revenge that Big Money and the cop would be celebrating some occasion and that Big Money would be drinking with the cop. Big Money told Fast Money to fill his glass along with the cop's glass with ice. Fast Money done as told.

Both men were rushed to the hospital before the night was over. Fast Money took this opportunity to rob his father. He had peeped his father's stash spot in the wall at the head of the bed he shared with Fast Money's mother. Fast Money stole every dime of the stash. In the only act of kindness he ever showed, Fast Money gave his sister ten thousand dollars of the money. The two of them caught a cab to the bus station where they departed, never to see each other again. Fast Money never saw his parents again. He did learn that the cop had died and his father had to have half of his intestines removed. He would have to wear a bag for the rest of his life.

Fast Money had traveled the country as a hustler of every sort before stumbling up on Pine Bluff, after leaving Texas and traveling through Arkansas. He had been on a six-month hustling spree after being paroled from a Texas prison for attempted murder of two men who had tried to rob one of his whores at a motel.

Fast Money was traveling with the fifteen-year-old daughter of one of the whores when he was pulled over by a fat patrolman for running a red light in Pine Bluff. It was after 2:00am and Fast Money had not seen the cop as he sped through a caution light on the expressway passing through town.

Fast Money was on parole in six states and still owed fines in five others. He also had cases pending in three. Fast Money had never served over a year in prison at any one time but had served over six years in combined time in different states. Fast Money had fully embraced his father's philosophy of money over everything. Fast Money had few friends and none who he hadn't crossed in one way or another. Friends to Fast Money were simply pawns to be sacrificed when the king was in trouble of being checkmated. He was the king and no one on the board was more important than him. And especially not the fifteen year old daughter of the hooker in the car with him on that fateful night he was stopped for running a red-light in Pine Bluff.

Fast Money recognized the look in the cop eyes who had pulled him over. It was the same look the cop he had killed in Nashville had had for his sister. In a repeat performance of his father's dirty deed, Fast Money traded the crying girl to the cop for his freedom. The mother of the girl in the same way that he had robbed his father, robbed Fast Money and stole his car.

Fast Money awakened to find the car, whores and six months of hustling money in the trunk of the car gone. He was left alone and near broke at a roadside motel in Pine Bluff.

Fast Money called the cop from the night before and told him his story. The cop who saw great potential in Fast Money who had peeped his fetish for young girls told Fast Money to stay put. He stopped by the motel later and gave Fast Money a thousand dollars and a kilo of cocaine. He told Fast Money to bring him back twenty thousand dollars. That was the beginning of a prosperous relationship for both parties. Fast Money stayed in Pine Bluff and decided that with the cop protection he had that he would make it his base of operation. Once the cop made detective thanks to Fast Money feeding him arrests of those he encountered in the drug trade, Fast Money felt invincible. A nomad at heart, Fast Money still traveled the country doing his dirt but he would always retreat back to Pine Bluff where he operated with impunity thanks to his cop friend who had become head of the drug task force and who sold him confiscated drugs at the minimum.

What was once a perfect setup was beginning to crumble down around Fast Money. He realized now that his troubles had began when he had decided to setup a naive country boy as a fall guy to fill his cop friends arrest quota. If not for the trouble with Broke, he wouldn't have the trouble with Michelle. If not for the trouble with Michelle, he wouldn't have the trouble with Cream. No trouble with Cream and he wouldn't have needed Poochie. No business with Poochie and he wouldn't have any business back in Nashville.

If not for his crisis in Pine Bluff, Fast Money wouldn't need his crisis management team. He told Benny and his crew to keep an eye on Cream during his absence. He wanted to be able to find him upon his return. The men Fast Money would be bringing with him were fully capable of finishing the job Grizzle Hound had failed to do.

***

Fast Money found Big Cleve and Little Cleve at their favorite hangout. This was the Hot Babe's strip club. The club was owned by Daryl McQuiddy an old friend of Big Cleve. Fast Money had first met the big muscular black man in the Nashville County jail. Fast Money was there on an assault charge which was later dropped. The two men became friends over chess games, Big Cleve who considered himself a master of the game was impressed when Fast Money had checkmated him in ten moves. Lil' Cleve was Big Cleve's younger brother. He was an inch shorter than the six feet nine inch Big Cleve and weighed ten pounds less than his three-hundred and fifty pounds. He was called Little Cleve because he was the younger of the two.

Fast Money didn't want to stay in Nashville longer than it was necessary for Big Cleve and Little Cleve to gather their things for travel. A ragged figure was waiting between parked cars when Fast Money walked outside McQuiddy's Hot Babe's club. The figure called out to Fast Money as he walked past him. Fast Money turned to see the raggedy looking man pointing a gun at his head. Big Cleve and Little Cleve were supposed to have been behind Fast Money. If he had known they weren't Fast Money would have been more aware of his surroundings.

The man pointing the gun at Fast Money couldn't believe his luck. The frail old man had murder in his eyes. He had waited many years for this moment. The man had recognized Fast Money earlier when Fast

Money had first arrived. He wanted to kill him so bad that he had killed an off duty cop to take his gun. The cop had been trying to run the beggar off the lot for most of the night. When the man saw Fast Money, he lured the cop to a secluded area and hit him upside the head with a brick he had picked up off the ground. He continued to hit him until the cop was dead.

Fast Money turned towards the voice that he recognized immediately. "Dad," he said surprised. Big Money never got a chance to reply. Big Cleve crept up behind him and grabbed his gun hand with his left hand. He used his right hand to shove the twelve-inch Plexiglas knife he carried into Big Money's back. The knife punctured Big Moneys back and entered his chest.

Big Cleve held him high in the air impaled on the knife before tossing Big Money's body ten feet away onto the parking lot.

Big Money was breathing ragged breaths of air as he desperately tried to crawl to nowhere in particular. Fast Money's cold-hearted mother had left Big Money years ago while he was still in the hospital suffering from the broken glass Fast Money had fed him. She took the whores and all he had left in the world. Big Money never recovered from the loss. He swore to kill mother and son if he ever saw them again. The thought of killing Fast Money was still on his mind when Fast Money drove over Big Money's head and crushed the thought and life out of him on the parking lot. This cruel fate dealt to a father by his son was the only act of kindness either had ever shown the other.

Big Cleve was relaxing with the remote on Fast Money's couch. He paused on a picture of Detective Jones that appeared across the TV screen. Detective Jones was the subject of a news update about his death. The anchor woman said that Jones was being sought on numerous felony charges stemming from the abuse of teenage girls at the time of his death. One of the girl's lawyer was speaking to the press in front of the Pine Bluff courthouse. Each time one of the lawyers of Detective Jones victims filed a motion the press would run his picture and give an update on the story.

"Yo Fast Money, ain't this your man right here?" Big Cleve pointed to the TV screen. Fast Money who had been busy packing stuck his head into the room.

"Man, that nigga look like a Gila monster." Lil' Cleve said laughing with Big Cleve.

Fast Money stared at his old crime partner. He knew that if the Feds had caught up with Jones that Jones would've told them all he knew. He would've told about Fast Money procuring him young girls, about drug deals and most damaging, about murders that would've buried Fast Money in prison for life. Fast Money had tried to call Jones at his old number but it was disconnected. Jones had been lucky in this regard. Fast Money had plans of killing Jones before the Feds could catch up with him or before whoever killed him had killed him..

Fast Money got a sense of urgency after watching the news account of Jone's fugitive status. He move fast back into the bedroom to finish packing. What use to be a sweet hustle was no more. After lying low in town to gather up outstanding debts, Fast Money was now packing to leave Pine Bluff for good. He planned to be gone within the next couple of hours. As soon as he settled some old scores.

Fast Money's Pine Bluff eyes had finally given him something he could use. The parties he sought were presently at P.A.P.A.'s headquarters located in an old school they were renovating on west thirteenth. You cat's ready," Fast Money asked the Cleve's. He made a show of zipping up the suitcase filled with money. The Cleve's stared wide eyed at the money. It was the reaction Fast Money expected. He knew that as long as he possessed the suitcase he would also possess the men. Like the demon he was, Fast Money would lead the men to hell and back before they would one day awaken and realize that both him and the money were gone.

***

"May I help you," Verla asked the herculean figures standing in front

397

of her desk. Verla didn't know the men but based on their physiques and demeanors, she figured the men were friends of Brick's from prison.

"We're looking for Broke and Clean, the smaller of the two men spoke. We're old friends of theirs. Someone told us we could find them here." The man smiled at Verla.

'They're painting the gym floor across the street," Verla said. "Just follow the sidewalk once you cross the street and you can't miss them."

"I'm sure we won't," the bigger man said.

"Thanks beautiful, maybe next time I can come looking for you. Would you like that?" The smaller man said. Verla held up her wedding ring finger and smiled. "Oh, I'm sorry, but you're still beautiful."

"Thank you," Verla said smiling.

***

Lil' Shelia was sitting in the backseat of Sherry's car. She was resting her arms atop the car seat as she sat forward running her mouth to Sherry and Michelle. "I'm just saying," Lil' Shelia was saying. "I'm not a painter, I'm a comedian. I make people laugh for a living. There are no parallels between painting and being a comedian."

"Ooooooo, you and your newfound self-expression," Sherry sighed and said. "The whole world has become one big joke to you. Well guess what, my little vertically challenged cousin and friend, today you're a painter, ha! ha! the jokes on you."

"You will most definitely be in my next act," Lil' Shelia said.

Who that?" Sherry asked as she stared at the two herculean figures crossing the street towards the gym.

"I can't tell you who they are but I bet you I can tell you from where they came. Them prison muscles," Lil' Shelia said, "Niggas don't get that big on the street. Too much other shit to do. Them muscles come from jacking off and lifting weights with nothing else to do." Lil' Shelia was laughing hard which caused Sherry and Michelle to laugh.

"Everything's a joke," Sherry said laughing.

I know one thing ain't no joke," Lil' Shelia said. "It ain't gone be no joke when I pee all over the backseat of this car you don't let me out." Lil' Shelia was squirming in the backseat waiting anxiously for Michelle to let her out the car as Sherry parked.

"That's what you get for drinking that big ol' fountain drink." Sherry said. "Drink was big as you."

"Ha! Ha! Very funny," Lil' Shelia said. "Maybe you should think about being a comedian." Lil' Shelia jumped out the car and ran towards the entrance of P.A.P.A.

Who that SUV belong to parked on the side of the building," Sherry asked Michelle. Sherry noticed the SUV which was barely visible as if the driver was not trying to be seen.

"Oh Shit!" Michelle shouted as she opened her door in a rush to exit the car. "That's Fast Money's SUV," Michelle said as she jumped out the car. Michelle was in panic mode. "I thought those two men looked familiar." She said. "They from Nashville! Cream!" Michelle was off and running.

Broke! Sherry said the name softly to herself as fear gripped her body. She also recognized the men. Sherry was running fast behind Michelle. Both were rushing to save the men they loved.

Broke, Cream, Rabbit and Stone were painting the far wall of the gym. Reggae music was blaring across the boom box speaker system sitting on the floor. Four beer cans sat next to the men. Everyone was laughing and talking without paying any attention to the front door of the gym.

Is it just me, Rabbit said, "or is Brick going for the longest supply and beer run record in history." The men all laughed. Rabbit turned to pick up his beer off the floor.

"Oh shit!" Rabbit said. "We got trouble."

The gym door was opened and Big Cleve and Lil' Cleve had walked unnoticed inside the building. Lil' Cleve was a step behind Big Cleve as they walked towards the men. Both men had pulled out their guns. Rabbit alerted Broke and the others to the danger. The men all stood stunned as they watched the approaching men.

Big Cleve was already counting his money as he leveled his gun at Broke. Lil' Cleve made a target of Cream. Both men had been easily identifiable by the description Fast Money had given his shooters. Big Cleve and Little Cleve thought it was foolish of Broke and Cream who stepped towards them to make such easy targets of themselves. They didn't know that both men were trying to protect the women they loved.

Michelle and Sherry had followed the Cleve's inside the building. The men were so focused on Broke and Cream that they didn't pay any attention to what may have been creeping up behind them. They would have already shot Broke and Cream if not for Fast Money who was supposed to be bringing up the rear, telling them to wait for his entrance.

That's close enough nigga, Big Cleve waved his gun at Broke. The men were located towards the center of the gym near the three point line of the goal nearest the door. This is where Broke and Cream had rushed to confront the men.

"You too pretty boy. Fo' I bust a cap in your ass right here." Lil' Cleve stepped towards Cream.

Cream watched Michelle through his peripheral view. Michelle raised the fire extinguisher she had taken off the wall near the gym door when she entered the building. Broke also watched Sherry as she raised a broom she had taken off the wall as she entered. Sherry held the straw broom with two hands like Broke had taught her. Sherry was a martial art student and was prepared to use her skills to save the man she loved. Sherry was waiting for Michelle to strike first. Broke held his breath as he thought back to Sherry's vision of two men with guns threatening his and Cream's lives.

Broke and Cream would have preferred for their women not to get involved in their troubles. All it took was for the men to turn and see them and both girls could be killed. That's why Broke and Cream had made targets of themselves and walked towards the men maintaining eye contact with them to keep the men focus away from the women they loved creeping up behind them. Rabbit and Stone had made it to the half court line where they paused after the threats by the Cleves. Stone's face was a stone mask of anger. His massive fists were balled up beside his legs as Stone breathe angry breaths of air.

Michelle swung the small fire extinguisher with all her might. The hard metal casing struck Little Cleve across the head. Sherry took her cue from Michelle and came down hard in a downward motion with the hard end of the broom across Big Cleve's gun hand.

"I-Yigh!" Sherry yelled.

"Shit," Big Cleve shouted out in pain. Lil' Cleve crumpled silently to the floor. Sherry held the broom in front of her in a fighting stance as she backed away from the angry Big Cleve. Big Cleve called her a black bitch and went at Sherry after he saw Cream go after the gun he had dropped after the blow to the hand.

"I-Yigh!" Sherry jumped up and kicked Big Cleve in the chest. Big Cleve stumbled but shook off the kick and struck Sherry hard with his good hand. Sherry shrieked in pain and went down hard to the floor. She landed off balance back against the gym wall where she struck her head and crumpled over to the floor.

"Sherry!" Broke screamed Sherry's name. He hadn't made it to Big Cleve and Sherry fast enough after dodging Cream who had dove for Big Cleve's gun. The lost of a second had caused him to make it to Big Cleve just after he struck Sherry. Broke stared at Sherry who laid dazed against the wall. He then turned his attention to Big Cleve.

Broke ran up to Big Cleve and kicked him in the chest. Big Cleve staggered and growled. Broke followed the kick with a roundhouse to the head before rushing Big Cleve with a flurry of punches to his head and body that had the giant man stumbling backwards and grunting loudly after each blow. Big Cleve was helpless with his broken hand as Broke continued to pound him. The fight wouldn't have been much different even if he had had both hands. Broke used every skill he knew to totally annihilate the big brute. The thought of Sherry lying in pain had him in kill mode. Big Cleve fell to the floor after a final kick from Broke. Broke straddled his body and placed Big Cleve in a death lock chokehold. Every vein and muscle in his body were visible as he proceeded to choke the life out of the ruthless killer on the floor.

"Boom! Boom!" Gunshots caused Broke to turn towards the door from where the shots came.

"OK killer, that's enough." Fast Money knelt and held a gun to Sherry's head. Sherry was still dazed and stared at Broke through glazed over eyes.

"Now I know you don't want me to shoot this pretty little thing right here, and you know I will." Fast Money smiled at Broke. "Now get your ass off my man and get over there with the rest of your posse." Fast Money waved the gun in the direction of Cream and the others who were all gathered together near the basketball goal after rushing to help Sherry. Fast Money had stepped inside the building and grabbed her before they could get to her. The men all formed a protective barrier around Michelle.

"Baby do as he say," Sherry said in a weak voice. Sherry remembered her vision and knew that it was unfolding before her eyes.

"Yeah baby, do as I say, or I might just have to take darkness here with me and do her before I do her." Fast Money taunted Broke. He rubbed Sherry's face with his free hand. "What's up baby, you want to ride with a winner for a change. No sense a pretty little thing like you going for Broke when you can have Fast Money. Black meat is a hot commodity these days. I know you want to be a star." Fast Money kissed Sherry on the forehead.

"This time nigga there won't be no reprieve," Broke was furious as he stood off Big Cleve.

Big Cleve and Lil' Cleve were both regaining their senses.

"Fool," Fast Money said. "What the fuck you think I'm here for, to play games. Stop making threats you gon' be too dead to carry out. You! pretty boy," Fast Money turned to Cream, "Drop that gun. You too George Foreman." Cream and Stone had picked up the Cleve's gun. "Drop them or Ms. Chocolate Delight is gon' be thinking out loud with her thoughts flying all over the place. Now!" Fast Money demanded.

Cream and Stone dropped the guns they held to the floor. "All right boys, now slide them over to me. I see my boys 'bout got their senses back. This should all be over in a minute. You'll be dead and I'll be on my way. Should've stayed out my business nigga." Fast Money said.

***

Lil' Shelia was searching frantically for a weapon of some sort. She had recognized Fast Money as he crept across the street.

Lil' Shelia had just walked outside of P.A.P.A., when she noticed him as he pulled a gun from his waist. "Fuck," Lil' Shelia swore. "I'm a got damn comedian; I'm not no fucking super hero." Lil' Shelia ran as fast as she could towards the open door after not being able to find a weapon.

Big Cleve was standing on shaky legs. Little Cleve was in a kneeling position trying to shake his head clear. Fast Money was kneeling in the doorway. "Well tricks, I guess I'll see you in hell." Fast Money kicked the guns towards the Cleves.

Lil' Shelia never slowed as she ran and dropped kicked Fast Money as he stood off the floor. Fast Money who had shoved Sherry towards Broke grunted loudly and fell towards the floor. He managed to break his fall by pressing his hands to the floor. The gun was still in his hand pressed down onto the floor. Cream ran and kicked Big Cleve away from the gun Fast Money had slid to him. He picked up the gun and hit him twice upside the head knocking Big Cleve back out to the floor. Little Cleve didn't fare so well. Stone was so angry that he walked over to the still kneeling Little Cleve who turned to see him just as Stone raised his massive fist high into the air. Stone brought the fist down in a brick busting blow. And just like the bricks that he busted with his fists, Stone cracked Little Cleve's skull. A sickening crunch could be heard before Little Cleve crumpled over dead to the floor.

Broke ran and kicked the gun out of Fast Money's hand before he could recover. He stomped Fast Money unmercifully. Broke was in the process of choking Fast Money out when Brick walked into the gym. All it took was one look around for Brick to know what was happening. Brick was quickly angered by what he saw.

Brick walked over to Broke. "Let him go," Brick said. "He's not getting off that easy. I got something special for this nigga. We gon' make him suffer for invading our sanctuary. Broke! I say let him go!" Brick pulled at Broke's arm. Broke was intent on killing Fast Money. He had zoned out and was about to do just that when Brick grabbed his arms. "Stand down brother," Brick held Broke's arm. Broke released his hold on Fast Money and kicked his body away from him.

Broke rushed over to Sherry who was being assisted to stand by Michelle. Stone was cradling Lil' Shelia who had fail and hit her head after kicking Fast Money in the back. Lil' Shelia was semi-conscious. Stone said he was going to walk her across the street where M.A.M.A., and P.A.P.A., had a small clinic.

Broke and Cream were both hugging the women they loved." Baby don't ever risk your life like that again," Broke kissed Sherry and held her tight.

"I didn't risk my life," Sherry said. "I was trying to save my life. Baby there is no life without you. I told you, the day you die, I die. So I'm going to do whatever it take to keep you alive. That's how much I love you," Sherry cried in Broke's arms.

"Sherry's oath is my oath," Michelle told Cream. "So you better teach us how to fight, well, at least teach me, Sherry all ready know how to fight."

"I got to go and check on Lil' Shelia," Sherry said.

"She's fine, Broke said. "She just bumped her head, Stone took her across the street to the clinic to get checked out by Doretha. Maybe you should go and get checked out yourself."

"I'm fine," Sherry said. "I'll put an ice pack on my head once we get home."

***

"Look I done told ya'll, I'm not no damn super hero and I'm not no painter either. I'm-a..."

"We know, you're a comedian," Sherry and Michelle said together. "I guess that hard head finally came in handy." Sherry said laughing.

"Speaking of hard head, I better call and tell my baby what happened to me. I might can get some sleep tonight." Lil' Shelia was propped up on a pillow in a clinic bed.

"Well we all owe you our lives and I just want to say thank you." Michelle leaned over to hug Lil' Shelia.

"Woman please," Lil' Shelia said. "We all put our lives on the line today. That's what we do as black women, that's what we've always done. Put our lives on the line for our men and families. You bet not start crying." Lil' Shelia stared at Sherry who was about to cry. "You the cryingnest woman I know. Ol' soft self."

"Forget you shrimp." Sherry dabbed at her eyes. Lil' Shelia and Michelle were also dabbing at their eyes.

***

Brick was furious about what had happened. He stumped Fast Money's arm and shattered it above the elbow. Bitch ass nigga, you bring this shit to our sanctuary." Brick kicked Fast money hard upside the head. Fast Money laid moaning in pain on the gym floor.

Poky who had been called along with Sleepy and Scacehead walked back into the gym after hiding Fast Money's SUV to be disposed of later. "I think Mr. Fast Money only stopped to make a considerable donation to the causes of M.A.M.A. and P.A.P.A.," Poky tossed Fast Money's briefcase filled with money onto the gym floor. He unzipped the briefcase and the men all stared at the stacks of money. "It won't pay for all his sins but it's a good down payment." Poky said.

***

Fast Money watched through semi-conscious eyes as Brick beat Big Cleve to near death with a board lined with nails. The men were in a wooded area somewhere outside of Pine Bluff. Fast Money had been around killers all his life. He had seen and even done some gruesome things. Yet in all his adventures, he couldn't recall ever seeing a terror like the one before his eyes. Fast money knew fear for the first time in his life. If there was any consolation in knowing fear for the first time, Fast Money was at least grateful that it wouldn't last long before death took its' place. The thought of all the pain he would soon experience at the hands of the diabolical man swinging the board caused Fast Money to drop his head in fear. Fast Money again realized that when he had first chosen Broke as his fall guy he had sealed his own fate. His dying wish as Brick approached him with the board now dripping with Big Cleve's blood was that death would be swift. He also wished that he had left that black ass nigga, staring down at him next to the crazed man, the fuck alone. The three men were all buried in lime pit graves on the wooded property owned by a shell corporation created by Brick. Fast Money and Big Cleve were still breathing when the dirt was tossed on them.

***

Brick called a meeting in Altheimer at Broke's family home. The meeting was for all the executive staff of M.A.M.A. and P.A.P.A. An old army buddy of Broke's father now lived at the home. Tech-9 was a derelict on the streets of Pine Bluff when Broke saw and recognized him. Tech-9 was also special forces like Broke's father. His field of expertise was in demolition. Tech-9 use to hunt with Broke and his father. He was always like a father to Broke. Tech-9's government name was Oscar Jones. Friends called him Tech-9 because he was a technical genius in the field of technology and explosives. He could make bombs out of most anything.

Tech-9 had not asked Brick what he wanted with the explosive devices he had given him which were used to kill the two cops on Harding Street. Just as he had never asked his government employees what they had planned for his devices. Tech-9 knew that the men and women of M and P fought for a greater cause than the government he once served. The same government that had abandoned him and left him as a homeless man on the streets of Pine Bluff.

Brick stared out at the faces of the men and women of M and P. "This is it," he said. "We are the vanguard of black people. It will be naive of us to think that the forces of evil aligned against us will release its' hold on us without a fight. It's evident that in our fight for change we must first change the way we fight. We must change the way we think, communicate and the way we view our mission in life." Brick stared around at his forces sitting in a circle.

"We must do whatever it takes to take whatever it takes to take back what have been taken from our people over the years and still being taken on a daily basis. Pride, dignity, respect, self-love and aspirations to do for self and kind are just a few of the things we must take back."

"People have died and people will always die in this war. Those who were in the belly of the beast with me know how far we must go. We spent many nights in our enemy's prison thinking and planning for this opportunity to be free to lead our people forward. What we didn't plan on was for the women we love to join us in this fight. I think it's safe to say that when we chose our women we chose wisely. They have all proven their worth in battle. It's us who must ask ourselves if the battle is worth our women."

"Old enemies have been destroyed but new enemies will emerge. Therefore we must train and prepare to meet all foes, we must be as clandestine as the C.I.A., and just as thorough. We will infiltrate every gang or street organization on the streets of Pine Bluff. Nothing in Pine Bluff will move without our knowledge. In order to help the people we must protect the people. In order to protect the people we must know the evils they face and the plans of those who would harm them. We're not trying to stop the drug dealers or gangsters from doing what they do. Not as long as it doesn't interfere with what we do. If ever our two forces do so happen to clash over philosophies we will make sure that our forces will be the greater force because we have the greater cause.

Broke and Tech-9 are going to teach us non-verbal communication, hand-to-hand combat, weapon training, discipline and strategy. This will be out training grounds. We're going to come here each weekend for training purposes. M and P will recruit only the tried and true to join us in our cause. By rights given to us be the God we serve we are dedicated men and women united for His cause to fight for black liberation. Our oaths will be oaths of death to never betray our cause. What happened the other day will never happen again. We were lucky this time. Thanks to the unselfish and brave acts of three courageous sisters we're still here as a whole. Next time we will be prepared.

"Brick I hear what you're saying," Lil' Shelia said. And, I agree that we need to fight. But, I don't know if you know, but I'm a comedian. I'm not a revolutionary." Lil' Shelia had a concerned look on her face. Brick laughed. Everyone joined him.

Michael Rogers

Chapter 49

The prosecutor sat snugly in his boat while sipping from a beer can in his hand.

He was amusing himself by watching his cork bounce gently up and down in the water. The prosecutor figured it had to be a snake or a turtle that was nibbling on his bait. If not for the fact that he was near drunk and already packed up to leave, he would've already reeled in his line and tossed his bait into another area of the small private lake. Instead, he sat and watched the bouncing cork. He figured he would try one last time to snatch whatever it was on his line out the water. The prosecutor placed his drink in a holder and fired up a cigar from his shirt pocket. It was a beautiful day and he had already filled his cooler with fish. He was now relaxing and thinking about an upcoming case that he was scheduled to prosecute. It was the case of four black men who were accused of raping a young white girl. The prosecutor knew all too well that the girl was lying. Still, he couldn't wait to convict the four boys of the crime. The prosecutor squint his eyes from the sun as a motor driven boat approached him coming from across the lake. He wondered who was driving the boat. He hadn't seen anyone else on the lake all day. The waves being generated by the big bass boat caused the small aluminum boat that the prosecutor was in to rock in the water. The prosecutor had an angry scowl on his face as he glared up at the men in the boat as the boat turned broadside and threw water all over him into his boat.

"Got dammit," the prosecutor angrily said.

The prosecutor was fuming mad as the boat circled him and caused his boat to rock in the water. His anger turned to fear when he saw who was driving the boat. The prosecutor was knocked from his boat by the men with a long pole. He landed with a splash on his back in the water. His life jacket was still in the boat where he had removed it so he could better relax. With fear in his eyes, the prosecutor tried desperately to swim back to his boat. His attempts were being thwarted by the men in the bass boat who had hooked his boat and was pulling it away from him. Because of age and one too many beers the prosecutor could only tread water for a few minutes before he began to sink to the bottom of the lake.

***

Sherry was lying in Broke's arms as she read aloud an article detailing the death of a federal prosecutor in a boating incident on a private lake. The article read that the prosecutor's death was an accident.

"Don Smith," Sherry said the prosecutor's name again as if she was trying to recall it to memory.

"Ain't that the prosecutor that BeBe said was a racist," Sherry hugged Broke as he took his keys off a bookshelf. Ain't that's the one that was going to let Cassius Lee off with that light sentence before he was killed by an assassin?"

"I think so," Broke said.

"Hmmph," Sherry said as she followed Broke to the door with her arms around him. "The Lord works in mysterious ways," Sherry said.

"Yes he do," Broke kissed Sherry on her forehead. "All right little woman," Broke kissed Sherry again, "I'm fixing to go, me, Brick, and Cream gon' take dad's boat back to Altheimer. I should be back before dark."

"I'll be waiting," Sherry said. "Just like always."

Sherry stood in the doorway watching as Broke drove off. She missed him from the moment he left. Broke was everything to her. Sherry felt that her life was complete, that God had blessed her with all the joys of happiness. There was nothing she wouldn't do for Broke. Sherry was not the naïve little country girl anymore. Since being around the men of P.A.P.A. and the women of M.A.M.A., Sherry was anything but naïve. Still, it was only for Broke that she would allow herself to be free of her inhibitions. Sherry was still smiling within as she flopped down on the couch and began again to read the paper.

"Noooooo!" Sherry almost screamed as she jumped off the couch and ran to the door. She flung open the door and tried to stop Broke as he turned the corner. Sherry screamed after Broke before running back into the house. She snatched up the telephone and frantically tried to call Broke only to hear his cell phone ringing on the couch beside her. Sherry was a nervous wreck as she again read the heading above the article in the paper for the second time.

ALTHEIMER HUNTERS FIND THREE BODIES IN WOODED AREA

Bodies believed to be that of missing skinheads…

The end

Michael Rogers

COMING SOON

Michael Rogers

About the Author

Michael Rogers was born and raised in Pine Bluff, Arkansas. He spent 22 years in Federal Prison as a first-time drug offender before his release on September 10, 2015.

Mike has written over forty books. His goals are to self-publish his books and to use the proceeds from his book sales and other writings to help bring awareness to the plight of other non-violent offenders like himself who are still in prison.

To his fellow prisoners, Mike sends this message.....

The Great Frederick Douglass was once forced to ride in the boxcar of a passenger train because of his color and discrimination. Two white women who knew him, asked him if he felt degraded as the Great Frederick Douglass for having to ride in the boxcar.

Frederick Douglass replied that no one could degrade his great soul. He said it was not him who should feel degraded for having to ride in the boxcar, but rather, those who would place him there.

As non-violent prisoners serving unjust prison sentences in prisons across America, know that it is not you who should feel degraded for being in prison under such unjust laws; but rather those who would pass such laws that would keep you there.